THREE SHATTERED SOULS

BOOKS BY MAI CORLAND

THE BROKEN BLADES

Five Broken Blades
Four Ruined Realms
Three Shattered Souls

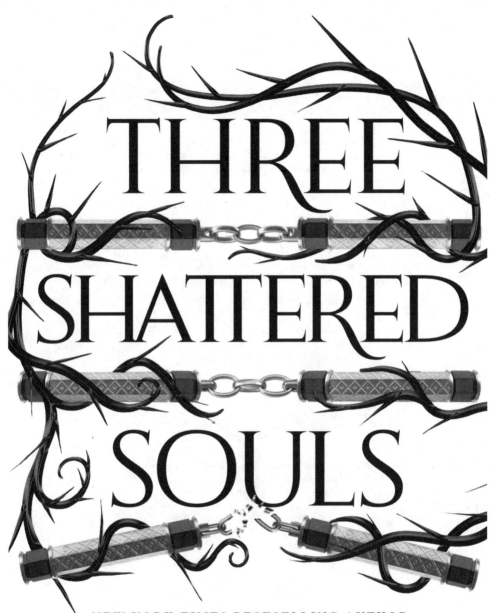

THREE SHATTERED SOULS

MAI CORLAND

RED TOWER BOOKS™

Entangled Publishing, LLC
644 Shrewsbury Commons Ave., STE 181
Shrewsbury, PA 17361
rights@entangledpublishing.com

Red Tower Books is an imprint of Entangled Publishing, LLC.

Visit our website at www.entangledpublishing.com.

Edited by Liz Pelletier
Cover, edge, and case design by Elizabeth Turner Stokes
Edge image by Yousuk Yang/Shutterstock
Endpaper original illustration by Juho Choi
Interior map original art by Elizabeth Turner Stokes
Interior map images by Siam Vector/Shutterstock,
T Studio/Shutterstock, Rollercoastershark/Shutterstock
Interior design by Britt Marczak

HC ISBN 978-1-64937-915-3
Ebook ISBN 978-1-64937-676-3

Manufactured in the United States of America
First Edition July 2025

10 9 8 7 6 5 4 3 2 1

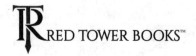

RED TOWER BOOKS™

For my heart and my sunshine
&
my man of steel

Three Shattered Souls is a dark adventure fantasy full of hard-earned loyalties, devastating betrayals, and warships on the horizon. As such, the story features elements that might not be suitable for all readers, including depictions of violence, blood, death (including the death of family and animals), suicidal ideation, imprisonment, injury, poisoning, burning, drowning, alcohol and drug use, sex work, classism, sexism, colonization, indentured servitude, graphic language, and sexual activity. Rape, child sexual abuse, torture, and genocide are discussed. Readers who may be sensitive to these elements, please take note, and prepare to meet the Dragon Lord…

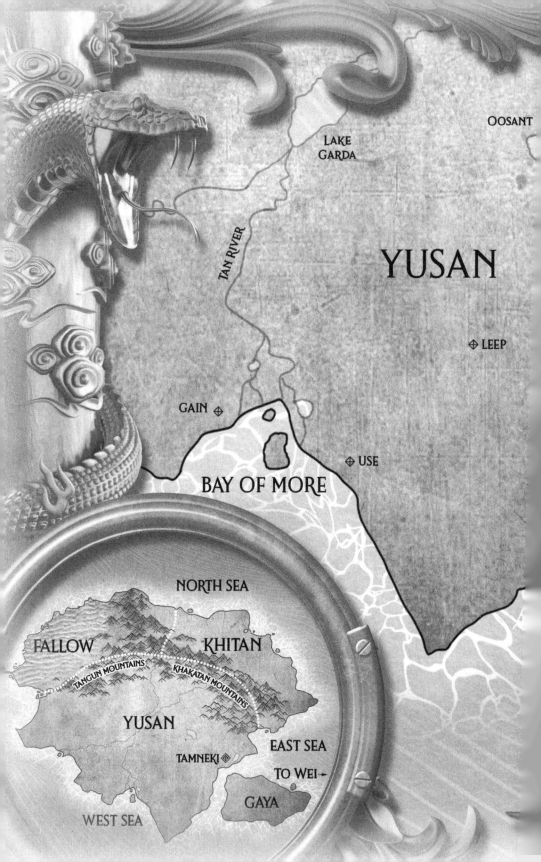

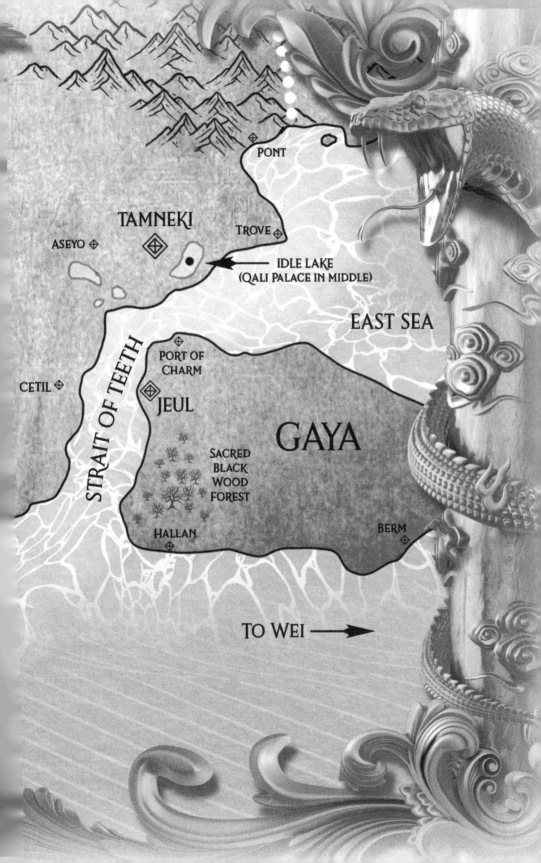

Main Characters

AERI (*AH-ree*)... A Thief, Princess of Yusan, King Joon's Daughter

MIKAIL (*Mick-ALE*)... The Former Royal Spymaster of Yusan, Prince of Gaya

ROYO (*ROY-oh*)... A Strongman from Yusan

~~EUYN (*YOON*)... The banished Crown Prince of Yusan, King Joon's Brother~~ (deceased)

SORA (*SOAR-a*)... A Poison Maiden from Yusan, formerly indentured to Count Seok

TIYUNG (*TIE-young*)... Count Seok's Son, recently escaped from Idle Prison

Other Characters of Note

KING JOON (*King JUNE*)... The King of Yusan

QUILIMAR (*QUILL-i-mar*)... The Queen of Khitan, King Joon and Euyn's sister

GENERAL VIKAL (*VY-cal*)... General of the Khitanese Armed Forces

COUNT SEOK (*Count SEE-ock*)... The Southern Count of Gain, Yusan

~~DAYSUM (*DAY-sum*)... Sora's Sister and Count Seok's Ward~~ (deceased)

~~COUNT BAY CHIN (*Count Bay Chin*)... The Northern Count of Umbria, Yusan~~ (deceased)

~~COUNT DAL (*Count DAHL*)... The Eastern Count of Tamneki, Yusan~~ (deceased)

~~GENERAL SALOSA (*General Sah-LOW-sa*)... General of the Yusanian Palace Guards~~ (deceased)

ZAHARA (*Za-HAH-ra*)... A Yusanian Spy, formerly a Poison Maiden named Hana

FALLADOR (*FAL-lah-dor*)... The Pretend Exiled Prince of Gaya

~~AILOR (*ALE-or*)... Mikail's father~~ (deceased)

GAMBRIA (*GAM-bree-uh*)... Fallador's Cousin

UOL (*OO-ul*)... Priest King of Wei

AUTHOR'S NOTE

Korea has a rich mythology and vibrant culture all its own. And as a Korean American adoptee, I drew on my own personal story and experiences to fashion the world of *Three Shattered Souls*. However, it is worth noting that this story is neither historical fiction nor fantasy based on the real world; it takes place in a unique setting that is inspired by my research of Korean myth, legend, and culture. Creative license has been taken throughout, but it is my hope that readers will leave the story with their lives enriched, as mine has been through the writing of this book.

—Mai

Previously, in The Broken Blades Trilogy

Five of the most dangerous liars in the land came together with one mission: to kill the God King Joon of Yusan. However, King Joon used his own attempted murder as a trap for the blades. His real intention was to have his daughter, Aeri, bring him the killers so he could acquire the Golden Ring of the Dragon Lord from the neighboring realm. Although the team was able to take the relic, Euyn, the banished prince of Yusan, was killed by the Queen of Khitan.

Now that Aeri has both the Golden Ring and the Amulet of the Dragon Lord, she possesses new powers along with a terrible prophesy to fulfill. She broke strongman Royo's heart by lying to him about the Sands of Time. They and Sora, a poison maiden desperate to save her sister, just landed on Gaya, a former realm and current colony of Yusan. Joining them is Mikail, the Yusanian spymaster who recently discovered he is lost Gayan royalty. The four would-be assassins narrowly escaped from Khitan with Mikail wielding the stolen Water Scepter of Wei.

With three relics in their possession, the other realms will descend on the remaining blades. But fractures and secrets among themselves might doom the group before the usurper of the Yusanian throne can even wage war against them. The only way to survive is to defeat the world, but who will be willing to pay the ultimate price when the Dragon Lord returns?

CHAPTER ONE

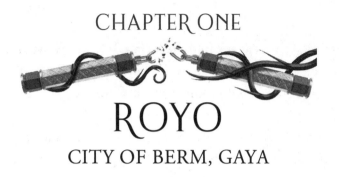

ROYO
CITY OF BERM, GAYA

We're really fucked.

I mean, not right now. We're safe at an inn on Gaya, but I've thought about it since dawn, and overall, we're screwed.

Mikail stands by the window of the room, looking down at the white sand and the blue sea. We got the Golden Ring and made it out of Khitan, which should've meant that we won. Instead, we lost Prince Euyn, found out that Mikail is the last Gayan royal, stole a relic from Wei—an empire that routinely slaughters Yusanians—drowned a bunch of people, and discovered Aeri was lying this whole time.

All of that was yesterday.

I rub the scar on my face as Fallador and Gambria talk to Mikail's back. They lied, these two. Fallador was supposed to be the exiled prince of Gaya, and Gambria was supposed to be his royal cousin, but they're not. They only came clean because we had to get the fuck out of Quu Harbor. With Aeri passed out, Mikail was the only one who could wield the Water Scepter.

The relic gleams in his hand. It's five feet of gold with a sapphire the size of my fist at the top. The metal and gem alone make it valuable, but it's the etherum, the god magic, that allows it to control the sea.

"…you weren't the only one. Mikail, are you listening?" Fallador asks.

Mikail turns and blinks his teal eyes like he's surprised they're here.

Gambria frowns as she folds her arms. "He wasn't listening at all."

I clench my jaw. They should give him a fucking break. He's doing okay for a guy who found out his whole past was a sham and whose lover was killed in front of him.

I'm about to say something, but Mikail smiles as if nothing's wrong. "I was paying attention, but for argument's sake, why don't you repeat what you said?"

Gambria huffs. What she lacks in height, she's got in attitude. But Fallador's nice enough. He just nods.

"Your birth parents were the Miats, the royal family of Gaya," he says, starting again. "You and I were switched as infants, in keeping with a long tradition."

Mikail strolls over and sits on the sofa across from Fallador. They both have warm brown skin and light eyes—Fallador's are green, not teal, but that's easy enough to overlook in babies. I guess they could've been swapped, but why?

I got a lot of questions, but I try to stay quiet, since I'm not really a part of this. I'm only here because I was pacing in the hall. Mikail opened his door and said I'd wake the entire place with my feet, so he invited me in.

"What tradition is that?" Mikail asks. He relaxes against the cushions as Fallador leans forward.

"Two hundred years ago, when Gaya became a colony, the Miats began secretly safekeeping the youngest child. They would switch that prince or princess with a commoner so that if Yusan broke the colonial treaty and attacked again, the Miat bloodline wouldn't die out. Really, it was done so there would always be someone to wield the Flaming Sword of Gaya."

That's the thing King Joon stole about twenty years ago.

Mikail picks at a bloodstain on his pant leg. "Why weren't the children told?"

Fallador frowns. "They were all told the truth when they came of age. However, that couldn't happen with you. Not with the Festival of Blood." He pauses, his eyes wet with tears, but then he shakes his head and refocuses on Mikail. "We thought you were gone along with the entire royal bloodline. I believed I was all that was left, and so I…had to…"

The ball of his throat bobs. He sniffles and looks away.

Gambria rests a hand on Fallador's shoulder. "So we kept up the facade in Khitan. By the time we discovered that you'd survived, you were already a spy for Yusan and everyone believed that Fallador was the exiled prince. At that point, we thought it safest not to say anything. If someone wanted to kill the last Gayan royals, they'd come for me and Fallador. And you were protected as spymaster… despite your best efforts."

"That's pretty shit reasoning," I blurt out.

She eyes me with pure contempt and continues like I said nothing. "We thought you'd be at greater risk if you knew the truth."

Mikail looks from her to Fallador and back. "Are you two actually related?"

"No," Fallador says with a sheepish grin. "Gambria's parents worked in the palace kitchens. She saved my life, secreting me away in a crate on a cargo ship right before they rounded up my…our family. We whispered that we would be cousins when we landed in Khitan."

So everything they said was a lie.

I wait for Mikail's reaction, but he just nods. He's taking all of this pretty well. Too well, if you ask me. But maybe lies aren't a big deal when you trade in them.

"Who else knows the truth?" Mikail asks.

"No one," Fallador says. Mikail raises an eyebrow, but Fallador doesn't blink. "Everyone who knew died that day. I only told Gambria after you first made contact with me eight years ago. As you can imagine, that was an…intense moment between us."

She gives him a hard stare, and even if I don't like her, I get her anger. They'd been through so much together, and he still hadn't told her the truth. He didn't trust her enough, love her enough, or care enough to give her honesty. I ball my hands in fists—that's a betrayal I can relate to.

"Well...your friends also know," Gambria corrects, her blue eyes darting over toward me. "Speaking of, what exactly is the plan?"

Yeah, what are we gonna do? Aeri has the Golden Ring of Khitan and the Sands of Time, and Mikail's got the Water Scepter. That leaves only the Flaming Sword of Gaya and the Immortal Crown, and King Joon has both of them. Nobody knows where we are... yet, but they'll search every realm to find us. We've got three relics. We're hunted now.

"Sora and Aeri are still asleep?" Mikail asks.

"Yeah," I answer.

Mikail shifts the scepter around, and a worry line forms on his forehead. A chill hits me in the warm room. I haven't seen that wrinkle since Euyn offered to bet his life for the Golden Ring. Come to think of it, I've never seen Mikail worried about death or danger for himself, but it's different with people he loves. Losing a loved one can send you to a place worse than death. I know that better than most.

He reaches for the metal pitcher on the table and pours another glass of water. I think this is his sixth cup today.

"We have to get to the city of Jeul and dispose of Governor Yong," Mikail says. "That is the plan—to free Gaya." He pauses and glances at me. I must look as confused as I feel, because he continues. "Jeul was the capital when Gaya was a realm, but the colony is still ruled from there. It's on the northwest side of the island."

Fallador tilts his head, and Gambria arches an eyebrow.

"What about the Yusanian garrisons?" Fallador asks. "There are around six thousand soldiers occupying the island, and most are stationed near Jeul."

My stomach drops at the number, but Mikail spins the scepter as he shrugs. "Once we take the capital, I'll offer the king's guard a choice: flee or die."

What?

"What?" Gambria shouts. "Take the capital with what? Humor and charm? You have no army, no navy. All we have is the skiff we stole from that warship and the clothes on our backs."

Fallador speaks before Mikail can answer. "Even if we can take Jeul…" He trails off and shoots Gambria a displeased look. "If you let the soldiers go, that will just be more men opposing us."

Mikail stops the scepter from spinning with one finger. "Are you proposing I kill them all?"

Fallador's eyes widen, and he shakes his head. "What? No. But we'll need our own soldiers—a great deal of them."

"We will rally the people of Gaya," Mikail says. "But I doubt we'll need as many as you think with three relics in our possession."

Gambria and Fallador look at each other as I try to figure out how Mikail thinks this'll work. Yeah, we've got the relics, but six thousand soldiers is a shitload of men when there's six of us. And we don't know what using two relics will do to Aeri. These relics don't give without taking.

Oh good. I'm worried about her again. I kick at the empty chair near me. Way to learn my lesson.

Gambria and Fallador keep eyeing each other, but no one says anything. The silence continues until it grates on my skin.

"Speak." Mikail hits the arm of the sofa. It's weird for a guy who doesn't have much of a temper. He's really not himself, but I guess that's tough to be when you don't know who you are.

"Adoros, this island has been under Yusanian rule for two centuries," Gambria says slowly. "And it has been fully absorbed for nearly twenty years. I told you that it's not the homeland we remember—that place is gone. Two decades is long enough for a generation to forget, to be loyal to Yusan, not Gaya."

"That's impossible," Mikail says, anger moving his features. "I've been in touch with spies. There is always rebel activity on the island."

She frowns. "A generation has been taught that Yusan liberated them, and you want to say it's not possible."

"A yoke is not liberation—even animals know the difference," he says. "A generation is alive who remembers the Festival of Blood."

I feel like I'm watching a tuhko match, my head going from side to side as they argue. I don't know who's right, so I keep waiting for the next point.

"Not everyone joined in the Gayan rebellion," she says. "You know this. The people who knew the truth are dead or they were on the winning side. Cowardice has a way of erasing bravery."

He waves a hand. "The people remember."

"Because you've spoken to so many of them?" Gambria's cheeks color as she raises her voice. "Just because you don't want to believe the truth doesn't make it false!"

I move closer to Mikail. I'm not his guard, but he doesn't need this woman yelling at him. And I'm happy to throw her out for free.

Gambria exhales and then stands. "I'm going to get some air."

Without waiting for a reply, she leaves the room. There's not a sound until the door clicks closed.

Good riddance.

Mikail stares off again, his eyes vacant. He looks like he's caught between worlds, sleepwalking while awake. I remember that feeling. After my girlfriend was killed nine years ago, it was like the Road of Souls was calling me but I was stuck here. It's why I was okay with death. Being the one left behind feels like a curse, not a blessing. And now, Mikail looks the same.

I shudder. If he goes looking for death, he'll find it. And then what happens to the rest of us?

"She does love you," Fallador says.

Mikail blinks, really trying to be present. He grins, faking being casual. "She has an odd way of demonstrating it."

6

Fallador shrugs. "Love is like water. It can take many different shapes, go through many different stages and forms, and yet it remains the same."

Is that true? I swallow hard and think about Aeri, still asleep in the other room. Are we just in another stage? No, the ache in my chest says otherwise. There can't be love without trust. She didn't trust me enough to tell me the truth, and I can't trust her for shit. It's a form of something, because I still want to make sure she's okay—even now—but it's not love.

"Are you sure you're...all right?" Fallador asks Mikail.

He reaches forward, placing a hand on his arm. Their eyes meet, and I pick the absolute worst time to clear my throat. They both stare at me. Without Gambria here, I'm the odd man out.

"I should… I should go patrol," I say.

If there was a subtle way to leave, I couldn't find it.

Mikail pulls away from Fallador and nods. "That's a good idea."

I'm nearly out of the room when I notice Fallador shake off a disappointed frown. He's hiding what he feels. Can we trust him?

Can we trust anybody now?

CHAPTER TWO

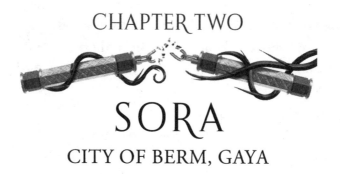

SORA

CITY OF BERM, GAYA

I cover my head with a pillow. Royo might have the heaviest feet in the four realms. He's been pacing, creaking the floorboards in the hall on and off since a little after dawn. Meanwhile, I've been tossing on my bed in this nice seaside inn as the ocean breeze flows through the windows.

We're temporarily safe, and I know I should rest while I can, but my mind is ill at ease. I can't stop thinking about Daysum, Tiyung, and what will become of us all.

It seems foolish now, but before Euyn died, it had started to feel like the five of us could survive anything together. We'd lived through our assassination attempt failing in the arena, the Marnan attack, and an avalanche—just to name a few close calls. But now it's clear that we're not invincible—even Aeri, who can sink ships at will. Royo must be worried about her, too.

Not that he'll admit it.

I turn, rearrange my long hair on the feather pillow, and try to fall back to sleep. Moments later, I give up. I'm undeniably awake. I slip out of bed, throw on my heavy dress and boots, and open the door.

Royo is right outside. He jumps backward with his hand reaching for a blade.

"Good morning," I say.

"Oh. Sora." He's breathing hard, and with some effort, he lowers his broad shoulders. "Hi."

"Were you about to knock?" I point to the wooden door.

"Yeah, no, I was… No. I just went… I wanted to… No." He nods, then shakes his head.

I asked the wrong question.

"Do you want to come in?" I gesture to the room.

"Is she… No, I'm fine out here." He shoves his hands in his pockets. He has on slacks and an undershirt that's straining to contain his chest. Inside that shirt, there's a broken heart spilling out.

He peers around me to Aeri, who is still asleep on the other bed. Last night, we decided it was best for someone to keep an eye on her, and I volunteered. It was nice to have the company. I used to sleep in the same room as my brothers and Daysum, and then there were nineteen other girls in the bedroom hall in poison school—at least at the beginning. After that, Hana used to sleep by my side every night until she died. It's easier to sleep when someone you love is near.

"I was just going to stretch my legs," I lie. "Want to join me?"

"Yeah…yes," Royo says.

I smile and lock the door behind me. He watches like a hawk, as if I can mess up turning a key. He's still protective, although he'd deny it. Broken hearts grow thorns as they stitch themselves back together. His has twice the armoring now.

We take the stairs down to the lobby. It's a smaller traveler's inn of two floors and twenty rooms, but they offered a good dinner.

Royo and I walk up to the desk, and the girl behind it smiles and says good morning. They speak Yusanian here.

I'm about to respond when the innkeeper steps behind the desk. I'm not sure how old he is, maybe forty, but he's balding with a thin black mustache and hungry brown eyes.

"Going out for the day, miss?" he asks.

"Yes," I say. "Is there a dress house nearby?"

The girl gives me directions while the innkeeper continues to stare at me. A chill runs down my spine in the warm lobby. Something about him makes me want to flee. Luckily, though, the interaction is short-lived, as there is a shop just a few blocks away.

"We're going to a dress shop?" Royo asks, opening the door for us to leave.

"You don't have to come, but I'm out of place in this." I gesture to my clothes. I lost the fur cape in battle, and I left the chest armor in my room, but I'm wearing a cold-weather gown and it's tropical in Gaya. The last thing we want is to stand out any more than we already do.

I look back over my shoulder as we leave and see that the innkeeper is still staring at me. A creeping suspicion takes hold of me, but I shake it off. Maybe I just don't like the feeling of being prey again. It was different in Khitan, where women had equal rights, but we're back in a Yusanian territory now.

As we step outside, the salty sea air reminds me of my home in Gain. For better or worse, it's a familiar feeling. Yet this island is different from anywhere I've been. Mikail said Berm is the second largest city in Gaya, but it's much smaller than Gain or even Use. If I had to guess, fewer than ten thousand people live here. The houses are whitewashed with patches of seagrass in front and high palm-thatched roofs. Black timber stilts protect them from a surging sea.

I limp slightly as I walk down the paved, sandy road. My pinkie toe remains blackened from when I froze on the way to Lake Cerome, but at least I can't feel it. Three of my other toes are red and still painful to walk on.

"Are your feet okay?" Royo asks. He stares down at my boots and then at me.

"I'll be all right," I say. "How are you?"

"Fine."

I side-eye him. We are many things, but none of us is fine.

He sighs. "Angry, hurt, sad, lonely, feeling like the king of fools—pick any one of those, I guess."

He kicks a rock, and it skitters down the street.

I nod. I understand what he means, and yet I don't know how he feels. I haven't had someone I love lie to me the way Aeri deceived him. But I did keep secrets from someone I love. Daysum would claim she could handle knowing everything when I knew she, in fact, could not.

"Some truths are held back out of love," I say.

He shakes his head. "You can't keep secrets from someone if you love them."

I stare into the distance. "You can if you think the truth will needlessly hurt them."

Royo opens his mouth and then closes it as we continue down the street.

Aeri and I spoke as we lay in our beds last night. We talked about how she didn't tell him or anyone else about having the amulet. Honestly, I wouldn't have told anyone, either. The relic is quite literally life and death. She used it to save Mikail in Oosant, Royo on the Sol, and to get me away from Seok in Khitan. Then with the ring, she turned two warship hulls to solid gold right before my eyes. She may have drowned two kings who fancied themselves gods. Of course she'd keep the Sands of Time a secret. Most people would slaughter her to take a relic that powerful—including her own father. And if Royo had known, it would have put him in harm's way.

There are weights you bear alone because the truth will crush someone you love.

But not all secrets are kept out of caring. Euyn didn't tell me about my parents—that they never sold me and Daysum, or that he hunted my father for sport. He also never told anyone that he didn't believe he was Baejkin. The truth can also be withheld out of selfishness or self-protection. I just don't believe that was the case with Aeri. Not with Royo, anyhow.

"She thought you'd be in danger if you knew the truth," I say. "Her father and many others would've tortured you until you broke.

She kept you in the dark to keep you safe."

"Yeah, because we're nice and safe now," he deadpans.

I laugh in spite of the situation. We certainly aren't. No one is until we figure out how to end this. Aeri said it best on the steps of the palace in Khitan: the ones we hate die first.

But how?

We have powerful relics, but we are just four people, six with Fallador and Gambria—if we can trust them. We were lucky to survive facing the empires one time. I doubt we'll survive again without an army on our side. How do we win? How does Seok die and Daysum live? How do we murder and save at the same time?

Royo and I keep walking in the humid air. It's not raining here, but Mikail mentioned that Gaya is so far south that the monsoons swing above it, the same way the rains don't reach west to Fallow.

Here, the tropical sun shines all year. Palm and date trees shoot up into the sky, their shade a welcome relief from this heat. Sweat glistens on Royo's brow and wets his shirt. Although we pass a forge, a bread house, a stable, and a tannery, I don't see any dress houses.

I start to think we missed a turn as we come to the end of a street. We were so busy scanning the storefronts that we're nearly at the base of a fortress before I notice it. Royo stops short as well. He blinks and wipes his brow with the back of his hand.

The garrison is built up on a green hill, and the soldiers patrolling it are Yusanian king's guard. Their tan uniforms with black leather armor are unmistakable. The red flag with the black snake flies from the turrets, waving in the ocean breeze.

Royo looks at me out of the corner of his eye and then crosses the street, away from the fort. He motions with his chin for me to follow because the last thing we need is to be detained by the king's guard. I doubt word has spread to look for us yet, but there's no need to draw attention to the fact that we're here.

I'm about to cross the street when something draws my eye. Two soldiers are talking to a shorter woman. She laughs, and I stop in my tracks.

I know that laugh. I heard it in a sleigh in Khitan.

Gambria is talking to king's guard.

I freeze. This isn't right. I don't know where Mikail and Fallador are, but we left Aeri alone at the inn. Gambria knows that she has two relics, and Yusan would pay good money for that information. Mikail says that Gambria is loyal, but is she? Enough gold can tempt even the strongest hearts.

Dread pools in my stomach, and my pulse pounds. We need to get back to the inn.

I cross over to Royo and meet his eyes. His breathing has sped up, and his muscles are tensed. We walk quickly to the end of the block, his jaw locked and spine rigid. As soon as we round the corner, we start running.

CHAPTER THREE

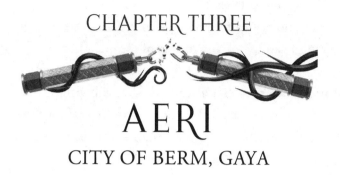

AERI

CITY OF BERM, GAYA

I slept like the dead next to Sora. I wake up gradually as a hand pulls at my ankle. I groan at yet another dream about Prince Omin. Another where he's touching me before I kill him. It's been seven years—when do the nightmares end?

But there's the briny scent of the ocean and multiple men breathing. It's not Omin—no, he's dead and I'm awake.

My reality is somehow worse than a nightmare.

I open my eyes with a start as Yusanian soldiers pull me from my bed. My heart pounds, my mind frantic. How did they find me here? They already have my arms, and they're yanking me out of the sheets. Mikail said to rest, that we'd be safe here. But the king's guard have already found us.

Wait… Sora. Where is Sora? She was just asleep in the bed next to mine.

Desperate, I turn my head every which way, but all I see are king's guard in black leathers. They're not steel-plated palace guards, but there are a bunch of them in here.

I flail and manage to slip out of the soldiers' hands. My freedom lasts for just a second before they grab my wrists again and pull my arms behind my back.

"Royo!" I yell, terror clawing at my throat. "Royo!"

A sweaty palm clamps over my mouth. His fingers smell like

onions. I'm going to be sick.

I twitch and try to pull away as my gaze darts around for help, for anything I can use or any means of escape. There are five soldiers in this second-story room, and there's nowhere for me to go. Sora is gone. Either they took her already or she fled without me.

No. She must've been taken. She wouldn't have left me behind.

Two of the soldiers pick me up and start carrying me. I twist, kicking out, and a third takes my legs.

It's hopeless.

My palms sweat, and my heart flutters against my ribs. Wherever they're taking me, it's somewhere away from my friends, away from Royo. No. I need a weapon, but my dagger is still buried under my pillow. I'm unarmed and dressed in a slip. My stomach sinks, and then my ring and amulet vibrate on my skin, begging to be used. Yes, I'm not powerless, but I can't get to them with my arms held. Wait… I don't have to. The two relics work with nothing more than intention now that their power is multiplied.

Weirdly, the soldiers don't try to remove the ring or pry the Sands of Time from my chest. The relics are fused to me, but they must not know I have them.

They're going to find out.

I'm about to turn the soldiers into gold when Mikail bursts through the door. He has the Water Scepter in one hand and a flaming sword in the other. He looks every bit a warrior king.

Everyone freezes. Except for Mikail.

He springs into deadly action, swinging his fiery blade. With one smooth motion, he slices into the three soldiers who have me. They drop me and grab their midsections. I land hard on the woven mat and roll out of the way of guts and blood splatter.

The soldier closest to the door takes off running as Mikail slits the throats of the groaning men. There's a brief scream in the hallway, and then Fallador appears with his sword dripping blood.

The last soldier backs away from Mikail with his hands up. He says something as I get to my feet, but I can't understand him. He must be speaking Gayan.

Mikail tilts his head, staring at the man's uniform. Anger contorts his face, his teal eyes ablaze. He swings his blade and slashes the soldier's throat. A fountain of blood sprays out, splashing Mikail's shirtsleeve.

The man clutches his own neck and then falls to the floor, gurgling.

I look down. I'm standing in my white slip, with four soldiers bleeding out on the ground and Mikail and Fallador staring at me. That's the scene Royo and Sora come running into. Sweat shines on both of their faces. Royo has a dagger out and brass knuckles on; Sora has a throwing knife ready, but they stop as soon as they take in the room.

"Well, good morning," I say. I smile at Royo, but then my legs give out.

I fall, slamming into the side of one of the beds. I manage to brace myself, clawing onto the mattress. For a second, fear swallows my next breath. I can't feel my legs at all. Royo and Sora rush to help me, but I wave them off. I hang on to the sheets and almost sob when the feeling in my legs returns. I get back on my knees and stay there, breathing hard.

"I just stood very fast," I say. "That's all."

It's a bit of an understatement.

Taking a deep breath, I get back to my feet. My knees, my legs are solid. All good, no lasting toll from the relics.

"What was this?" Royo's amber eyes dart around as his broad chest rises and falls. Gods, he looks good in that shirt.

"What happened?" Sora asks.

"How did they know we were here?" I wonder as the three of us talk at nearly the same time.

"The king's guard came looking for us first and then you," Mikail says. As usual, he's unaffected by slaughter. He casually uses a guard's shirt to wipe blood from his sword before sheathing it.

"But how did they know our exact rooms?" Fallador asks as he drags the other soldier's body into the room from the hallway. He tosses him onto the heap. The fake prince has been a good addition to our ring of liars. "We would've heard them kicking in other doors—they didn't."

Everyone stops and stares. It's not a coincidence—that's for sure.

"Because Gambria betrayed us," Royo says.

We all turn our attention to him. At first, I think he must be wrong, but I look around. Gambria is the only one not here. I doubt she slept through all of this, so maybe he's right. But Sora said Gambria saved them by the ice caves. And she helped us get to the palace in Quu. Why do that and give us up now?

"That's not possible," Fallador says. He wrinkles his nose at his bloody hands.

Sora sighs. "We just saw her talking to the king's guard."

Fallador shakes his head. "She would never betray us—not to Yusan."

As soon as the thought enters my head, it makes sense. Gambria did save them in Khitan, but that was before the events of Quu Harbor.

"I mean, she might not betray you normally, but she loved Quilimar, didn't she?" I ask.

The room goes quiet.

"Love leads to betrayal," I add.

I ignore the tick in Royo's jaw muscle at my words.

"Did you leave any of them alive to talk, Mikail?" Sora asks. She rests her throwing knife on the table and closes the door, all business.

He shakes his head. I guess that's the downside of killing so quickly—no witnesses, no sources.

"I suppose we'll have to ask her when she gets back," Sora adds.

Fallador peers out the window. "We need to find her and leave as soon as we can. The garrison commander will send reinforcements when the soldiers don't return. Sneaking out now will save us a lot of headaches."

"But what if more soldiers are lying in wait and it's an ambush?" Sora asks. "What do we do?"

I...hadn't even considered that. My mind is slow. It feels like I'm dragging my head through mud this morning. I'm not sure if it's the relics or just being so shocked and tired.

Mikail looks around with sharp eyes. "I don't think it's an ambush. There would be more soldiers pouring in, and the perimeter would be surrounded. I'm certain there's one or two guards downstairs and one or two outside, but they're just waiting for us to be brought out."

"Why, though?" I ask. "Why try to take us in with so few men?"

"Because they don't know we have the relics," Mikail says. "I assume someone reported us as suspicious but not as being fugitives. Quu happened so recently that even if Joon survived, he couldn't have alerted the full king's guard to arrest us." He pauses and shakes his head. "No, someone saw six strangers and notified the garrison."

I take in the five of us. We look like outsiders. We should've stopped at a dress house yesterday, but everyone always groans when I suggest a new wardrobe. As if clothes don't shout the world about you to anyone who'll listen.

A gentle knock on the door startles me. I grab the throwing knife Sora set down and reach for the dagger under my pillow. Mikail's sword burns to life. Fallador grips his blade, and Royo turns toward the door.

"Who is it?" Sora asks in her wind-chiming voice. She, of course, continues to look rested and radiant.

"Gambria," a woman's voice answers. It sounds like her.

Royo and Sora meet each other's gazes, and I feel like I'm missing something, but Fallador nods and moves to open the door. Royo adjusts his brass knuckles, his biceps flexing. Gods, I missed him. He's ignored me since I woke up on the skiff and he discovered I'd lied about having the Sands of Time, but he did just try to save me, running in from wherever he was. I saw it—he still cares. Hope bubbles in my chest, but then it bursts because caring isn't forgiveness. Even if he loves me, he won't ever be able to move past me lying a second time.

Fallador tiptoes around bodies and organs and opens the door slightly, but Gambria bursts in, holding a knife to the throat of a Gayan man. She throws him on the ground, and he lands on a dead body. The man flails and sputters, staring at the soldiers' open wounds. His feet skid along the bloody mat, and his jaw drops, but he's too shocked to scream.

What is happening? Who is this?

Gambria says something, but it's in Gayan and I can't understand her. Whatever it is makes the man tremble. I think she's saying *tell him*, but even though I pick up foreign words quickly, I only know a few in Gayan because it's considered a dead language.

Gambria's totally unfazed by the gore and bodies in the room as she stares hard at the man. I finally recognize his mustache—he's the innkeeper.

She says something else, pointing to the dead soldiers in the room.

"I... I...reported you," he says in Yusanian.

"I think that's fairly obvious," Fallador says. "Why?"

"Because you're out of place and came without luggage. Innkeepers, all citizens, must report strangers in order to protect Gaya."

Mikail's eyebrows rise slightly. "I understand protecting Gaya, but why would you say anything to the Yusanian king's guard?"

He sheaths his sword, but the tension in his shoulders says he could still kill a man in seconds.

"Because we are Yusanian." The innkeeper's eyebrows knit.

Gambria gestures with her arms in a move that translates to *I told you so*.

Now I'm sure I missed something.

Mikail sighs. Then he reaches out, grabs the innkeeper's head, and, with a brutal twist, snaps his neck.

Ugh. We're in so much more danger than we thought. And we haven't even gotten breakfast yet.

CHAPTER FOUR

TIYUNG

THE KHAKATAN MOUNTAINS, KHITAN

I hold a lantern as Hana and I approach the cave system that will take us under the Khakatan Mountains and back into Yusan. I need to return, but my steps are slow and deliberate. Weeks in Idle Prison stole my strength, but it's fear that makes my legs leaden.

Plus, I am still grappling with the fact that my father has taken Qali Palace. Somehow Seok went from being the southern count to sitting on the throne of Yusan, but however he accomplished that feat, he must believe I'm dead. I should be. I would've been ashes if not for Mikail's father's sacrifice. When Ailor heard the assassins coming, he pretended to be me, borrowing my noble necklace. He saved my life. And he was murdered for it in the dark of the cell.

We reach the cave mouth. It towers overhead like a hungry demon about to consume us. Darkness is all I see. I stumble back a step as fear grips my spine and my innards twist. My palms sweat in the cold. I've seen what happens in the dark. I can't go back there again—not into a lightless place, not to Yusan. There has to be another way.

"I… Maybe we should continue to Quu," I say.

Hana stops and pushes her hood back, shaking off snow. She stares at me, her beauty striking. Her eyes are the same brown as her hair. Her lashes are long, her face perfect, even as her full lips curl.

"You think, all things considered, that you can help Sora more by running into a land-and-sea battle in Khitan than by returning home and talking to your father, who has just appointed himself the new king of Yusan?"

I grimace. We heard the war drums at the border. We know Gayan and Yusanian troops are invading Khitan. And during this chaos, my father usurped the throne.

So I walk.

The daylight fades behind me, and I utter a noisy sigh.

"That place will cling to you, if you let it," Hana says. "Don't let it."

She keeps her chin high, but her expression changes, her eyes haunted. She must've gone to Idle Prison not only to communicate with me but in her role as a royal spy.

"It's easier said than done," I mutter.

She growls in disgust. "You think I don't understand suffering and the way it scratches and gnaws at your mind? It is a weight that constantly pulls at your neck, and it can drown you on dry land if you're not careful."

I wince. She's talking about her suffering at the hands of my family. She and nineteen other girls were selected by my father to become poison maidens. They were subjected to poisoning for almost ten years. Nearly five hundred weeks of torture. Only three survived, and then they had to murder at Seok's command. If they refused or died, their siblings were sold as pleasure indentures.

Hana looks me in the eye again.

"You are more than what you endure," she says.

She keeps walking, and I put my head down. I rustle up some bravery and trudge into the darkness, adjusting my heavy pack. Hana managed to acquire more supplies, even with people taking cover from the impending war. We'll need the food, firewood, and lamp oil for the trek back, but I'm surprised commoners parted with anything. Then again, there's always hope that tomorrow will be better. That the money she offered will buy them a brighter future.

We continue into the cave for bells, our two oil lamps burning a small path through the dark. I tell myself I'm fine, that I'm not back in a dungeon as Hana checks markings on the walls, but I'm not fine.

I keep seeing wet blood on the ground, and when I look again, it's gone.

I'm not sure how long we walk before we finally stop, but it felt like weeks. Hana puts her lantern in an alcove next to charred wood. A firepit here means there's a place where the smoke will vent to the outside. And this spot is protected on three sides. It'll do for a camp for tonight.

"Can I ask you something?" I inquire as I set down my pack.

She looks at me.

"Why are you coming back to Yusan when you were free in Khitan? If my father finds out you're alive…" I trail off. We both know he'd torture and kill her. It doesn't need to be spoken.

"For Sora." She blinks and then returns to arranging the logs I carried in.

"Does she know you're alive?"

I can't believe it hadn't dawned on me to ask. But before we escaped from Idle Prison, Hana was in charge of the questions, and I was a prisoner. Now, I'm the son of the king…somehow. I run a hand over my clean-shaven chin. My father's ambition is truly boundless.

Hana shakes her head just enough for me to know the answer. It's strange she didn't tell Sora that she'd faked her own death, but I suppose she couldn't risk making contact when Sora was still in Gain. But now the path will be clear for them to reunite—if we all survive.

I swallow the feelings of jealousy that rise in me. I don't want anyone else to have Sora, but that's not a fair thought.

"She'll be thrilled," I say.

Hana looks to the side as she takes out the fire starter, and then she nods. "She'll be relieved."

"You'll be able to be together." I unfurl my sleeping bag and try to sound pleased. It's harder than it should be, but I do want Sora to be happy, even if that's not with me. She deserves at least that much.

Hana stops striking the flint and stares at me. "You really don't know her at all, do you?"

"I do, I—"

"Tiyung, once she realizes I'm alive, she will never love me again."

I can feel my brow crease. "Of course she will. She'll—"

"I abandoned her and my brother, the two people I loved most in the world, just so I could survive. For myself alone. She would never have done the same, and no matter what, she won't be able to forgive it."

"She did," I say quietly.

The memory replays in my head of finding Sora hiding by that moss-covered boulder in the woods. She'd fled from Gain after she murdered her first victim. I was the one who dragged her back as she begged me to let her go. I drove her forward as she told me of the horrors she'd endured in poison school and about the man she'd just killed for my father—all while she begged me to report him to the king's guard.

Shame floods me in waves of hot and cold, but I don't shrink from it. I make myself remember the terrible cowardice and complicity I'm capable of. Only by owning your mistakes can you really hope to change.

Hana shakes her head again.

I lean forward. "Sora ran into the Xingchi forest three years ago and…"

Hana arches an eyebrow. "You think you just caught her?"

"I…had to."

She sighs, and her shoulders droop. "Kingdom of Hells, do you ever doubt your own greatness, Tiyung?" Hana takes a deep, steadying breath. She balls her hands into fists and then releases them. "Sora stopped running. She went far enough to have second thoughts and then no farther because I would've been left behind.

Because if she fled, she would've left Daysum to the wolves—the very thing I did to Nayo—the difference being, I didn't turn back. I didn't let anyone catch me. She had a moment of weakness after taking a life for the first time. I've lived for only myself."

I sit on the ground next to the firepit as I think back to that day. Hana can't be right. Sora didn't *want* to be caught. But...she wasn't moving, and she wasn't well hidden when I found her. I had to push her back to Gain, but not wanting to return isn't the same as actively escaping.

"I had to become another person in order to go on," Hana says. "It cost me everyone I loved. I mean it when I say I'm not Hana anymore. Hana died two years ago when I made that deal with the nobleman. I let him live, and he helped me kill Hana."

The space fills with quiet regret, with choices that can't be unmade.

"She'll understand," I say gently. "Nayo did."

Hana stares at me. "You don't know a thing about Sora."

She shakes her head and then lights the fire. She's not vicious, just resigned, and that's worse. I turn the lamps down to conserve the oil.

"You don't believe I love her," I say.

Hana hesitates. She pulls out a dinner pot and runs her hands over the metal. "At first I thought you just fell for her beauty, and that's surely a part of it, but the more I think about it, the more I believe you love the concept of her."

She's wrong, but it's pointless to argue about my own feelings. I love Sora from the arch of her foot to the depths of her soul. I love all the ways she's strong and every weakness. I'd know her in a hundred lifetimes, and I'll love her through all of them.

We sit silently as Hana prepares a rice pot, filling it from the water bladder. Curiosity soon gets the better of me, though.

"What concept is that?" I ask.

Hana meets my eye. "Atonement."

The word knocks the wind out of me.

No. She's not right. But something about atonement sticks in my mind. Something about it feels true. Is that what I'm searching for? Am I doing all this to atone for who I was and what I let happen, or do I truly love Sora? When I was in Idle Prison, I asked Ailor if he thought redemption was possible, and he gave his life thinking I could make amends. Is that what this is?

Nothing but the crackling of the fire answers me.

"So then, if you're right, neither of us love her enough," I say.

Hana nods and then smiles slowly. "Finally, something in common."

CHAPTER FIVE

SORA

CITY OF BERM, GAYA

Today has been very odd. Gambria might've betrayed us, but she also picked up casual clothes for everyone—a strange dichotomy. I change in her room, tossing on a plain white dress and shoes. At least now we'll blend in.

But as I tighten my sandals, I'm still not sure if we can trust her.

I sigh at yet another mystery as I hurry down the hall of the inn. I take a final look at the six bodies in my room, then shut the door. We're meeting in Mikail's suite, and we don't need a well-intentioned traveler or maid stumbling upon all this.

"Here, wait," Aeri says, coming up behind me. She slips a privacy sign on the handle.

I can feel my eyebrows knit, but I guess that's as good of a plan as any.

"Are you all right?" I ask.

She shrugs. "I'm good. Wait, do you mean from the attack or the relics?"

Her golden eyes examine me. They're so brilliant that they still catch me off guard.

"Both, I suppose."

"Yeah, I'm good." She shrugs again and smiles.

I stare as she traipses into Mikail's room in her sky-blue dress. She's such an odd person—the combination of light and dark. But

I'm relieved that Aeri is safe despite me leaving her alone, asleep and unprotected.

I linger in the hall, blowing out a sigh. I can't make these kinds of mistakes—not with so much hanging in the balance. Not only do I love Aeri as a friend, but we need her to take the throne of Yusan. She doesn't want a crown, but she is the only one who can change things.

Gambria eyes me as I walk into Mikail's suite. The door doesn't shut properly because the frame is broken. Soldiers must've kicked it in, but I push it as closed as possible. We won't be here for long. We just need to figure out where to go. That's harder than it sounds, because where is there a safe place for us? Not Wei, certainly not Khitan or Yusan. Maybe Fallow, but those lands are lawless. Euyn and Mikail barely made it out of there.

The others are waiting, but I pause next to Gambria and whisper in Khitanese, "Why were you talking to soldiers?"

Gambria stares down at her sandals and then meets my eyes. "I realize it looked suspicious, but I was trying to find out what happened in Quu. If anything has been heard about King Joon or... the queen."

She holds my gaze even though her eyes are glassy.

I nod. It's difficult to exist while not knowing what's become of someone you love. I haven't heard anything about Daysum since Seok said he sold her to the pleasure houses. Sometimes I can manage to push it all aside, but most of the time I feel like I'll scream or burst from lingering in this space of the unknown.

"Was there any news?" I ask.

"Nothing yet."

I search her face, schooled in the ways women lie, but I can't tell. I don't know her well enough, and her real emotion for Queen Quilimar hides anything else. I suppose we can't know for sure right now. Of course, we'll find out if Gambria ultimately turns on us.

It's not a comforting thought, but not many are.

"So I have a plan," Mikail says. He has blood on his sleeve, a lot of it, but he's unbuttoning his shirt to change.

"This ought to be good," Gambria says. She goes and sits next to Fallador. We're all ignoring the pools of blood and the six dead soldiers littering the floor.

That makes twelve we murdered today. Twelve people. My stomach twists, and I wring my hands. I try to remember that they would've killed any of us if they'd known who we were, but it's a dozen more souls to tally against us in the Kingdom of Hells.

I rub my palms on my cotton dress. Maybe I should stop keeping count, since this won't be the end of it. I made this exchange long ago—letting Lord Yama write the total in exchange for Daysum's life. No sense in regretting it now.

"What's the plan?" Royo asks.

Mikail tosses on another shirt. Scars old and newer crisscross his back—marks of all he's endured. Some people think scars are ugly. I think they're badges of being a survivor.

"We go to Cetil and regroup there." He pauses and takes in our puzzled expressions. "It's a Yusanian town across the Strait of Teeth from Gaya. I have sources and a safe house there, but it's close enough to get to Jeul in less than a bell."

"Yusan?" Gambria asks. "And how are we getting there?"

"On the skiff," Mikail answers.

The skiff has oars and a single sail, but the way he spins the scepter, I know we won't be using either.

"You shouldn't use the scepter unless you have to," Aeri says. "The toll sharply increases every time."

Mikail waves his hand. "Let me worry about that."

I'm not sure Mikail is in his right mind—actually, I'm certain he's not. Then again, I'm not sure any of us are all right. But Mikail has been taunting death since Euyn was murdered. We have to stop him because eventually, Lord Yama accepts all offerings.

Mikail looks at each of us. No one is exactly leaping at the idea. Yusan seems like the worst place to go. "I'm open to suggestions, but we don't have the means to stand and fight. We need time to figure out what happened in Quu Harbor, and we've already worn out our welcome here." He gestures to the bodies in the room.

"All right, then. Let's go," Aeri says, standing.

Royo and I exchange glances. I suppose that's that.

We all grab our weapons, but I stop as an idea hits me. If we're going back to the coast of Yusan…

I make my way to Mikail, my heart fluttering. I didn't think we'd be able to get to Gain this soon, but maybe we can. Mikail has the Water Scepter, and if he thinks Yusan is safe enough for us, then maybe we can rescue Daysum before sunset.

"Mikail," I say. "If we're going to Yusan, can we stop… Is it possible to go to Gain?"

Something crosses his face—a ghastly expression. It's so fleeting, I barely register it, but it chills me to the bone. I hold my breath, waiting for his response. His lips part, his shoulders falling.

"Sora…" Mikail begins. Then he pauses because footsteps pound down the hall. They're as heavy as Royo's, but it's more than just one man.

Soldiers.

Mikail pulls me behind him and draws his sword. It flames to life just as two king's guard come through the door. Their swords are drawn, but they pause, taking in the scene in front of them— the six of us gathered by the sofa and the six soldiers dead on the ground.

Royo moves first. He grabs one of the soldiers and pulls his arms back until they snap with a sickening sound. Fallador runs his sword through the man's chest. At nearly the same time, Mikail leaps onto the sofa. He's on the back of the couch for a moment before he jumps and pierces the neck of the other soldier from above.

His speed and aim are unnatural. I didn't have time to move, let alone jump from the top of the couch, and now the guard is dead.

"Right," Mikail says. He lands on sure feet, then shakes blood off his sword. "Let's get to that skiff."

Fourteen dead today. I really must stop counting.

CHAPTER SIX

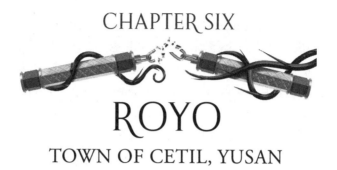

ROYO
TOWN OF CETIL, YUSAN

Turns out Mikail was right: we needed to get the fuck out of Berm. As we ran to the skiff, another soldier tried to stop us. He faced off with Fallador, spinning and whipping around his nunchuka. He was pretty good, but he was so focused on showing off that I was able to get behind him. I grabbed a rock and bashed the guy's skull. I'm not sure if I killed him or what, but I pocketed the nunchuka—they're the nicest I've seen.

A bell later and we're back in Yusan on a small, rocky beach. There's a town above us built into the hillside. This has gotta be Cetil. It's nothing like Tamneki or Quu—it's just a sleepy little spot. Mikail wasn't kidding when he said it's real close to Gaya. I can still see the island and even the walls of the city he called Jeul from here. He said we'd be safe, but he also said that about Gaya. I grip the nunchuka hanging from my belt. I don't trust this place, even if I trust Mikail.

I can admit I was wrong about him—he saved us all in Khitan. But I don't trust his friends. We didn't need new people with us—we already had enough issues.

"What's this?" Aeri says.

She's still standing next to the skiff. She reaches down and pulls out a long tube that had been hidden in the side of the Weian boat.

We all move closer as she opens it. Of course she rummaged through the compartments. Once a thief, always a thief. Same as being a liar.

She opens the tube and slides out a long cloth. Inside, there's a wooden walking stick that's about as tall as Sora.

Fallador strokes his chin. "What do you think that's for?"

Aeri stares at the stick and then Mikail. Her tipped golden eyes shift, and she smiles. "I think Wei built this to hold the scepter—to disguise it. It's the same size and around the same shape."

Fallador's eyebrows come together. "Why would they try to camouflage the scepter? Everyone knew they had an unsinkable navy with the relic."

Aeri shrugs. "For the same reason they had this escape skiff—in case things went wrong."

Mikail closes his fist around the scepter. He's been weirdly possessive about it. But then he relaxes his hand and angles it closer to the walking stick. "It is around the same size, but how does the scepter fit in? Is there an opening at the bottom?"

Sora shakes her head. "I don't see one."

Aeri feels along the side of the walking stick, and then all of a sudden, it pops open. Just splits in half. She must've pressed a spring.

She smiles, delighted. I cross my arms and pretend it doesn't pull at my heart.

I'm not going to act like I can turn cold to Aeri. I can't, but I got enough dignity to keep my distance. She's who she is, and all she's gonna do is hurt me.

Prince Euyn is dead, and with him went hope. People don't change, and neither does the world. We're broken pawns on a crooked board in a game we didn't ask for. All I want now is to make sure whoever goes on the throne will free Hwan, and then that's it. I'll walk away and be on my own. I'm better off that way.

Mikail studies the thing with his brow furrowed. He slides the scepter in and then closes the case. As he picks it up, it looks like a simple walking stick.

"Incredible," Sora whispers.

"Now you'll be able to carry the relic anywhere," Aeri says, still beaming.

He smiles back at her. "I'm glad you found this."

We follow Mikail as he leads us to a long stone staircase built into the hill. When we get to the top, we're in a cobblestone town square. Now that we're up here, I can spot a small harbor down the coast. We could've used that, but Mikail probably wanted to avoid us being seen after all the shit in Berm.

He strolls through the square like he knows it, but I guess when you're a spy, every place feels like home. It's nice, though—not as hot as Gaya with lots of shade trees. But we're still south of the monsoons, so it's sunny. A market, temple, and shops line the square. The houses in the hills are nice but small.

Mikail stops for a long time at a drinking fountain. His arms shake as he leans down, but then they stop. When he's finally done, he leads us through the town and up a dirt road.

Fallador has looked over at him a few times. "This is where you grew up." He smiles. "Where you could see Gaya over the water."

Mikail nods.

Fallador stares at the island. "I see why you love it still."

"Our people just need to be shown the truth, and the island will remember who they are," Mikail says. "I'm sure of it."

Gambria and Fallador exchange skeptical looks, but neither says anything back.

"Isn't Gayan history written in their Temple of Knowledge?" Aeri asks.

"There isn't a temple anymore," Mikail says. "It used to be in the sacred tree of Alta, but Yusan burned it and the sacred woods to the ground at the end of the Festival of Blood."

Anger and outrage stab at my chest, and I clench my jaw. I grab the green temple key that's still in my pocket, then force myself to let go. Why am I mad about a bunch of books? It ain't bread or ale. Not blood or bone. I shake my head. I need to get it together. So what if they burned a Temple of Knowledge? Books are the least of anybody's worries when men are dying.

Still, it's a kind of violence to erase the history of a realm. It feels like something was pulled away from all of us, even though I'm not Gayan.

"I heard the temple still exists," Fallador says.

Mikail turns and eyes him. "That's not possible."

I tap the key in my pocket. "Wait. The priest guy in Khitan said the key would work on Gaya, too."

"You're right, he did," Mikail says. "But I thought he was speaking theoretically."

"There were Gayan scrolls on the Rule of Distance," Sora adds as we walk. "And that went into effect years after the Festival, right? The temple must still stand...somewhere."

Mikail's face takes on that look of his when he's deep in thought and coming up with a plan that's likely to kill a bunch of people.

We continue up the dirt road.

"Where are we going, anyway?" Aeri asks after a few minutes. She's paused next to Sora, who's now in the back. I can't tell if Sora is out of breath or they both are.

"A safe place where we can wait until we hear news out of Quu," Mikail says, slowing his pace. "It's a little farther this way, up by those olive trees." He points about fifty yards ahead.

We continue into an orchard. We're in pairs like we were on the skiff again—Fallador and Mikail in front, Sora and Aeri together, and me stuck with Gambria. I'm not sure who's got a bigger problem with this—me or her. But I'm not the one who ratted us out to the king's guard, so she can fuck off.

Bees buzz, and it should smell like flowers and lemons, but it doesn't. I sniff. There's the salt of the ocean and the loam of the earth, but something else is in the air. It kinda smells like a campfire after you stomp it out. I don't know why, but it makes the little hairs on my neck stand and my skin prickle. I don't like it.

"Just a little more up this way," Mikail says, looking back at us. His eyes are bright, but there's something in his voice. He sounds unsure, suddenly leery.

I shift a dagger into my hand, and I catch Sora doing the same. Gambria silently cocks her crossbow.

Yeah, everybody else feels it, too.

We all crest the hill at the same time. Mikail smiles, clearly expecting something nice, but then his jaw drops. There should be a house here, but there's not. It's just the charred remains of what had been one.

We circle together, pulling out weapons, and I scan for danger. Gambria puts her bow to her shoulder, but there's nothing to shoot. It's quiet. Whatever happened was a while ago.

Nobody's here.

Still, we move as one because nothing about this feels right. There's something on the ground up ahead. I'm not sure what it is, so we go slow.

When we get close enough, Aeri draws a breath. It's a half-eaten donkey. The way the head is almost detached means men killed it, but other animals scavenged from the carcass. Probably those fucking hael birds.

Mikail falls on his knees next to the animal, and a swarm of flies lifts into the air. He looks like he's going to scream, but he's silent, his face all anguish.

I look from him to the house and back again. Why's he so upset? Whose house is this?

A red stain by what had been the front door catches my eye. I draw my nunchuka, wishing I had an axe. Sora is by my side with her blade drawn. Gambria and Fallador stay back by Mikail. Aeri walks halfway to us but stops, torn between staying and going.

Sora takes a deep breath as we creep forward another step. Her other hand has a vial. Probably poison. Seems useless, but I saw what she could do with poison dust in the banquet hall in Khitan.

My stomach clenches as we keep moving, and I grip the nunchuka and my dagger tighter.

One step, another. I think we both expect the red stain to be blood like in the Temple of Knowledge. There's gonna be a body, or a few of them.

We reach the door, and I see that it's not blood—it's paint. The word *Baesinga* is written in red on what had been the threshold stone. I look around, but there's just rubble. No people, no corpses. I relax my shoulders although I'm still confused.

"What's that mean?" I ask. "*Baesinga*."

"It's an old word for traitor," Sora whispers.

Mikail lets out a cry so loud, birds take flight. It's the sound of inconsolable grief and raging anger, and it rattles me to my core. His hands dig into the dirt as his neck arches back. He screams until he doesn't have air left in his lungs.

It's the same sound he let out after Euyn died. Maybe worse.

Tears well in Sora's eyes. Fallador and Gambria stand stock-still.

"I don't understand," Aeri says, moving around in a circle. "What happened? Whose house was this?"

"My father's," Mikail says on a ragged breath.

Oh fuck.

My stomach twists, and a cold dread like I've never felt before hits me. His father didn't survive this. I just know it. Everything Mikail did to save him, everything we all did, and his father is still gone. Ten Hells. What if all the people we're trying to save are already dead?

CHAPTER SEVEN

MIKAIL

TOWN OF CETIL, YUSAN

After I get to my feet, I toss the scepter onto the ground, find a shovel, and start digging a hole. Spade in the earth, dirt up and over onto a pile. That's all I focus on—moving dirt. It feels good to do something, anything with this soul-sucking grief. Shovel, loosen earth to make a hole, repeat.

One motion, one thing at a time to keep madness at bay.

Anything, everything to keep from thinking about what I lost.

Once the hole is big enough, I gesture for Royo and Fallador to help me. Royo looks like he'd rather be somewhere else. His face takes on a shade of green I haven't seen since Euyn was seasick, but he helps anyway. We pull the remains of Sticks, my father's beloved donkey, into the hole. Then I start covering it. Spade, dirt, back into the ground.

The palace guard killed the animal for no reason.

The last time I visited Ailor, he was practically in love with the creature. He'd bought Sticks to help with the harvest, and it was like he had another son. He smiled and joked as the donkey nudged him and stole his hat. I was happy that Sticks had brought youth back to his life. I'd done similar for him when he found me in Gaya and raised me from a scarred little boy to a man. He'd lost his wife but gained a son. Now there's nothing I can do aside from stopping the scavengers. But I can do that much.

The others are searching the area, looking for any signs of my father, but I already know they won't find him. Not here.

Qali Palace guards took him. They are the only ones who would write *Baesinga* on a house—the only ones who mark traitors to the throne. Joon had said he would take good care of Ailor, but I thought it was an idle threat. I thought he wouldn't dare touch a decorated war hero. Or maybe that's what I'd wanted to believe. Somewhere in the rubble is my father's medal of valor.

Stars. He gave everything to this realm, and it wasn't enough.

Ailor must be in Idle Prison, or he's already dead. Zahara hasn't been in touch, but I'll send eagle post as soon as I can. I'd march on Qali to free him right now, but I have to wait and bide my time. My whole life has been a long game, and I'm so tired of holding still while everything gets stripped away, but I remind myself that impatience results in disaster. We need resources, weapons, and men before we face Joon. I didn't come this far and go through this much to fail. Not when I'm this close.

Still, useless rage boils my blood. He'll pay. I swear on the stars and to the gods, Joon will pay. I'm not sure how much blood it will take to quench this grief, but I know how much I'm willing to try.

I pat down the dirt over the donkey's remains, and I think of all the souls I will steal from Lord Yama. Aeri already took care of General Salosa and Count Bay Chin. She turned them to gold sand statues, dead at the bottom of Quu Harbor without a chance for their souls to be reborn. I'll bury the rest of the palace guard—right here, if I can, and Joon and Quilimar along with them. I'll have my revenge, and it will have to be enough.

My hands shake as I drop the shovel. Will it be enough? My heart thumps an irregular beat. I'm not sure I can handle losing more, but there isn't much more that can be taken from me. I keep expecting to see Euyn setting up traps or looking over my shoulder, but he's dead. And now my father is gone. The five other people here are the only family I have left. And if they die, I'll surely be with them.

The ones we hate die first.

It's what Aeri said. That is the promise I cling to. They will die first. I pick up the scepter and look for the others.

Baesinga.

I'll show Yusan what treachery looks like.

I find everyone gathered at a wooden table by the patio. Somehow, the patio and table remained intact. It's a sunshiny day, and I can almost imagine that we are visiting with my father. He'll come out of the kitchen with a baked fish any moment now.

Then I look at the charred house and grip the staff.

This isn't a picnic, and the time for daydreams and memories is over.

"Is it drinkable?" I point to a pail of water in the center of the table.

Depending on the crime, the palace guard is not above salting the earth and poisoning the well of a traitor. But I'm dying of thirst, so I'm willing to risk it.

"I tried it for poison," Sora says. "It's clean."

I nod and lift the pail. There isn't anyone I trust more than her.

I gulp down so much water, so quickly, that the front of my shirt becomes soaked. I should sip slower, but using the relic causes unbelievable thirst. The scepter pulls water directly out of my body, and now the toll is twice as bad as it was the first time. Aeri had tried to warn me, but there was no choice. We didn't have time to slowly row the boat out of Berm. Besides, if the Weian bearers can survive two years constantly using the staff, I'll be fine.

Sora walks over, her beauty actually enhanced by a simple cotton dress. Her purple eyes are filled with sincerity and shared grief.

"Mikail, I'm so… I'm so sorry," she says.

"I know." I do. I know if Sora could take this pain away, even if it meant her own suffering, she would. She understands loss and useless rage better than anyone.

"He's probably been taken into custody," she adds.

I nod. I have to believe that—believe he's still alive and being held. But people don't survive Idle Prison. Not really. Even if they live, they're not the same. That place takes away all you are from the outside in.

She draws a long breath, hesitant to say something, but her expression morphs from concern into resolve. I smile—she's still made of steel.

"I hate to ask, but seeing this... Is there a way we can go to Gain? I... I have to know."

My cheeks tingle as the blood flows away from them. Today has actually gotten worse.

Sora had started asking about Gain when we were in Gaya, but then soldiers came crashing into our room and there wasn't time to answer her. And then, shamefully, I simply forgot between wielding the scepter and finding my father's house.

From the bottom of my heart, I don't want to tell her about Daysum. Yet I owe her the truth.

I put the pail down and swallow hard. "Sora, walk with me, please."

Her worry line shows, but she nods. "Of course."

I offer her my arm, and she takes it.

We stroll down the groves we came through. When we first climbed up this hill, just a little while ago, I was a different person. I was excited, hopeful, and relieved. I thought I'd find my father pressing olives in front of his home and arguing with Sticks. I thought we'd be safe under his quiet care for at least a night or two, the same way I was as a boy. I used to wake up from endless nightmares and find Ailor tired but stoking a fire. I'd sit next to him, and without asking me what I'd dreamed of, he'd read stories of a hero named Mikail.

It will be the same for Sora—there will be a before and after. And I can only hope I can provide some comfort to her the way my father did for me. I didn't have the words to tell her in Loptra, but now, being here, I think I do.

"I used to eat olives and lemons off these trees as a boy," I say. "Absolutely stuff myself. There are also capers that way. The combination with fish was frequently dinner and lunch. You'd think I'd have gotten sick of it, but I never did."

She smiles and looks around at the grove.

"But that was after Ailor saved me from the Festival of Blood," I say. "My family, both my birth family and my childhood family, were slaughtered, as were tens of thousands of others. Ailor was a Yusanian captain who found me after that night of terror. His orders were to kill all survivors—anything with a heartbeat. But instead, he smuggled me back here and raised me as his son. He'd recently lost his wife, and he was living here alone before me."

"Oh, Mikail," she says, her lashes wet. She squeezes my arm. "He sounds like a good man."

"He is. We sat right here on the property and watched as they burned the victims on enormous pyres. You could see the smoke and flames for miles. Some of the ash carried all the way over the strait."

"That must've been…" Sora sighs. "I don't know. I can't imagine it."

"Everyone I loved, everything I knew was gone. The island was so close but out of reach for the rest of my life. Gaya had changed overnight, and suddenly there was nothing there for me anymore. Instead, I became Mikail—Ailor Vee's son. And so, I know what it feels like when I tell you now: there is nothing for you in Gain."

Sora turns to me, a line marring her forehead. "Of course there is, there—"

She stops, and her light skin turns whiter. She draws a shaky breath. I know she's going to ask me about her sister, and I'm going to have to tell her. I've put it off for as long as I could. Maybe longer than I should've. But now, there is no escaping the truth.

My heart drums steadily as I wait. Sora closes her eyes and inhales. Then she exhales and stares directly at me.

"Daysum is dead," she says.

"Yes."

She exhales again. Or really, the air is knocked from her lungs by the impact. She lets go of my arm. I truly wish I didn't have to do this, but I'm also glad that I am the one to tell her. I'm the only one who really knows how she feels.

She shakes her head. "When?"

"A sunsae ago," I say. "More."

She nods, but the pieces are falling into place in her mind. Her eyes move rapidly. I brace myself and wait.

"But how do you know? You couldn't have just found out. We haven't been to a messenger house since... How long have you known?"

I draw a breath. My own delay brought about this moment, my own actions and inactions. "Longer than I should've. I wanted to tell you in Loptra, but—"

She startles and takes a step back. She shakes her head as if she didn't hear me correctly. But she did. I made sure to stand on her hearing side.

"Loptra?" she repeats.

"Yes."

Backing up another step, she puts her hands in her hair. Then she pulls and screams. The cry echoes around us.

I have to stop myself from shuddering.

As soon as I said the city, it felt like Loptra was so long ago. Over a week has passed since I found out, but we were constantly running for our lives or in the midst of incredible danger.

"There wasn't time to tell you, Sora," I say.

She shakes her head. "We waited for days in Vashney..."

I close my eyes slowly. She is right. We waited for Aeri and Royo to meet us after we survived the Marnan attack. But we had a mission, and I was dealing with Euyn's wound and his spiraling conspiracy theories. I thought telling her would only distract her, put her at risk. "I wanted to tell you when we were safe."

I realize how hollow it sounds, but it's also the truth.

She laughs. "You know, I just spoke to Royo about how some secrets are kept out of love and others out of selfishness." She stares off and then shakes her head. "I murdered men and women because I thought it would save Daysum. And you let me. Knowing it was already a lost cause."

"Sora… We killed for each other."

"If your father was dead, would you continue on?" She examines me, waiting to pounce on any tell, any lie.

I sigh. I already think he is. "I wouldn't want to know."

"But I did." She slaps her hand to her chest. "And you made the choice for me. And so did Euyn. And so did Seok. And so did the king." She stops and stares at Gaya across the Strait of Teeth. "This whole rotten thing can burn."

I remain silent because she's not wrong.

"And you can burn with it," she says.

She stares at me with such intensity that I straighten my spine. I don't grab for my sword, but I consider it. Not to hurt her, never to hurt her, but to defend myself.

But she's not attacking me. Not physically.

Sora walks past me, and even though I want to reach out for her, I let her go. I tell myself she didn't mean that. She said it because she needs time, but deep down I'm not sure she will change her mind. I am the one who broke our bond.

Taking a breath, I stare at the ground. This used to be a safe haven for me, a place of respite, but Ailor is gone and now we need to go somewhere else. I need a new plan—always a new plan. I have to go back to the others and tell them something. I have to lead because their lives are in my hands.

But I'm so very tired.

I let my shoulders fall. I allow the weight of all that's happened to register for a moment. Just one. Sora's hate, my father's loss, finding out my real identity all too late. But I don't think about Euyn's murder. I can't.

After one second, I gather myself again. I didn't survive to stop now. Sora asked if I'd keep going if I knew the truth, and I didn't spare it a thought. I have no choice. I always have to move forward.

Resolved once more, I turn to walk back to the patio, but there's Aeri standing just a few yards away. She must've overheard everything. With a sigh, I know there's no sense in denying it. I did what I thought was best for Sora, for all of us, and if I had to make the choice again, I'd do the same. One hundred more times, and I would still do no different. Sora was so broken after hearing her sister was sold that we couldn't risk having her shatter. It would've put everyone in danger to have her that distraught—not just herself. If Sora chooses to hate me now, then she does. I stand by the decision, and I'll bear the consequences.

But there's something off about Aeri. I squint as a feeling of wrongness drapes over me. I take a step closer. Her eyes are open, but she's not moving at all. I thought she was speechless, but her hand is slightly raised, and she's leaning forward. It's like she's turned into a statue.

It's like she's frozen.

I wave a hand in front of her eyes. She doesn't blink.

"Aeri," I say.

Nothing.

I clap my hands in front of her face, and she doesn't move.

Stars, what is this?

CHAPTER EIGHT

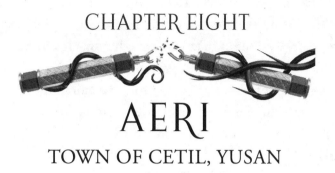

AERI

TOWN OF CETIL, YUSAN

Mikail has a very concerned look on his face. He comes into focus slowly, which is strange, but there he is, a foot away from me.

"Aeri!" he yells, his voice strained.

I shake my head and blink. I must've spaced out for a second. I went to find him and Sora after I heard her cry, but now he's standing in front of me, looking very bothered. Which, I mean, makes sense. We just found his father's house burned to the ground, his mule slaughtered, and his father missing. It would be weird if he were okay. Then again, he's done a decent job of faking it with Euyn dead.

"Hey, are you all right?" I ask.

"Me?" He points to his own chest, his eyes wild. "Aeri, you were just not moving for a full minute."

I have no memory of that, and I'm sure he's exaggerating, but the look in his eyes tells me he's genuinely worried. "I... I don't remember that."

He shakes his head. "I couldn't snap you out of it. It was like you were frozen in..."

"Time?" I fill in the blank.

He pales.

We stand silently in the orchard. Maybe this is the toll. I was surprised that sinking two ships made me pass out but didn't seem to have any other ill effect. The amulet alone was stealing years off my life. Using that with the ring has to do something terrible. Nothing is free in Yusan, particularly etherum. It's just odd that I don't remember it, that I didn't feel any pain.

"Do you think this is from using the two relics?" I ask.

Mikail rubs his forehead. "I'd have to think so. You didn't find anything about the multiplication properties in the Temple of Knowledge?"

"No, but I don't think any human has ever had two relics."

He frowns. "Your father did during the War of the Flaming Sword."

"I read that he didn't use the sword, though," I say. "Which…if he could've, he certainly would've. Do you think that's because…"

I trail off, trying to think of how to phrase it, but my mind is muddy again. It almost feels like I'm in two places at the same time. I shake my head and force myself to focus on Mikail, on the dirt path and the breeze coming from the Strait of Teeth. I make my mind be present.

"Is it possible the sword was bonded to you as a child?" I ask. "You're the only royal survivor, and the amarth said something about relics not being useful while the wielder still lives."

Lines appear on Mikail's brow. "I suppose anything is possible. Fallador had mentioned needing the Royal Gayan bloodline to use the sword. It would be odd for him to know the relic was bound to me and not mention it, but I think that's a question for our friends."

Mikail gestures back to where the house stood.

"Where is Sora?" I ask, looking past him.

"Oh, she… She needed some air," he says.

He avoids looking at me, and it's weird.

"Should I go find her?" I ask.

He sighs, glancing down the orchard. "I think she probably wants to be alone for a little while. I doubt she'll go far."

"But maybe I should…" I shift my weight. I don't like anyone going off on their own. We now have a history of things going very wrong when we split up.

Mikail nods. "All right, bring her back."

He continues up the path, his scepter hidden in the walking stick, and I go the other way. I'm not sure what happened between them, but Mikail looked oddly guilty and overall weird just now.

Still, it's a far better walk moving downhill. The climb was steep, and Sora had to stop a few times to catch her breath. I wasn't winded, but my legs continue to feel strange. Well, sometimes I feel them and sometimes I don't. And now I have that…whatever that was in the orchard.

Best not to think about it.

I swing my arms as I walk and continue through the groves, calling Sora's name occasionally, but nothing answers me except for birdsong. I can't imagine her ignoring me, but she did have a five- or ten-minute head start.

"Sora? Sora!" I call.

Worry creeps in as I continue without an answer. The little hairs on my arms stand, and I scan for danger, but there's nothing at all.

Where could she be?

Good gods, why do we keep splitting up?

Annoyance floods me, but I'm not actually annoyed at Sora. I'm angry that we're constantly in danger, and now I'm concerned because she's gone.

I take the paved road down until I'm in the quaint little town of Cetil. I search the town square, and I finally spot her. Relief floods me, and I release the tension in my shoulders—she's safe. Everything is okay.

Sora is perched on the ledge next to the drinking fountain. It's a quiet space and she's dressed demurely, but we're strangers and everyone always stares at Sora. People in the market keep looking over. Her black hair shines like onyx in the sun.

"There you are," I say.

She lifts her head, and her eyes are rimmed with sadness, her cheeks flushed. But she's not crying. She's furious. Her hands are balls, gripping her skirt. I haven't seen her this way since she was dancing with Seok.

I drop down next to her, my earlier relief gone. "What happened?"

"Daysum is dead."

She says it so casually that it takes a second for me to react. Gods, what? Sora's sister is dead?

I cover my mouth with my left hand, then remember the ring and switch hands. My mind wants to deny it, but Sora has no reason to lie. I look her over. I expect her to break into pieces the way she did in Quu after Seok revealed that he sold Daysum, but she's weirdly calm. Unsettlingly so.

Honestly, it's freaking me out.

"I'm so, so sorry, Sora." I take her hands in mine.

What a ridiculously tiny phrase that is. I might as well try to bandage the ocean. I internally cringe and wait for her reaction.

"Mikail… Mikail has known for weeks."

Oh. Oh no, that's not good. That's why he had that look on his face. And why she left.

She smiles, but it's a hard sneer. I really didn't think her face was capable of that. She almost looks ugly…for Sora. Which means she looks like a normal person for a second.

"I'm sure he was waiting for the right time to tell you," I say.

I'm not actually sure of that. Not at all. He could've decided not to tell her. I wasn't looking for the right time to tell Royo about the amulet. I had that moment in the Light Mountains, and as much as I wanted to be honest, I chose to protect him instead. It sounds like it was the same for Mikail. And now we're both in total shit for our decisions.

"I…" I start speaking, but I trail off because I really don't know what to say. I want to comfort her, but there is no comforting this kind of a loss. Saying "there, there" doesn't work when someone's heart was ripped out.

"I need Seok dead, and I need you on the throne," she says.

Sora is calm like Idle Lake, but it's masking the horror beneath the surface. Both are kind of terrifying, honestly.

"All of this has to end," she says. "We can't keep going the way we have been—not us and not this realm. It has to be you. That's the only way things will change."

I nod, even though I don't know anything about ruling or how I'd even take the throne. I am Baejkin, but I am a woman, and the people won't support me. But Sora needs this right now, even if it's not a promise I can keep.

"Okay, Sora," I say.

Her eyes search mine, and all I think is, *I will try.*

She squeezes my hands. "I'm all right."

"Are you sure?"

"No." She smiles slightly. "I can't absorb any of this. But at least there's some comfort in…knowing." She looks to the side. "She… she can't suffer any more, at least."

Sora watches the water continuously flowing out of the fountain. I sit, eyeing it as well. The water comes from a source—snow melt or a stream—and it flows down to here.

All of what Yusan is, what Gaya has become, starts with Tamneki, with the king in Qali Palace, and then it flows throughout the realm. That's where it will have to end—we will have to go to the source.

"I'll stay with the group until we can crown you, but I don't trust Gambria," Sora says.

"I…" I immediately lose my train of thought. There's so much I want to say, but my mind is definitely not the same.

Sora blinks at me and then squints. "You're a little off…"

I gesture but sigh. It's so like her to care about me, even when she's suffering. "It's the relics."

"But you haven't used them since Quu Harbor."

"No, but I think—"

All of a sudden, bells start ringing. My back goes rigid. Sora and I both look toward the sound. It's coming from the temple.

Good gods, what now?

"The king is dead! Long live the king!" the town crier says. He's a short man with a broad chest and a booming voice. He holds a scroll in his small hands. He repeats the same two sentences as he walks around. It's not until the third time that the words really sink in.

Sora faces me, her eyes wide. "King Joon is dead?"

"What king?" I ask.

We exchange glances as we stand. We have to go tell the others. My father is dead? I guess he drowned in Quu Harbor and word is just spreading. That means I killed him, but I can't deal with that right now. The bigger question is: Who is on the throne? How is there a new king so quickly?

Whatever happened, it can't be good.

Sora gives me her hand, and we head back to the others.

CHAPTER NINE

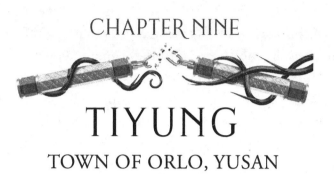

TIYUNG

TOWN OF ORLO, YUSAN

It's nearly two days before the first sliver of daylight appears. It's faint, but it's hope on the horizon, and it pulls me forward like a cirena call. We made it out of the Khakatan Mountains. There's light after all this darkness.

I exchange relieved glances with Hana.

As we come out of the cave, I breathe in the rainy air and savor the fact that although it's not sunny, it's not dark. The gray morning sky is so welcome over pitch black. A weight lifts off my chest, making it easier to carry on.

A little town called Orlo sits nearly on the border, just a short walk from the caves. We make our way toward it, pulling up our hoods to protect from the drizzle. We'll need horses or a carriage to take us to Tamneki, but as we come into the town, Hana stops at a bread house first. I suppose she's hungry, and I am, too, but it's a strange errand. Stranger still is that the shelves are all empty.

But it's warm and dry and smells like baking as we step inside. My stomach growls at the empty promise of food.

"Good day," Hana says.

"Good day, miss," the old woman behind the counter replies. Her long gray hair is twisted into a low bun.

Hana eyes the empty shelves and bins. There isn't a single roll left. "Busy morning?"

"Yes, miss. The army." The woman sighs and wipes her spotted hands on a dish towel. Hana's eyes dart over to me and then back to the woman as she continues. "First they come and then they go, but I have nothing left to sell you today."

The Yusanian king's guard "appropriates," meaning takes, everything it needs as it marches through the realm. Shopkeepers are supposed to be reimbursed, but judging from the baker's weary tone, it isn't true.

"Oh, I see. Maybe we shouldn't take the Northern Road back to my mother, then," Hana says with a frown. She's speaking to me, but really, she's trying to pull more information out of the old woman. I thought the woman might be a source, a spy for Hana, but now I don't think so.

The baker shakes her head. "I wouldn't. You'll be behind the army the whole way as they return to the new king. Unless you have food to last you for days, you'll go hungry."

"Thank you for the advice, halmi," Hana says.

Halmi technically means "grandmother," but we also use it to show respect to elders. Hana reaches into her purse and leaves five bronze mun on the counter. A kind tip but not a remarkable amount. The woman eagerly scoops up the coins. It's all she'll make today.

Hana walks out, and I follow her. The shop woman casually spoke about the new king. She has to mean Seok. But what happened in Quu, then? Where is King Joon? And more importantly, where are Sora and the others? How is the war already over before it began?

"We need to go to Pont," Hana says.

She strides quickly down the street toward the stables. I'm not sure why we are checking the stables. If the army came through, they took all the horses first.

Still, I hurry to keep up, rushing down the wet cobblestone streets. "Why Pont?"

"It's the nearest city with a messenger house, but it's also on the Coastal Road. We'll have to take the longer way back to Tamneki to avoid the army."

Hana is all drive and determination, so I keep my doubts to myself.

We get to the stables, and as I expected, all the stalls are empty.

The stable boy appears and tells us that the only animals left are two donkeys. Hana and I exchange glances. It's not great, but the ground by the Khakatans is rocky, and riding is better than walking. Especially because I don't really have the physical endurance for a long march.

Hana pays for the donkeys and a cart. She tips the boy a silver, and he rigs and hitches everything for us. Once he's done, I take the reins, and Hana slides in beside me. We put our packs in the cart. It's such a small bench that we're touching as we slowly pull down the street.

We pass a bathhouse, which I could use, but I'm sure we'll stop at a traveler's inn once we get to the coast.

Hana's eyes are vacant as she stares into the distance.

"Why do you look like that?" I finally ask.

She shakes her head and looks at me. "Because of what the baker said."

"About the army taking her goods?" I ask.

"No," Hana says. "The commoners and the army already know there's a new king, and if they accept it so readily, that can only mean that word has spread that Joon is dead."

She's right, and it would only help us if that were the case. King Joon's death would mean that Sora and the others no longer have to take the Golden Ring. Sora isn't safe with my father in power, but in a new realm anything is possible. Is it true, though? How did the king die with the Immortal Crown keeping him alive?

"Is he really dead?" I ask.

"That's exactly the question we need to answer."

CHAPTER TEN

ROYO

TOWN OF CETIL, YUSAN

Bells chime, and it had better not be a fucking water invasion. Fallador and Gambria turn toward the sound. They've been chattering in Gayan, which I can't understand for shit. Occasionally, Mikail translates, but mostly he spins the scepter and stares off at nothing. His eyes look, but they don't see.

The bells stop after a minute, so at least it's not a war. Not today, anyhow. But it's not a holy day, either—there aren't any during monsoon season because of the old thought that the gods can't see us during the rains. So what was that?

"Aeri and Sora are still in the orchard?" I ask.

Mikail shakes his head. "No. Sora needed some air, and Aeri went to find her."

Ten fucking Hells. He left the girls alone. Again. Nobody learns a thing.

I slam my fist on the picnic table. "And you said nothing?"

"She needed some space," Mikail says. "It's a safe town. I grew up here."

It doesn't sound like he gives a shit. Maybe there is no such thing as team to Mikail.

I get up too fast and slam my thigh into the wood. It'll bruise, but I don't care that it smarts. I have to find them.

I stomp off the stone patio, hoping nobody got kidnapped again.

My heart thuds, my neck flushes, and I curl my hands into fists. The only thing that keeps me from breaking into a run is that Sora is no fool. She wouldn't just wander. But why'd she leave? Why did she need space from Mikail in the first place?

I've just made it around the charred house when I see them— Sora and Aeri walking up the path. Relief makes me exhale, and then anger squeezes my chest.

"You can't just leave like that!" I yell.

My words hang in the air. It wasn't what I meant to say, and my voice is louder and harsher than I wanted it to be.

"I'm sorry, I didn't mean to scare you," Sora says.

There's something real off about her, but I don't know what. I was yelling at Aeri, though, not her. I hate it—the worry and now relief. I hate that she has control over me.

"Well, you did." I shove my hands in my pockets. "There were a bunch of bells."

Aeri nods. "We heard them, too—it's why we came back. We were in the town square, and the crier said, 'The king is dead! Long live the king.'"

Fucking what? "What?"

I gesture for them to follow me because the others will want to hear this. King Joon is dead? So that means he didn't survive Mikail flooding the harbor. Either he drowned or he was killed by the Khitanese army. Either way, that's gotta be good news. It was half of what we needed to do: kill the king. Now, we have to replace him with somebody better.

We get back to the patio, and Aeri repeats what she said.

Fallador's mouth opens, Gambria's eyes shift, but Mikail remains staring at nothing. I thought they'd be cheering, celebrating, but it looks like a funeral pyre here.

"The town crier said Joon is dead?" Mikail asks.

"Yes," Sora says.

She won't look at Mikail. I don't know what happened when they were in the orchard before, but they're both acting weird.

"I don't get it." I look from face to face in the group. "This is what we wanted. We were supposed to kill him. It's good that he's dead, right?"

The Baejkins are now all dead except for Quilimar, but she wasn't really Baejkin. It's a good thing, so why does everybody look more upset?

"*If* he's dead." Mikail suddenly stops spinning the scepter. "Someone has usurped the throne of Yusan and *wants* everyone to believe he's dead."

I wipe sweat from my forehead. What am I missing? "But you flooded the harbor while the three realms were fighting. Maybe all the rulers are dead."

"I mean, we can hope," Mikail says. But he looks real skeptical. "The crown makes Joon's death unlikely."

"Who took the throne?" Aeri asks.

Nobody says a word.

"If it's a king, it's not Queen Quilimar," Sora says. "I doubt it's the priest king of Wei. Yusan would be in chaos if we were suddenly under Weian rule, so it has to be someone Yusanian."

"Seok, the eastern count?" Fallador asks, looking only at Mikail.

Sora's back goes rigid. Seok's the guy who owns her—Tiyung's father. Hate like I've never seen before fills her eyes.

Ten Hells, she's terrifying.

"If he's alive," Mikail says. "Or Rune, the western count."

"What do we do?" Gambria asks.

"We go to Rahway." Mikail taps the stick on the ground, having decided.

Everyone stares at him. Even Sora.

I shake my head like there's water in my ear. "Rahway? The city way the fuck out in western Yusan that it took us weeks to get to?"

Pirates, the isle, traveling with Aeri. All of that flashes through my mind. Holding her while she shivered, looking at her in that robe.

No, I don't need these thoughts right now.

"That one," Mikail says. "I've been thinking about it since yesterday. We need soldiers more than anything else. Now, we also need a place where we can wait while we see if Joon is actually dead and figure out who sits on the throne. We're in danger for the sole reason that the king is not someone we put there. Then add the relics." He points between himself and Aeri. "Rune was on our side for the assassination. If Seok took the throne, Rune will align with us just to keep the southern count from taking over the realm. Conversely, if Rune slithered his way to Qali, we'll find out quickly in his city, and then we might actually have an ally in Tamneki."

"What makes you think we can trust him?" Aeri asks. "He's a nobleman like the others."

"He also killed a dog for the spectacle," Sora says.

Mikail shrugs. "A lack of other options. Plus, we don't need trust—just self-serving alliances."

All of a sudden, the memory of being in the King's Arena plays in my mind. King Joon had survived Sora's poison kiss, and Mikail was knocked out. I was struggling against palace guards, trying to save Aeri. A well-dressed man I thought was the western count came up to me.

"Was he a little taller than me, around the king's age?" I ask. "Diamond collar on his chest?"

Mikail nods.

"He told me something weird in the arena," I say.

Mikail raises his eyebrows. "What was that?"

"I was being held by the palace guards, and he said not to fight, to surrender now to fight another day."

Fallador exchanges glances with Mikail. Sora blinks. Aeri tilts her head. Gambria continues to eye me like I'm a water buffalo wearing pants.

"He must've had a backup plan already in place," Mikail says to no one.

"Maybe he owned the laoli," Aeri says.

That warehouse in Oosant with all of those drugs had to belong to somebody rich. Maybe it was Rune's. It was closest to his territory.

"I asked him why he was helping us when we were at dinner in Rahway," Sora says. She speaks like the words taste bad.

"What did he say?" Aeri asks.

"He said: *Isn't it obvious?* But I wasn't following. He noticed and changed the subject."

The hell does that mean?

"Perfect, it's settled then." Mikail stands and brushes dirt from his pants. "We'll go to Rahway to find answers."

Gambria and Fallador rise as well.

"Aren't we all forgetting that it's going to take weeks to get there from here?" I ask. "Even with a fleet carriage."

"It won't," Mikail says. "We'll go by sea."

"Rahway is landlocked," Aeri says.

Mikail shakes his head. "Not really. We can go around the coast of Yusan and then up the Tan River into Lake Garda. Rahway sits where the Sol meets the lake. We'll be there in a couple of bells."

"Mikail…" Fallador, Aeri, and Gambria all say his name at the same time. Nobody wants him to use the scepter.

He sighs and runs a hand through his wavy hair. "I guarantee that by the end of monsoon season, every king's guard, Khitanese, and Weian spy will be hunting us, if they aren't already. We need protection and answers—and we need them fast. We're in a time of instability, but everyone is moving quickly. The faster we get to Rahway, the quicker we have answers of our own, the better our chance of surviving."

I don't know why we keep having to make such shit choices, but reluctantly, I nod.

We go down the path back to the town. The walk downhill is totally different than the feeling going up. Mikail and Sora have changed the most, but even Aeri seems different. She smiles, but there's a hollowness to her.

Or maybe I'm just reading into things.

We stop at the market. The girls grab food, and I'm sure Aeri is going to look for dresses and makeup. I turn away to stop staring at her.

Dignity. I need some fucking dignity, but at least there's a weapons table right in front of me. I test the edges of a new battle-axe, and it's razor sharp. I'm about to haggle for it when I hear Fallador whispering with Mikail. At first, I think they're speaking in Gayan, but they're not. I can understand them.

"I know that look," Fallador says. "What's troubling you?"

"I'm missing something again." Mikail blows out a breath, obviously frustrated.

"About what?"

Yeah, what is it, and why didn't he say it before?

I slide to my left to get closer, but I knock into a couple of swords. They clang into each other, but I catch the hilts before they drop. The wrinkled old merchant frowns at me, but he's bargaining with someone else.

"Why the end of the monsoon season?" Mikail wonders. "As soon as I said it before, I thought about how Joon was very clear that we needed to return with the ring before the season ended. Why?"

Fallador pauses. "I doubt he wanted to leave your task open-ended."

I move to the side of the stall where I'm still hidden, but I can see them. Mikail is stroking his chin, and Fallador stands just a step too close to him.

"He doesn't act without a reason," Mikail says. "It was a clue, but what?"

Fallador looks around. "Should we ask his daughter?"

"No, she—" Mikail begins.

"Are you going to buy that?" The same wrinkly old man stares at me. I realize I've lifted the axe to my shoulder.

"I'm thinking about it—seeing how it feels."

With that, he quiets down, so I can listen again.

Mikail shakes his head. "…and don't alert the others. It's just something sticking in my mind."

He walks away. Fallador reaches out for his hand, but he moved just a second too slow and Mikail was already out of reach.

Fucking great. More secrets. And I missed what he said about Aeri.

I'm going to need the axe.

I turn to the shopkeeper. "Yeah, I'll take it at six silvers."

CHAPTER ELEVEN

SORA

THE WEST SEA

Daysum is dead.

May the gods guide her soul. May Lord Yama have mercy on her. May her deeds weigh lighter than a feather.

I sigh as I make my way through the standard death prayers while sitting aboard the skiff. I think something is wrong with me. Daysum, the girl I've lived my whole life for, is dead, and I feel nothing. I've barely shed a tear.

I think I'm broken.

Aeri looks over at me again, scanning with her golden eyes. She lays her hand on mine. She cares, and she doesn't have to. She wants to help, and that's something. There is a great deal of unkindness layered with indifference in the world, and her compassion is a gift. So I open my fist and weave my fingers with hers.

I brace myself for questions, but she sits quietly. She's kind enough to recognize that I don't want to talk, and that isn't easy for her.

We silently hold on together as the world blurs by.

Mikail uses the scepter to wield us along the cape of Yusan, a good distance from the shore. The sail on this skiff is white—meaning it doesn't fly any nation's flag. We have it unfurled so that we don't draw more attention to how unnaturally fast we are moving. Not that it matters. If anyone is closely watching us, the sail won't fool them.

Fallador sits with Mikail at the front, and Aeri and I are in the middle, which leaves Gambria and Royo together in the back. It's hard to tell who dislikes it more. But we won't be on this boat for long.

It's barely a bell before we reach the Bay of More, the curving inlet between Gain and Use. We traveled an impossible distance in that short of a time. It's even more impossible that yesterday morning we were in Quu Harbor.

I twist my hair. I suppose we exist among miracles and horrors now.

Moments later, we sail up the Tan River. Named for the colored silt that's often in the water, the Tan flows from Lake Garda into the bay. Even though we're sailing against the current, it's far faster than any other way of getting to Rahway.

I have mixed feelings about returning to the western city. Count Rune is far from a good man, but I suppose Mikail is right—we don't have many options, and they are all bad men.

The only good nobleman probably died in Idle Prison. I take a moment to absorb the possibility that they're all dead—all the people we're fighting for. That not just Daysum but Tiyung, Ailor, and Hwan have gone to the Kingdom of Hells.

Yet I still feel nothing.

Royo scans the horizon with a spyglass, and it distracts me from my thoughts.

"What are you looking for?" I ask.

"Pirates," he says, not taking his eye off the water.

"Those are on the East Sea," Gambria scoffs. "We're all the way in the west now—on a river."

Royo takes the glass down for just long enough to glare at Gambria. "There are pirates on the Sol."

Tension crackles, and I'm a little concerned that one of them will push the other from this skiff.

"I haven't heard of pirates in the southern region, but I suppose we can't be too careful," I say.

They both seem to accept that, or at least they return to staring out of opposite sides of the vessel.

One conflict put to rest. A hundred more to go.

We speed along the Tan and pass the floating city of Speculator. The city sits high on the engorged river. Memories return, and I think about the man I murdered here. He was the eighth mark for Count Seok, the name scrawled on the back of a card—Brookson Veil. I remember his name. I remember all of their names.

In order to find him, I had to ride to Allegiance, a city at the northernmost edge of Seok's territory. After studying my mark, I saw he coveted other people's possessions, so I charmed my way onto the arm of another high-ranking nobleman. He was the one who introduced me to Veil, and then I let myself be seduced away.

A day later, Veil took me onto his pleasure yacht and almost immediately to the cabin below. I can still feel his wine-laden breath on my neck and the way he kissed my ear, gripping me from behind. He was practically pushing me down the stairs to his bed, he was so eager to claim his new prize.

I murdered him with a large dose of Erlingnow. He was dead within seconds, but then I had to figure out how to escape on a moving ship with servants and guards above us. It was well into the evening, and I stared at the Tan River from the lower-level deck.

Jumping in was the only solution, but I hesitated.

There were not only blood pike but sharks in the water. Yet I was buoyed by the lights of Speculator. I thought I could make it, so I held my breath and leaped overboard. I hit the cold water and swam against the current, keeping the city lights in my sight.

But I underestimated how fast the river was flowing downstream.

The current carried me for a mile before I was able to drag myself onto the shore, my limbs shaking until they gave out.

It was one of the most terrifying nights. Even now, that feeling of helplessness grips me. I exhale. My fingers twitch around Aeri's, and she pats my hand.

I look at her and remember that horrible night is over. I'm not swimming right now. I'm on a skiff.

With another deep breath, I calm my pounding heart.

But all of it, all the worst moments of my life, were because of Seok.

Fallador and Mikail casually mentioned that he may have taken the throne of Yusan. I grit my teeth at the thought of him being king, but any coronation will have to wait until monsoon season ends. The celestial gods can't see Yusan during the monsoons, and therefore they can't bless a new king. But once he is coronated, Seok will be guarded behind the walls of Qali Palace and it will be impossible to get to him. We have to cut him down now, before it's too late.

I exhale a short laugh. I've finally become the merciless killer Seok always wanted me to be, and I'm coming for him.

Aeri tilts her head while blinking at me. She probably said something, and I missed it.

"What was that?" I ask.

"We're almost there," she says.

I finally notice where we are. We entered Lake Garda while I was lost in my thoughts. It's a beautiful lake twice the size of Lake Cerome. The water is cerulean, and the shore is dotted with towns. Last time I was in Rahway, I could only see where the Sol ended, but the full expanse is breathtaking in the dusk.

The city of Rahway appears out of nowhere. There was nothing on the horizon and then Mikail pushed us closer, and now there's the sandstone metropolis in front of us. The monsoons don't normally reach this far west, so the sky is lit up in ribbons of bright pink and oranges, making the beige city shimmer.

So much water has rushed down the Sol that some of the harbor of Rahway is submerged, but Mikail pulls us toward the raised portion of the port. Then he hides the Water Scepter inside the walking stick, and we use the sail to take us the rest of the way to a dock.

Aeri found a dress with long sleeves at the market in Cetil. The lace of the edge somewhat hides the ring, and the high neckline conceals the amulet.

With the relics now disguised, we disembark into the Port of Rahway. Mikail offers his hand to help me out of the skiff. He searches my face as I take it. I think he's looking for forgiveness or at least acceptance. I turn away.

I'm not sure this gamble will pay off. There's nothing to stop Rune from betraying us all, but desperation makes for strange friends. We'll have to trust that he'll need us as much as we need him.

As we walk, I apply a dash of Oxerbow on my lips, just in case.

CHAPTER TWELVE

MIKAIL

CITY OF RAHWAY, YUSAN

It takes a surprisingly long time to get an audience with Rune. It's ten bells at night, and we're still waiting in his overly ornate study. I glance at the mahogany shelves. He can't possibly need this many leather-bound books. He certainly hasn't read them.

Part of the delay was our fault. Aeri insisted on going to the tailor to dress all of us for this audience. Then we had to wait for Royo to be outfitted because nothing premade fit him. We killed time in a tavern while the seamstresses worked, all of us thankful for cold ale and a good supper. But we've been at Rune's villa for almost a bell now. It took that long to clear the guards at his gate, then his entry hall, and now we've been in his study for twenty minutes.

I lean against the bookcase and spin the Water Scepter. This is getting excessive.

Royo paces, wearing down the expensive area rug as Sora and Aeri read on a fainting couch. Coju and water were left out for us on a bar cart. Sora said they're both clean, but no one is drinking. Not after he poisoned a dog the last time we were here.

Just as I'm about to chance it, the study doors open. Fallador and Gambria stand while I continue to lean on the shelf.

Count Rune strolls in wearing a dressing jacket over pants and a shirt. Rather shockingly, his noble collar is missing.

"Forgive my lateness," he says. "I had a previous dinner engagement."

It's hard to tell if it's a lie. He takes in all of us as we're variously posed around his office.

"Your Majesty," he says, his eyes wide. He bows to Fallador. "I do apologize for the delay. My servants failed to recognize you."

It's clear from Rune's tone that he's going to order the whipping of someone.

Fallador smiles. "I'm hardly royal, Your Grace."

I suppress a laugh.

"And you must be Gambria Miat," Rune says to Gam. He takes her hand and kisses it. "My lady." Then he looks around. "Where is Prince Euyn?"

"He is in the Kingdom of Hells," I say. "Your Grace."

Rune raises his eyebrows. "I'm sorry for that. But that does explain how we have a new king who isn't Euyn."

"And who exactly is it?" I ask.

A slight wrinkle mars Rune's forehead—he's surprised I don't already know.

"My old friend, Seok of Gain, now occupies the throne." Rune can't help but curl his lip as he spits out the words.

The room falls silent—no heavy footsteps from Royo or page-turning from Sora. It's who we suspected, but having it confirmed somehow makes it worse. I'm not sure how the southern count accomplished taking Qali, but the throne was empty for some time as Joon conspired with Wei.

Rune eyes me. "I'll admit, I'm surprised you're still alive. But that's always the case."

I shrug.

The good and the bad news is that Rune is exactly how I remember him. He makes his way over to the coju on the bar cart and selects a bottle. But he stops, looking at Aeri and Royo. His eyes linger on Aeri. "And who are they? Sora, of course, I remember."

Sora stares at him. "Your Grace." She stays seated but eventually inclines her head.

He grins as he grips the neck of the bottle.

"That is Joon's daughter, Naerium, and her strongman, Royo," I say.

Rune stops with the coju bottle open. "Princess Naerium?" His snakelike yellow eyes shift. "I thought she passed to the Kingdom of Hells years ago."

"You and me both," I say.

"The pleasure is mine," Aeri says. She stares directly into his eyes, still seated on the couch in a short green dress with long sleeves.

Aeri is a far cry from the silly girl I first met in this city, or even the one I thought was steel in a ball gown in Khitan. I like the change. Although, frankly, I think it's me altering my opinion, not any difference in her.

Rune bows formally and then looks her up and down. "I see the resemblance to your mother, Soo Lin, Your Majesty. I'm now awfully sorry about the wait, as I am your most humble servant."

"I'm certain that's true," she says.

Rune takes her hand and moves to kiss it. The motion causes her lace sleeve to shift, revealing the Golden Ring of Khitan. Rune audibly gasps and backs up a step. The crystal bottle stopper falls from his hand and rolls onto the expensive rug.

"Is that…" He stops and blinks, attempting to gather himself. He fails. I've never seen him this thrown. It's enjoyable.

"There's much to discuss," I say.

"I see," Rune says. "She really is Princess Naerium. How extraordinary." He doesn't take his eyes off the Golden Ring. His stare is as hungry as a prisoner in Idle's. "I thought you were trying to pass off a charming fake." He looks at me. "Come into the dining hall. I'll have my kitchens prepare supper for all of us."

"And here I thought you were late because you just had dinner," I say. "We already ate."

"Dessert and wine, then," he says with a shrug. "Your Majesties, please follow me at your leisure."

He inclines his head again.

Gambria and Fallador follow the count, but the others stay back by me. We gather by the walnut wood desk.

"Are you sure this isn't a trap?" Aeri whispers.

"It certainly feels like one," Sora adds, looking around.

I spin my walking stick. "It might be, but I'm not worried about it."

"Yeah, but shouldn't you be?" Royo asks.

The guards took his axe and Gambria's crossbow at the door. Those were just a little too conspicuous for a dinner meeting. Royo has nunchuka, but I can tell he'd rather have the comfort of his weapon of choice.

"No," I say.

"Why not?" he asks.

Sora and Aeri look at me, waiting for my answer.

I smile. "Because the river is at high tide."

CHAPTER THIRTEEN

TIYUNG

CITY OF PONT, YUSAN

We finally reach the city of Pont, and I stretch, my backside aching. The donkey cart was terribly uncomfortable after only a bell. It was another five of being jostled around before we reached the coastal city.

Hana is negotiating for halibred horses, as she handles the money. I have no gold and no way to access any. I'm no longer a nobleman with my father's accounts. My purse was taken before I was locked in Idle Prison, and it's not like anyone handed it back as we escaped.

I laugh to myself. This is what Seok had threatened if I disobeyed him—that I wouldn't have a bronze mun to my name. And it happened because his ambition nearly got me killed.

"Something funny?" Hana asks as she hands me the reins of a horse. She stares at me with an eyebrow raised.

"Not really, no," I say.

"Don't crack up on me, please," she says. "I really don't have the time to deal with it."

It's fair enough.

We ride and reach the dry warmth of the messenger house. I stand by the fire as Hana writes out coded messages and sends three eagles. I'm not sure who she is contacting, although I assume one is Mikail. I don't bother to ask, though. I can spare her the burden of lying to me.

Our next stop is the market. During monsoon season, most markets are held in any available vacant warehouses. Bigger cities, like this one, have a central market house.

As soon as we walk in, the food hawker stalls tempt me with the smells of ready-to-eat snacks and meals. Crispy fried shrimp with eel sauce and warm custard buns call to me. My stomach growls loudly, and Hana sighs.

"All right, we can stop for food first," she says.

I'm so excited that I ball my hands in fists and race over to the stalls.

Hana gets rice cakes and delicately nibbles them off a skewer. I... don't. I buy half a dozen pork buns, and I'm polishing them off in one bite each. The same desperate prison hunger drives me. A plate of squid fried noodles and a cherry cake later, and I'm finally full.

Once we're done eating, we head to the arms table. Although my prison guard uniform is long gone, I still have the sword. It's not enough, though. Hana selects two sharp daggers, another sword, and several throwing blades. It's doubtful that with the rain and the army on the move there will be highwaymen, but we can't be too careful. Desperation makes people bold.

I know that better than most.

Hana slips change into her coin purse and tucks it back inside her cape. Her purse is velvet and looks suspiciously like the one I used to have.

We leave the market, and I stow our goods in the saddlebags. I hope we'll check into a traveler's inn next.

"Where to now?" I ask.

"It's not that much farther to the next town on the Coastal Road," she says. "We should try to get there before dark."

We're drenched, and I could use a warm tub and a dry bed, but the sooner we reach Qali, the better for Sora and everyone else. We mount our horses and continue on.

The cold rain pelts me as we ride, the drops hitting like tiny knives. The sea breeze only makes it worse. I close my cape around myself and focus on the horizon, scanning for danger. This part of the Coastal Road can only be navigated during daylight, and even then, it requires full attention because there is a five-hundred-foot drop-off down to the East Sea to my left. It's a far cry from the gentle road Sora and I first took out of Gain.

If only I'd burned her sister's indenture—Daysum would be alive right now. But I couldn't find it, no matter where I looked. Even my mother couldn't locate it.

"I can almost hear you overthinking," Hana says.

I smile.

"What about?" she asks.

"How did Daysum die?"

Hana blinks, surprised, then sighs. "I couldn't tell. Not violence, as far as I could see. There weren't any marks on her. It could've been an overdose, or, if what you told me was correct and she was sick, she died naturally." A few seconds pass before she adds, "Gods guide her soul."

Hana isn't religious, but prayer can't hurt.

"Gods guide her soul," I repeat.

If there's any justice, Daysum will spend her three years in the second hell, Elysia, before being reborn. The same won't be true for my father or uncle. But what about my mother? How will Lord Yama judge her?

"Is my mother at the palace?" I ask.

Hana's eyebrows rise. "I'd imagine so, but I haven't confirmed."

I grip the wet reins. I should've sent an eagle to my mother's country villa. I'll send one when we reach the next city.

"Nayo said she was kind." Hana's voice is monotone, and her mouth slants.

"But you don't believe that."

"I'm glad she wasn't cruel. Nayo said she was patient yet firm with all the wards. He believed she was loving, even, but I think that anyone who knew what was happening, if they were really kind, wouldn't have been able to live with it."

"You're mistaking being kind with being a selfless person," I say. "I don't know many of those."

"I don't, either." Hana sighs, then looks at the sea.

I suppose my mother's kindness did stop her from reporting my father. But it was also, undoubtedly, self-interest. Women can't hold their own land or title in Yusan. If Seok were arrested, my mother would've lost everything. And she was raised noble and wealthy and has never known another way of life. On top of that, she still loves my father. You can love someone even if you don't love what they've become.

"Kingdom of Hells." Hana pulls on her reins and stops her horse.

I grab the hilt of my sword and look around, trying to spot an ambush. My heart races from her tone. But there's nothing but empty road, rain, and sea.

"What? What is it?" I ask.

I don't notice any danger, but that doesn't mean we're safe.

She points at the East Sea. "Look."

The visibility isn't ideal with the rain and mist. At first, all I see is the dark blue of the ocean and whitecaps from the monsoon seas. The horizon is empty otherwise. But then I narrow my eyes. There's something strange about the sea.

"Is that..." I begin. Then I shake my head. It can't be.

"I think it is," Hana whispers. She reaches into her saddlebag and pulls out a spyglass. She stares through it, and her full lips drop open.

"What?" I ask. "What did you find?"

She closes her mouth, opens it, and then exhales. She hands over the spyglass. I give her a quizzical look. What has her this thrown?

I put the glass up to my eye.

"Gods."

It is what I thought. The whitecaps are actually Weian ships in the distance. My stomach lurches, and I start counting. There are ninety, maybe a hundred of them battling the waves, their blue sails billowing and white bodies undulating. If that weren't bad enough, in the front, leading the navy, is a white boat flying a red flag with a black snake in the center.

I search the rest of the sails, but I don't see the trident of the priest king's ship. And is that…a purple flag? I catch the glimmer of the golden eagle, which means one warship is flying the standard of Khitan.

The rough seas are tossing around the fleet, but I'm certain that the Weian navy is coming from the north and they're within striking distance of our coast.

And Yusan and Khitan are with them.

My mouth goes dry.

My father has triggered a war of the realms.

CHAPTER FOURTEEN

AERI

CITY OF RAHWAY, YUSAN

The western count is a strange man. Sora said he is a sadist, and I see it, but he's also refined, smooth, and surprisingly charming. He's handsome in an older-man way, and he smells like desert blossoms and cedar. But there's cruelty in the line of his mouth and amorality in his eyes. He's like those beautiful venomous snakes that dance to music that Royo and I saw in Rahway during the night carnival.

Good gods, that feels like a lifetime ago.

As highest-ranking royalty, I sit at the head of an absolutely enormous table. I think it's one piece of wood, but, if so, they built this room around it. Fallador is to my right, and Count Rune's seat is to my left. Mikail is next to him, and then Royo. Gambria and Sora are on Fallador's side. There's still room for like forty more people.

Mikail has shared what happened in the throne room at Qali and then the banquet hall in Khitan. We have lost so much—Mikail most of all. He hesitated some as he described Euyn's death, the pain echoing in his pauses. I don't know what the victory will ultimately cost, but I'm beginning to wonder if it will be worth the price.

It's interesting to see what Mikail discloses and what he hides, though. He's allowed Rune to believe that Fallador is royalty, and he hasn't mentioned the Water Scepter. The story he's told has been vague on the timing so that our appearance in Rahway isn't suspicious, but otherwise, he's mostly told the truth. He did leave out the amarth, but they were quite unbelievable as a whole.

The story sounds like a lie, even without the prophecy from a bird. It seems impossible that we made it through so much, yet here we are.

"So, you now have three relics," Rune says as a servant pours him another glass of liquor. "And the rulers of the realms, if they are still alive, are all aware that you have them."

None of us have eaten or drunk anything despite a lavish display on the table. Servants place even more desserts down. The little plum cakes are so cute that I reach for one. Sora discreetly shakes her head *no*. I pull my arm back. She hasn't had a chance to try them for poison.

"Two relics," I correct.

Rune points to Mikail's walking stick. "Three with the Water Scepter of Wei. I'm impressed you were able to take it, Mikail, even if Fallador is the one who should be holding it."

No one moves, but my breath catches. How does he know? What has he heard?

All eyes shift to Mikail, who shrugs one shoulder, confirming what the count said.

Well, I suppose we were never going to fool him for long. And he still believes Fallador is the royal.

Rune smiles. "I remain your steadfast ally even as the realms unite against you. But Crown Prince Euyn has passed, gods guide his soul, so who will now take the throne? I recall he was our initial replacement."

"We think we have a man," Mikail says. He means Tiyung, but again he's as vague as possible. If Seok is king, that would mean that Tiyung is free, unless…

"That wasn't a real question," Rune says. "I am your answer."

The room falls dead silent.

"Now, with me as king and the Prince of Gaya as an ally, Yusan can reach new levels of greatness." Rune inclines his head to Fallador, and then his eyes lock on me. "With you as my queen, of course."

What? His queen? My cheeks tingle as blood leaves my face.

Royo starts coughing. He swallowed the wrong way. His face turns red, and he reaches for a glass of water, but then he thinks better of it and continues to cough into his sleeve.

"Sorry," he mutters.

I'm glad I didn't eat the cake, or I'd be choking, too. Did I just hear the western count correctly? Does he really intend to marry me? Someone young enough to be his daughter? I freeze, my fingers icy.

Sora's violet eyes are wide as she stares straight ahead. Gambria's face is skewed like she smells something foul. Fallador reacted quickly, but he's back to pleasant and unaffected.

"I think the countess might have some objections to that plan," Mikail says smoothly.

Rune traces his finger on the rim of his glass. "Ah, but she cannot, as she has walked the Road of Souls since I saw you last."

Oh good. He's single.

Of all of the conditions I thought the count might have, I didn't see this coming. Neither did Mikail, judging from the quick shift of his eyes. I know Royo definitely didn't.

But Rune has just named the starting price for his assistance, and it's the throne. He knows how much we need his help, and he wants the realm in return. We should've expected this.

And now he wants an answer.

"I'm quite astonished and flattered by your affections," I say. I do my best to sound like Sora as I also try not to run out of the room.

"It would be a marriage of convenience, Your Majesty," he adds, then lowers his eyes. "Although you'd come to enjoy it."

The corner of his mouth lifts as he sips coju.

I can almost feel the vein on Royo's neck throbbing from here.

"I'll have to consider it, my lord," I say. I catch Mikail's eye, and he tips his chin quickly. It was the right answer.

"In return, you would align with us, give us the men and mun to kill Seok?" Sora asks, leaning forward.

Rune nods. "How else would I get him off the throne, my beauty? He won't simply abdicate. People like us, we don't back down."

In the history of Yusan, there has only been one abdication. From what everyone's said, I doubt Seok would make it two.

I'm thinking about what Rune wants, all of what he wants, when a servant appears in the doorway. Rune's eyes slide to the left, and then the servant disappears. Someone else has arrived here at nearly midnight. Someone Rune doesn't want us to see.

"I'm sure you are all exhausted from your travels," he continues. "And apparently famished." He gestures to all of the untouched food. "You have my vow that you are safe and welcome here. Rest, and we will begin our plans tomorrow, assuming my terms are acceptable. In the meantime, I will have my servants prepare your baths and take your trunks."

"We seem to have misplaced our luggage again," Mikail says. "Lousy porter service."

Rune sighs like it's the most distressing thing he's heard tonight. "I'll send my tailors and seamstresses in the morning."

"That's very generous of you," Fallador says.

Rune smiles. "Of course. We are friends here, and I treat my friends and lovers well." He eyes me as he says *lovers*, and I think Royo might pass out. I'm not far behind him, but I'm determined not to let it show.

The count sips his drink and remains seated even though I feel like he's rushing us out. It's strange for him to quickly end the audience, given how badly he wants the throne. Perhaps he wants us to sleep on it, but that doesn't feel accurate. It most likely has something to do with the exchange with the servant earlier.

When none of us move, he finally stands. "I'll bid you good night, then. We will iron out details in the daylight."

Just as we're pushing back from the table to rise, an absolutely gorgeous woman in a gold dress appears under the archway to the dining room. Seriously, this woman might be prettier than Sora—which I didn't think was possible. She's an inch or two shorter than Sora but with a sands glass–shaped body and warm brown skin. Her ebony hair falls in gentle waves that remind me of the South Sea, and her eyes are emerald green.

We all look from the woman to Rune. Ah, this is who he didn't want us to see.

He clears his throat. "My distinguished guests. May I introduce Misha of Jeul, my newest courtesan."

Sora knocks over her water glass. It rolls off the table and shatters on the floor.

CHAPTER FIFTEEN

SORA

CITY OF RAHWAY, YUSAN

What in the Kingdom of Hells is Sun-ye doing here?

She stares like she doesn't know who I am. I open my mouth, but then I realize that if I expose her, who she really is, she'll be killed. We weren't friends in poison school, but I also don't want to see her dead.

"Are you all right?" Rune asks me.

"I apologize." I allow myself to blush and step out of the way as a servant rushes to clean up the shards. "I'm not myself. Earlier today, Mikail told me that my sister passed on. I thought I was doing well with the news, but I am not. Would someone be so kind as to show me to the powder room?"

Sun-ye puts on a kind and concerned face that I know for certain is an act. "Come this way."

I look to Rune for his approval, and he nods. "A servant will show you to your room when you are ready."

I incline my head. "Thank you, Your Grace."

My mind races as I calmly approach the archway. Sun-ye smiles, and then we silently walk down the vaulted hall together, passing tapestries and paintings. Our steps are as light as a butterfly's wings. Madame Iseul taught us well.

We turn down a hallway, and Sun-ye points to a door with yet another fake smile. I swing it open and then walk into the powder room. As I enter, I drop the dagger from my sleeve into my palm.

The door swings shut. Sun-ye pushes me, and I pull her. We land up against gilded wallpaper, a breath away from each other. I have a fistful of her hair, and my blade is to her throat. Her knife is alongside my neck. If either of us moves an inch, it's a kill.

I smile. "Sun-ye."

"What are you doing here, Sora?" she asks through her teeth.

She's more gorgeous than the last time I saw her, expensively perfumed, and also out for blood.

"It's a long story. I could ask you the same."

Her green eyes track mine. Hana was smartest, but Sun-ye was by far the most vicious. "You're not here for him?"

"No. But I assume you are."

She doesn't look away. That's confirmation enough.

I raise my eyebrows. "That's quite a mark."

"Seok promised if I did this, he would free Rayna," Sun-ye says.

Rayna is her sister—her twin. Which makes her twenty-three years old and the last sibling held by Seok as his ward. He claims they live an idyllic life, being tutored by his wife without duties or toils. Of course, he forgets to mention that every moment they have to worry about losing their sisters and being sold as pleasure indentures. But that's just a small detail to him.

He must be desperate if he's risking his favorite to kill Rune. Then again, Rune is the last count remaining—the last competition for the throne, if King Joon is really dead.

"He doesn't know I'm here," I say.

Sun-ye slightly eases the pressure of her arm on my chest, testing my response the way you would with a wild animal. I also very slowly loosen my grip on her thick hair.

"He made me a similar offer," I say. "He sent me to kill King Joon and then sold Daysum when I failed."

Her gaze probes mine, looking for a lie, a tell. I hold her stare.

"I'm sorry, Sora." There's no emotion in her voice, but I know she means it.

"She's... She walked the Road of Souls," I say.

Something about saying it to Sun-ye makes me absorb the truth. My eyes sting, and I sniffle. My sister is dead. All I was living for. Everything I suffered, everything I did, and it all came to nothing because I failed. My breath catches, and tears start streaming down my face. I keep my chin up as the drops fall onto my neck.

Sun-ye releases me but keeps her dagger out. I'm surprised, but I do the same.

"I am truly sorry," she says.

Nodding, I wipe my face. I know she is. I'd feel just as bad if anything happened to Rayna. We all lived under the same axe, waiting for it to drop on our loved ones. After the first year, not one of us cared if we lived or died. We only made it through for our siblings. Now, all that's left is revenge.

Sun-ye and I both immediately fix ourselves—another of Madame Iseul's lessons: to look perfect at all times.

"There are moments I think it would've been better for Rayna to have walked the road," Sun-ye says to the mirror. "But she is all I have. I... I can't lose her."

It's as open as Sun-ye has ever been. Is it a ploy? Maybe, but to what end? She will be dead if I expose her, and we both know it. No—more likely, it's sympathy from someone who is foreign to the emotion.

"How did Daysum pass?" she asks.

"I'm not sure, but he sold her to Sterling."

Sun-ye doesn't react aside from the muscle in her cheek twitching. She knows exactly what kind of man Lord Sterling is and what he does. Daysum was thrown to the wolves. But regardless of how she ultimately died, Seok is to blame. "He has always made good on his threats."

It isn't much of a reaction, but it's more than I expected from her.

"When did he send you?" I ask.

"Around three weeks ago." She combs her fingers through her perfect hair. "He called me to his study and offered me this deal— my freedom and Rayna's if I kill Rune. I arrived here last week and observed first. But it didn't take me long to meet the count. It never takes these men long."

She likes men more than I do, but that's not saying much. Sun-ye is a more efficient killer than I am. She was better paid, taking marks outside of the protection of the south—reportedly as far as Gaya. In poison school, she claimed she would continue to murder for Seok even after her indentures were paid. She looked at him as a father when we were young, hers having died when she was a baby. Still, last I knew, she was only halfway to her sum. It's not a surprise for her to be in the west, but something isn't adding up.

I stare at her, looking for a tell. "If you came to Rahway a week ago, why is Rune still alive?"

Sun-ye sighs. "Sadly, the terms entailed getting close enough to watch him and his affairs first. I am to report back until I'm given the signal. This report may finally change things." Her red lips turn up in a smile.

Maybe I should've exposed her in the dining hall.

"You won't report anything." I casually adjust my lipstick.

She arches an eyebrow. "No? Because we're such good friends?"

There's hate but also hurt in her tone. I turn toward her, surprised.

"No, don't give me that pitying look, Sora," she says. "You never bothered with me before. It was you and Hana against the world until she died."

It's simply not true. We all tried to befriend Sun-ye in the beginning, but she took to Seok and hated all of us. Her anger is still aimed at the wrong people, but that didn't sink in once during all those years in school, so I doubt I'll have any success in swaying her tonight.

"It is the world against us." I gesture to her and to myself. "Does Pier still live?"

He was the delivery boy she fell in love with. The one Hana and I kept hidden as long as she kept our secret. We stumbled on them in the woods together, but Sun-ye already knew about us by that point. It was mutually assured destruction for years, not a friendship.

She draws a breath. "He does. I was sorry to hear that Hana passed."

She's not. Her green eyes are as clear as fountain pools as she stares at me.

"Do you even have that emotion?" I ask with a sigh.

She shrugs. "Not really, no. I truly don't know how you carry on feeling everything you do. It's exhausting to even watch it."

"At this point, I carry on just to torture and kill Seok. I don't care about what happens after that."

She turns and eyes me, a slight wrinkle in her perfect brow. "In that case, maybe my report will be blank."

I raise my eyebrows, testing if she's serious. Has she realized the truth? Has she changed her mind?

She puts out her palm. No weapons. I slide my dagger back into place in my sleeve, and then I shake her hand.

Allies for now.

CHAPTER SIXTEEN

TIYUNG

THE COASTAL ROAD, YUSAN

The warm baths, dry beds, and hot meals were exactly what we needed. But at daybreak we continue on toward Qali. It'll take days to reach the palace. We'd looked for a carriage at the stable in town, but unsurprisingly, they're all rented during monsoon season.

Hana looks unbothered as she rides, stunningly beautiful as always. Her features are different from Sora's—she's taller and curvier where Sora is more delicate. My father searched for unique beauties, thinking he'd have a stable of poisoners to suit every man's tastes. He must've been so disappointed that only three survived.

All that torture, all those families torn apart, just so he could maintain or increase his power. He said one day I'd understand. I aim to live a life where that's not the case.

Every now and then, Hana pulls out her spyglass. The Weian ships are no longer visible, but I know they're continuing down the coast just as we are. I hope I'm wrong—that they are actually sailing back to Wei—because a war of the realms will be disastrous for Yusan.

I grip my reins at the thought. If King Joon is alive and still possesses the Immortal Crown, my father will die. That much is certain. But getting to someone who has taken Qali Palace is easier spoken than accomplished. I don't think anyone, king or not, has ever successfully sieged Qali. Which means it will be a war and thousands of people will die.

Would my father surrender to avoid that? No, absolutely not. He's proven time and time again that he doesn't care about the lives or deaths of others.

I cough and shake again with a worrisome chill from this rain. Hana looks none the worse for wear, but maybe she's from the northeast like Sora. The truth is, I don't know. I lack basic knowledge about the woman who saved my life.

"Where are you from originally?" I ask.

"Oh, no. Not small talk, Tiyung. My nerves can't handle it," Hana says.

I glance at her. "You don't have any nerves."

Her lips curl up into a grin. "You'd be surprised. I'm from a small town in the west. Your father searched the entire realm for girls to become poison maidens. Imagine my luck that he found me."

"Where in the west?" I ask. "My mother was from Pact on the Yew River."

Pact is technically in the west, although the river marks the border to the south.

"Way out west," Hana says. "Almost in the foothills of the Tangun Mountains."

I nod. "Like Sora and the Khakatans."

She cringes slightly at the name and then drops her shoulders. "Similar in that they are mountains and we both grew up poor. But my climate was drier, more desert than hers. My town was nearly to Fallow."

Poverty did force most parents to sell their children to my father, but with Sora's father, Seok threatened to kill the entire family. After swords were drawn, my father told me to wait by the carriage. I was still surprised when he came out later with indenture bills and the girls. I asked what happened, and he said all men can be bought—it's just a matter of the amount.

It always seemed off to me. Her father had been so determined to keep them, but maybe Seok was right. Maybe everyone has a price.

I wait for an insult from Hana. One inevitably follows any mention of my family, but her barbs don't come.

"Why are you being nice to me?" I blurt out. Blood rushes to my cheeks. I hadn't meant to say that aloud.

She sighs. "I suppose I realized that you are genuine."

I sit straighter, buoyed by the compliment. "Not totally useless, then?"

She arches an eyebrow. "I wouldn't go that far."

A feeling bubbles in my chest—the possibility of friendship. Hana has warmed to me since we escaped from Idle, and I've changed her opinion some. But a voice in my head reminds me that she only helped me because I saved her brother. She is not actually a friend. I never had friends until Mikail, Euyn, Royo, and Aeri. Hana is settling a score because she doesn't want to be in my debt, but she doesn't need to do a thing.

"I am sorry," I say.

She stares at me. "For what?"

"For what was done to you, and Nayo, and Sora, and Daysum. And all the others. I should've been stronger and braver. I should've stopped my father."

She takes a breath and adjusts herself in her saddle. "Don't flatter yourself, Tiyung. You were just a kid when it all started, and you're mostly useless as a grown man. You couldn't have stopped your father. And you've taken large steps to right his wrongs. You're not the one to blame."

I can't help it. I grin.

She rolls her eyes and looks away, but a small smile plays on her lips, and it lightens the heaviness in my chest.

Maybe I do want atonement, but there are worse things to desire.

CHAPTER SEVENTEEN

AERI

CITY OF RAHWAY, YUSAN

It takes a while for Sora to join us in the bedroom hall. She was gone for so long I started to worry, but she seems fine. She walks gracefully toward us, incredibly beautiful in her shimmering pearl dress. Maybe I was wrong before. Maybe she's prettier than Rune's new courtesan.

Six servants stand outside the six bedroom suites. Once again, Royo won't be sharing a room with me. He hasn't looked at me since I said I would consider marrying the count. He's angry, but that's nothing new. I really don't know what he had expected me to say, though.

No, sorry, my heart belongs to the strongman who won't talk to me. Ridiculous.

It's not like I want to marry someone my father's age, but it would've been dangerous to refuse outright. I can't tell Royo that, though, because he's not fucking speaking to me.

Frustration courses through me until I stomp my foot. All five people turn and stare at me. I look behind me like they're eyeing something else.

"Can we trust him?" Gambria whispers. She's speaking Yusanian, so she wants the rest of us to understand her. Otherwise, she talks to Mikail in Gayan. I'm picking up pieces here and there, but old Gayan is complex.

"Stars, no," Mikail says. "Rune won't kill us if he thinks he can use us—and he certainly believes he can. But everyone should sleep armed just in case."

Sora and I look at each other—that's not great. I already killed a man on an estate like this. I hope not to make it two.

Everyone lingers in the hallway, reluctant to separate.

"Should we sleep in pairs?" Sora asks.

Mikail strokes his chin. "It's not a bad idea."

"I'll take Mikail," Royo blurts out.

Sora turns her whole body toward him. Fallador tilts his head. Gambria quirks an eyebrow. I pretend that doesn't hurt.

"Okay…" Mikail says slowly. "Sora, do you want to share a room with Aeri again?"

She nods. "Of course."

"All right, it's settled, then. Choose your rooms."

Sora and I take the middle bedroom. Mikail and Royo are to our right, Fallador and Gambria to our left.

Although it's not Royo, I'm glad it's Sora and me again. A warm feeling of security fills my chest as I close the door behind us. This second-floor room is grand with very high ceilings, large windows, and a marble fireplace for the desert night. There's an elaborate crystal chandelier and gilded paneling on the cream-colored walls.

"Well, that was an interesting evening," Sora says.

I laugh.

"What did you think of Rune?" I ask.

Sora draws a breath. "Too much." She stares at the walls and then the servant waiting by the door. "Talk after baths?"

I nod. The chambermaids follow her into the baths, and Sora leaves the door open for safety. Finally alone, I pull throwing knives out of my cloak and tuck them under the pillows and between the mattress and frame. Once I'm done, I sit on the bed, spinning a dagger, waiting for any noise or sign of danger.

Around fifteen minutes later, Sora comes out in a white robe, her hair in a turban. Gods, she's still beautiful damp with no hair. What kind of unfair shit is this?

The servants drain the tub, refill it, and it's my turn. I hand off my blade to Sora and walk in. The fresh water is so hot that steam rises in the tiled bathroom. The scents of roses and lavender bubble up with the bath. Little soaps in the shapes of flowers line the edge of the tub. I smile, filled with glee.

A servant helps me undress, and then I relax against the sloped wall of the clawfoot tub. The tension in my shoulders loosens as the girl washes my hair. Sora won't let anything happen to me. I'm safe here.

The other woman comes over with a sponge. I see the resemblance. I think they're mother and daughter.

As they bathe me, I realize I could get used to this royal treatment. It had been my birthright until Joon decided it wasn't.

The western count wants me to be his queen, and Sora wants me to rule alone. I don't want either, but between the two, I'd rather sit on the serpent throne with Royo as my…

I swallow hard, thinking about how he wanted to room with anyone but me.

Well, he'd rather be court jester than king consort at this point.

Absentmindedly, I tap my fingers on the side of the tub, and my ring clangs. The servant girl pauses. She's young, maybe fourteen, and too inexperienced to pretend not to notice it. I remember how even Rune reacted to the relic. I submerge my hands in the water. I should've bathed myself, especially now that the amulet is fused to me, not hanging from a necklace. The girl continues to massage my scalp, but my earlier ease is gone.

I finish my bath, and the girl wraps me in a white robe just like Sora's. Poor Sora. I still don't know what to say about Daysum, and maybe I should say nothing, since she's deep in denial. It's best for her not to absorb it right now. We all push forward because there is no going back.

When I walk into the bedroom, I notice that Sora has closed all the drapes. Her hair is down to dry and comes to nearly her waist.

"So refreshing, right?" She gives me a dazzling smile.

I nod. It was, before I realized I shouldn't have shown the relics. "Yes, but now I'm really sleepy."

"Me too."

There's only one bed in the room, but it's plush, dressed in silks and satins, and the size of three normal ones. I take the left side, and Sora slides in on the right. I took this side because this way, if she faces me, she'll be able to hear me.

The gray sheets are a soft satin. They feel like clouds against my legs. I lie on my side, and Sora does the same a couple of feet away.

"Where did you disappear to tonight?" I ask. "Was it really the powder room?"

Sora silently eyes the servants pulling down the chandelier to turn out the lights. They leave the oil lamps on our nightstands. Whatever it is, Sora doesn't want to say it in front of them.

"It's a very long story. Tomorrow?" Sora asks.

"Sure."

I yawn. I didn't even realize how exhausted I was until we lay down. Then again, my day started with a kidnapping attempt in Gaya and ended with a marriage proposal from a count. It was a lot.

After the servants leave, we put out the oil lamps. Thoughts churn in my mind. I need to say something, anything to her.

"Sora?" I whisper as my eyes adjust to the darkness.

"Mm-hmm," she says.

"I love you, and I'm really sorry about Daysum," I say.

She reaches out on the bed and takes my hand. "Thank you, Aeri. I love you, too."

A few minutes later, Sora is asleep. Surprise, surprise, she sleeps gently, looks like a doll, and doesn't even drool.

Ugh.

I lie awake. I expect sleep to hit me hard. Instead, my thoughts turn to Royo—how he looked when I woke up on the skiff, how he ran into the inn to save me, and how he choked when the count proposed tonight. He's so close, but he's constantly out of reach. It's an awful feeling to miss someone who is right here. I know he cares about me, but is that enough when he doesn't trust me? I wish he felt differently, but then again, I wouldn't change anything about him. The same attributes that keep us apart are also what I love about him.

So, that sucks.

I sigh, shifting under the covers. At least tomorrow will be simpler.

Maybe.

I close my eyes and try to rest. I'm almost asleep when I notice there's a third person breathing in the room.

CHAPTER EIGHTEEN

MIKAIL

CITY OF RAHWAY, YUSAN

Royo is a strange bedmate. Euyn would be very confused if he could see us from the Kingdom of Hells.

I smile to myself as I peel off my bathrobe. Between his jealousy and his conspiracies, he'd have as much of a sense of humor about all of this as Royo does. But it is, in fact, funny.

Royo turns out his light and stiffly gets into the other side of the bed, folding the sheets around himself from roughly five feet away. He was going to sleep on the floor, but I pointed out that he was welcome to stay at the foot of the bed like a pet. And so here we are.

He obviously didn't think through the logistics of sharing a room when he dodged staying the night with Aeri.

I stow the Water Scepter away, placing it under the bed. As I sit on the soft mattress, I'm reminded of the last time I was here. I pulled Euyn into the wardrobe with me and came up with our assassination plan, and then I took him on the bed. He was definitely not five feet away from me, hugging the edge like it's his last bronze mun. Royo would be far more comfortable in Aeri's bed if he could just let go of her deception. And he should. People lie. We are frail, flawed creatures. It seems silly to hold being human against someone.

"You know, I've never found any benefit to hanging on to the past," I say to Royo's back. "We exist in the present for a reason."

He grunts.

"You should consider forgiving her," I say. "It was an impossible situation."

He flops over on the mattress with an exasperated sigh. "Why does everybody keep saying that?" His fist lands on the bed with a thud.

I lift an eyebrow. "You're right. Surely everyone else isn't being objective and you're the only one seeing things correctly."

He shoots me a death stare, then runs a hand over his scarred face.

"She hurt me," he says to the ceiling.

It's so plain, raw, and unexpected that my heart squeezes.

"I understand the feeling," I say.

His eyes search my face, and I hold his gaze. In the words unspoken between us are Euyn's death and my complicated feelings for him. I hurt him. He disappointed me. We deceived each other greatly and loved fiercely. We forgave too much and too little at the same time. Loving anyone is complicated; loving a Baejkin is a mess.

But there were moments of pure joy. Even growing up with Ailor, happiness wasn't pure because Gaya was always on the horizon. With the sweetness of lemon cakes and bedtime stories also came the tart sourness of having survived the Festival of Blood. Of home being unreachable. But with Euyn I could lose myself in the way that being in love absorbs you completely. Not only sex but the voracious way loving someone ties your souls together.

And now, I'm just unmoored.

"You know, there's very little happiness in any of the realms," I say. "If you've found some, I'd do a better job holding on to it."

Royo responds with another sound that's halfway between a sigh and a grunt.

Really, what does she see in him? There must be something, because Euyn liked Royo, too. He trusted him, and he didn't easily trust anyone—even me. People say there can't be love without trust, but you're never more vulnerable than with someone who has your heart. It would be foolish to unquestioningly trust them.

I suppose, at my core, I am different from Royo.

"Is this Rune guy serious about wanting to marry her?" he asks hesitantly. His whole body tenses as he waits for me to respond. He doesn't want the answer, but he needs to know.

"He's completely serious," I say. "Marrying her would give his bid for the throne legitimacy far above Seok. She would wear the Immortal Crown until she passed it down to her son."

After the audience with Rune, Fallador whispered that I should also consider marrying Aeri. Not for love but for the alliance. He has a point. It would unite the royalty of the two kingdoms, guarantee a free Gaya, and give us safety. As safe as royalty ever is.

He's forgetting, of course, that Royo would murder me before our vows.

"A son," he says through a locked jaw.

"That's always the end goal in Yusan," I say. "The continuation of the bloodline."

I doubt Royo is going to sleep a drop on that note. Still, it's been a long day, and we need to try. I turn off the oil lamp after drinking another glass of water. The thirst has mostly stopped, and in its place is intense physical pain.

As I lie down, every inch of my body feels like it was beaten. We killed over a dozen men and I barely broke a sweat, so it's not that—it has to be the toll, the aches of massive dehydration. The only similar pain I felt today was telling Sora about Daysum.

I clench my teeth until they hurt, and then I sigh. I suppose if I'm going to ask Royo to be honest with himself, I should do the same. The truth is, I'm unfairly angry with Sora. I shouldn't be upset with her at all, but I am. What I did, I did for her. We are similar enough that I don't understand why she can't see it. I'm hurt that she views it the same as Euyn's secrets when I was only trying to protect her. I easily forgave Fallador and Gambria for withholding my parentage because they thought it was best. Why can't she?

I rub my forehead. Again, I already know the answer—because she wouldn't have done the same. She would've told me the truth. She would've been unable to keep it from me as a matter of honor.

I'm still awake and stewing over it when a brief, sharp scream punctures the night.

Sora.

Royo is already on his feet. I grab my sword and scepter, and we race toward the door.

CHAPTER NINETEEN

AERI

CITY OF RAHWAY, YUSAN

There's someone else in this room. I hold my breath. Sora has a delicate breathing pattern when she sleeps. I listen closely, and there it is. Another exhale, just a hair out of sync. It's not a servant or a guard. The only person who would sneak in here is an assassin.

Someone gave us up.

Again.

I hold my breath in the dark and soundlessly grab the throwing knife from under my pillow. Someone is always trying to kill me. It's exhausting. It's exactly what I feared would happen if people knew I had the amulet. But if I had the choice to hide the Sands of Time and have Royo die in front of me, or save his life and risk my own, I'd make the same decision a thousand times over.

The breathing is coming from the left side of the room by the windows. I catch a movement. Either a breeze is blowing the drape or someone is creeping closer. I grip the handle of the knife, but I can't see anyone. It's dark, and I don't have Euyn's unique aim. If I light the lamp and miss, I'm dead. And worse, Sora could be killed.

What do I do? My heart pounds. My palms sweat. I need to protect us.

My ring and amulet vibrate against my skin. I could use them, but there's the toll. The weirdness in the orchard makes me hesitate until there's a footfall on the parquet floor.

I'm out of time.

I sit up, leaning past Sora, and put out my hands.

Turn enemy hearts to gold.

As soon as I wish it, a golden halo surrounds me again. It lights the room like a chandelier, illuminating not just one assassin in all blacks but two. A light breeze blows the drapes to the side. They must've scaled the villa walls and snuck in through the window.

It doesn't matter now, though—they're dead.

As the glow fades, the two people both clutch at their chests, dropping a rope and a dagger onto the ground as they crumble.

Sora sits up, grabbing the comforter. She lets out a startled scream before covering her mouth with her hand. As the room darkens, she lights the oil lamp. Then she stares at me with her eyes wide.

"Aeri, what just happened?" she asks.

I'm about to answer when the door bursts open. I have my hands ready, although I don't really need to use them. They just guide my intention.

But I lower my arms.

Royo runs into our room in his underwear with his dagger drawn. Mikail follows him, also in his underwear, his blade aflame and the scepter in his hand.

I smile at the sight, and then I'm falling out of the bed.

The next thing I know, I'm standing up, looking down at my feet. So, that's strange. Beneath my bare soles is a street, but it's not paved—it's made of ash. Tipping my head back, I look up above me. The sky is red. Funny. I've been here before, but where am I?

"Aeri!"

I blink, and there's Royo. His face is inches from mine.

"Your voice sounds like thunder," I murmur. "I follow like lightning."

He shakes me. "Aeri, Aeri, what are you saying?"

I squeeze my eyes shut, blink a few times, then look around. We're on the parquet floor of the bedroom suite in Rahway, and that's weird. I was just somewhere else. But there's no more ash on the ground or red sky overhead—just gray satin and lamplight.

Confused, I close my eyes.

"Aeri!" he yells. I blink hard and focus on Royo's pained voice. "Aeri, stay with me."

"For tonight, and tomorrow, and tomorrow, and tomorrow," I say.

Royo wraps his arms around me and grips me tight. It's too much at first, and I struggle to breathe. But then I finally realize who is holding me and relax into him. Why would I need air when I'm reaching the heavens? I lean into his neck. He's on his knees next to me, holding up my torso. His face is pained, and tears swim in his eyes.

"What's wrong?" I ask.

"You were just…frozen," Sora says. I look past Royo to Sora standing in her white robe. She also looks very concerned, gripping the tie at her waist. "Your eyes were open, but none of us could get you to respond until Royo called your name."

Oh, okay, that makes sense. Same thing as earlier.

"It went on for longer," Mikail says with a troubled sigh.

I sit up with Royo's help. Mikail is examining the two bodies on the ground. His eyebrows knit as he stares at them. I'm sure he's wondering how they died.

"Oh, I killed them," I say. "I turned their hearts to gold."

Royo's eyebrow arches as his face skews, but then he shakes it off. He puts his arms under me and lifts me. I'm weightless against him as he sets me on the bed. He treats me so gently, like I'm a porcelain doll he might accidentally break. He knows very well that's not the case. He's picked me up before under different, naked, circumstances.

"So much for being safe," Mikail says, frowning.

Sora avoids looking at anyone. There's something she's not saying, but I'm not sure what. I bet it's related to whatever she couldn't tell me earlier.

"Where's Gambria?" Royo asks.

"In the room with Fallador, I assume," Mikail says.

"But you don't know."

His skepticism is clear as day. He's accusing her of being a traitor. Again, she knew where we were staying, and she was conveniently absent while we were attacked. But Rune also knew where we were, and the servant girl who washed my hair saw my relics and knew which room I was staying in. Any one of them could've betrayed us.

Mikail shakes his head. "We can't prove it was her."

Royo slaps his hand on his thigh. "How many coincidences do we need? Or does one of us have to die for you to doubt your friend?"

Mikail is silent.

"Royo has a point," Sora says. "They're palace assassins, so it's unlikely Rune sent them."

Mikail shrugs. "Unless he is on Seok's side."

Oh.

CHAPTER TWENTY

ROYO

CITY OF RAHWAY, YUSAN

Aeri's okay, but I'm gonna get my axe back and kill this fucking guy. I don't care if he's a count. I don't care if he's got an army that'll take out Seok. Rune tried to murder Aeri.

Or it was Gambria.

Or maybe Fallador.

It also could've been servants tempted by the fortunes they'd get for the relics.

I run my hand down my face. There are always too many potential traitors.

"You're saying this whole thing could be a setup by Rune?" I wave my hands generally to the room.

Mikail nods. "It's not beyond him to fake friendship while trying to kill us. Alliances shift quickly at a time like this. Seok can always make him a better offer—or we can."

He looks at Aeri, and my hands itch to wring Mikail's neck as I realize what that means. He wants Aeri to agree to marry the count for our safety. Because if she was engaged to him for real, he would keep her alive, at least until he could take the throne. My stomach turns at the thought of her marrying him and knots at the idea of him hurting her. It's like my guts are trying to claw up and choke my heart.

The fuck she will marry him.

"Did you know them?" Sora asks Mikail, gesturing to the assassins on the ground.

Sora looks concerned, but something about her isn't right. She keeps squeezing the belt of her robe. I've been thinking it's grief for her sister, but she's been off since she came back from the powder room. Her eyes shift a little bit when she talks. I don't know why, but it's weirding me out.

Mikail takes a breath. "Rose and Avalon—upper-level assassins. Avalon could've been a spy, but he preferred this side of things."

"Were they trying to kill Aeri or me?" Sora asks.

We all silently stare. It hadn't even dawned on me that they might be here for Sora, not Aeri. Tiyung said Seok wants Sora dead, but if it's the southern count, how'd he know where to find her? An eagle would take a full day to reach Tamneki and another to get back. We just got here.

None of it makes sense. Nothing ever does.

"They're not alive to talk," Mikail says. "It's possible they were here for both of you."

Both? The thought that we could've just lost both Sora *and* Aeri is a gut punch. It's hard to even inhale.

My hands shake as I think about how Aeri lay on the floor with her eyes open, not blinking, not moving. Mikail clapped in front of her face, shook her, and nothing brought her back. Sora checked for signs of poisoning, but there was nothing.

All I could do was stand there and relive losing her in the hot springs. I was certain I lost her for good this time.

I clasp my hands behind my head. Ten fucking Hells, my heart can't take it. I wish I could just rip the organ from my chest. It would make things a lot easier. But I need her heart now, too, in order to go on.

Love, or whatever this is, is a fucking fool's game.

But when I thought she was really gone, I forgave everything. If I could do it then, that means the only thing holding me back now is pride. And I'm standing here in my underwear, so pride is a real lost cause.

Aeri stares at me with her golden eyes, hopeful and waiting—it's like she can read my thoughts. I kinda wish I had on clothes.

I go over to the table, pour her a glass of water, then hand it to her.

"Thank you, Royo."

I nod and tuck a strand of hair behind her ear. Her face lights up with joy, and the expression lifts my heart, too. But I step away. I need to keep my distance until I can think this through.

"So, do we confront Gambria or Rune?" Sora asks.

Mikail sighs, rubbing his forehead. "I think we say nothing and see what happens in the morning when whoever it was realizes their plan failed. We should switch rooms and get some sleep, though. I'm sure you need it, Aeri."

"Mostly, I feel fine," she says. "Well, aside from getting frozen in time." She shrugs and looks at the floor. "Anyhow, what should we do about the bodies? We can't just leave them here, right?"

Mikail and Sora exchange glances. Aeri has a point.

"Throw them out the window," I say.

Mikail shrugs. "As good a plan as any."

He waves me over after patting down both of the bodies.

We pick up the guy first—Mikail called him Avalon. He's a lot heavier than I expected, but he does have a gold heart now, and I know how heavy gold is.

Sora skirts over to the drapes and throws them apart. The window is open about a foot, which allowed these two to slither in.

She frowns and shakes her head. "I swear I locked the windows when I closed the drapes."

"You probably did," Mikail says, carrying the guy's legs. "Assassins can all pick simple window locks. One of the first tests we put them through is getting out of a locked room."

Sora opens the window wide, and we toss the guy out onto the bushes below. We go back, pick up the girl, and do the same. The assassins are younger than I first thought—probably a few years younger than me—but I don't give a shit about their lives. They would've killed Aeri and Sora if they could've and then went on to their next jobs. It's us or them, and it's sure as fuck not going to be us.

"Royo, why don't you see Aeri to safety?" Mikail suggests. He's closed the window, and he's staring at Sora with a troubled look. I was right—something's weird about her.

"Should I… Should I stay with Aeri?" I ask.

Mikail eyes me, and something like approval flashes on his face. "Yes, that's a good idea. They're better protected separately."

Sora stares right back at him, challenge written in her expression.

Fantastic. Another mystery.

But, whatever. I go back to the bed, where Aeri is already trying to stand.

"Don't bother," I say.

I scoop her up against my chest, grab my dagger, and carry her out of the room. Still in just my underwear.

CHAPTER TWENTY-ONE

AERI

CITY OF RAHWAY, YUSAN

If I'd known all it would take was an assassination attempt to get Royo talking to me again, I would've paid them myself.

"I really am fine, Royo."

I'm sitting on the bed in his room after he carried me in. If I hadn't already fainted, I might've swooned at the way he lifted me up and took me here.

He pauses, looking unamused as he sets window traps. He's using knives and melted candlewax so that if anyone opens the windows, the knives will either fall on them or clatter to the ground. It's ingenious. I wonder if he learned it from Euyn.

It takes a while, but eventually, Royo is satisfied. He closes the drapes and then walks over to me. But he stops a few feet away, idling by the nightstand.

"Aeri." He stares at the oil lamp, and the flames reflect in his amber eyes.

I hold my breath, waiting, torn by hopeful anticipation and dread. Is he going to say he can't ever forgive me? Or give me a chance and ask me why I didn't tell him about the Sands of Time? I try to prepare myself for heartbreak, but no one can really soften a death blow, so what's the point?

He traces patterns on the nightstand with his fingers and then looks at me.

"I never thanked you," he says.

Okay, I didn't see this coming. His scarred face is sincere, almost boyish. I want to take it in my hands and kiss him, but I hold still.

"What for?" I ask.

"For killing Bay Chin and saving my life in the harbor."

Oh, right. That was a bunch of murders ago.

"But you shouldn't have done it," he adds. "Now they're hunting you."

I can't summon more than a shrug. I've been hunted my whole life—every young girl is prey for the appetites of men. At least now I have the relics to protect me and the people I love. And I have Royo…maybe.

I stare up at him. "The amarth said I'd have to choose between loves, but that's easy. I would choose you every time. I don't care what the consequences are."

His fingers twitch by his sides. He wants to reach out for me—at least he's thinking about it. My heart swells.

Just reach out for me, and you have me.

But he balls his hand into a fist.

I deflate. So much for that.

"Mikail and Sora think I should forgive you," he says.

I nod along eagerly. "They are very wise and always right."

His lips twitch, and he almost cracks a smile. Almost. Then they drop into a frown and he runs a hand over his short black hair.

"You hurt me, Aeri."

I sigh. "I know I did."

"Did you not trust me enough to tell me the truth?" he asks. "Did you think I'd take the amulet from you?"

The thought had never crossed my mind.

"Not at all," I say. "I wanted to tell you, but if you knew, my father could torture you. And you were loyal to Euyn, and I… I wasn't sure if he'd kill me to take it. My family is… Well, they're not opposed to murdering each other under the right circumstances.

And the relic is so very valuable, Royo. It manipulates time. Imagine what it could do in the wrong hands."

The neckline of my robe is open enough for me to touch it as I gesture. He stares at the sands glass that is now embedded into my skin by my collarbone.

"How long have you had it?" he asks.

"Since I was twelve."

I watch as his brow furrows. He must be putting together the timeline. He knows everyone thought I died at twelve—another of Omin's young victims. I really don't want to think about what happened back then, but I'm just so happy he's talking to me. That we're together again. The past, no matter how horrific, seems very distant right now.

"I stole it from Prince Omin's wrist the night he tried to attack me," I say. "I didn't know what it was—I thought it was a gem, but I aged four years in minutes because of it. It's how I'm nineteen but I look your age. It literally steals time from me in order to freeze it."

The lines on Royo's brow deepen. "It was on your necklace before."

"Yes."

It's almost like I can see him remembering that moment camping, when we kissed under the swirling lights of the night sky. I pulled away because he grazed the necklace. I couldn't explain it then, but I can now.

"Is this how you saved us on the Sol?" he asks.

I nod.

"And how you took the crown?"

"Yes. It's how I stole almost everything. My sleight of hand is pretty good, but it's not that good."

He's silent. Etherum is a heavy thing to understand. But for me, it feels like a weight lifted. It lightens my whole being to have him know the truth about me. For the first time in my adult life, I can actually tell someone everything. I can be close to him, to Sora without the barrier of secrets. I mean, yes, I'm also hunted from now until I die, but there's an upside.

Royo rubs his face. "It explains a lot, but what is happening to you after you turn things to gold?"

"I'm really not sure. I thought… Well, this is going to sound…" I trail off. I don't need him second-guessing his decision to speak to me.

"Just say it. You haven't worried about sounding weird before."

I raise my eyebrows. That's true enough. "I thought I saw a red sky and a road made of ash. It was so real."

I close my eyes, and I can still picture it. The sky was red like the Yusanian flag, and there were pieces of bone in the fluffy ash.

"That's…odd. Is the god magic causing you to see the future? Like the huge birdman?"

Gods, I hadn't even considered that. Could the relics be causing visions? I think about it for a moment. I want it to be true, but something in my heart says no.

I shake my head. "I don't think so. The relics have a price. Using one eventually kills the wielder. I can't imagine that using two actually benefits you—if anything, it has to kill you faster."

Trouble lines form by his mouth at the thought of me speeding to my death. But that's been the reality since I was twelve. Everyone dies. The difference is in who you can save.

"Do you want to sit?" I ask. This whole conversation has occurred while Royo's been standing next to the bed in his underwear.

He shakes his head. "No, no. You get some rest. I'll keep watch."

I ignore the stabbing pain caused by his rejection.

"You have to be tired, too, though," I say.

"I'm good. I'll go to bed after you wake up." He stands straighter.

My shoulders droop, and my chin falls. "Oh. I thought… Never mind."

He walks over to the dresser and puts his clothes back on, which really is a shame. The muscles in his legs look especially good like this. He tosses on his undershirt and pants, then lights a candle and brings it over to the nightstand. His thick fingers turn off the oil lamp.

"Get some sleep," he says.

I lie down. I move the pillow and find a dagger under it. Royo's. I take it by the hilt and slide it under the pillow next to me.

"Royo?" I say.

"Yeah?"

I take a breath. I don't know why it's so hard to apologize to him, but he deserves to hear it. So, I make my mouth work. "I'm sorry I hurt you. I didn't mean to, but I know it's all the same."

Hurt remains whether you intended to do it or not. If you stab someone, they still bleed. It doesn't matter if it was a jab or an accident.

Royo draws a big breath, then nods. I don't know if he accepted the apology, but he didn't reject it, so that's better than I'd hoped for.

"It's not all the same."

He reaches down and pulls the blankets over me. He lingers and gives me a look. Just one. But in his eyes, there's forgiveness. I'll take it whether I deserve it or not. Forgiveness is a gift you can earn later.

I turn my head, and I'm asleep within minutes, dreaming about a better tomorrow.

Assuming we survive the night.

CHAPTER TWENTY-TWO

TIYUNG

THE COASTAL ROAD, YUSAN

The novelty of riding in the rain has officially worn off. I'm developing sores from being constantly wet, and my cough is concerning. As we make our way south, it's turning warmer, but the wind and rain make the change negligible.

We've only passed four other travelers this entire time. People try not to ride any distances during the monsoons, as the roads can get washed out and bridges are often impassable, but we don't have a choice. Not after what we saw. A war of the realms is coming, and we are running out of time.

"Should we tell the king's guard about the Weian fleet when we get to Trove?" I ask. It's the next closest city that's large enough to have a manned fortress.

Hana's mouth falls open. "Have you lost your senses?"

Maybe. I mean, it's possible, but why is she acting like this is the worst idea I've had?

"And if Sora and the others are aboard the Weian ships, do you really care enough to tell the throne of Yusan?" she adds.

The thought hadn't even crossed my mind. We still don't know what happened in Khitan. Every time we stop in a messenger house, I hold my breath as Hana asks if there is anything for Nabhi of Kur. She's gotten two letters, and neither were from Mikail. One was from Nayo—he is safe and no longer near Tamneki. The other message, she didn't show me. She just said it was from a "source."

"You really think they could be aligned *with* Joon?" I ask.

It doesn't seem likely when they just tried to kill him weeks ago. Then again, he worked with Bay Chin, so I suppose he can look past his own attempted murder.

Hana shrugs. "I think that anything can happen in a war. Euyn is his brother, and Aeri is his daughter. Stranger things have occurred than royal families forgiving blood betrayals. Maybe they were able to get the ring and give it to him. Maybe there was some other wrinkle. But we do nothing until we know for certain. Yusan doesn't have the navy to match Wei's, regardless of a few days' head start. So we'd risk dooming our friends and still not help Yusan either way."

"I see your point," I say.

She raises an eyebrow. I'm sure it's rare that men listen to and agree with her, especially the nobility. It must be hard to be a woman like Hana—so intelligent and yet constantly underestimated.

"What is your plan for when we get to Qali?" she asks.

I draw a breath and blow out a heavy sigh. I've put off any thoughts of dealing with my father. But now we are running out of time.

"You don't have one, do you?" she asks. Something in her tone says that she hopes I prove her wrong.

"I…let him know I'm alive." My voice rises at the end like it's a question. My words hang in the air, and they don't sound impressive.

She drops her reins and wipes her face with both hands for an extended amount of time. I think there's a long-suffering sigh in there.

"Tiyung, Sora's life depends on you. I've risked everything to help you. I don't think it's overselling it to say the fate of the realm depends on you. We should work on this plan of yours."

"All right," I say.

Talking to my father has never been easy. I can use all the help I can get.

CHAPTER TWENTY-THREE

SORA

CITY OF RAHWAY, YUSAN

It was a tense night, and now it's an equally tense morning. We all decided to act like nothing happened in hopes that the traitor will slip up and reveal themselves today. But as we sit at a sumptuous breakfast with Gambria and Fallador, they seem normal. I study her, and I just... I can't tell.

Mikail is eyeing her, too. He had questions for me last night, but I'm convinced the walls have ears here. I knocked on them, and Mikail did the same. We couldn't prove any were hollow spying walls, but instincts shouldn't be ignored. I said we'd take a walk today and I'd tell him anything he wanted to know. He picked up on the fact that I recognized Misha, so he wasn't fooled by my act. He wasn't supposed to be, though—just Rune.

The western count waltzes in as soon as I think of him. Gambria, Mikail, and I all stand. Eventually, Royo does, too. Aeri and Fallador, as royalty, keep their seats. Decorum first until the end of the realm.

"Good morning," Rune says. "I trust you all slept well."

He's suave—freshly bathed, wearing a gold-embroidered jacket and his diamond collar. Most of us are in the same clothes as yesterday. The tailors measured us a bell ago, and they are working on new attire. Aeri, of course, is in the second dress she picked up in Rahway. It's white and gold with a pearl neckline.

"The baths were delightful," she says.

Well, that much is true. It was nice to be able to soak in the tub…
before the murders.

I search the western count for a reaction, and it's slight, but
there's a tell. His left eye closes just a little.

He clears it almost immediately, maintaining his carefree air as
he takes his seat. "I'm glad you thought so, Your Majesty."

"Something wrong?" Mikail asks.

He pierces a slice of mango with his knife. I tried everything on
the table, and nothing was poisoned. Everyone is famished enough
to eat, but they are still hesitant as they poke at eggs and corn cakes.

Rune sighs as servants make him a plate from the array of dishes.
"My guards discovered palace assassins on the grounds last night."

Fallador's eyebrows rise as he sips his coffee. "Really? From Qali?"

"Indeed. Stranger still was that they were already dead when we
found them in the hedges."

We didn't mention the assassins to Gambria or Fallador, and
their shock is genuine. At least, I think it is. She pauses with her fork
midway to her mouth. Fallador clangs his cup in its saucer.

"The gods work in mysterious ways," Mikail says. He taps his
walking stick and slices apart a fried egg. The yolk bleeds onto his
potatoes.

"Ah, so it was you," Rune says. He splashes coju into his orange
juice. It's a choice at nine bells in the morning. "Very well. I am glad
you took care of them and no one was disturbed last night."

Gambria's eyes narrow slightly. Is that a tell, or is she simply
annoyed with Mikail for not mentioning anything?

She catches me staring and lifts her eyebrows.

"Could you please pass the congee?" I ask. It's over on her left.
The dishes were all prepared to be served family style, which made
it easy for me to sample for poison.

Gambria smiles pleasantly and reaches for the bowl.

"I received eagle post this morning with news that should interest
you all," Rune says.

Everyone turns toward him. The count takes his time sipping his drink. Of course he loves this, keeping us on edge and painfully waiting.

He delicately sets down his glass. "The Queen of Khitan lives, along with General Vikal. The queen rules from Quu and has signed a treaty of everlasting peace with Wei. I am told the priest king of Wei drowned or was variously slain in the harbor along with the general of his guards; however, his son now rules. Bay Chin perished, as did the general of our palace guards. However, no one seems to know if Joon is dead or alive. He is certainly not confirmed dead, no matter what rumors Seok spreads."

Gambria sits back in her chair, her face awash with relief. Mikail's face doesn't give away anything, but I know he must be vexed that Queen Quilimar still breathes.

"To the death of one tyrant," Fallador says. He stands and lifts his coffee.

The rest of us stand and raise our glasses to the death of the king of Wei.

As we lower our drinks, there's a split-second look between Fallador and Rune. It causes the little hairs on my arms to rise as my senses go on alert. They know each other—it was the glance of co-conspirators.

We retake our seats, and I shake off a chill. We've been accusing Gambria, but what if Fallador is the spy? By being in the room with Mikail in Gaya, we didn't suspect him, but he knew where we were staying in both locations. He's charming and friendly, but he lied to Mikail for years. It could be him. That could also be how Rune knew we had the scepter.

"Does the news change your plans?" Aeri asks Rune.

"Not at all, Your Majesty. Forces loyal to me are already marching on Tamneki. We will meet them in the capital and take back the throne from Seok. If your father is alive, we will be there to support his claim and oust the usurper."

What did he just say?

Everyone stops eating. Six pairs of eyes blink at Rune.

"Wait, you want to work with the guy who wants us all dead?" Royo asks. He's speaking out of turn, but he can't help himself. King Joon alive would mean we die as traitors, but Rune wants to align with him.

Rune sips on his coju and juice. "Is there anyone who hasn't tried to kill you all?"

There has to be someone, but the list isn't long.

Mikail shrugs. "A few."

"An imposter sits on the throne of Yusan," Rune says. "Should Joon have survived the battle in the harbor, he will have not only the Immortal Crown but the support of the king's guard. You have a shared, immediate goal of taking down the enemy. Shared needs make for an alliance, no matter how great the rift."

"And once Seok is dead?" Mikail asks.

"I marry Naerium, and then we arrange for a quiet end to Joon. The rest can be sorted later."

He waves a careless hand, but the details contain our fates. Royo grips his steak knife so hard, I worry he'll snap the ivory handle.

Yet Rune's wave reminds me of the last time I was here, when we were plotting to kill the king. I put down my spoon.

"Your Grace," I say. "If I may?"

"Of course, Sora. What is on your mind?" He smiles as his eyes undress me.

I ignore it.

"The last time I was in Rahway, when I asked why you were helping me, you said, 'Isn't it obvious.' What did you mean by that?"

Rune smiles. "You have quite the memory."

I stare at him, not letting it go. He was the one who told me that Seok intended on destroying me, even if I succeeded. That Tiyung was supposed to kill me.

Rune finishes a bite of egg and corn cake, once again stalling.

"I thought that you were aware of my history with Seok and the questions surrounding Tiyung's parentage. I was mistaken."

He catches me sipping my juice. It takes all of Madame Iseul's etiquette training not to spit it back into my glass. What did he just say? Did he just imply that Tiyung is not Seok's son?

My fingertips grow icy as I process the thought.

Rune smiles, swirling his glass. "What you have to understand about the high nobility, my dear, is that there aren't many of us. The greater your rank, the more that's true. Princess Naerium is in rarified air. As am I. As are Seok and Joon. To make things worse, we were around the same age as young men, which means we were courting the same women. The web gets tangled quickly when there are so few players."

I'm listening, but I'm trying to jump ahead and figure out what this has to do with Tiyung.

Rune must realize I am not following him, so he continues, "The Countess of Gain, formerly Olivia of Pact, was engaged to me before she ran off with Seok. There was a rumor that Joon also fell in love with her and wanted her hand—I don't think that's true, however."

I shake my head. "But what does that have to do with Tiyung?"

"Olivia and Seok married quickly. Less than a year after she was sharing my bed, in fact."

Aeri's eyes widen. Royo sucks in a breath. They must realize what he's saying. But I am lagging behind.

One corner of Rune's mouth lifts. He's enjoying my confusion almost as much as he'd enjoy my torment.

"You don't find it curious that Seok has only one child?" he asks. "I always have. This realm requires heirs. I have four sons. Bay Chin had six sons and many daughters. And Dal fathered five girls before finally having a son. But Seok only has Tiyung...if that. I find that both strange and obvious."

My stomach twists with a sinking feeling, my left ear ringing.

Kingdom of Hells, Rune is saying that he fathered Tiyung. Memories of the last time we were in Rahway swim in my head. The way he insulted Ty at dinner had seemed oddly personal, but at that point I didn't care. Yet, for the reasons Rune just stated, I have always wondered why Tiyung was an only child.

"I hope that answered your question, Sora," Rune says with a grin.

CHAPTER TWENTY-FOUR

MIKAIL

CITY OF RAHWAY, YUSAN

Rune thinks he fathered Seok's son. Truly, the nobility of Yusan has too much time on their hands.

There's a silver blur at the corner of my eye, and Gambria's dagger stops right at my throat. She's breathing hard, a hair away from slicing open my neck. I stare down at her and smile. She got the drop on me.

"The lack of effort is offensive, Mikail," she says in Gayan.

She tosses the dagger to the side of the sparring ring. I asked her to accompany me to the armory after we finished breakfast because we have something to discuss. We were supposed to be fighting with only bamboo poles, but she had the dagger stashed somewhere in her training rough spun.

"You have to be prepared for anything," she adds.

I usually am, but the complicated parentage and deceit at the top of Yusan has taken me by surprise. Joon or Omin fathered Euyn. Quilimar wasn't Baejkin. And now Tiyung's bloodline is in question. I'd simply forgotten we were sparring. Plus, last night still weighs on my mind.

"Is that any way to address your sovereign?" I ask.

Gambria inhales and rolls her eyes.

Shifting my pole, I hit her three times before she can react. I get her right knee, left shoulder, and then push her by her stomach until she falls out of the ring.

She lands in the white sandpit three feet down. I've won.

I extend my hand to help her up, but Gambria waves it off. She colors red and springs to her feet, wiping the sand from her brown tunic.

I leave the ring in search of water. The scepter leans by a table where there's a pitcher and towels. With large gulps, I down a glass, still trying to replenish my body with salts and water so that this pain will go away. I think it's less severe than yesterday, but scale is a tricky thing. It's hard to tell if a temple or stadium weighs more when it's crushing you.

As I finish the water, I study the inner courtyard of the armory. The armory takes up the entire west wing of Rune's villa. This open-air training section provides natural light and air. The space is impressive. Not only do they have a wide variety of weapons, but the raised black sparring rings, sandpits, and woven mats are the best I've seen. It makes sense. Rune is the most warlike of the counts—well, when there were four. We seem to be down to one.

But I didn't ask her here to spar. Not really.

"I have a question for you," I say as Gambria joins me by the table.

"Why didn't I challenge you in archery?" she mutters. "That's my question."

I smile. "We'd have to go to the other hall for that."

We stand quietly. I use silence as a tool, spinning my wooden pole. She's too curious not to take the bait. Nearly everyone reacts the same—it's human nature.

"What is it?"

I turn and face her. "Do you want to go back to Khitan?"

Her eyes drift as her brow furrows. She's trying to figure out where I'm going with this rather than just answering honestly. Disappointment floods me, but it's not a new feeling. I've been keeping it at bay since last night.

"It's a simple question," I say. "Your wife and lover are there. I suspect that's where you'd rather be. So why do you stay?"

"I don't have a lover other than Lyria," she says. "I assume you mean Quilimar, but that's long in the past."

"Feel free to respond at any time about Khitan."

The bamboo sparring pole is far lighter than the Water Scepter. When I first used the scepter to get us out of Quu Harbor, I'd worried about dropping it into the East Sea, but the etherum causes it to cling to my palm when I'm wielding it.

At least the scepter is loyal.

"I don't understand what you're getting at," Gambria says.

She has always been sharp, cleverer than Fallador. But her slyness is working against her. She's being dishonest, and by trying to evade me, she's only making it more obvious.

She grabs her pole again and enters the ring.

Fair enough.

I saunter in, using the raised bridge, and I bow to her. She does the same. Then I drop into a ready stance.

Gambria attacks immediately, now fueled by ego and anger. She's faster than I remembered, and despite being shirtless, I actually break a sweat keeping up with her. But a flame this bright dies quickly.

"You don't care about Gaya," I say, parrying her blows. "Or really Yusan, for that matter. Not enough to risk your life."

She doesn't deny it.

"So my question remains: What is stopping you from returning to Khitan?"

She's panting as she strikes again. She swings at my head, and I duck with a sigh. I'm tired of taking it easy on her. She's left her side exposed this entire time instead of alternating strikes.

I twirl the pole and punch at her ribs, knocking the air out of her.

Gambria stumbles back a few steps, her eyes wide as she clutches her side.

"One could think you have to be here," I say. "Because otherwise, who would relay information to the crown?"

She colors red. "You are the spymaster, Mikail. You think I'd spy for that bloodletter? I would never stoop that low."

Real hate flashes in her eyes, and it explains so much. She doesn't feel the way Fallador does about my position as spymaster—she views it as a betrayal of what we held dear. And when it comes to Gaya, I suppose it has been. I've ordered the assassinations of rebel leaders on the island. It doesn't matter that I also sent them forewarning. I did it, and some still died.

"Of course you wouldn't," I say.

She pauses and knits her eyebrows. I hook my pole behind her knee and upend her again. She lands on her back on the black floor of the ring, struggling to inhale. Casually, I drop the pole on her thighs and step on it so she can't kick up at me. I'm not sparing her any pain. Not this time.

"I said *crown*, not Yusan." I reach into my pocket and take the card out of my rough spun pants. "You know, it's a funny thing about messenger houses. You can never quite be sure the letters arrive at their intended location. So many things can happen between sealing the clay and someone opening it."

I drop the letter onto Gambria's chest. It says:

My love,
They have the ring, the sands, and the scepter in Rahway. We seek Count Rune's assistance to take the throne. Align with the count, and Yusan is yours.
Forever in love

Gambria's blue eyes fill with terror. She doesn't have to read the message because she knows every word.

She swallows hard. "Where did you get that?"

"I found it on the assassin who broke in last night." I shake my head and sigh. "How many eagles do you think are sent from here to the palace in Khitan? It's so sloppy, Gambria. Did you think Seok wouldn't have spies watching the messenger houses? You almost got them killed."

She shakes her head. "I hadn't meant to. I would never help this realm."

That part is true. She hadn't even coded her message, not thinking her letter would be intercepted and used. Of course, betraying our whereabouts and plans to Quilimar was intentional. Love and loyalty go hand in hand with dishonor and betrayal.

I hesitate. I know what must be done, but I also understand what it is like loving a Baejkin. She's fallen into a trap, and what's worse is that it's so pleasant that she doesn't want a way out.

"I swear on my parents, on Gaya, that I never meant to hurt them!" Gambria says.

She shouldn't have mentioned Gaya. Ire rises in me at her using our homeland's name, and I think about killing her right here.

I lean down closer to her. She winces as I press on the pole.

"Because I once loved you, because Fallador continues to, I will give you this chance to flee now with your life. Cross paths with me again, and it will be one time too many."

"Mikail, I—"

She wants to explain that she was merely trying to help the woman she loves. But I have no interest in hearing it. She knows that I am the true prince of Gaya. She has known me since we were children, and she has no loyalty to me. To the home we survived. I can forgive a lot of betrayal, but not this. The island comes first.

"Go before I'm dressed." I pull my shirt back on.

She tries a few times to speak, but then she shakes her head. "I wish you peace, Adoros."

I spit. Peace is for the weak. I swear and I vow that those will be the last words she ever speaks to me.

CHAPTER TWENTY-FIVE

ROYO

CITY OF RAHWAY, YUSAN

Aeri and I are back in our room after a weird breakfast. I shake my head from the politics. After all of this, Count Rune wants to keep King Joon on the throne?

I ball my hands in fists. It's just more of the same. Like that game I used to play as a kid where people switched chairs. Except when it's royals and nobles, a bunch of innocent people die just so they can change seats.

Aeri stares at me as I prowl by the windows. All the traps are still in place. I checked as soon as we got in to make sure the servants hadn't touched them. I also swept the room for weapons, hidden traps, and spies.

I shake my head. Maybe Euyn wasn't paranoid—maybe he just had to deal with people constantly trying to kill him.

New clothes sit on the dresser and hang in the wardrobe, but Sora said not to put on anything before she has a chance to check it.

Apparently, you can poison clothes.

I run my hand down my face. We aren't safe here. I wanna leave, but we aren't safe anywhere. At least this place is swank with satins and goosedown. So that's something.

"You have to be tired," Aeri says, watching me. She's over by the dresser, inspecting the new clothes.

I only slept from when she got up at dawn until the tailors

knocked at eight, but it's okay. I can sleep in the Ten Hells.

"I'm fine," I say.

She's unsurprised by my reaction. Her eyebrows rise a little, but that's it.

"Try?"

Her golden eyes plead with me. She looks beautiful in her white dress. Pearls line her long neck. I want to see that neck arch as I...

I shake it off, shoving my hands in my pockets. Doesn't matter. Maybe I am exhausted if I'm thinking about getting that close to her again. Forgiveness isn't forgetting. I have forgiven her—I did last night. But I'd have to have no memory to let her hurt me again.

I eye the bed, trying not to think about what I want to do to her. So that's all I'm thinking about.

Fuck my life.

"You'll wake me if there's any sign of trouble?" I ask.

She laughs. "I think you'd notice the room glowing."

That's not funny. I turn and stare at her.

She smiles. "Yes, of course I'd wake you, Royo."

Aeri closes the drapes and lights a candle by the armchairs. She pulls a leather-bound book out of the nightstand and curls up in a seat. She must've stolen the novel from Rune's study, but who knows when she did that? I have a feeling it was while we were all waiting there last night.

Still a little thief.

A time thief.

I lie down and stare at the ceiling. I don't get how she did it—how she saved me on the Sol—but it explains how I woke up with a splitting headache in the lifeboat. Aeri's given up part of her own life to save me, Sora, and Mikail. Every use of the sands costs her, but she did it anyway. She was ready to leave the amarth egg, just so I'd live. If she had to, she'd marry this count to protect all of us.

My stomach turns at the thought, my hands digging into the pillows. Yeah, he's got more power and money than I could even dream about. Yeah, he's a decent-looking old guy. But she can't marry him. He'll never understand her, never love her. And if she becomes his wife, I'll never see her again. Not to patrol, not to hold her. Nothing.

I bite down on my lip.

"Aeri," I say.

"Yes?"

I open my mouth, but what do I want to say? *Don't marry one of the most powerful guys in the realm and become queen of Yusan? Live with me in a drafty, smelly shack once this is all over?* She's a princess— she deserves a life of luxury and spoils. There are hopes, and then there are delusions.

I crush the thought with a sigh.

"Wake me up in a couple of bells," I say.

She looks at me, and a little wrinkle forms on her forehead. She knows it wasn't what I was gonna ask.

"Sure, Royo," she says.

Regret floods me, weighing down my chest. Somehow, I know I'll look back at this moment and wish I'd said what I felt. But the moment's already gone. I turn over onto my side and close my eyes.

CHAPTER TWENTY-SIX

SORA

CITY OF RAHWAY, YUSAN

At eleven bells, I take Rune's luxurious carriage into town on the pretense of going to the messenger house. I had to give an extensive explanation before I was allowed to leave the villa, but I slide onto the velvet bench, and minutes later, we get into Rahway proper. We navigate the shining stone city, and then the cream-colored coach pulls up to a cobalt blue shop. Traffic comes to a halt for the count's carriage. People quite literally stop in their tracks.

"I'll wait here for you, miss," the coachman says as he helps me down. He's an older man, probably around fifty, with short gray hair.

"There's no need," I say with a smile.

"I insist."

"All right," I say, deflating. I have to figure out a way to lose him. I smile. "Actually, that's great! Once I'm done, you can take me to the gem houses for a new necklace or two, and then the cobblers. I want to get fitted for a few new pairs of boots and shoes. I also need to find the best beauty house. Do you know where one is? Oh, you probably don't. I'll just visit them all, since they're all so different, you know? And I also need a new coin purse. This one is too out of date."

I do my best to sound like Aeri, and the coachman's eyes glaze over. The concerns of women are frivolous in Yusan, even when they exist to cater to men's tastes.

"So just wait here," I say. "I have to send a few messages to my family, and then we can start the day of shopping. Unless you have to go back before six or seven bells."

"I am needed back at the villa, miss," he says eagerly.

"Oh, okay." I force a frown, then shake it off and smile. "I can hire a coach for my return, in that case."

The coachman nods and opens the shop door. I drop into the messenger house and stroll to the ledge to select a pen and a slip of paper. I keep my eye on the window. It's only a few moments before the luxe carriage rolls away.

I exhale. Thank the gods.

Rahway is busy with horses, carriages, and pedestrians. People constantly come in and out of the messenger house. Because we're in Yusan, the pace still slows during the monsoons, but not as much as the cities where it rains.

I wait five minutes after the carriage is out of sight before I toss the blank paper into the fire and leave out of the other side of the building.

Now, I have to find a dress house in a city that all looks the same. Rahway was purposefully designed to be uniform, and even the squares and fountains look alike. But despite a few wrong turns, I manage to reach the Kingdom Dress House at precisely noon. A sign on the door says they are out for lunch and will be back soon.

With a steadying breath, I pull the brass handle. It opens. It's fairly dim inside the store. The only light filters in from the crowded shop windows.

"You're late," Sun-ye says.

She's seated on a divan in a body-hugging purple dress with a high slit in the skirt. The space is filled with mannequins, mirrors, and fabric walls, but no one else is in here. She must've paid off the shopkeeper.

"I'm on time." I point up above us as the noon bells ring out. She had been very specific about how, where, and when to meet before we left the powder room last night.

"Which is late."

I throw my head back in frustration. Sun-ye is still terrible. But how terrible?

"Was it you?" I lower my voice and take a step closer.

She blinks. "The assassins?"

I nod.

Her whole low-cut dress moves as she sighs at me. "Why would it be me? If I attacked you, you'd expose me. How would that benefit me?"

"Perhaps you counted on me dying first."

"No, I think I've seen enough of us die." Her green eyes take on a distant look.

Seventeen. We watched seventeen girls die. One, Seok killed by hand—Plia. He had all of us gather, and then he grabbed Plia's blond hair and slit her throat. She had rebelled, refusing Madame Iseul's pleas to take more poison. He made us watch until she died, choking on her own blood. She'd just turned thirteen. After that, no one else refused the dosing. The rest of the girls died horrifically in the bedroom hall instead.

Madame Iseul initially administered poisons and antidotes, but as we aged, some of the poisons had no known remedies. She microdosed us and hoped for the best. When we survived, she upped the dose. Most died.

And then Hana made eighteen.

Sun-ye shakes her head, then stares at my face. Her hand trembles on the cushion. I've seen the same tremors in my right hand. Sun-ye notices my line of sight and rests her arm behind the back of the divan. "It wasn't me, Sora."

I stare at her, but I can't tell. I think she's being honest, but it's pointless to keep questioning her about it right now. The traitor will reveal themself.

"Why did you want to meet?" I ask.

"Originally, I wanted to tell you something interesting I'd heard, but now it's to warn you to escape from Rahway before tomorrow."

Chills careen down my spine although I hold still. Sun-ye is not prone to dramatics. If she's warning me like this, the situation is dire.

"Escape?" I repeat.

She laughs. "Did you think I had you meet me under all of this cloak and dagger because you were free to move about?"

I hadn't even considered that we were prisoners of the count—even after I had to beg to go into town. Did we willingly walk into a trap? Or is it just me he wants to capture?

"Just me?" I ask.

"No, your friends, too. Rune wants the relics, and you brought them to his door. None of you are free—not that we're ever free." She reaches into her purse and pulls out a velvet pouch with a tiny spoon. I know those velvet pouches. I saw them in Oosant—that's laoli.

The spoon is tied to the pouch by a golden string. Sun-ye reaches into the bag with the spoon, holds the heaping white powder beneath her perfect nose, and inhales. Then she does it again on the other side, sniffling as she wipes her nostrils.

Laoli is an extremely potent pain reliever, but she's not in obvious pain. It looks far more recreational, which means she's addicted.

"Sun-ye..." I say.

Her shoulders drop. "Spare me, Sora, please. We're all going to die. If you can get through this life unmedicated, good for you. But you didn't have to pleasure Rune last night."

I feel immediate sympathy for what she's had to endure. At least murder is fast and over with, while being a courtesan is a long form of torture. But then confusion hits. I take a small step forward.

"Wait. Can we do...that?" I ask.

She narrows her eyes, trying to figure out if I'm serious. Then she lets her head fall back with a groan. "Good gods, Sora. How lucky that you've never had to use that pretty little head of yours."

"But Seok said..."

"And how would he know? How would that even work? We've *been* poisoned. We didn't *become* it." She pauses and gathers a breath. "He said our bodies are poison to keep his lecherous brother away from us, and his son away from you, because he wanted sole control. We can only kill men with applied poison, or my lover would be long dead by now."

I...don't know whether that makes me feel better or worse. But I do feel terrible about Sun-ye having to bed Rune. I want to reach out for her, but she doesn't want my sympathy or anyone's, really. Sympathy is for the weak, and she is strong.

Instead of extending a hand, I cross my arms.

"What was the interesting thing you wanted to tell me?" I ask.

A little relief shows on her face, but she clears it, serious again. "After you left Gain, Seok realized that Tiyung had burned your indenture. He was furious. But I assumed you already knew that, since Tiyung was so in love with you."

I nod, trying not to think of him or where he is now. But I am surprised that everyone realized his affections except for me.

"Seok had four indenture certificates left in his possession. Daysum's. Mine. Rayna's and one other."

I glance around the shop as I try to absorb what she's saying. Sun-ye was undeniably Seok's favorite, but there's no way he'd trust her with this information. "How would you even know this? Seok would never show you where he kept them."

She looks at the laoli again with greedy eyes, but she puts it away. Not because she won't take another dose but because she refuses to look weak in front of me.

"Obviously he didn't show me, Sora," she says. "But his head of household likes to talk."

"Never to me."

"No, Irrad hates you."

I sigh. Where is she going with this? "Who was the fourth?"

"Hana."

The room silently spins as Sun-ye stares at me.

"But why…" I shake my head as soon as the thought enters my mind. It's not a real possibility. It's a baseless hope, a delusion. Hana died two years ago in the southwest. I know this. But the certificate… "What are you saying?"

"I'm saying that he still has her indenture. That is all I know. I thought it was interesting."

She shrugs, but that isn't all she's saying.

"You think she could still be alive," I whisper.

She runs a hand over her silk dress. "I think that when Seok confirmed a poison maiden's death, he immediately burned the document linking him to the girl. That way he could deny ever having owned her if he were caught. It's speculation after that. Maybe he kept it just in case. I don't know."

I can't even process the thought that Hana might still be alive somewhere. I've hoped it so many times, but I haven't dared to really think it.

Someone tries the door, and the shop bells chime. My spine goes rigid. I'm so startled that I have to suppress a scream. Sun-ye slides a dagger into her hand from under the cushion, but the door stays shut. It must've locked behind me.

I twist my hair over my shoulder. It's the talk of escape that has frayed my nerves. That's all.

"Why do we need to leave Rahway today?" I ask.

"Other than the fact that someone tried to kill you last night?" Sun-ye tilts her head. "I don't know how many reasons you need, but I assume the assassins sent word to Seok that you're here. You'll be hunted by tomorrow. If you leave now, you'll at least have a head start. But more than that: someone gave you up. It was either one of your own or one of Rune's servants, but he didn't know. He has people he can't trust, and the tide will turn against him quickly. I can only hope it happens by sundown. But he has his own uses for you and your friends, and unless you want to be his slaves, I suggest you leave."

"Thank you," I say. "I don't know how to…"

"I want something in return," she says. Of course she does. Sun-ye doesn't act from the goodness of her heart. I would've gotten suspicious otherwise.

"What is it?"

She stands and comes closer to me. She doesn't walk so much as glide, her movements effortless. Her perfume is sweet like rose apple poison. Madame Iseul really did her work well.

"A promise that Rayna will go free," she says. "The countess took her to Qali Palace after Seok seized the throne. She's in there, somewhere."

"Done."

Sun-ye shifts her weight to her hip, and she stares up at the ceiling. "No, actually give it thought, Sora. That means you can't allow your friends to drown or destroy the palace with everyone inside."

The thought is brutal, ruthless, and incredibly practical.

I shake my head. "We wouldn't do that."

"Why not?"

I debate whether to tell her the truth. We were never close, but we also never exposed each other. I decide to give my reason but be vague on details. I hope, in the end, it doesn't harm us.

"Because people we love are being held in Idle Prison."

She blinks, then shakes her head. "Sora… They aren't. The first thing Seok did after taking Qali was empty that prison and release all of the detainees. If they're alive, they're free."

My heart races—Mikail's father might be free, and maybe Hwan, the man Royo is trying to save. They'll both be so relieved. But in truth, neither of them was my first thought.

"And Seok's son?" I ask casually.

Sun-ye rolls her eyes. "Dead, thank the gods. He was killed in his cell and burned sometime before the coup. Seok lost his mind when he found the sapphire collar. He hasn't been right since."

My face tingles as blood drains from it. My lungs feel as if they are collapsing. I try to soothe myself by remembering that this is what I wanted—Seok to have nothing left. But hearing that Tiyung is dead makes me want to clutch at my chest and fall to the ground. I don't dare show what I'm feeling, though. Sun-ye would only use it against me.

"Oh."

She takes another step closer. "Sora, promise me Rayna's life. Swear it on Daysum's soul or I will kill you right here."

She still has the dagger in her palm as her eyes search mine. There's no doubt that she means every word.

"I swear and I vow it," I say. "On Daysum's soul, I will do everything I can to make sure Rayna walks free."

I don't know that I can promise Rayna's life or anyone else's. Nothing seems certain or easy. All we can ever do is try to survive the plans of powerful men. But I will keep that promise till my dying breath.

Sun-ye examines my face, looking for any falsehood, but then she nods, satisfied.

"Good. Now go." She points to the door.

I don't embrace her. I just turn and walk out.

I leave the shop and close my eyes, lost in a haze. Then I shake my head. From when we were in the throne room and King Joon sentenced Ty to Idle Prison, I knew he might die. Logically, I knew he wouldn't survive the dungeon even if he managed to live. But I'd kept a little hope secreted away in my chest—just a small, fragile thing. Now he's gone and the hope is shattered, leaving nothing but shards in my chest.

I take a few steps, then lean against the building. I hadn't realized how much I needed to believe Tiyung would make it, even if it would hurt Seok more for him to die. But I've lost Daysum and now Ty. I'm just empty. I keep moving, though. I always have to go forward, a shell battered by the tides and abandoned.

Again there's no one to blame, to lash out at, other than unreachable men. I wander the streets and pass statues of the cruel gods and the kings who think they're deities. Everything was so different last time I was here. I was afraid but ultimately hopeful that I could change the realm. Now I know I can't. There's no winning in Yusan. Not for broken souls like us.

The four of us are all we have left.

Then I stop cold on the sidewalk as a thought grips me. If Sun-ye knew, Mikail must have found out, too. Maybe at the same time he heard about Daysum.

He kept another secret? Justified as another false protection? Did he hide this to keep me going forward like a puppet with himself as master?

Anger surges through me, sending heat into my hands and face. I've long reached my limit of lies, betrayals, and grief. And I won't have an owner again.

I drop my dagger into my palm. Enough.

Gripping the hilt of my blade, I stride back toward the villa.

CHAPTER TWENTY-SEVEN

MIKAIL

CITY OF RAHWAY, YUSAN

It's late afternoon by the time I've bathed, dressed, and calmed myself enough to find Fallador. After making casual conversation with two of the house servants, I learn that Gambria left the villa and the "prince" is in the library. I find him exploring the shelves but not really reading anything. Fallador is wearing a western-style cream-colored tunic and brown pants—it's a good look for him, but he is a chameleon. Ever blending, ever altering. Does his loyalty change as well?

"Searching for answers?" I ask.

Fallador turns and grins at me, but the smile doesn't reach his eyes. He's bothered by something—Gambria, I assume, yet he's playing it off as if everything is normal.

"We should take advantage of the beautiful day," I say in Gayan. "Join me for a walk?"

"I'd be delighted."

We make our way under the arches and along lavish halls until we step outside onto the massive stone terrace. This part of the house overlooks the sprawling, manicured gardens, unlike the patio off the eastern dining room that nearly touches the Sol. The sun shines on the right angles of the hedges, illuminating the elaborately pruned trees. Two white swans swim in a central artificial pool. It's all very symmetrical and rigidly controlled.

Fallador and I stroll the crushed stone paths, staying away from the tall hedges and flowering bushes where servants and spies could hide and overhear us. As I walk with the hidden scepter, Fallador looks away but forces a smile when our eyes meet.

"Something troubling you?" I ask.

He grins. "Oh, just a few things. It's good to walk with you, though."

He's right—it is. We're honored guests in a place I couldn't have imagined as a boy. Under other circumstances, it would be a pleasant time.

"I want to apologize for Gambria," he says. "She found me before she left and confessed what she'd done. I'm grateful to the gods that your friends weren't hurt."

I stop and stare at him. "By that you mean grateful Aeri murdered them first?"

He shrugs. "I believed Gambria when she said she never intended it."

I inhale and look away. This is why I had to wait to seek out Fallador. I knew he'd defend her, and I hardly have the patience for it.

"Love is a cloak that can cover even deeply held beliefs," he says. "You know this better than anyone."

I stare at the swans floating in the pool. I've heard that these birds mate for life—seems like a much simpler existence. Certainly easier than loving a Baejkin.

"You're referring to Euyn?" I ask.

"Among other things." Fallador stops in front of me. "You haven't spoken of him, you know."

His eyes are full of concern. Not because he cared for Euyn but because he knows I did.

"There doesn't ever seem to be the time," I say. It's true. This isn't the time to mourn him. Even now, the sun rapidly moves across the sky, and we need to make our plans. We are constantly in a race against time, gods, and men.

Fallador utters a heavy sigh. "Grief doesn't wait, Mikail. You loved him, and he is gone. That is a tremendous weight to bear alone."

I shrug. The weight doesn't matter when there's nothing you can do to shake it.

He takes a step closer. "I had Gambria to share the trauma of survival. You were alone by necessity—but you don't have to stay that way. You can rest some of it with me."

It's tempting, and there's a pull in my chest, my shoulders gravitating to him. Fallador has an almost hypnotic way of speaking, and there's always been a hint of something there. We always find ourselves a step too close, a glance too long. But is he just a charming fraud?

"I *thought* I had you and Gambria." I grit my teeth. The betrayal stings like lemon on a wound no matter how I try to avoid it.

Fallador nods slowly as he stares at the swans. "She loves someone who cannot return her love. At least not at the depth that could sustain her. Instead of accepting that, she keeps giving more of herself, as if sacrificing all that she holds dear will create enough love for both of them. Like priests to the gods, it is a one-sided affair."

There's something in his tone that makes me feel like he's also talking about me. Either my love for Gaya or Euyn—possibly both, as he has that way of double-speaking. Before today, I have always trusted that Fallador was sincere, but I also believed he was the prince of Gaya. I trusted Gambria, and she turned traitor. What is he now? What does he truly feel?

Fallador stares at me, then looks away with a frown. "Mikail, what will you do when you're done fighting the world?"

I breathe out a laugh at the idea of being done. "I highly doubt I'll survive for long enough to worry about the aftermath."

He closes his eyes, then reaches his hand forward and brushes his fingers against mine. That spark lights up inside me that I always feel with him. A call toward home.

I think. Things have never been clear with Fallador.

Our hands have just touched when Sora comes storming down the path behind Fallador. There's something in her shoulders, her walk. She has the same look as when we were aboard the fleet ship and she found out that Euyn hunted her father.

It's pure fury.

My muscles react faster than my brain. I pull Fallador out of the way just as she slashes at me with a dagger. She catches my shirt and tears it. My arm stings as metal cuts my skin.

"You knew!" Her voice rings out with pain.

She draws back to strike again, sloppy and full of emotion. I don't know why she's so upset, but I can't exactly ask her. I reach out and catch her arm with my hand. I hold her wrist in the air, away from me.

Fallador has regained himself. He takes Sora's other arm and pins it behind her back. A knife falls out of her hand and clatters onto the ground. I stare at the small blade. It would take a lot more than that to kill me.

"You knew!" she says through her teeth.

I search her face, trying to figure out what would upset her like this with Daysum already dead. I come up empty.

"I legitimately don't know what you're talking about, Sora," I say. "I knew about who? Gambria?"

Her eyebrows knit. Anger leaves her face for a moment, and confusion takes its place. She shakes her head.

"Tiyung," she says. Those two syllables contain a world of grief.

She crumples, going slack against Fallador and me. He holds her up, puzzlement scrawled across his face as she begins to cry.

"What? What about Tiyung?" I ask.

"He's dead," she whispers.

Fuck.

CHAPTER TWENTY-EIGHT

AERI
CITY OF RAHWAY, YUSAN

Did Sora just attack Mikail? What is happening right now? Royo and I run down the steps of the terrace, heading toward where Fallador restrains Sora. Gravel crunches under my boots as we hit the paths. Everyone wonders why I prefer short dresses—it's because I can run away so much faster in them. This time, though, I sprint full speed *at* danger.

I pull a throwing knife from the side of my dress and one from the band on my thigh. Royo slips on his brass knuckles. My relics vibrate, but I don't want to use them. Not until I figure out what happened. I don't want to kill Mikail, and I'd rather not kill Fallador.

Yet I know in my heart I'd slay both to protect Sora.

Royo breathes hard, his broad chest rising and falling. We're both winded by the time we reach them. But my heart feels lighter, being a team with Royo.

That is, until I get closer.

Tears stream down Sora's face. Mikail has a hand to his forehead while Fallador just looks confused.

What is this? What's going on?

"What did you do?" I ask Mikail.

He stares at me, eyes widening. "*She* just tried to attack *me*, but other than that, I don't know." He runs his hands over his wavy hair and sighs, his shoulders slumping. "That's a lie—I do know. She thinks Tiyung is dead and that I knew and didn't tell her."

Oh shit.

His words knock the air from my chest. Poor Sora—first her sister and now Ty. I don't know what exactly Tiyung meant to her other than a hope for tomorrow, but that is a tremendous loss. For all of us, but especially her. And there's only so much loss someone can take without breaking.

"Oh, Sora," I say, clasping my hands together. "Rune told you this?"

Earlier, I let Royo sleep because I enjoyed watching him rest peacefully. He's so much younger, less guarded when he's asleep. Years leave him, and he's just...mine. I thought nothing was happening at the villa, that at most we'd miss lunch. Apparently, we missed a lot more than that.

Sora shakes her head. "Not Rune."

"Where did you hear this, then?" Mikail asks. His expression sharpens, his features alert. His shirt is torn, and he's bleeding. A purple stain spreads on his sleeve as his red blood mixes with the blue of his shirt. He doesn't seem to care, though.

She looks down at the gravel. "Someone I know."

Mikail eyes her. "The courtesan?"

I glance at Sora. I thought they'd seemed familiar last night. For a second, I wonder if Misha is a poison maiden—she's certainly pretty enough. But then I remember that if she were a poisoner, Rune would already be dead.

Sora looks to the side—that's a yes. She moves her shoulders, silently asking for Fallador to release her. Mikail tips his chin, and Fallador lets her go. There is a dagger on the ground and also a knife. They're both Sora's. I recognize those decorative handles—we picked them up in Cetil.

"Sora, I swear and I vow that no one told me he died," Mikail says. He pauses to let his words sink in. "Last I heard from my source, he was alive. I assumed nothing changed because I had someone in Idle watching out for him. I will send word as soon as I can to confirm, but don't lose heart. I don't put it past Rune or anyone else to spread a rumor that he died."

Her purple eyes move rapidly as she tries to sort out who is telling the truth and who is lying. Poor Sora. It's harder than it should be.

"Why did you mention Gambria?" she asks.

I look at Mikail, Fallador, Sora, and then Royo. Once again, we're in shambles and she's not here. She has a funny way of disappearing right before blood splatters the ground.

Mikail draws a breath. "She was the reason the assassins found us yesterday."

No one makes a sound. Even Royo holds his breath.

"You mean found Aeri and me," Sora says.

Tension crackles between them as Sora faces off with Mikail. Fallador slides closer to Mikail. Royo moves a step nearer to Sora. I wring my hands. This feels like when we were outside of the warehouse in Oosant and Tiyung wanted to spare the barmaid and her father. Only, this time, it's worse. We've all been through too much for this to be happening now. But maybe it's happening because of what we've suffered.

Mikail casually waves the walking stick, trying to defuse the situation. "You were the target, but she betrayed all of us."

"How do we know this guy wasn't in on it, too?" Royo points a thick finger at Fallador.

"I wasn't." Fallador's eyes are wide, and his face is earnest. "But you have no reason to believe me."

He's right. Only time can prove loyalty—and we don't have enough of it.

"So is Gambria dead now or what?" Royo asks.

Fallador flinches at the blunt way Royo just phrased it, but I'm certain we all want to know.

"The latter," Mikail says. "She's gone back to Khitan."

In other words: he let her go.

Conversation stops. So, Gambria did, in fact, set us up. She might have done the same in Gaya. I could've died either time, but Mikail let her go because they have history together. What a terrible time for him to discover mercy.

I swallow the hurt clogging my throat. I thought he cared, and maybe he does, but not enough.

"We have to leave Rahway tonight," Sora says, finally breaking the silence. She side-eyes Fallador. She doesn't trust him, and maybe we would be foolish to trust anyone else now. But she says it so definitively that she must have heard something.

"Why?" Royo asks.

She hesitates. "Because we aren't safe here."

Mikail looks from Sora to Fallador and back. "What do you want to do, Sora?"

"We will tell Rune that we have to leave but we will meet him in Tamneki. In the meantime, have Fallador stay with Rune and report to us on the western count's plays and plans."

She wants to get rid of Fallador. I don't blame her, even though, honestly, I like him. But there's a lot she's not saying.

"And where are we going in the meantime?" Mikail asks.

"To Oosant," she says. "We need to figure out who owned the warehouse. I saw one of those pouches today, and it jogged my memory. The drugs belonged to either Seok or Rune, and we need to know which. Locals in the borderlands must know something. They couldn't have snuck that much laoli in from Gaya without anyone seeing."

We all weigh the idea. I'm surprised Sora would want to return there, given how the gang kidnapped her, but she's stronger than anyone I've ever met. Plus, we did kill everyone, so maybe there's not the same danger. The drugs do seem to be tied to all of this. It was too much money to not involve the counts...or my father.

But I don't know why she thinks we need to go right now.

Mikail studies her. "All right, Sora. Be ready to leave in a bell."

Sora stares back at him and nods. She lifts the hem of her long dress and steps over the blades on the ground, headed back toward the villa. I hesitate for a breath because something feels very strange about all of this, but then I turn and follow her. Royo is at my side.

We exchange glances. His brow is furrowed, and he's rubbing at his scar. So, I was right—something was strange.

We catch up with Sora on the stairs. Fallador and Mikail have stayed back on the path.

"Get all of the weapons you need from the armory," Sora says quietly.

Royo nods. "We'll need 'em for Oosant."

"We're not going to Oosant," she says.

Royo stares at her, and I'm sure I look just as confused.

"But you just said—" he begins.

"We're going to the Temple of Knowledge," she says. "We have to figure out what happens when all of the relics are combined. But more than anything, we need to get far away from here."

"Why?" I ask. It's been weird, blacking out, but it doesn't seem that urgent.

"Because I think Rune will use Fallador to kill you and Mikail in order to present the relics to King Joon."

I pause on the steps as my pulse thuds in my throat. Something about her theory feels right. My father has the other two relics. With mine and Mikail's, he can become the Dragon Lord and impose his will on all the realms. My amulet and ring vibrate, the etherum rising to the threat. But the danger is in my mind.

For now.

I shake my head. "But we looked for information on the multiplying powers and the legend of the Dragon Lord, and we didn't find anything in Khitan."

"Because King Joon's spies had gotten there first," Sora says.

I realize what she's saying. We have no way of knowing if they destroyed information before we reached the temple. And if my father's plan had always been to reunite the relics, he'd make sure we wouldn't find anything.

"So, we go to the temple here?" Royo asks.

Sora shakes her head. "No, it could also be compromised. We have to go back to Gaya."

"Mikail wasn't sure it existed," I point out.

"We have to try," Sora says.

Returning to the colony would mean either taking a riverboat and then a ship to the island, or Mikail using the Water Scepter. I don't think we have time for a riverboat.

"You mean with Mikail?" Royo asks.

Sora nods. "Of course."

We get to the terrace and stop at the top of the stairs. The worst effect of the relics is how the toll has slowed my thinking. Why did she just lie to Mikail, then? Why the ruse?

Royo shakes his head. "I don't get it. Why not say all this before?"

She tilts her head. "Because Fallador was standing right there."

"But he…" I begin, and then I trail off because I'm not actually sure of his loyalty, and that's the issue.

Sora glances at me. "You didn't notice? Mikail doesn't trust Fallador, either."

CHAPTER TWENTY-NINE

MIKAIL

CITY OF RAHWAY, YUSAN

"You're bleeding," Rune says, arching an eyebrow at me.

The five of us wait in the count's study as he sorts through papers, putting his stamp on some and burning others. Generally, he looks like a man wrapping up his affairs. But he's paused for long enough to notice the blood on my sleeve.

"Mishap by the hedges," I say with a shrug.

Sora shoots me an apologetic look, but I've already forgiven her. There's only so much someone can take before they snap, and she's well beyond her limit. Besides, she wasn't actually trying to kill me. If she had been, she wouldn't have used a blade. She's a poisoner, not a fighter.

Rune's eyebrow reaches higher. He, of course, doesn't believe me for a second.

With a wave of his fingers, he dismisses the bookkeepers, noblemen, and advisors who'd wanted his ear. Then he takes the chair behind his desk. He leans back, effortlessly gaining control of the room.

"What can I do for you all?" he asks.

"Settle a debate, if you would," I say. "Do you happen to know anything about Oosant?"

I spin the walking stick as I wait for him to answer.

"Other than that it's a city that lies in the old borderlands? No."

He pauses and strokes his chin. "But somehow, I don't think you're asking me random geography questions. What is this about?"

He steeples his fingers in front of his face as he waits. His air is casual, but he can't keep his eyes off the hidden scepter. Rapacious hunger is difficult to conceal.

"We found something there that we need to investigate," Aeri says. "You haven't heard any rumors about the city, Your Grace?"

Rune shakes his head. "Not a thing, Your Majesty."

I watch him closely, but these men are all skilled liars and manipulators. They rarely have obvious tells.

"Oh, come on, you gotta know something," Royo says. He slaps his hand against his thigh. The sound echoes in the high-ceilinged room.

I close my eyes for a long-suffering blink.

The count slowly turns his head toward the strongman. He looks at him as if he's a rat scurrying across the dining room floor. "You may wait outside."

Royo flushes, and his gaze, of course, falls on Aeri. She stares blankly back at him. It's a smart play—he's only supposed to be her guard. Still, real pain registers on his face, and I feel for him. A man like him can only lose when playing the games of the nobility.

When Royo finally looks at me, I gesture with my chin for him to leave.

He storms off, dismissed. His footsteps resound down the hall toward the entryway. Stars, I forgot how loud his feet are. The chandeliers actually shake.

"I think I'll join him," Sora says, rising from the couch. She faces Rune. "Will you excuse me, Your Grace?"

Rune nods. She inclines her head and leaves on light feet.

Two down, two left.

"My strongman is a bit overzealous," Aeri says.

Rune looks her over, taking his time at the hem of her dress. "Hard to not be with something so precious in your hands."

It's a good thing Royo left when he did. He would've choked the count.

Rune then turns his focus to me. "But what is all this about the border town?"

"We think Seok has a substantial amount of laoli stored in Oosant—over a million mun's worth," I say. "But we need confirmation."

Rune's eyes narrow. He's trying to figure out if I'm bluffing, which means he really hadn't heard about the drugs. The warehouse wasn't his. I leave out the part where we killed everyone and set it on fire. That doesn't seem relevant right now.

"I can escort you to Oosant," he says. "I will be traveling that way to meet my army."

"That's so very generous," Aeri says with a smile. "It should only take us a day or two there."

Rune taps his fingertips together. "I'm afraid that won't be possible, Your Highness. I will be traveling by fleet coaches to reach the capital as quickly as possible. I can't afford that much delay, but you will be able to make some inquiries while we water and feed the horses."

"We will meet you in Tamneki, in that case," I say.

Rune shakes his head. "I can't allow that. The borderlands are notoriously dangerous. Too much so during an upheaval. It isn't worth the risk."

"Ah, yes, we were having such a peaceful journey otherwise," I say.

Rune sighs his annoyance. "I would feel much better if the two of you were in my personal coach with armed men. Surely, you don't disagree."

What he means is that we are not free to go, as Sora had expected. The price of his help is not only the throne but being prisoners until he sees a fitting end for us. The three relics were too much temptation. He won't allow us out of his sight because he wants to be able to take the relics if need be. Or use us in a power exchange if the tides turn that way.

I think about drowning him, but I have more pressing matters.

"Of course," Aeri says, smiling brightly. "I'd feel much safer that way, anyhow."

"It's settled, then," Rune says. He straightens a stack of papers. "We'll leave first thing in the morning."

Sora comes back into the study, her pretty face marred by worry. "Excuse me, please, but Royo is threatening to quit."

"I..." Aeri sighs. She runs her hands over her short skirt as she stands. "I'll go speak with him. I'm sure this is nothing an additional diamond won't resolve."

"I can provide other guards for you, my relic queen," Rune offers.

"I appreciate that, but Royo has been reliable since Umbria, and I trust him. Let me see if I can't settle things first, Your Grace."

She acts like she is just vexed by a good servant as she leaves with Sora. But the count's snake eyes track her. His jaw muscle ticks.

"Young hearts are wild," I say, shrugging a shoulder.

"And foolish," Rune says. "I'll have to dispose of him soon."

Of course. Counts do not tolerate common competition. I was the one who said that to Royo about Bay Chin. Rune will kill Royo as soon as he can—probably in Oosant. I need to buy him time.

"After the nuptials, obviously," I say. "You don't want her too distraught to say 'I do.'"

"Why would her emotions matter?" Rune looks genuinely confused.

Ah, there's the cruelty. He's masked it so well up until now.

The yelling reaches the office. It's Royo's deep voice and Aeri's higher one. They're fighting the way they did outside of the traveler's inn in Capricia. I rub my forehead.

"Perhaps you should go intervene," Fallador says to me.

I roll my eyes. "Stars, give me strength."

Fallador stares at me as I remain in place, and then his eyes dart toward the door. Rune can't see his face from where he sits.

"I'd like a word with His Grace in the meantime," he adds.

Right—they must have private plans to discuss. I bow to Rune and take two steps out of the study.

"Mikail," Rune says.

I'd almost made it. I stand still, and my heart thuds, but my hands are steady. They are always steady. I glance over my shoulder, making sure to remain casual. "Your Grace?"

"See my healer, and she will get you sewn up," he says.

I incline my head to him.

With quick but not hurried steps, I make my way through the entryway. Servants open the heavy wooden doors. Down the stairs from the villa, Royo and Aeri are still yelling at each other. They're both red and in the midst of an animated argument. Sora stands to the side of them, her hands out, trying to calm them both but being roundly ignored.

"I'm leaving on the next carriage outta here!" Royo yells.

"By all means, take mine," a voice says.

The four of us turn, and there is the gorgeous woman from last night—Misha, the count's new courtesan. She stands by her rented carriage, looking unamused with her hands on her hips.

"You are at a great man's home, acting worse than the slums of Jeul." She walks gracefully as servants scurry to open doors and announce her.

I exchange quick glances with Sora. She rapidly moves her fingers by her dress, motioning for all of us to get in the carriage on the side away from the villa's entrance. Sora is last, looking at Misha. They give each other almost imperceptible nods.

As soon as Sora closes the door, we ride off, headed to the Port of Rahway. I watch out the back, waiting for Rune's guards to notice that we escaped.

CHAPTER THIRTY

TIYUNG

CITY OF TROVE, YUSAN

Soaked to the bone and uncomfortably chilled, we stop at the messenger house when we finally reach Trove.

I write out a message to my mother, taking my time in the warm and dry house. Then, I coat it with clay. I no longer have my seal, but she'll recognize my handwriting and code—if it actually reaches her in the palace.

Hana sends two envelopes and mine. She also receives an envelope. She cracks the clay and uses a blade she'd stashed up her sleeve to open the letter. With her brow furrowed, she takes a pencil and decodes the message. She's expressionless as she reads it, and then she tosses everything into the fire.

We leave the shop once the papers are ash. I study her as we walk to our horses. Hana is so good at playing it cool that I can't tell if she's heard anything.

"You know what I'm going to ask," I say.

"And this time I have an answer. Sora, Mikail, Royo, and Aeri are alive—they're in Rahway."

The news makes me stop in the middle of the street. My heart pounds in my chest, and I feel like I'm about to burst with joy. I hadn't dared to hope they survived Quu Harbor, not after hearing there was a battle on the seafloor with massive casualties. But they're alive, and not only that, they are back in Yusan.

Everything is wet and muddy in Trove, but somehow, it's now the most beautiful city I've ever seen.

Until I almost get hit by a horse.

I skirt out of the way as a halibred rears back. The animal snorts, and the rider shouts very colorful things about my parentage.

Hana shakes her head. She grabs my hand and pulls me toward where we tied up our horses. She makes a sign of apology to the rider, and he's so struck by her beauty that his mouth hangs open as he rides away.

The constant rain barely even registers. I feel like I'm floating from the news. I look over and expect the same reaction from Hana, but, if anything, she seems troubled, with a line forming between her eyebrows. Is she just concerned about how Sora will react to finding out that she's still alive? No, that doesn't seem to be it. There's something she's not saying.

Wait. She would've told me the good news in the messenger house if that was the only thing she'd heard.

"What is the bad news?" I ask.

The corner of her mouth tips up, although her eyes stay sad. She clears both as she unties her horse. "Your father believes that you are dead. He is claiming the five blades murdered you, and he's put a substantial bounty on them."

I exhale and throw my leg over the saddle. As I sit, I try to grapple with what she just said. Because of Ailor saving my life, I knew my father would think I died. I didn't bother to send a message to him because he'd just dismiss my letter as fake without a seal. But I never thought he'd blame Sora and the others. It was King Joon who'd ordered my imprisonment and death, and obviously Seok knows that, so there's something else at play.

Hana and I ride down the street.

"How much is the bounty?" I ask.

Hana stares forward. "A million in gold."

A chill runs through me—that's a fortune.

"Gods," I say. "A million for the five of them?"

Hana inhales like she's bracing herself. "No. A million for Sora, a million for Aeri, a million for Euyn, and a million for Mikail. If they're brought in alive."

Kingdom of Hells. The blood drains from my face, and my arms tingle. Four million in gold is the highest bounty anyone has offered in the history of the realm. That's equal to the purse in the Millennial Championship. Outside of the counts, no one has that kind of money. And even then, the richest, which had been Dal, had only twice that. Every servant, commoner, nobleman, and bounty hunter will be looking for them now. Plus all the king's guard. There won't be safe quarter for them anywhere in the world. They'd be hunted through the Outer Lands.

My father has done this for a reason, and it's not grief over losing me. I'm just not sure what it is. Why does he want them alive? And why did he leave out Royo?

Good gods, I thought a war of the realms was the worst news we'd have.

"Do we go to Rahway now?" I ask Hana.

"No."

Hana is so calm and steady, but why did she dismiss that out of hand? We have to do something. With four million at stake, anyone and everyone will turn them over. Panic and uselessness turn my stomach. They'll be captured within days, even if they are dangerous killers in their own right. You can't win, fighting against the realms. They need our help.

"We have to at least try..." I say.

"They've already left Rahway. The rumor is that they're headed to Oosant, but they're smart. I think they spread disinformation."

"Who is telling you this?" I ask.

I haven't inquired about Hana's sources or expected her to tell me. But if we're not going to try to reach Sora, I have to know all of this is legitimate.

"A source who helped me before," she says. "There's the inn up ahead."

She points to a green-and-gold sign for The Maker's Inn. Usually, I feel a wave of relief when we reach a traveler's inn, but not tonight. Predictably, Hana has only answered as much as she wanted to reveal. It's like dealing with a more attractive version of Mikail.

"Is the source someone we can trust?" I ask.

Hana bites her lip. "I wouldn't go that far."

I shake my head. "Then how can we…"

"Our interests align for now. That is all. And that is enough."

I suppose it'll have to be, because I don't have a better plan. Riding two weeks away to somewhere they already left with my sword drawn doesn't seem like much assistance.

The stable for the inn is located across the street. We put our horses in to feed, and I offer my hand to help Hana dismount. She actually accepts it. I take her overnight luggage out of the saddlebag and carry it with mine.

It's still monsoon season, but Trove is a busy place. It's the largest coastal city before Tamneki. I'm not sure if Hana is troubled by something she's not sharing or the bounty, or if she's just gotten lulled by how quiet the coastal towns have been, but she doesn't look before she steps out onto the road.

A two-horse carriage comes right at her. She's about to be trampled.

"Look out!" I yell.

I drop the bags and pull her by the waist, grabbing her wet cloak. Taken by surprise, she struggles, but then she falls, landing against my chest. I wasn't expecting her full weight. My boots slide on the stones, and I lose my footing. The next thing I know, we're careening backward. We fall and land in the street runoff, both of our heads splashing into the gutter.

I stare up at the rain as my head lies in muck. This is so disgusting that I can't even countenance it.

"You really know how to save a damsel," Hana says.

I can't do anything but laugh. This is pretty much how my hero efforts end—in murky horseshit.

Hana laughs, too. She stands up first and then extends her hand. I take it and get to my feet. I really don't want to think about what I landed in, but I now stink. I try not to make a face, but I have to breathe through my mouth.

"Thank you, Ty, for saving me," she says, eyeing her matted hair. "But next time, just let me die."

Despite smelling like gods know what, I smile. She called me Ty. But then my grin fades as I think about the others. I thought I'd be relieved when I found out Sora and the others were alive, and I am, but tomorrow I will need to leave for the palace so I can try to talk sense into my father before someone collects on the bounties. They will have to survive until then, and we will all have to get through the coming war of the realms. I have less than a day to figure out my father's real scheme and a way to stop him. But first, I need a bath.

CHAPTER THIRTY-ONE

ROYO

THE WEST SEA, YUSAN

The sea wind whips around my head, a constant whooshing sound filling my ears.

Mikail is at the front, leaning forward with the scepter in his hand. The relic causes this boat to move unnaturally fast when he focuses. Etherum makes us cut through the water like we got twenty sails, a dozen men rowing, and a favoring wind.

I sit alone at the back to watch for danger, but we're far from Rahway. I breathe out a long exhale and lower my shoulders. Our plan worked.

Before we went to Rune's study, the four of us met in the coju cellar and came up with a plan of escape. Sora said that the count wouldn't just let us go—to Oosant or anywhere else. He'd been keeping close tabs on us since we arrived. Mikail knew it was a possibility that Rune would try to trap us, but we had to risk it in order to find help.

I hadn't even realized we were prisoners, but it made sense. The count knew about the relics, and he had his own play. Either he wanted to turn us over to King Joon, Count Seok, or he wanted to use us himself. Who knows?

We didn't want to stick around to find out.

I had to find a reason to storm off and make it look real. Then Aeri would try to soothe me. We then had to make a scene loud enough for Mikail and Sora to intervene. It worked, but we had to wait on Mikail. Aeri was worried he wouldn't come out, so we shouted at each other, the emotion real. She called me hellishly stubborn, and I called her a liar. Once Mikail walked out, Sora had a carriage take us to the skiff with the help of Rune's courtesan.

I think the girl, Misha, is a poison maiden. She's gotta be. Nobody looks like that except for Sora. If I'm right, at least I don't have to worry about Rune.

One worry down, a thousand to go.

I shift in my seat. We made it out, but it's already sunset on the water and we haven't reached Gaya yet. I don't like the idea of being on the cruel seas at night. We didn't have much of a choice, though. We had to leave while we still could. I asked why we didn't just kill Rune, and Mikail said he could prove useful. I disagree, but at least I got my axe back. I grabbed it on my way out.

I also have a spyglass. I look off the stern toward the setting sun, but I scan to the sides, since nobody is following us. Yusan is to the port side. I swing to starboard, to the South Sea, and there's something weird in the distance.

We're moving so fast that the wind roars in my ears, but there's music coming from somewhere. High, melodic notes. And that's not right. Sora's not singing, and there's no music on the ocean. I continue to look through the glass until I spot the source of the sound. Far away, nearly on the horizon, there's a rock outcropping. And…women.

"What the fuck is that?" I ask.

Everybody but Mikail turns to the right to look at where I'm pointing.

"I don't see anything," Aeri says.

Right. I have the spyglass. I hand it up to her. She holds it to her eye, and then Sora does the same. My palms itch, eager to get the glass back, to let me look again. Eventually, Sora gives it over, and I put it to my eye.

"Are those...women?" she asks.

"On rocks?" Mikail asks.

He stops using the staff to talk. Without him focusing, the god magic doesn't work. We slow down, and the singing becomes clear. It's fantastic. One of the best sounds I've heard in my life. We have to get closer. Mikail immediately puts the staff back in the water.

"Cirena!" he yells.

I'm barely listening to him, though. We start to move away. *No.* We can't. I need to swing the mast so we sail to the rocks.

I get to my feet, but Aeri dives at me. She tries to put her hands over my ears. I dodge her and move my head.

What is she doing? I need to hear more of that sound. She tries again, and I toss her arms off me. Those women are stranded. They need me. We have to get to them! We need to turn. We have to save them! Ten Hells, I'll swim there myself if I have to.

Aeri's golden eyes stare at me. I've just noticed the look on her face when her lips mash against mine. She slips her hands over my ears, but it's hard for me to notice because, at the same time, she jumps and wraps her legs around me. We fall back against the bench, and she straddles my lap in her short dress as she kisses me. That plump lower lip and her taste that's like a sugar house fill my senses.

I know I was just thinking something, but for the life of me, I can't remember what. She wraps around me like a vine, and my hands crawl all over her like they got a mind of their own. Heat flushes my face and chest. There's a small part of me that says I shouldn't do this, but fuck if I can remember why.

Ten Hells, I've missed her. I press my fingers against her skin, savoring the feel of her body, her smell.

Hunger burns through me, and the bottomless kind of appetite I feel with her returns. She's pressed against my pants, and I need to feel more of her. I bite her lip. More. I need to have her right here. I want her writhing beneath me while she moans my name.

I move to shift her under me, but then the boat rocks. I reach out to steady myself, and I suddenly remember we're on a skiff. With Sora and Mikail. In the middle of the sea.

Wait, what the fuck just happened? What am I doing? Why is Aeri on top of me?

What is going on?

I break from Aeri's kiss, or maybe she does first. I dunno, but we're both panting. I adjust my pants. I was just about to take them down. I was just about to…

I run my hand down my face.

"I think we're safe now," Sora says.

I lift my head to look at Sora, and Aeri rises off my lap. Sora is up at the front, half-tackling Mikail. She slowly lets up and removes her hand from Mikail's head. She'd had her lips up against his other ear. With her right hand, she'd covered her own.

"What the fuck is going on?" I ask.

"That was a cirena," Mikail says.

He shakes his head and then pats Sora's hand. She smiles back at him. I guess they're okay now. Can't hold a grudge about every murder attempt, I guess.

But what did Mikail just say? A cirena?

"I thought they were just a myth." I'm sweating, and my arms are shaking. Definitely not a myth.

Mikail blows out a breath and rights himself, fixing his torn shirt. "No. Normally, they hunt well into the South Sea. I don't know why they're this far north, but all that matters now is that we reach Gaya."

He resumes his position at the front of the ship.

"What are they really? I saw beautiful women on rocks," Sora says.

"Me too," Aeri says.

Mikail has the staff in the water, but we're not moving yet. He looks back at us. "They're enormous sea beasts that make their tentacles appear like stranded women. The rest of their bodies are like octopi, hiding under the surface. The sound they produce is hypnotic and goes on for miles. They lure sailors in and then pluck them from their boats to feast on them."

I close my eyes, remembering how strong the urge was. The way I *needed* to save them. I was willing to grab the sail and steer us right to the beast.

I wipe my forehead. Ten Hells. We almost got eaten again.

But Aeri and Sora saved us. My desire for Aeri was greater than the sound. Which is really awesome for keeping my distance from her.

"Wait, why did Sora cover one ear?" I ask. "Don't they only affect men?"

Mikail shakes his head. "They affect anyone attracted to women."

That's right. She'd loved a girl in poison school.

"I can't hear them in my left ear," she says. "Hearing loss. So I only needed to cover my right. I whispered to Mikail about Gaya to keep us going, away from them."

That was really smart.

We start moving, and Sora sits down next to Aeri. The wind blows over our hair and ears, cooling our skin. I grip the seat with my legs still shaking. The sun is nearly below the horizon now.

I really fucking hope nothing else tries to eat us tonight, but there are more rocks ahead.

CHAPTER THIRTY-TWO

AERI

CITY OF HALLAN, GAYA

We land in the port of Hallan on Gaya. Mikail said Hallan used to be a thriving city, catering to pilgrims who visited the sacred black wood forests and the lumberjacks, artisans, and mills that used the wood. The city is now a shell of what it used to be because my father burned down the forest nearly twenty years ago.

We tie up the skiff and walk out of the port. Somehow, even this close to the ocean, this city smells like a campfire nearly twenty years later. So, the rumors of it being magical must be true.

It's after dark, and the town is covered in low fog, making it hard to see. I stick out my arm and can barely make out my fingertips. Everything about this place says to leave and find somewhere else, but we think the temple is around here, so we have to stay.

"We should probably all room together tonight," Sora says. She pulls her cloak tighter around her shoulders.

No one argues. Four blades are better than one.

We make our way through the fog and find an inn at the edge of town. This city seems far older than Berm, the streets worn and winding—more like Umbria than an island. The three of us wait outside while Mikail rents a room at the Canopy Inn. We need to go unnoticed, since our last trip to Gaya ended in disaster. Somehow, even being over six feet tall with teal eyes, he is the least distinct of the group.

Mikail comes out and gestures to Sora, who joins him inside. Royo and I wait a few more minutes. I fold my arms to block the chill because the fog makes my skin damp and my cloak is light. Royo looks over and waves me to him. I stare for a second, puzzled. But then he opens his arms. I rush to him and nuzzle against his chest. I let out a contented sigh, his warmth surrounding me.

We haven't spoken about what happened on the skiff. I hadn't meant to make out with him—or, well, I did, but it wasn't like I'd planned it out. I was just trying to save him, and I wasn't even sure it would work. Kissing him was the only thing I could think of to distract him. Royo's too strong, too capable of evading me, otherwise. Not that I minded, though. A pleasant shiver runs along my back as I think about wrapping my legs around him.

A minute later, we walk into the once grand inn. The ceiling is high and lined with black beams, and the woven rugs are ornate but worn down. Same with the couches and chairs in the empty lobby. Everything is from before the forest burned.

We take the marble stairs up to the second-floor corner room. A placard on the wall calls it the royal suite.

Ironic.

I knock twice on the door, and Mikail lets us in. The suite has two bedrooms and a living space with a couch.

Mikail goes to the water pitcher and starts guzzling down glass after glass. He grimaces. He must be in severe pain, but he doesn't say a word about it.

"So are we just here for the one night?" Royo asks Mikail, but there's no response.

"Mikail?" Royo says.

Mikail stares at him like he's confused. "Yes?"

Sora and I exchange glances.

Royo blinks. "What's the plan?"

"Rest tonight, and we'll leave to find the temple tomorrow. We'll get supplies for the forest in case it takes a few days to find it. I assume it's hidden, probably underground now, but we'll see."

Mikail's answer is fully lucid. He must not have heard Royo the first time. It's been a long day. Still, there was something unsettling about his confusion.

He wipes his mouth with the back of his hand and then looks at Royo. "You're sharing a bed with me again, right?"

Royo's jaw drops open. Sora suppresses a laugh as Mikail grins.

"It was a joke," Mikail says. "You should share a room with Aeri—to protect her." Then he turns to Sora. "I can take the couch."

"We should talk." Her fingers worry the beading on her purse.

He nods and drinks another glass of water. He's, of course, thirsty from wielding, but my stomach growls.

"Anyone else hungry?" I ask.

The three of them stare at me, but Royo and I missed lunch. I've been hungry since I was watching him sleep. Not only am I starving, but I'd like to avoid this uncomfortable moment. I'm sure they need to discuss what happened on the path and maybe what happened with Fallador. Sora did kind of try to kill him, and she's too good of a person to just let it lie. Still, it's better if I'm not here for it. Apologies are better without an audience.

"I could eat," Royo says.

My heart leaps. Before Rahway, he would've rather starved than leave with me. I smile at him. His lips twitch, and then he looks away.

"Don't go far," Mikail says.

Memories of Oosant flood my mind—the gang, the feeling of being prey, the worry of leaving, knowing we'd soon be attacked. "We'll eat downstairs and bring you back supper."

"That's kind of you," Sora says. But she's not looking at me. She's eyeing Mikail. He turns to face her as well.

Royo and I hustle out and close the door behind us.

CHAPTER THIRTY-THREE

SORA

CITY OF HALLAN, GAYA

Aeri and Royo leave like Mikail and I might draw blades…again. Instead, after both looking at the door, we sit on the patterned couch.

"Is your arm all right?" I ask. "Does it need stitches?"

He looks down at his torn, bloody sleeve. There's an angry red line where I made a cut with my dagger. It looks deep, but it doesn't appear to be bleeding anymore. "It's fine. I put salve on it before we left Rahway."

"I am sorry, Mikail," I say.

He smiles that easy, unaffected grin. "We're fine, Sora. I promise."

He's being gracious, and that makes me feel worse. I stare down at the floral cushion. "I…"

"I forgave you the moment after it happened," he says. "We've all been through a lot—no one is at their best. And that is not where the standard is set. We're just dealing with hardship and setbacks as they come. You thought I knew about Tiyung. I understood your rage."

He makes it sound so logical, but it wasn't. I had no other outlet for my feelings, and I chose to take them out on my friend.

"We have been through a lot, especially you, but you haven't attacked me," I say. "You've saved me—from the gang, from my own mercy with the Marnans…"

He shakes his head. "It's not about keeping score with each other.

It's about settling them with everyone else. I'm with you to the bloody end, Sora."

Tears prick my eyes. "And I'm with you."

I rest my hand on his despite my nerve damage making it tremble. He notices but doesn't say anything. There is a lot going unsaid in our group, and we've all gotten by on words unspoken. But I know better than anyone else that tensions, unreleased, can boil over.

"Do you want to talk about Euyn?" I ask. I search Mikail's face. He hasn't spoken much about him, and while I might not be the ideal person to talk to because of how I felt about him in the end, I am here to listen.

"No." Mikail looks to the side and shakes his head. "It's not that I don't want to speak with you about him—I know you're grieving as well—but it feels like if I open my mouth, I may never stop screaming. So it's better to not."

"I understand."

Maybe there is no benefit to trying to process things now. That rabbit hole might lead too deep, and there isn't the time or space to put ourselves back together if we come undone. It's probably why Daysum hasn't been on my mind much. The grief is too much to take on, so I ignore it.

"I know you do, Sora," he says.

I tap his hand. "Numb comfort it is, then."

"Cheers." He raises his water glass to me, then finishes it. He sets it on the coffee table. "So, Misha is…"

"A poison maiden—the last one aside from me."

Now that we're out of Rahway, I feel more comfortable telling the truth. Fallador and Rune won't find out, and there's no one to overhear us.

Mikail doesn't react at all. Sun-ye's beauty made her suspect from the start, I'm sure.

"It's as smart as it is desperate on Seok's part," he says.

"Oh, she told me something today, but with everything that happened… I didn't get a chance to tell you. She said that Seok emptied Idle Prison when he took Qali. If your father was brought there, he's free. Hwan, too."

I smile brightly and wait for him to show some kind of joy. Instead, he just nods.

"You're not…happy?" I ask.

Mikail sighs, and his shoulders curl. "It's good news, but I… Seeing the house… I don't think he survived. I've made my peace with it…as much as I can."

"I can't do the same with Tiyung," I say.

"Nor should you. I believe he's alive. Survival in that place comes down to whether or not you have something or someone to live for. And he does."

I shake my head. "I don't know that I'm—"

"We're going with false modesty now?" He arches an eyebrow at me. "I'm not saying what he is to you, but what you are to him— that's what matters in Idle."

"And Fallador is…" I trail off, allowing him to fill in the sentence.

He blinks. "What about him?"

There's the tell again in the corner of his mouth. Surely, he knows I've caught the glances and the affection between them. Mikail relaxes in his presence in a way that I've never seen before. I would think he was seeking solace after losing Euyn, but that's not exactly it, either.

"I don't know. You tell me," I say.

Mikail rubs his forehead. He opens his mouth to speak and then closes it. Then he does it again. Sometimes we don't have the words to express what someone means to us. Sometimes they aren't necessary.

"Something?" I ask.

He sighs. "That's a good way of putting it. We've known each other a long time. And it's always been a line I didn't want to cross for any number of reasons, which I suppose makes him special. But now I don't know. Trust is a tricky thing, and this isn't the time for affection."

"I hope one day you'll figure it out," I say.

He smiles kindly at my dreams of the future. "I doubt it. This… We won't all survive this, Sora."

I grip the cushion as a cold wave of apprehension washes over me. It's the first time he's spoken of any kind of defeat. Normally, he's all fiery sword and vengeance. Mikail sounding resigned makes my empty stomach knot. But I suppose it's logical—there are only so many times the four of us can walk away from battling the world.

With all these odds stacked against us, it seems ridiculous to fight. It's easier to lie down and die. To wait for the realms to descend on us and accept our fate. But we need to keep going. If for no other reason than this: Why should we make it easy for them? They've tried to ruin and break us, but we're still here. We'll go down swinging a blade in a burst of blood.

"I've survived worse at the hands of powerful men, Mikail," I say. "And so have you. And it was at a time when we didn't have each other, or Aeri, or Royo. The gods have handed immense power to the two of you in order to change things—not just for ourselves but for the four realms."

I get up and grab the water pitcher. I pour him another glass and one for me, and my hand hardly shakes at all.

"To defying the odds," I say.

He taps his glass to mine, and light shines in his eyes again. "To the bloody end, Sora."

CHAPTER THIRTY-FOUR

ROYO

CITY OF HALLAN, GAYA

Aeri ordered way too much food. There have to be a dozen different plates in front of us, and that's not counting the banchan. But we're at a table that can fit six and we're the only people in the large dining room of the inn. Everything looks good, but I don't got a lot of hope for a tavern without customers.

She catches me eyeing the spread and pauses with her chopsticks in the soup dumplings. "We didn't have lunch, Royo. And we're bringing a lot of it upstairs."

She says it like it's normal. But nothing about her is.

I like that.

I pick the plate with plum-covered roasted duck and spoon on some oyster noodles, which the server said are a house specialty. I cut a super small bite and put it in my mouth. The salty sweetness of the duck hits my tongue, and I immediately reach for my knife. Either I'm starving or this is actually good.

Aeri eats in that distracted, birdlike way of hers, sampling dish after dish until she figures out which one she likes best.

I keep an eye out for any danger, but it's real quiet in here and we're not that suspicious. If you didn't know Aeri had two of the relics of the Dragon Lord, you wouldn't guess. The neckline of her dress hides her amulet, and she keeps her left hand mostly under the table. I still wish I had my axe—they made me leave it behind on the boat because it was too noticeable. I have a dagger, a few knives, and the nunchuka, but it's not enough. Not to protect her. A thousand swords and I'd want more to keep her safe.

"What are you thinking about?" she asks, reaching into the bulgogi.

"I want more blades on me," I say.

She laughs, and the sound echoes in the empty room. "Of course that's what you're thinking. This egg custard is really good—it's sweet." She points to a bowl with her spoon.

"Mikail has the stick, you have your…things, Sora has poison. It's all I got." I shrug and dig into the shrimp fried rice. It's a little greasy, but rice is good that way.

Aeri tilts her head. "You're so much more than a blade."

She says stuff like that, and my heart skips. I actually feel it jump up in my chest. Nobody's ever seen me or treated me like Aeri.

"I'm glad you were just thinking about axes, though," she says, helping herself to a piece of scallion pancake. "I thought maybe you were thinking about other things, like gorgeous courtesans or…me."

"I'm always thinking about you," I say.

The words are out of my mouth before I can think twice about them. Maybe I shouldn't have said that, but it's the truth.

Aeri's shoulders droop, and she closes her eyes.

"You okay?" I ask.

She looks at me. "I waited my whole life to find you, that's all."

"Aeri…" I ignore the fluttering inside my ribs. I hit my hand to my chest to make it stop. It's just indigestion—that's what I'm going with.

"In a strictly-friends way, of course." She rolls her eyes and sips some water.

But her golden eyes shimmer, and I remember her scent as she kissed me. The craving for her surges through my limbs. I need this strange girl more than I need air. Her right hand rests on the table, holding her chopsticks. I reach out with my palm up.

Aeri drops the chopsticks so fast, they clatter on the table. Then she slips her hand into mine. I take her fingers, bring them up to my lips, and kiss her hand. She beams like the Sun God, then gets out of her chair, leans across the table, and kisses me. Her soft, plump lips mash against mine. That voice in my head yells that this feeling won't last. She'll betray me again, or some other thing will happen where she'll get taken from me. The good is fleeting and makes you feel worse when it's pulled away, but the bullshit goes on forever in these realms. I gotta protect myself.

I fail.

I break away first, but I stroke her face. She smiles contentedly as she leans into my palm. But those gold eyes and what she can do come at a cost.

"What happens if you get stuck in time?" I ask. "Really stuck."

She blinks as she sits back down. "I don't know. I guess that's why we're going to the temple—to try to find out. But I know you'd bring me back, so I'm not too worried about it."

She shrugs and digs into the glass noodles.

It's not a promise I can make. I don't know how I've been able to bring her back. But for her, I'll try anything.

My stomach knots on the good food because I don't know if trying will be enough.

CHAPTER THIRTY-FIVE

TIYUNG

CITY OF TROVE, YUSAN

I've taken two baths since arriving in Trove, but I'm convinced I still have an odor. I sniff, trying to discreetly smell myself, but it's impossible to tell over the scent of food in this crowded tavern.

Hana sits across from me in the booth, looking lovely, as always. She sips her ale as I demolish a second lamb shank with vegetable stir fry and rice. I hunch over my meal like someone will try to steal my plate. I hope one day this ravenous hunger fades, but I doubt it will. The same way I still need to sleep with a fire and the oil lamps lit.

Hana looks at me over the rim of her glass. "You're going to choke yourself before your father gets the opportunity."

I stop cutting into the shank. "Very funny."

Unsurprisingly, the poison maiden has executioner humor. But between burning Sora's indenture and essentially faking my death, this joke hits a little close to home. My father might be happy to see me or furious. Or both. And he's certainly not above throttling me.

Her lips turn up in a smile as she relaxes against the wooden booth. We are warm and dry after changing into fresh clothes. I threw out my old ones as soon as we checked in. I'll need another cloak before we leave. It's warmer, this close to Qali, but it's still raining.

I'm nearly through with my second plate when I realize Hana hasn't spoken in a couple of minutes. I find her staring off.

"What are you thinking about?" I ask.

She sighs. "Sora."

It's a strange thing to have in common—being in love with the same woman. But there's no better commonality to have binding you than love. I've moved past my jealousy, I think. At my core, I truly want Sora to be happy, whether that's with me, Hana, or anyone else.

At least that's what I tell myself.

"She'll be all right," I say. "She's a survivor, like you."

Hana shifts in her seat, staring at me. She eyes me for so long, I begin to worry that I have food on my face or that I do, in fact, smell.

"I will admit," she says, "I've misjudged you."

"Join the club. They have swords." I finish my last bite.

She smiles. "I'm…sorry."

I put my fork down and wipe my mouth with a rough napkin, then toss it to the side. "Hana, there is absolutely nothing you need to apologize for."

She looks to the side. "I don't know if that's true. This time tomorrow, you'll reach Qali."

She sounds a little off, and I suppose I am, too. I want to reach the palace, and yet a part of me would rather stay here and avoid the future.

We go our separate ways tomorrow. Hana can't risk Seok's wrath—therefore, I will have to go into Qali alone while she flees to Tamneki. From there, she'll try to find Sora and the others. That's been the plan since we came back to Yusan. We're just gloomy about it now. Maybe it's the weight of knowing that we probably won't see each other again. My father has too many enemies who'd like me dead, and she is one double-agent spy against the world. With a war of the realms at our doorstep, many people will die, including one or both of us.

But there's Sora. And for Sora, we'll try.

A fiddler and two other musicians start playing. He's actually quite good. My parents used to have musicians and balls in Gain, but that stopped fifteen years ago after an assassination attempt on my father's life. It was my "friend's" father who stabbed him in the collarbone, just missing his neck. The only reason he missed was because I'd screamed and Seok had turned to look at me at the last second.

After that, there were no balls, no friends. Instead, Seok began searching for girls to become poisoners. My father became who he felt he needed to be. I've survived by being his opposite.

Tables are moved out of the way, and people clap and begin to dance as the fiddler plays a familiar tune. I drum my fingers on the sticky table, tapping along to the beat.

"Do you dance, Tiyung?" Hana asks.

I raise my eyebrows so fast, my face hurts. "Are you asking me to dance with you?"

"No, just making conversation. I wouldn't dare try to pull you away from licking your plate."

I laugh and wipe my mouth again. This is too heavy a night, too somber for dancing. Which is exactly why I slide out from the booth and stand. "Would you do me the honor of a dance?"

She smiles. "I thought you'd never ask."

I refuse to waste our final moments in dread.

Hana is, of course, a great dancer. I spin her as I put a hand behind my back, in the normal pose for gentlemen. She twirls, and then I take her arm and catch her waist. She links her arm in mine as we spin through the crowd. It isn't long before people move to the side to clap and watch us. Her footwork is impeccable as she floats, her dress billowing.

"Madame Iseul taught you?" I ask.

I pick her up by the waist as she jumps, and then I place her back down. It's far more graceful than when I tried to save her.

She nods. "Where did you learn? You're better than expected."

"Tutors and my mother. The nobility must dance at balls, especially heirs," I say. "It's a great slight if you don't."

"Ah yes, your friends' parties," she says.

"I don't have any friends," I say. "Except for Sora and the others. And you."

She looks away for a moment. "I guess we'll see."

I'm not sure if she means her, Sora, or anyone else, but it has the same feeling of hitting a false note, an off moment that sours the experience. The song ends, and I kiss her hand as is customary, but there's a shift between us. All that's left is a sneaking suspicion that I'm missing something important.

CHAPTER THIRTY-SIX

MIKAIL

CITY OF HALLAN, GAYA

We made it through the night and the morning without being attacked, so that's something. But if Aeri spends a minute longer looking at wrap dresses in this market, our streak might be over. Even Sora looks annoyed.

"Just pick one," Royo says, throwing up his arms. "Or get them both. We're going camping, not to a ball."

He's grumbling, but they're as close as they were in Khitan. Like I told her, he just needed time.

Aeri picks the white-and-blue-patterned dress she'd gone back to a few times. She pays the shop worker and pockets the change.

We finally have all the supplies we need…and then some. Actually, we could survive a full sunsae with everything we bought. We were running low on mun until Aeri pulled out a diamond to sell this morning.

She can also turn anything into gold, but that's a last resort.

The market is surprisingly full for a city that's seen better days. I consider asking locals about the temple, but it's not worth the risk of discovery. Loyalty has been hard to come by, but enemies have been plentiful. By now, Rune knows we escaped, and Seok is aware we're alive. We're being hunted, and there's no reason to leave a trail.

As we walk out of the market, we pass a messenger house. I think about sending a message to Fallador. By asking for a private word with Rune, he helped me escape, but was that intentional? We didn't tell him about our plans in case he was working for Rune, yet it seemed like he picked up on them. Whose side is he really on?

Without an answer, I continue down the old stone street. The only people I can trust are the ones walking with me. We will, in fact, meet Fallador and Rune in Tamneki, but it will be at the head of an army.

I hope.

Ever since Berm, I've been thinking about Jeul, the old capital that bore the worst of the Festival of Blood. I am certain the Gayans there feel far differently about Yusan than those who live in the southeast. Rebel and spy reports came from the northwest side of the island. It's what I'm counting on.

We leave the skiff tied up at the port and take horses out of the city. If needed, I can use the scepter to call a boat to us. But with aching pain from my joints to my muscles and an ever-present headache, among other issues, I'd rather not do it.

The four of us ride in a line west to the sacred woods. Or where they once stood. A normal forest would've grown back after a fire, even a purposely set one, but from all accounts, the enormous trees belonging to the earth goddess never regrew. And yet Joon didn't suffer for desecrating a goddess's prized possession.

Sometimes I wonder if the gods are even watching us. And if they are, why don't they act? Why are they indifferent?

I grip my reins despite the pain curling my hands.

"Are you all right?" Sora asks. She's riding next to me. Aeri is to her hearing side, so she turns her head, waiting for my answer.

"I'm just thinking about the woods," I say.

"Mm-hmm," she hums.

I smile. I thought I was a great liar before Sora. Last night, she asked me to sleep in bed with her because she didn't buy me claiming to feel fine on the couch. I'm glad she insisted. It was good to sleep on the feather bed. I doubt I would've slept at all on the lumpy sofa.

We ride west for two bells. It's just the dirt road and green field around us under a clear blue sky. The fog burned off by dawn, and now it's warm but not hot. The breeze feels refreshing, lifting spirits on the floral air. Aeri laughs as a butterfly lands on Royo's head. Sora smiles. On an open road with my friends, I can almost forget why we're here. Then, as we crest a hill, there it is—a wall of fog and death.

The sacred woods of Alta, or what's left of them, are covered in a dense mist said to be the goddess's tears. The immense ebony trees stand without leaves or needles. Acres and acres of charred woods linger like reapers in an area that had once been teeming with life. The zone of death extends far up the western coast, nearly reaching Jeul.

I claw at my saddle, but we continue forward.

"Is the ground...ash?" Aeri asks.

It appears so. I ride forward until my horse won't step any closer, and then I dismount and try to pull the animal forward. Begrudgingly, he walks until we reach the border of the ash, where he refuses to move another foot. I pull his reins. He rears back and whinnies, his eyes full of terror.

Animals can sense forsaken ground.

The horse calms when I allow him to back up a few feet. Finding the temple would certainly be faster on horseback, but something tells me that's not going to be an option.

I hold the reins, debating about where to tie him. The closest grass was on the other side of the hill, but the horses could be stolen. We could leave them here, but if we don't return within a day or so, they'll die of hunger or thirst.

Royo has also dismounted. He's carrying his pack and Aeri's on his back. He also has Sora's in his hand. I'd offer to help, but I'm in enough pain just carrying my own pack and a water bladder.

"I'll tie the horses back by the hill." Royo drops all the bags and takes rope out of his pack. "You said it could take a few days to find the temple, right?"

"It could," I say. "But thieves could take the horses from the meadow."

Stealing a horse is punishable by death, but that hardly matters when you're starving or addicted to laoli.

"They could take 'em from here, too. If the gods will it, they'll be around when we get back." He shrugs and takes the horses to where there is grass and a stream.

I suppose the muffled moans I overheard last night are the reason for his startlingly good mood. If I asked, Royo would claim it's because Hwan might already be free from Idle Prison, but that's not it at all. We don't think Hwan was ever moved there. No, it has everything to do with the way Aeri looks at him. Doesn't matter, though. I should be grateful that Royo is in a good mood at all.

He returns, and the four of us walk toward the towering charcoal woods. Each tree is over ten feet wide and reaches well over a hundred feet into the air, most over two hundred.

Sora steps a delicate foot on the edge of the woods. She pulls up the hem of her dress, and her boot sinks down until the ashy soil reaches her calf.

"It's like a bed of ash," she says.

Aeri frowns at her new shoes.

"The ground has wept ash since the festival," I say. "The land was blessed, and now it's cursed." I shift my pack to take a sip of water from my canteen. The bladder is enough to refill all of our canteens ten times. I try not to wince with pain as I move the pack. "Let's go."

It's unsettling at best, entering the mist-covered dead woods. The ground is spongy ash underfoot, and there's not a sound. My senses tell me that this is hopeless, that the temple is long gone, but Sora and Aeri are right—there were recent Gayan scrolls in the Temple of Knowledge in Khitan. Yusan wouldn't bother with making a Gayan translation, not for a colony. The temple must still exist somewhere. And because Yusan believes they burned it to the ground, they would assume the Gayans, now under Yusanian control, wouldn't need one.

The Gayan Temple of Knowledge used to be housed in the magical tree of Alta, which was said to be two hundred feet in circumference and three hundred feet tall. But despite the massive size, I'm not sure where it is. Something tells me it's dead center in these woods. I'd rather have more than a gut feeling, but information on the temple also disappeared.

The four of us continue into the forest, and the mist soon closes in around us. I have a compass, and so does Royo, but the visibility is poor, and the trees are dense.

We're not more than a hundred yards in when my skin prickles. It feels like there's a feather dancing over my shoulders. I turn each way, certain we're being watched. But that's not possible. There's no one else in these woods. Still, I switch the walking stick to my left hand so I can grab my sword hilt faster.

Bells and bells pass as we continue into nothing but the sound of Royo's heavy breathing. Nothing lives here—it's why the horses spooked and why reasonable people would steer clear. But this soil is nothing compared to the funeral pyres after the Festival of Blood that were so large the ash blew all the way over to Cetil. The black specks were the remains of people whose only crime was to live on Gaya. Mothers and sons. Grandfathers and infants. They all burned.

I sip more water. We can't give up, no matter the odds. We may not win, but we'll take as many to Lord Yama as we can.

Yet as the sun gets lower, my hope begins to fade. I knew it might take some time to find the temple, but how long? The woods span thousands of acres. What if the temple is far north? That will take days and days of walking. What if we miss it to the west or east? Then we'll have to circle back.

What's worse is that I'm not sure I'm leading everyone in the right direction, especially when I've been unusually confused. It's part of the toll of the scepter, I think. But we need to reach the temple. We have to find out what happens when the relics are reunited, what is happening to Aeri, and also if there's a cure for this toll. I haven't told the others about my confusion, but they noticed last night.

"This is a good spot to stop," Royo says.

He points to two trees that had once grown together. The fused trunks will guard our flank and then some. With how dark and foggy it is, there's no real option to keep going.

I drop my pack, and my muscles are instantly relieved. I refill my canteen again and start taking out supplies.

Royo tries to dig down through the ashy soil, but it keeps filling back in again. He gives up and starts stacking wood and rocks into the shape of a firepit.

Once again, it feels like spiders are crawling along my back. I shift and scan with my hand on the hilt of my sword. I check behind us and then around the sides of the trees. My swift motions alert the others, but there's nothing. Just woods, mist, and three concerned faces staring at me.

Euyn would've gotten a kick out of me turning paranoid. He finally would've had a rapt listener for all of his traps and scanning techniques.

Tears prick my eyes, and I'm not sure why. Why now? My first instinct is to dismiss the feeling. But what is the point of that? Does our love not deserve mourning? Or is it that I don't want to cry in front of the others? I'm safer among these three people than I am in the rest of the world.

I sniffle and then sit on my sleeping bag. Sora's worry line appears on her brow before she wraps her arms around my shoulders. Aeri takes my hand. Then Royo comes over and slaps me on the back with his meaty palm. It really hurts, but he rubs his hand in a circle to wipe away the pain.

"I miss him, too," he says.

Those little words burst a dam inside of me. All the emotions I've kept at bay since the banquet hall spill out. Maybe I needed someone else to say that they've missed Euyn. I missed him for the years of his banishment, but this is something else. This is a deep, dark cavern of longing that can't be filled. It felt good to murder the king's guard. To do something with this rage. Even the pain of using the scepter has been better than dealing with this emptiness, this hole in my heart.

I let my tears fall as my nose runs and my headache worsens. I cry for Euyn and my father—the men who chose me, who loved me, and who paid the price for it. They're gone. And yet I remain. Deep sobs rack my chest, and I reach deeper. I cry for what happened here when I was a boy. The family I knew and lost, and the family I didn't. I cry for the victims until I'm wailing on the forest floor.

Then I move to wipe my face. But Sora, Aeri, and Royo hold me until I have no tears left. Sora adds salt to my water to help me feel better. Aeri places a blanket over me. Royo lights a fire, which beats back the dark. This isn't an alliance—this is a family. One to live for and die with.

I lie back on the sleeping bag as my breathing slows enough for me to be able to drink. As I stare at the fog, I can't see any of the night stars. But maybe that's not a bad thing. The stars tell our future. Maybe together with a starless sky, the four of us can write our own destiny.

CHAPTER THIRTY-SEVEN

TIYUNG

THE PALATIAL ROAD, YUSAN

It's morning, and we're in the indoor market in Trove, but Hana doesn't speak to me much. Actually, come to think of it, I don't think she's said anything at all. I handed her the cloak I wanted and the breakfast sandwich I needed, and she paid for them without a word.

We stop in the messenger house one last time. We're so close to Qali that my mother could have gotten my letter and responded within a day. I hold my breath as the man behind the counter checks, but once again, there's nothing for me. There's nothing for Hana, either. She doesn't seem surprised.

We get back onto the Coastal Road. Once again, we're being pelted with rain, but this ride feels different. Hana seems like she's in another realm. She looks and speaks to me as much as she did after we escaped Idle Prison. When I was not much more than her ward.

The rift started last night, but I'm not sure what caused it. Perhaps this is just how she is. Maybe after so much loss in poison school, she had to figure out a way to shut off her feelings before a goodbye. Or maybe I simply don't mean anything to her. The sting of that and the drops of rain hit my cheeks. Maybe I'm a fool for thinking it had been real friendship.

I sigh and adjust my new cloak.

We ride for bells in silence. Hana focuses on the road. I think about what needs to be done. As soon as I get to the palace, I have to persuade my father to remove the bounties. I'll explain how I escaped from the prison with the help of one of Mikail's spies and one of Euyn's loyal palace guards. I will also tell him about Ailor and warn him that the Weian ships are coming. I will claim that I didn't contact him until now because I didn't want to risk the messages getting intercepted. Instead, I rode down from my hiding spot as soon as I found out he was king.

My stomach turns, and I slouch. It all vaguely makes sense without mentioning Hana or Nayo, but Seok doesn't settle for surface answers. I gulp. I am many things, but I'm not stronger or cleverer than my father. But this time I have to be. He cannot know she's alive. He'll hunt her to the ends of the Outer Lands.

It's late afternoon when we come to a crossroads. This is the turn off for the Palatial Road. Hana slows her horse, and I do the same.

"Be well, Tiyung," she says. Her posture is stiff, her manner cold.

I had been thinking about what to say, how I wanted to thank her for all she's done for me, but something feels so strange about all of this that what I say is, "Be well, Hana."

She looks relieved and nods to me.

I pull my horse onto the Palatial Road—the three-mile-long stretch of nothingness. The road is paved, but there's not a tree, a plant, or a blade of grass to the sides. Nothing is allowed to grow near the palace because even weeds could hide attackers. They burned this entire section and carted in a thin layer of salted sand hundreds of years ago. The closest greenery is Westward Forest, miles to the other side of Qali.

Hana continues down the Coastal Road without looking back. I tell myself it's for the best. She cared about me, or she wouldn't have saved me so many times. Certainly, she wouldn't have risked her own life. But then I'm struck by another thought: What if her end goal was to deliver me here all along?

To whom, though? Definitely not Seok.

What if I'm about to be captured or killed? What if there is also a bounty on me?

I shake my head, raindrops streaming down my hair, and I try to calm my racing heart. No, I'm being paranoid. My thoughts are spiraling, and I have to stop. There is no bounty on me because everyone, including my father, believes I died. I clear the rain from my face as I stare up at the gray sky. I didn't make it out of the tenth hell just to fall apart now.

With a sigh, I gather myself, sit up straight, and adjust my shoulders. I shaved in Trove, and I'm as presentable as I can be, given this ride.

I spur my horse and summon some bravery. I am still Seok's son, and he is now the king of Yusan. I will not cower or hesitate.

Still, I swallow hard as I ride closer to the white palace. The archers on the walls all train their arrows on me. And that lake ripples gently with rain.

I shudder.

My father has added king's guard at the land end of the bridge. I expect that the men will be from Gain and they will know me. But as I ride up, I don't see any familiar faces among the ten soldiers.

"Halt," one man says. He's in his late thirties—a lifer in the king's guard. "Who goes there?"

"I am Tiyung. Count... King Seok's son and heir," I say.

I grit my teeth to stop myself from wincing. I'd practiced saying King Seok many times only to still fail.

Murmurs echo around me. I wait as the soldiers defer to the man who spoke. He must be their captain. He gestures, and a runner goes sprinting down the bridge to the palace. I casually sit atop my horse as if this whole procedure is tediously boring. It's what other princes would do.

Rain falls steadily. The men don't speak to me, and I sit with my chin raised as if I am above their chatter. I avoid looking at that lake.

Eventually, the runner returns. He whispers to the captain, who nods and then gestures with his arm.

"Sire," he says with a bow.

The soldiers all part to allow my horse to cross. They lower their heads as I pass.

The second my horse steps foot on the bridge, I shake with a violent chill. It feels like invisible hands grip me, squeezing my neck and chest, yet it's nothing more than fear. But this fear is reasonable. Last time I was this close to the lake, I thought the palace guards were going to throw me in and feed me to the iku—the monsters swimming under the surface. I was then locked in the sunless dungeon beneath the lake. I can still feel those doors closing overhead.

I can't help memories rising to the surface and bringing fear along with them, but I continue. Bravery isn't the absence of fear; it's persevering despite it.

But something is wrong here. The entire palace feels off. The way the guards blocked access to the bridge was strange, but it also feels as if Qali itself dislikes a usurper on the throne.

My back muscles are tight, my spine pulling me to turn around. Yet I have to press on. For Sora, for the others.

In front of the palace stands one figure. Bile rises in my throat, but I force it back down. This was the point—to see my father. I make myself sit upright and try to will the tremors to stop.

As I get closer though, I realize it's not my father but my mother. She waits under the raised gate with her hands clasped.

My chest swells, and my heart drums with joy. All the negative feelings and baseless suspicions vanish. It's been a while since I've seen my mother. As usual, she looks beautiful, her long blond hair in a braid down her left side.

She wears a ruby-and-gold crown atop her head—the crown of the queens. I wonder what my father wears, because it can't be the Immortal Crown. I suppose I'll find out soon enough.

Once I'm within a few yards of her, I dismount from my horse, and a stable boy takes the reins.

"Mother." I open my arms as I walk to her.

She waits under the portcullis and then embraces me, kissing the side of my face. She has that familiar scent of lilacs and vanilla, but there's an off note, too—sweat, maybe. As she hugs me, I can feel her tremble as she whispers in my ear. "You must leave this place now. Wait for a message in Tamneki."

CHAPTER THIRTY-EIGHT

SORA

THE SACRED WOODS, GAYA

We rise after a restless night. I slept in a tent with Mikail, or at least I tried to as he tossed and turned. I'd lay a hand on his shoulder, and he'd still, but not long after that, he'd be thrashing around again. I'm not sure if it was dehydration or emotional pain disturbing him, but I'm glad he wasn't alone.

I sigh and stretch by the campfire. Even if I'd been on a feather bed, I wouldn't have rested much. We'll sleep better tonight after we find the temple.

At least, I hope.

It's still foggy—I assume it always is in these woods, but it's light enough to be morning. Mikail makes a delicious-smelling tea over the fire, and Aeri passes out red bean buns she picked up yesterday. They're a little stale, but not with the hot tea. It was kind of her to think of us all.

We eat our breakfast and drink our tea in the eerily silent woods, then pack up camp and start walking again.

We travel for bells through monotonous woods and thick fog, following as Mikail leads the way. I stopped trying to lift my dress long ago, accepting the ruin. Aeri still sighs at her shoes.

Every now and then, Mikail's body goes rigid, like he senses danger, but I look around and find nothing. He then continues on like it didn't happen. I think this is part of the toll, but I'm not sure.

I'm glad he allowed himself to cry, to be comforted, last night. As he tossed around in the tent, I lay there and tried to search for the same well of emotion. I came up dry, and it doesn't make sense. I loved my sister with all of my being, so it's not a lack of emotion. I tried everything I could to save her, so it's not a lack of caring. Maybe I'm simply exhausted from what I've been through. I did everything I could, and I still failed. I hate having to carry on, having to live in a world without Daysum. I hate being the survivor again. I suppose my one comfort is that once Seok is dead and Aeri is on the throne, I won't have to carry on anymore. My business in this world and life will be done. I'll go to a secluded cottage somewhere and wait for the Kingdom of Hells. Or maybe I'll run to it.

I glance over at Aeri as she brushes hands with Royo. They smile and blush. Gentle happiness ripples across my chest. It feels like watching the children chase butterflies in the meadow in Gain. A fleeting, feathery joy. A moment over too soon but never forgotten.

She has all she needs in him, and he, even more so. Love was never all I needed—not once Seok invaded my life.

We pass around dried meat, nuts, and berries as we continue walking into the afternoon. We brought plenty of provisions for meals, but it looks like finding fresh water will be a struggle. It's a good thing Mikail has the water bladder.

"Okay, how do we know the temple is on this path?" Royo asks. "We can't see for shit."

My hope is being tested, too. I don't tend to question Mikail's skills, but we can only see three or four trees away with the fog.

Mikail pulls out a folded piece of paper. "I charted the dead center of the sacred woods from an old map I saw at the Canopy Inn. This is where I think the last temple stood. It shouldn't be too much longer. We should reach it by sunset."

I breathe out a sigh of relief. At least that will give us a starting point. I ignore the fact that something in his voice sounded uncertain.

We continue on.

"Can't Royo use the key to find the temple door?" Aeri asks.

"It's probably underground now, but once we get there, we can try that," Mikail says. "It's a good idea, Aeri."

Royo grins down at her. She looks at him like she's soaking up the sun.

"Sora," Aeri says in a singsong way. She caught me staring at them.

I flip my hair and pretend to be looking up at the sky. But then I see something. There, towering into the mist, maybe fifty feet away, is a black wall. But it has…branches.

My breath catches, and I place a hand over my heart.

"That's it," I say. "It has to be."

I point to the northwest. There, beyond two more trees, is the sacred tree of Alta. Nothing else could be this large.

The three of them follow my arm.

"Ten Hells," Royo whispers.

Aeri's mouth drops open. "Is that even a tree? How is that possible?"

"It was," Mikail says with a sigh. "The first grown by the goddess Alta. She's only worshipped as an earth god on Gaya. Yusan doesn't have an equivalent. We believe she was the lover of the God of Knowledge, hence the temple being in the tree. She's also known as the lover of the God of the Seas."

The religions of the four realms are a little different. Sometimes they overlap—like we all have sun and sea gods. Other times, they don't. We unite in prayer but diverge on why.

We approach the tree with slower, more hesitant steps than we've taken since we entered the woods. Although the tree stands, it's burned to a crisp like all the others. But I can still make out the marble lintel of the door, see the grooves where there used to be fountains. I assume inside there were domes and mosaics. But these doors haven't been opened since before the fire. The way this is charred, they spent extra time burning this down.

The four of us genuflect to what used to be. This ground is holy, and Yusan burned it out of spite. The temple and the forest posed no danger to them. They wanted to erase the history of the island and take away their gods. I grip a fistful of ash as I kneel. I know what that feels like.

Yet despite all the brutality and the horrors, somewhere, the temple survives. Now the question is where.

"Royo, maybe it's time to use your key," Aeri says.

Mikail stays down on one knee while the rest of us stand.

Royo sighs, looking skeptical, but he pulls out the key. He strikes the ground with the key in his fist just like he hit the ice in Khitan. We look around for any change as he strikes again. I assume the ash will move just as the snow did. Aeri eyes the nearby trees. He hits it to the ground a third time, and this time holds it down.

"Nothing?" Mikail asks. He's still staring at the old temple.

"Not yet," I say.

Royo stands and slips the key back into his pocket.

Aeri has wandered a little bit away, looking at the trees.

"It has to be around here somewhere," she says.

Mikail sighs. He puts his hands to his forehead to salute the temple and then stands. "It doesn't, though. We were hoping it was still in the same location, but we didn't know for certain."

"But what better place to disguise a temple than by the one that used to exist?" Aeri asks. "Knowledge is power, and that's why these temples are hard to get to. It's why the temple in Yusan is carved into a sheer mountain face and Khitan's is under a lake. They're not supposed to be interfered with. Plus, if the Gayans rebuilt anywhere else, Yusan would've noticed. It's in the woods…somewhere."

I look at Mikail. Aeri is right.

"Okay, let's search," Mikail says. "We already came from the south, so let's go east and swing north, keeping the tree in sight. Royo, continue to hit the key on the trees and the ground in case it helps."

We start moving in a circle around the temple. With a little hesitation, Royo strikes the key against a tree. He braces himself as if tapping the key on the trunk will make these enormous trees fall.

Nothing happens. He breathes out a sigh of relief. Mikail arches an eyebrow but doesn't say anything.

We keep moving to the north.

"I can't believe these trees can just stand, dead like this," Aeri says. "It's unnatural."

"Nothing about this place is normal," Royo says.

"They're so large, though, you almost have to wonder if—" Aeri stops mid-thought.

I wait for her to finish, but a sharp scream pierces the quiet.

The three of us grab our weapons, and Mikail's sword flames to life. He and I look for threats, but I don't see anything.

"Aeri? Aeri!" Royo yells. His pained voice rings into the air.

There's no response.

She was standing by that tree, and now she's just…gone.

CHAPTER THIRTY-NINE

TIYUNG

CITY OF TAMNEKI, YUSAN

I sip tea at the Palm Teahouse in Tamneki, watching the rain fall in the empty courtyard where Sora and I first met Count Bay Chin. I'm not sure why I came here, aside from the fact that I love any place that reminds me of her.

As I drink, I try to make sense of what happened at Qali Palace just a few bells ago. My mother is one of the most levelheaded people I have ever met. She is neither hysterical nor prone to overreacting. When she told me to flee, I grabbed my horse from the stable boy. She loudly called me a "charming fake" to Rayna, Sun-ye's sister, as she turned to walk back into Qali.

I sped away from the palace as fast as I could. I have no doubt that she just saved my life, but why was I in danger?

Am I a fugitive like the rest of them? No. My father spread word of my death when he put a bounty on them, so perhaps the fact that I am alive is too inconvenient for him. I am still his son, though—his only child. So what just happened?

I nurse my pot of tea because I'm not sure where else to go, and all I have for money is a single silver mun I received as change earlier. Tea in this expensive house will cost half of that.

What do I do now? I worry the edge of the varnished table with my fingers. I have no money, no supplies, no connections, no way to figure out where Sora and the others are. I hang my head in my hands. Things were so much easier when I was traveling with Hana. Hana.

I raise my head as I remember the strange look on her face when I said we were friends and she replied, *We'll see*. Her distant air today. Whatever just happened, she's involved in this somehow. Those messages she was sending as we traveled. I didn't see what she wrote or who she sent them to. What did she say? What did she do?

I curl my hand in a fist on my lap, now certain she betrayed me. Why did I even trust her? My family tortured her and her brother, and she's spent her life hating us. She didn't ever owe me loyalty. I'm just a fool.

But if she wasn't helping me because I freed Nayo, then who was she working for? Not my father, certainly. She could have still been a spy for the king, as Joon did grant her a new life and high status as spymaster. Or maybe she was working for someone else entirely. With Dal and Bay Chin both dead, the only other man powerful enough to make it worth her time would be Rune.

Was she also a spy for Rune? Is that how she knew the others weren't in Rahway?

Something about it feels true. I sit up straight. The alliance between Rune and my father was only ever surface deep to counteract the powerful northeast, but those alliances are no longer needed. Not with nearly everyone dead. If she is a spy for Rune, what does that mean for Sora and the others?

What does it mean for me?

I finish my tea and head toward the messenger house.

CHAPTER FORTY

AERI
THE TEMPLE OF KNOWLEDGE, GAYA

I fall for an unnerving amount of time. Well, I mean, any amount of time is unnerving when you fall inside of a hollowed-out tree. But I finally land on a pile of…scrolls. Some skitter and roll, and others get crushed by my weight. I'm half sitting, half lying down with the wind knocked out of me.

So, that hurt.

But all things considered, I'm in great shape for how far I fell.

I rub my backside as I get to my feet. I'm in a circular room, or more like a stone cavern. The walls are smooth, striated stone with… green grass beneath my boots, as if we're not underground. Confused, I look around. There have to be hundreds, if not thousands, of scrolls in a pile. But this is the strangest room I've ever been in. It's light like it's daylight in here, but even above ground isn't bright like this.

To my right, three Yoksa in gray robes stare at me. We've done it—found the Temple of Knowledge…sort of. I accidentally fell into their depository hole. But, hey, I'll take it!

"Hi. I'm Aeri." I wave at them.

The older woman with gray hair tilts her head.

With a short scream, Sora falls through the ceiling and lands on the scrolls. She has just oriented herself and moved out of the way when Mikail falls, but he's like a cat, landing on his feet with the walking stick for balance. Last is Royo.

"Feet first," Mikail yells.

"I don't know which fucking way is up," he says before he crashes onto the pile.

The three others look around the same way I did. This is so unnatural, so obviously created by a god, that it takes us a little while to catch up. The grass is real; the ground is soft enough to brace our falls.

The priests continue to stare at us. We must be the weirdest thing that's happened to them today. Or probably in years. Maybe ever.

Mikail gets his bearings first and grabs his walking stick. It held together despite the impact. He says something in Gayan as he takes a few steps closer to the priests while Royo curses in Yusanian and dusts himself off.

"Royo, they can understand all four languages," Mikail reminds him. "Do you have the key?"

"Oh, um, yeah." Royo fishes around in his pocket and pulls out the green key. I don't know how it stayed on him all this time, other than the God of Knowledge willing it.

The three priests exchange glances and then ask us to wait. We don't have a lot of options, so Mikail agrees on our behalf.

"What did you tell them?" Sora whispers.

"I said that we are pilgrims seeking knowledge and safe quarter and that Royo is the son of a keeper."

I mean, it's true. It's just leaving out some pretty big details.

A single woman returns. She has darker skin and reddish gray hair styled in locs. I think she's around fifty years old, but her skin is smooth and her cheekbones are high, so it's hard to tell her age.

"I am Braya, keeper of the Gayan temple," the woman says in Yusanian.

"I am Adoros Miat," Mikail says.

Sora and I turn. This is the first time I've heard Mikail use his real name. But will she know who that is with Fallador pretending to be the prince?

The woman smiles slowly. "I can see the resemblance to your parents. Gods guide their souls."

Mikail's whole face lights up, and then he inclines his head.

"And that makes him the keeper's son?" Braya says, gesturing to Royo.

Royo takes a step forward. "I am, ma'am."

She eyes him appraisingly. "Yes, you do resemble Snaw."

Royo's eyes go wide. That's the man he can't remember—the one who walked out on his family. The one the amarth mentioned. Royo thinks he was abandoned, but it isn't that simple of a choice for the keepers of knowledge. Maybe this will give him some comfort.

"She is Naerium, the twice-blessed princess of Yusan," Braya says, looking at me. I blink at her, wondering how she knew that. But she has already moved on to Sora.

"I am Athora Inigo," she says.

I turn my head and stare. I've only ever known her as Sora. Does everyone have a different, hidden name?

"Are we welcome in your temple?" Mikail asks.

She folds her hands. "Yes, Your Majesty. However, no information is to be destroyed, taken, or altered. We have a vow of silence within the temple walls; however, you may ask for assistance, and we will provide it. We require that your weapons remain outside the doors, as nothing can be learned at the edge of a blade."

Ugh, it's going to take forever for everyone to disarm themselves, but it's a fair term.

"You have my word and my vow that we will do no violence in your temple," Mikail says.

Unless we have to.

"Follow me, then," she says.

We start walking down the green grass of the cavern. Royo comes up alongside me.

"Don't do that again," he says, taking my hand.

"I didn't plan on falling down a hole, Royo." I laugh. "But noted."

"You scared me," he says.

This man. His words strike a chord in me from the base of my stomach up through my throat. I weave my fingers with his.

"I always want to be by your side," I say. "It's my favorite place in the four realms."

He grips me tight, the same way he laced his fingers with mine in the tent last night. I melt into his side, the same way I did after we fell back exhausted. Together, with Sora and Mikail, there isn't anything the four of us can't do. And now, maybe we'll find answers and a way out of all of this.

CHAPTER FORTY-ONE

SORA

THE TEMPLE OF KNOWLEDGE, GAYA

It takes a while for everyone to disarm themselves outside the temple doors. We're in a cavern under the dead forest, and yet, somehow, we turned a corner and there was a massive stone temple. The doors are black wood—ebony, not charred—just as they were in Khitan, but they aren't nearly as tall or ornate. Then again, this is the side entrance.

I twist my hair. Miracles and horrors. That's what we exist in now.

We leave a pile of blades by the door. Mikail takes his walking stick, and Aeri, of course, has her relics if things go wrong. I also have poison on me.

We pass through the doors and enter a space that's identical to the temple in Khitan. Everyone blinks as we look around. Again, the inside is beautiful with ornate mosaics on the floor and a large fountain in the middle with an altar beneath it. This must have been placed here by a god. Maybe the tree was a decoy or maybe the gods replaced the burned-down temple. It's hard to say.

The keeper and eight other priests silently move around the space. Some sit at tables, transcribing texts; some place volumes on the shelves. Like in Khitan, the shelves are built right into the stone walls. Above us is a second story, and there's a gilded dome at the top.

"How is this possible?" Aeri asks, eyes wide with wonder. "The temple was destroyed. We saw it."

"Alta, praise her name," Mikail whispers. "She and the God of Knowledge."

Braya turns and smiles. She clutches her hands, waiting.

"We need information on the relics of the Dragon Lord," Mikail says. "What happens when they are combined and what occurs if all the remnants are placed on the same person."

"Also, were there ever queens in Yusan?" I ask.

Mikail tilts his head just enough that I know he's questioning why I want that information.

Three priests begin to move as Braya gestures for us to take a seat at a reading table. Mikail and Royo sit facing the door. Aeri and I take the other side.

The first volumes and scrolls they place on the table aren't about the relics, but the history of Yusan. According to the texts, there have been two Baejkin queens over the last thousand years. Also in the texts are detailed accounts of King Theum invading the Temple of Knowledge in Yusan with his palace guard. He erased the history of queens not long after taking the throne. Although he didn't reveal his motivations, priests noted that his sister was very popular and considered a threat to his rule. Conveniently, she later died in childbirth.

I sit back. This wasn't that long ago—King Joon has only been on the throne for twenty years, and his father died after ruling for only ten. The information disappeared just thirty years ago. There are people alive in Yusan who remember that this realm had queens. No wonder I heard whispers about it.

I give Aeri a meaningful glance as I turn the book toward her. But then the priests arrive with scrolls and volumes on the relics.

It's far more than we found in Khitan.

I'm hopeful we can discover what is happening to Aeri and why King Joon wants all of the relics. Except as I read, I find that most of the texts are myth and legend—pure conjecture. The belief is that the Dragon Lord left his relics behind as gifts to the people. But no one knows what happens when all the etherum is reunited. King Joon allegedly had the Flaming Sword in the war with Wei, but he didn't use it. No other ruler has had multiple relics like Aeri. Perhaps the five relics were left on five different lands to make it difficult. Because if the Dragon Lord walks the earth again, that person would be imbued with god powers.

We're about halfway through the scrolls and books when another priest returns to the temple. I continue reading, but there's something strange in the way he's staring at us. He looks at our table and then something in his hands, then stares at us again. His expression fills with outrage.

My stomach sinks—whatever this is, it can't be good.

The priest pulls Braya to the side, and they have a silent but impassioned argument as the priest hits the paper and gestures at us. Mikail shifts in his seat, his eyes alert.

The man has a stockier build and thin gray hair. He strides up to our table, even as Braya silently urges him to stay behind. Mikail gets to his feet, and so does Royo.

"Leave now," the priest demands, his round face turning red.

I'm surprised he's breaking his vow, but he doesn't seem to care.

"You murderers will not use our temple to hide from your crimes," he says.

Which murders? Is this about Berm?

Aeri and I exchange glances as he slaps a piece of paper down. Unsurprisingly, it's a wanted poster. But the rest of it is a shock.

I close my eyes as my stomach twists, a sudden wave of dizziness making the room spin. The king of Yusan is offering a million mun each for our capture. Four million mun total. Because we murdered Tiyung.

CHAPTER FORTY-TWO

AERI

THE TEMPLE OF KNOWLEDGE, GAYA

"You are the ones wanted for murder, are you not?" the priest insists, hitting the table again.

I mean…sure, but we could use more specifics. I turn the poster. There is a decent drawing of me, a very good one of Sora, the same one as before for Euyn, and a good depiction of Mikail. Royo isn't mentioned, which is strange. I don't know whether to be relieved or offended, but the king is offering a million mun each because we supposedly murdered his son, Tiyung.

Sora blanches as she gets to the brutal murder part.

"We didn't kill Tiyung," Royo says. "He was locked up in Idle Prison by King Joon. Ty was our friend."

"We are here seeking knowledge," Sora adds. But her voice shakes.

Mikail looks relaxed but dangerous. "It's rather convenient that Seok is searching for the woman he owns, the two people who possess relics of the Dragon Lord, and the only other man who has a claim to the throne of Yusan, don't you think?"

"I think you are killers who are using a sacred temple to hide from the law," he says.

"So you heard nothing we just said, then?" Mikail sighs, gripping his walking stick. I'm positive he could kill a man with just the case.

Or his bare hands.

Braya, who's been standing off to the side listening, claps once.

The sound reverberates through the temple. Then she claps twice more. The Yoksa, even the one who broke his vow of silence, give her their attention. She points to the main temple doors. The priests walk with their arms out to the sides. They're clearing the space. That means us, too.

We still haven't finished reading, but Sora and I stand. The priests have been welcoming and helpful...up until now, and we don't want to abuse their hospitality. We all leave and enter an enormous cavern, three times the size of the repository room.

"Ronlo," Braya says. "You have broken your vow of silence to the God of Knowledge and are hereby stripped of your status, robes, and access to this temple."

Two priests hold the man's arms as another uses a dagger to cut apart the gray robes. Ronlo is left in a shirt and trousers. But he hands over the key.

"Reveal the location of this temple, and you will also lose your tongue," Braya says. "You are dismissed." She turns and takes a step away.

"You are the one who has broken your vow, Braya," Ronlo says. He pulls his arms from the other priests and fixes the collar of his shirt. "Your vow is to knowledge. Not to this island or its politics. Knowledge. Without passion or prejudice."

"My vow is exactly what I have kept," she says calmly. "The vow to the god is one of protection. When one side seeks to destroy knowledge, there is no neutrality. You may comfort yourself by saying that our oath is without passion or prejudice, but that is in the recording and sharing of all information, not in standing idly by while it burns."

"You allowed criminals safe harbor in a holy place, and the gods will judge you." He's red-faced and yelling as he points a thick finger at her face.

She arches an eyebrow. "You really aren't listening today. See him out."

Two of the priests take Ronlo's arms, and they disappear down one of the many tunnels off this cavern.

I stand outside the temple. What now? I'm not sure if we'll be welcome back, since they know we're wanted criminals. Well... except for Royo.

"You'd best return to your study quickly and be on your way," Braya says.

"We're still allowed in?" Royo asks.

Braya nods. "Knowledge transcends realms, class, or birth. And Ronlo was correct in that it also transcends politics—just not in the way he wished. We don't bend to the political agendas of the rulers of the realms in form or substance. If you heartfully seek knowledge, you are welcome here."

"The priest—the one you disrobed—will he report us to the king's guard?" Mikail asks.

She nods. "Most assuredly."

"Perhaps I should go stop him, then." His fiery sword is still by the other door, but Mikail hardly needs it.

The keeper shakes her head. "No bloodshed, Adoros. That is not how you win the hearts and minds of the island."

He sighs. "How can I do either when people have forgotten who they are?"

She reaches out and cups his cheek in her hand. "You give them something to remember. And not everyone has forgotten. However, we lost a third of our people that day, and our very identity was stripped from us. Grief has cloaked the island and distorted memories ever since. But the gods spared you for a reason. Go to Jeul. Reclaim your birthright, and the people will follow."

"That is easier said than done with four thousand king's guard stationed there," Mikail says.

Braya smiles serenely as she tilts her head. "Oh, Adoros, they were all called to Yusan weeks ago."

CHAPTER FORTY-THREE

TIYUNG

CITY OF TAMNEKI, YUSAN

I walk quickly through the rainy streets and over the canal bridges to reach the blue messenger house. The Tamneki central messenger house is a marvel. It is ten times larger than a standard shop with a parcel exchange, a two-story, glassed-in aviary, and dozens of workers devoted to emptying delivery canisters and sending birds on their way. The eagles are fed hundreds of pounds of fresh meat a day, watered, and rested on a strict schedule. Trained from when they can first fly, they are worth more than any of the humans who care for them and are treated better.

It's still monsoon season, but this house never slows. People come in and out, lines forming to receive and send eagles. There's also a large section to the side for cheaper land courier letters.

I shift my weight, tapping my foot on the marble floor as I wait for my turn at the eagle counter. I don't know if my mother sent a message or if she won't send anything until tonight or even tomorrow. She said to wait here, but surely she didn't know I only have five bronze mun to my name.

But I have to hope.

"May I help you?" the young man asks from behind the counter. He has a brown mustache so thin, I'm not sure why he bothers.

"Are there any letters for Cressen of Pact?" I ask, giving the name of my grandfather.

I drum my fingers on the varnished wood counter as I wait. I try to prepare myself for him to come back empty-handed. To do this again and again until I hear from my mother. I'll need to figure out where to sleep and how to eat on very little money. My empty stomach growls as my nails claw at the counter. The truth is, I don't know how to live that way.

The man returns after a few minutes with a red envelope for me. He then starts counting out gold mun. For the first time in my life, I think about reaching forward and stealing money, but then I remember that messenger houses also forward mun when special tassels are attached to the canisters. Bless my mother's soul—she sent me not only a message but funds to see me through.

She is the cleverest person I know.

I crack the clay. The letter is written in my mother's hand, but it is coded.

"Here you are, sir," the man says. "Fifty gold mun."

Giddiness makes me react too quickly, and I knock over the stack of coins. They clang as they hit the wood, but the man neatly slides the fortune into a little burlap sack. I slip the money into my pocket and give him my five bronze mun as a tip. I should leave, but there may be instructions in the note. I go to the ledge to decipher the code. Large wooden shelves line the walls under the windows.

My mother was my first tutor. She taught me simple coding for private messages, so I immediately recognize the numbers and signs. I take a pencil and paper and start deciphering it.

My son,

My heart rejoiced at seeing your face, but you come at a precarious time. Your father has not recovered from finding your collar and ashes. Joon still lives, and forces plot against us internally and abroad. Please, if you love me, stay away from Qali. Return to Gain now for your own protection. Your father will not abdicate, and I cannot risk you in his schemes. Remember that people with good hearts are but pawns in the games of god kings.

I love you always.

I stand still for a while as I try to process my mother's words. She is worried that I will be used by Seok or killed by his enemies, or both, and she wants me to seek safety. She is warning me that my father is not in his right mind. But I can't return to Gain. Sora and the others could be anywhere, but they are not in Gain. I shake my head. I'm in too deep with them to simply walk away.

After I burn my mother's letter in the messenger house furnace, I meander aimlessly until I find myself in front of the Fountain Inn. I swallow a laugh. Of course I'd come to the place I spent the night with Sora. I cling to any memory of her, but especially this one.

Now that I'm here, though, it's as good a place to stay as any. I walk up to the front desk.

"I'd like a room for the week," I say.

The well-dressed man behind the counter writes in his book with a fountain pen. "Very well, sir. That will be one gold mun for a deluxe suite for six nights."

It's a fantastic sum of money for just a rented room, but I slip a coin out of the sack and pay the man.

"Thank you," he says. "And now if you'd sign your name here for our records."

I take the pen, but I hesitate. If enemies are gathering against my father, I shouldn't use my real name or even my grandfather's. I write down Duri of Gain. I'm sure he won't mind.

The innkeeper nods at the name and then writes something else in the book.

He gestures with his arm out to the lobby. "If you would take a seat, sir, we'll have the servants prepare your room. Once it is ready, we will escort you to room 306."

I nod and then sit in one of the high-backed chairs that face the stairs. A flirtatious servant girl offers me a drink, and I accept a glass of red wine. She makes it clear that there is more on offer if I ask. I don't ask.

I've just taken a sip of the fruity wine when there's a sound I recognize—it's like the chiming of bells. I grip the armrests. I know that laugh. I've heard it several times over the last few weeks from Hana. I turn in my chair and catch that brown hair that matches her eyes. What is she doing here?

And what did she do?

I grit my teeth and let my dagger fall down my sleeve into my hand. Then I shift so I can see her clearly. She's on a settee, flirting with someone young, drunk, and overly important. He might be in the king's guard, or his father has a high administrative position. I hold my breath and listen.

"You must have heard something." She smiles, playfully pushing his shoulder. "I'd lie on fur blankets and be fed cherry water ice for the rest of my days if I had four million." She opens her cloak and leans back dramatically, acting like a silly girl. He enjoys the show.

"We are flooded with leads, but none of them are real. Besides, the poster is very clear that the killers must be brought in alive for there to be a paid bounty."

"I know one of them." She looks around like she's telling a secret. "One of the criminals."

He raises his eyebrows while swirling coju. "You do?"

She takes a sip of water and then eagerly nods. "Mikail, the spymaster."

"If you brought him in somehow, it would be a million mun for your pretty little wishes." He inches his hand closer to her knee.

She exhales, drawing his eye to her breasts as she shifts away from him. "I wouldn't even know where to start, though!"

"Last I heard, everyone is converging on Tamneki. But the four blades fled Rahway and certainly didn't go to Oosant. They have the Water Scepter, so they could have gone anywhere—even Wei. But you shouldn't get involved in our hunt. He's a very dangerous man."

The man's tongue is far too loose, but my gaze is on Hana's face. Something lights in her eyes. She has just figured out where they are. I'm certain of it.

"Would you excuse me? I'm feeling a bit drunk," she says as she stands up.

He stumbles to his feet. "Of course, Tria. I'll wait here."

She smiles flirtatiously. Tria? So she's assumed yet another name. Another disguise. Another lie.

I wait for her to get far down the hall before I follow. Instead of taking the turn for the bathroom, she slinks out the servant exit. I run down the hall and catch the door just before it closes. Then I grab her and slam her against the wall.

"Funny seeing you here," I say with my blade to her throat.

Hana's eyes tell a whole story. She's surprised I'm alive, relieved, and now annoyed, but definitely not afraid. She struggles, and I pin her to the marble facade of the building. She's five foot nine, but I have three inches and muscle on her. I've gained back my strength since escaping from Idle.

"You set me up," I say.

"I did what I had to in order to help Sora. Kill me if you want. I wouldn't do anything different."

She stares into my eyes, her face all resolve, and then she shrugs.

"What do you mean to help Sora? Who were you working with?"
"Rune."

"The western count?" I can feel the ridges in my forehead. "Why?"

"I needed help—a lot of it—when I escaped from your father. The nobleman I was supposed to kill brought me to Count Rune. He helped me get a position as an assassin and then as a spy in Qali.

In return, I worked for him."

"And you still do?"

She nods. "After we fled Idle Prison, and Sora and the others were sent to Khitan, I knew they'd need help. Rune claimed he was working with someone in their group, and he said he could aid them. He knew too much about their whereabouts, their plans, to be lying. I had no choice but to believe him."

I shake my head as she talks in circles. "But what does any of this have to do with me?"

"You were the cost."

My stomach bottoms out, and I loosen my grip on Hana. This whole time, she was probing me for information—not to help Sora but to give to Rune. That's why she wanted to know everything about my father and his businesses. She was pretending to be my friend in order to pay Rune for his assistance.

"He never told me his end goal, but I figured you'd be kidnapped or killed on the Palatial Road." She rights herself but doesn't try to flee. "But look, I'm glad you're alive, and I'm not working for him anymore. He doesn't know where they are."

Every word out of her mouth has been a lie. Heartfelt ones like these.

I gather an irritated breath. "That's reassuring."

Hana looks both ways before she speaks in a low voice. "I think I've figured out where they are. And together, we can help them. They need all the help they can get now."

She must think I'm the biggest fool in the world. She was willing to let me be taken hostage, tortured, or variously killed. There's no reason to believe her. In fact, I should probably use the blade in my hand because she's only a liability. But I'm not a cold-blooded killer like the others, and there had been that look on her face as she talked to the man in the lobby. She had figured it out.

"Where are they?" I ask.

She leans in and whispers in my ear. "I think they're on Gaya."

CHAPTER FORTY-FOUR

ROYO

THE TEMPLE OF KNOWLEDGE, GAYA

So we came all this way and didn't find shit. When they first gave us all these books and scrolls, I thought we'd get some real answers, but instead it's all guesswork and myth. Nobody's used more than one relic. At least not according to the priests. So, there are no answers.

But once the relics are assembled by one person, they think that guy will either become the Dragon Lord or the etherum will call the god down to them. I don't know what the difference is. Either way, the person would have unlimited powers for as long as their body could take being merged with a god. Which can't be that long—minutes, tops.

We didn't find out what is happening to Aeri. And now, I don't know why we thought we would. The Sands of Time was lost until she found it—no one knows what goes on when someone uses it.

I grit my teeth, pushing a book aside. We spent days on this. Now, we have a four-million-gold-mun bounty on us. Or...they got a million on each of them. It's kinda insulting to be left out, but whatever.

The rest of them finish reading and thank the priests, and then we arm ourselves by the doors. We have to go because the other priest is going to rat us out. I don't know why we didn't just kill him, but Mikail let him go.

The visit wasn't a total waste, though. Not for me, anyhow.

I make my way toward Braya as I slide knives back into my vest. I've wanted to talk to her for a while, but I couldn't because of her vow of silence inside the building.

"You really know my father?" I ask.

"I do. He has been the keeper of the temple in Yusan for twenty years now...stars, almost twenty-five. As younger priests, we make a pilgrimage to each temple before we become keepers. I studied at his temple for a year."

Well, that explains the guy walking out. Or at least where he went.

Braya tilts her head while eyeing me. "You look troubled."

"I guess it's good that he's alive. You know him better than I do, is all." I tuck my nunchuka into my belt.

Her brown eyes turn sad as she stares at me. "When the vow to a god comes into conflict with the vow to a family, there are no winners. Our elders instruct young priests not to fall in love, but love is the greatest of human emotions. Your father bled on the altar, and he was chosen by the God of Knowledge to be a keeper. If he didn't honor his vow, his life would have been forfeit."

I raise my eyebrows. This is the first I'm hearing of this shit. It was leave us for the temple or be killed? What kind of fucking choice was that? Was this why my mother always hoped he'd come home? What god holds a guy hostage from his family?

"So all the gods are cruel?" I ask.

Braya shrugs. "They are gods. They reap a price from mortals. As does anything in life."

"It isn't fair," I say.

"Who are we to question them? We are here to serve, not demand. I pray you find peace, Royo."

Peace doesn't seem real likely, but I put my hands to my forehead to salute her.

"If you take that tunnel, veering to the right where it diverges, you will come out at the edge of the northern woods. Only a day's ride from Jeul." Braya shoots Mikail a look.

"Thank you, Braya. But maybe we should stay, because if he revealed the location and the king's guard comes…" Mikail says, his hand on the hilt of his sword.

"Should it come to that, I will tell them that you were here and that I don't know where you are headed next, but you mentioned Tamneki."

Mikail grins. He embraces her arms and then kisses her cheeks. "Peace to you, Braya," he says.

"Give the people something to believe in again, Adoros."

With that, we get to walking. We lost all of our supplies when we fell down the tree hole, but we'll move a lot faster down here. The tunnels have green grass and are bright as day. None of this is normal, but what's been normal since I met Aeri?

We stay alert, but there's nobody else down here. When the smooth stone forms arches giving us two paths, we stick to the right. The compass in my palm says we're going every which way, but I don't think it's a trap. These are just winding tunnels.

I plod on, wishing I'd asked Braya a lot more questions. Had my father ever mentioned me or my mother? What was he like as a man? Was he funny or was he strict? Did he like tuhko? Did he ever regret the choice he made? But the moment's already gone, and I'm on to the next thing. That's life—chances that pass you by create regret.

Apparently, we're going to go capture a city—the old capital of Gaya. Did I even hear that right? We're just four people, even if two of us have god magic.

"What's the plan?" I ask. "We sacking cities now? The four of us?"

Mikail smiles. "No, we're going to Jeul, and I'm going to give the people something to believe in." He stares at his walking stick.

What the fuck does that mean?

I side-eye him, and there's that look again. He's coming up with something that will either work or get us all killed—maybe both.

But I don't got better ideas.

Aeri traipses alongside me, every now and then bending to touch the grass. She puts her hand in mine. She smiles, and the little hairs on the back of my neck rise as I look at her. While I'd die for Mikail's schemes without much bellyaching, I won't let him hurt Aeri. Deep down, I know he would use her powers to win—even if it killed her. I can't let that happen.

"You're going to impress these people by yourself?" I ask.

Mikail lifts an eyebrow. "Unless someone else has royal Gayan blood they haven't disclosed yet, yes."

I think we've all had enough of hidden royalty.

"How are you gonna do that?" I ask.

"I'm going to use the Water Scepter to inspire the people, drown Governor Yong, and take back my house." He says it the way someone says they're going to have a picnic, a beer, and then a swim.

"What about the soldiers?" Sora asks. She also eyes Mikail like he's lost his mind. The relic is taking a bigger toll on him than he's admitting. Maybe he's mad now.

Fuck. That would be the last thing we'd need.

Mikail grins. "Don't you remember the note Quilimar read? Gayan troops were at her border in Khitan. They aren't in Jeul."

CHAPTER FORTY-FIVE

MIKAIL
CITY OF JEUL, GAYA

The long tunnel led us to carved stone stairs that ended in another hollowed-out tree. A few steps later, we left the sacred woods behind and walked onto the Perimeter Road, the main roadway that circles the Gayan coast. I knew exactly where the road would be because I used to study maps of Gaya when I would get homesick as a boy.

"You don't mind that I look?" I asked Ailor as I pored over his war maps.

"It is your home," he said. "One day, you'll return again, Mikail—you should know it." He rested a warm hand on my shoulder.

"But you're my home as well," I said.

He smiled, true joy shining in his brown eyes. "Then you will always have two."

I take a breath as we ride into Jeul. I don't know where Ailor is, and I'm not sure what awaits me in the old capital.

We stopped overnight in the small town of Bramble. We were worn out from the day of walking, and we needed horses for the remainder of the trip. After a hot meal and a good night's sleep, I felt ready, but as we approach the ancient city walls of Jeul, I'm suddenly not as certain.

It's not that I doubt my ability to murder the governor, and he certainly has it coming—Gaya has suffered under his long rule, the people riddled with addiction, poverty, and constantly at the mercy of Yusanian soldiers. No, it's that I'm uncertain of how the Gayan people will react. Will my own people stand by me? Or will they be like the innkeeper in Berm? Do I have a home anywhere?

I grip the reins and hang my head. I've dealt with more than anyone should endure, and I have survived it, but I don't know that I could handle the heartbreak of losing Gaya—of Gambria being right.

"We're with you," Aeri says, looking over at me.

"To the bloody end," Sora adds.

Royo nods, too.

Then I remember that this is home. Right where I am now, wherever the three of them are.

I lift my chin as we pass the fortress. The soldiers are the scourge of the island. Not all the king's guard went to the war of the realms, but the fort is barely manned. My estimate is that they left a skeleton crew of five hundred, maybe a thousand soldiers for the whole island, and most oversee the laoli production on the northern end. Those numbers would be easily overwhelmed if the people are with us.

Are they?

I look around as we pass through the city gate. It's both familiar and not. I grew up not in Jeul but a small village outside of it. The old capital is the largest city on the island, and it could rival Umbria or Quu with its size and bustling feel.

We're not far inside Jeul when there, in the town square, are our faces. An enormous wanted poster hangs in the center, featuring life-size drawings of the three of us and Euyn. But I barely notice it because up on the hill, visible from any part of the city, is Rose Palace. The colonnaded white marble marvel was built by Alta and was the ancestral home of the Miats.

My house, occupied by usurpers for years.

I spur my horse, and we take the sun-brick streets toward Keen Hill.

"So what now? Are we knocking on the door?" Royo asks, riding beside me.

"Don't be silly," I say. "I'm going to make a scene in the backyard until the governor comes out to face me."

"Oh good," he says, running a hand down his face.

None of them like the idea, but I do have a plan. Keen Hill is steep. It's not nearly as large as Oligarch Mountain, but it's the highest point in the middle of the city, visible from any part of Jeul. And I will use that.

As I said to Royo, we can't just go to the front door of the palace. The grounds are guarded and patrolled like any of the counts' villas. There have been numerous threats on the governor's life over the last nineteen years. The city never warmed to the idea of a Yusanian living in the royal palace. Yet Gambria was told differently...allegedly.

Outside Rose Palace are the most beautiful terraced gardens in the world, and in the middle is the Fountain of Life. That's where we need to go.

We ride until we reach the groundskeeper's cottage near the base of the hill. Although all of Keen is technically palatial grounds, this area shouldn't be monitored much, as it's for workers and servants. We dismount and tie up the horses.

I've just tightened the knot when an older Gayan man comes around the nearest hedge. He's probably sixty years old, clean-shaven, and wearing trousers with a white shirt. He has wrinkles and freckles on his brown skin.

"Who goes there?" he says.

"Fugitives from Yusanian justice," I say in Gayan.

It's a gamble. He could call out an alarm, but I have to know what he—what the people—thinks of Yusan. Especially those old enough to remember the Festival of Blood.

"There is no such thing as Yusanian justice," he says. He stops and squints an eye at me. Recognition flashes after a moment. He knows me from the wanted poster. "What do you want here, son?"

"I'm going to kill the governor and free this island." I hold my breath, waiting for his response.

"Very well. Be on your way, then," he says with a nod.

Shock and joy fill my chest. I put my hands to my forehead. "Thank you, Uncle."

Aeri tilts her head, confused, but I gesture to the three of them, and we hurry up the base of the terraced gardens, scaling the four-foot retaining walls.

We've climbed two levels when footsteps approach. I put out my arm, and we stop behind a tall hedge. Readiness fills my limbs, my body preparing for the kill, but the patrolman continues down the path. We could take him out easily, but I don't want to murder Gayans unless I have to, and I don't want to kill anyone before I get to the fountain.

We scale another level. Seconds later, we all have to dive down behind flower bushes. I mistimed it, and a guard walking his patrol came too close. I breathe in the floral-and-dirt smell, my hand on the hilt of my sword, waiting, but his boots stomp past us.

My heart drums steadily with the anticipation, but I can't just murder the governor with my sword. I have to make a scene of it. I must let this island know that the Miats survived. It would be easier if I had the real Flaming Sword. If I had the Gayan relic, I could send fire arcing over the palace. I grind my teeth at another part of our identity stripped away by Yusan. I will pry the relic from Joon's dead body before this is all over. I swear and I vow it.

Enough on that for now, though. I have the Water Scepter, and that is enough.

Once the next guard is far enough away, we run to the spring of Alta. I take the Water Scepter out of the case. The golden staff vibrates in my palm, calling to my mind, eager for my command.

I'm ready.

CHAPTER FORTY-SIX

TIYUNG

CITY OF JEUL, GAYA

Hana and I left the Fountain Inn for Gaya as soon as the sun came up. We landed on the colony island less than two bells later at the Port of Charm.

It's been interesting traveling with Hana again. It's almost as if nothing happened because there's not much to say. She wanted to help Sora, and she was willing to sacrifice me to do it. Maybe I should be outraged, and I might be, if it had been for a different cause. However, I'd also do anything to help Sora, so it's hard to be too offended.

We arrived in Jeul a few bells ago, and our new problem became obvious as soon as we entered the ancient city. Jeul is the old capital from when Gaya was the fourth realm. It is deceptively large—probably around the size of Gain but not as sprawling. Right in the middle of the town square, a huge wanted poster hangs on the wall with their names and faces on it. As soon as I saw it, I realized that if Sora and the others are on this island, they must be in hiding. Maybe not Royo, because he was left off the poster, but otherwise, they have to be lying low. Four million is too much money for people not to turn them in. I'm not sure how we're ever going to find them.

I've only been to Gaya once before with my father. Half of the island is charm fields, and laoli is the colony's main export, but even though Gaya is a part of Yusan, it's not quite the same. The style of dress is unique; the food and architecture are different as well.

With no leads, it seems like we'll be here for a while. Hana and I visit the open-air market. She has supplies, but she needs new clothes to better fit in. The women mostly wear wrap dresses, the men short-sleeved shirts and trousers.

As we walk along the stalls. It's nice to get a break from the constant rain and chill of the monsoon season, but, of course, I'm hungry. I let my nose lead me. The food on offer is a mix of Yusanian and traditional Gayan, and the people are a mix, too. I get a plate of oyster noodles and follow Hana to the seamstress tables.

I thought everyone here spoke Yusanian, but as the shoppers converse with one another, they're using old Gayan. I studied the four original languages, but I never achieved fluency in Gayan because it's thought of as a dead language. The official language of the island has been Yusanian for two hundred years, but the tongue remains like that never happened, which is interesting.

Hana's theory that Sora and the others came to Gaya was based on the difference between the official Yusanian story and the reality of this land. Gaya is supposed to be a docile colony, but Hana said there is constant rebel activity, especially in this part of the island. Mikail would've known that as spymaster, and he could be trying to tap into allies sympathetic to their cause. At least they'd have a much better chance here than in Yusan proper.

Still, Hana seems…nervous, twisting her hair and jumping back when she sees someone with long black locks.

"Are you all right?" I ask.

She nods, but then she dabs her forehead. "It's just this heat."

"Let's find an inn, then," I say, finishing my plate.

We leave the market the way we came, but we're stopped at the edge of a large crowd. Thousands of people have gathered in the town square. I strain my neck, trying to see what they're looking at. Yusan sometimes hangs or whips criminals in the square, and it is always an event. I struggle to get a better view, but then I realize every single person is looking up.

One man stands on the palace hill by a fountain. He has a golden scepter in his hand, and he is making water shoot into the air and then flow unnaturally in shapes around him. The water circles and then bends and breaks to form a frothy tree in the air. The crowd whispers with praises of Alta. She is an earth goddess who founded Gaya the same way the Sky King lived in Khitan and the Dragon Lord ruled Yusan.

"Well, I think we've found them," Hana says. One corner of her lips rises into a smirk.

"What do you mean?" I ask.

She gestures to the man wielding the scepter. I can't make out who he is, but off to the side, two women and a man wait. And one has long dark hair like Sora, but we can't see anyone's face clearly from here.

"You don't recognize him?" she says. I shake my head no. "That's Mikail."

I stare up at the hill.

"He's using the Water Scepter of the Dragon Lord?" I thought a person had to be royal to wield the relics, and Mikail is a commoner.

"It's a long story, but yes." She pauses and smiles. "He must be the real lost prince of Gaya."

CHAPTER FORTY-SEVEN

SORA

ROSE PALACE, GAYA

Mikail pants as he pulls the Water Scepter out of the spring. The toll from manipulating the water with precision like this must be great, but Mikail barely seems fazed aside from his breathing. Instead, he faces the palace, waiting. The governor, two assistants, and a cadre of guards approach us. Mikail stands casually, locking eyes with Governor Yong.

He mentioned that the governor has been the same since the end of the Festival of Blood, which means he oversaw the subjugation of the entire island. The man is around my height with gray hair, darker skin, and an active build. He wears a suit that's a blend of traditional Yusanian and Gayan with a collar of onyx spanning his chest. He's not a nobleman, but because he rules Gaya, he has the same power as the counts. Maybe more.

Mikail stares at him, his eyes brimming with hate. I hold my breath.

"What is the meaning of all this?" the governor asks.

"I am Adoros Miat," he says. "You are trespassing on my family's home and this island. Flee now or die."

His voice echoes in the warm air. No one reacts until the governor starts to laugh. His men immediately join in.

"Do away with him." Governor Yong gestures dismissively with his fingers.

The ten guards draw their swords.

Royo grabs his new axe, pulling it from the strap on his back. Aeri stands with her hands out, her golden eyes waiting for a signal from Mikail. I slide both daggers into my palms. But it's Mikail who acts first. He stares at the guards as he places the scepter back into the spring.

Then he smiles.

Rather than forming a tree or another shape, this time, the liquid disappears from the fountain basin. I'm not sure what he is doing until the thirteen men in front of us start falling on their knees, clawing at their throats and chests. Their eyes bulge out, and a few of them vomit water, but the rest turn red and then purple.

Mikail is drowning them on dry land.

I didn't know the scepter could do that.

The men are crawling, desperately trying to breathe, but it's hopeless. They make gurgling sounds as their lungs fill with water. I don't want to feel sympathy for them, because I know what they've done. But I hope they meet Lord Yama quickly.

The governor gets the closest, crawling and pleading for mercy with his hands clasped, but Mikail doesn't break focus until they are all dead. Then he swings the scepter out. He jabs at the spring again, and a rush of water sprays up in the air. I crane my neck as Mikail sends tons of water miles above us into the clouds, and then slowly, the water falls down on Jeul as frozen little crystals.

He just made it snow on the tropical island.

A cheer rises from below us, and we turn and look down. There, gathered in the town square, are thousands of Gayans who just watched Mikail murder the governor like he was no different from common guards.

Mikail raises the Water Scepter in the air, and that draws another cheer from the crowd. He beams with sweat, but his face now glows with exuberance. A chill shakes me as I watch him bask in their adoration. It's a smile and an expression I haven't seen before. There's both hunger and satisfaction written on his face. He needs their love, but the allegiance of a people is a tricky thing. Yusan commands through might, Wei uses religion, and Khitan gives equality. What will sway the people here? Will freedom be enough?

My heart sinks. Somehow, I don't think so.

Mikail turns away first. He looks at the three of us.

"Let me show you my home." He smiles as he steps over the dead bodies. We all follow.

"Yusan changed the gardens," he says. "They used to grow food in colorful rows on half of these slopes, and the Miats would have a ceremonial first harvest dedicated to Alta. They would open the doors of the palace and feed whoever came, regardless of their birth. They'd all drink from the Fountain of Life. The spring runs from here down to the seven fountains in the city and provides water for all of Jeul, but the fountain is where Alta pressed her finger into the earth and made fresh water."

I listen, rapt, but then I remember that Mikail was only five when he left Gaya, so almost everything he's saying isn't what he remembers but what he has read. Yet he speaks with the passion of having seen and lived a life here. I suppose I'd talk the same way about Inigo. All our homes disappeared when we were children, in one way or another, so we cling to memories and stories. It doesn't make them any less ours, but it also may not be correct.

Five more guards come running toward us from the palace. Mikail shifts the scepter to his left hand and grabs his sword hilt with his right. Royo readies his axe. Instead of attacking, though, the guards take a knee from yards away.

They say something in Gayan, and Mikail responds. The guards then utter something as one.

"They are pledging their loyalty to me," Mikail explains.

"How can we be sure they'll be loyal?" Royo whispers. I'm not sure if he's talking to Aeri or Mikail, but it's a good question.

Mikail shrugs. "We can never be sure of anyone's loyalty, but I'll take even the show of it." He turns to the guards. "Go tear down the poster in the square and let the people know that their lost prince, Adoros Miat, has returned."

The guards salute him. Three leave and two stay.

"Welcome home, Your Majesty," one man says. He's around thirty, maybe thirty-five, and clean-shaven with very short black hair and an almost square jaw.

"What is your name?" Mikail asks.

"I am Teo, and this is my brother, Calier." He points to a man a couple of years younger who has blue eyes but wears an eyepatch on his left. "We were and remain loyal to the true Gaya."

"And how did you survive the Festival of Blood?" Mikail asks.

There's a subtle but dangerous shift in Mikail. If either of these men answers incorrectly, he'll kill them where they stand. I'm certain of it.

"We are both from Hallan," Teo says. "The slaughter ended before Yusan reached us, but not the destruction."

The sad memory of the burning of the woods plays out on their faces.

"I am going to rid this island of its oppressor," Mikail says. "Yusan will be thrown out. We will be our own realm once again and forever."

"You have our swords," Calier says.

They both place their blades on the ground and back up a step, taking a knee with their heads lowered.

Mikail touches each of their shoulders, accepting their submission.

"Do you want us to burn the bodies?" Teo asks.

Mikail glances at the men he just killed. "Not the governor—I have plans for him, but otherwise, yes."

I'm about to ask about those plans when two people come running into the garden. A man and a woman. I know exactly who they are, and yet they can't be, because Hana and Tiyung are both dead.

I start to laugh. I'm fresh out of room for more emotions and probably out of my mind, but it's uncontrollable. The giddiness spreads through my heart like blown poison in the wind.

"Sora?" Aeri says.

Her eyebrows knit, and she looks very concerned for my sanity. And she should be. I'm seeing ghosts. Mentally cracking was the last thing I needed, but I suppose this is what happens when you don't sleep or properly deal with grief.

I gesture in the ghosts' direction. Aeri looks that way, and her mouth falls open.

"Oh gods," she says.

"Ten Hells. Ty?" Royo asks.

Wait, Royo sees them, too? He must be cracking as well.

"Zahara?" Mikail says. "Tiyung?"

No, we can't all be seeing ghosts. Not the same ghosts in the same place. The world begins to spin. The next thing I know, I'm crumpling to the ground.

CHAPTER FORTY-EIGHT

AERI

ROSE PALACE, GAYA

We get Sora to the portico after she fainted in the garden. I say *we*, but really Royo picks her up as I fuss over her. Royo lays her down on a sculptural couch under the enormous colonnaded portico that encircles the palace. Servants who must've been watching the entire scene bring out a pitcher of water, glasses, and a washcloth for her head. Mikail thanks them.

Tiyung and the girl Mikail called Zahara follow us. It's immediately cool and comfortable in the shade of the palace. They both look terribly concerned for Sora, though.

I walk over to Ty and wrap him in a hug. "I'm so glad you're free and…alive. We thought you didn't make it. I'm glad it was just a lie." Then I turn my attention to the girl. "Hi. I don't know you. I'm Aeri."

The woman is stunningly beautiful. Not like Sora or Sun-ye, but she's around the same age and something entirely her own. Her thick brown hair is the same color as her eyes, and she has full, rose-pink lips and perfect sandy-brown skin. She's around my height, but she looks taller because she's all curves in the right places, where I am a fancy twig.

"Hello," she says hesitantly. "I'm Hana."

"What?" My voice comes out as a squawk. It can't be what I'm thinking. The girl Sora loved in poison school was named Hana. This woman is pretty enough to be a poisoner, but Hana died two years ago. This can't be the same person. Then again, how many gorgeous women named Hana does Sora know?

Mikail stops staring at the doors to the palace and turns his head. "Hana?"

"You know me as Zahara, but my real name is Hana," she says. "I changed it when I fled from Gain."

So, she is the same Hana. My eyes widen so much they hurt. Shocked is an understatement.

Well, that explains why Sora fainted.

"Can someone tell me what the fuck is going on?" Royo asks. He's been dabbing Sora's forehead with the cloth. It makes my heart overflow to see him be so gentle, so caring. The way he's taking care of Sora is the same way he handled that little ceramic bird when I first met him. I want to jump all over him, but I hold myself back.

Sora moans, coming to. I pour a glass of water for her and another for Mikail.

Sora's lashes flutter, and then she opens her eyes. I hold out the glass of water.

"Oh, thank you, Aeri," she says. "I'm sorry. I just got very dizzy."

"Are you sure you're okay?" I ask.

Sora nods and starts to sit up. But then she looks past me to Tiyung and Hana. She lies back down.

"No, never mind. I'm still seeing things." She puts her arm over her eyes. "It's concerning."

"No," I say. "They're both really here—Tiyung and Hana."

She shakes her head, and then tears slide down her cheeks as she sniffles. "They can't be, Aeri. They can't. They're both dead!"

"Let's bring her inside," Mikail says. He looks past us to the garden where they're building a funeral pyre over the top of the large firepit. It's going to smell like charred flesh soon, and that won't help anyone feel better.

I put my shoulder down to help Sora stand.

"Don't bother," Royo says. He hands me his axe and lifts Sora like she's a feather pillow. Again, my heart flutters, and I'm having truly inappropriate thoughts. I shake them off and follow along, holding the axe sideways.

I keep a look out for soldiers, but they must be near the laoli fields and not here.

Mikail leads us into the palace. The space is massive and full of windows. It has a greenhouse feel with two floors and an entryway that reaches all the way up to the very high ceiling.

The household staff of around forty people races to meet us as soon as we walk in. They all take a knee to Mikail. He speaks in Yusanian as he pardons them for serving the enemy and accepts them as his servants. I'm sure when this was a palace, they had a far larger staff, but it's been the home of just one man for almost twenty years.

This palace is built around a large courtyard with trees, flowers, and a fountain trickling into a central pool. The floors are black wood, as are the doors, and the rest is white rock. Because we came in through the garden, we must be in the private wing, and there's a large sunken living room in front of us. The six of us sit on the white couches and chairs. Well, Sora is half lying down, half sitting where Royo placed her. I take the loveseat next to her, and Royo sits so close to me that our legs touch. I look at him and smile, but we are all silent for a moment.

"I think I'm going to need explanations of how you're both alive," Mikail says, drinking a second glass of water. He points to Hana and Ty, and his arm shakes.

"We could use the same, honestly," Tiyung says. He speaks to Mikail, but his eyes dart over to Sora constantly. She still has her arm over her eyes.

Mikail nods. "Of course, but you first."

Tiyung nods and sits forward. "All right. I'll start right from when I left you. As you know, I was sentenced to Idle Prison. I thought I knew what that would be like, but I had no idea about the horrors waiting for me..."

CHAPTER FORTY-NINE

TIYUNG

ROSE PALACE, GAYA

I didn't realize how much there was to say until it all poured out of me. I tried to remember every detail of my captivity, especially my conversations with Ailor, but I made sure to give Mikail his father's message—that he loved him and he was the last thing Ailor thought of. Well, I tried to relay it. My voice cracked with tears and grief, and at times I had to stop and gather myself. Once I finished, Mikail stood and stared out the window, watching the funeral pyre burn.

Hana took over, starting from being purchased by Seok along with her brother, Nayo, to needing Rune's help after she faked her own death. Then she detailed our journey from Idle Prison to the Khitanese border and why we turned around and went back to Qali. I described what happened with my mother and how I found Hana in Tamneki. Then we explained why we thought to come here.

Together, we spoke for two bells. The others had questions for us, but really, surprisingly few, given all we said. I suppose we covered everything.

Aeri and Royo then told us what happened when they were sent to Khitan, the sad death of Prince Euyn, and all the places they've been since they fled from Quu Harbor. Neither Mikail nor Sora said anything.

We've all been sitting silently for a few minutes. It's a lot to process in every direction, but I can't take my eyes off Sora. She's really here. She's in turmoil, but she survived. Her heart is beating. Gratitude to the gods for sparing her spills over in my chest. With every breath, there's renewed hope for the future.

"So if what Hana said was true, Fallador was a traitor working for Rune this whole time?" Royo says, leaning forward.

Royo stares at Hana. I can tell he doesn't trust her, but it is difficult to trust a spy who just admitted to betraying everyone.

"It appears so," Mikail says. He retakes his seat. The only sign he's annoyed is how he clutches the arm of the chair. There's something off about him. For the first time, his hands are shaking. I think he's in pain, but then again, he just found out his father was murdered in Idle Prison.

Household servants arrive with food and drinks. It's a strange time for a meal, but maybe Gaya has different customs.

A pretty girl places a wine goblet and a plate of figs with honey and cheese in front of Mikail. The rest of the food is on trays and spread over the low stone tables. The servants then disappear as quickly as they came.

The six of us stare at the food we didn't ask for. It looks delicious, and my stomach rumbles even though I ate in the market.

Mikail eyes his plate.

"Don't eat that," Hana says. She was watching all the servants as soon as they came in.

He raises an eyebrow and passes the plate and goblet over to Hana. She sniffs them, the tip of her nose nearly touching the gray stoneware.

"They're both poisoned," she says.

Sora finally moves her arm away from her head. Her eyes are red from crying, but it still lights my chest with joy to see her face. She sits up and wordlessly gestures with her hand out. Hana gives her the goblet and plate. Sora sniffles twice and then gives up on clearing her nose. She takes a small sip of the wine.

"Xitcia poison," she says. "A lot of it. It's the type of toxin that causes euphoria before it kills you."

"It's in the honey, too," Hana says.

Hana and Sora taste the rest of the food, but nothing else was poisoned. Just what was meant for Mikail. Their lost royal.

Kingdom of Hells, that's somehow much worse than the staff trying to kill all of us.

Shock ripples through our group, and everyone eventually looks at Mikail. The tension claws at my skin, but his expression is neutral, almost amused.

His jaw ticks. "It appears I have some disloyal servants. Excuse me for a moment while I deal with this."

The five of us sit silently as he leaves the room. He's barely announced himself as royalty, and already someone has tried to kill him. I suppose I know better than most how people target those at the top, but this is particularly rapid.

"You're alive," Sora says.

I'm honestly not sure if she's talking to me or Hana.

"Yes," we both say.

Sora blinks, then focuses on Hana.

"I cried for you. I mourned you and prayed to the Kingdom of Hells for your soul. And you were alive this whole time."

Hana closes her eyes slowly. "I know, Sora."

"Not one word in two years. Not a letter or a hair ribbon to let me know you survived. Not even a blank card from Khitan, which I would've known was from you. Nothing to let me know you weren't dead, no thought to release me from my grief."

"Sora... I couldn't risk it."

Sora shakes her head. "You didn't *want* to because I didn't mean enough to you. I'm glad you survived and that Tiyung freed your brother."

She speaks without any emotion. Her words are plain but cut to the quick.

Hana sits straight and absorbs the impact. Her face is impassive, although her lower lip quivers just a little. Aeri reaches over and takes Sora's hand. I want to do the same with Hana, but she did just try to sell me out, and she devastated the woman we both love. Sora would never lash out in anything other than pain, but I feel the same kind of hurt that Hana does right now. Sora has barely acknowledged that I'm here. I didn't expect her to run into my arms, but I thought she'd have some kind of reaction to me being alive. Instead, she's only thinking about Hana.

I try not to let that sting. Sora owes me nothing.

"Why come to me now?" she says. "You'd moved on with your new life and forgotten me. What is it you want?"

"I never forgot you, Sora," Hana says. "I never could. But when I found out that you'd gotten swept up in the king's plan, I wanted to help you. He's still alive. We saw the Weian warships heading to Tamneki. One flew the Yusanian flag and another the Khitanese flag."

The group all shifts around to face her.

"You're positive?" Aeri asks. She sits forward, and Royo rests a protective hand on her back. "My father survived?"

I raise my eyebrows. Hana told me that King Joon was Aeri's father, but it's hard to believe. There's no resemblance, and I thought she was one of us. In the end, she did choose to double-cross her own father, so I see why they forgave her. It also makes sense that she has the ring and the amulet—only those with royal blood can wield them.

"We're positive," I say. "We saw the ships from the Coastal Road before they turned out of range of Yusan's scouts. They were Weian warships, but the front ship flew a Yusanian flag. The fleet should reach Tamneki in a day or two, if they haven't already."

For my family, the war will be a disaster, as my father will be exposed as a liar and a usurper. But the people of Yusan will be the ones who ultimately pay the price. Over two hundred thousand people live in Tamneki. It will be as bad as the War of the Flaming Sword, when Wei took their revenge on the capital.

It might be worse.

I'm thinking about the blood cost of men's ambitions when there's a sharp, high-pitched scream from the other side of the palace. It came from the direction Mikail went in. Alone. We all stand, grab our weapons, and then we run.

CHAPTER FIFTY

ROYO

ROSE PALACE, GAYA

Why the fuck did we let Mikail go alone? Yeah, he has the scepter, and yes, he's deadly, but he's still one guy. Enough people, and they could get the jump on him.

We don't learn a thing.

We sprint past the courtyard with its roses, then past the massive empty throne room, huge banquet hall, and shiny ballroom to the other side of the palace.

Fuck, why are we always running someplace?

But we don't stop until we get to the servant quarters where the sound came from. We reach an intersection and idle. No one knows which hall to take, but then there's another short scream. The five of us race toward the sound, flying into the kitchens.

I run in, my heart pounding, my muscles ready to swing my axe. But as we push through the doors, we're just in time to see Mikail slit the throat of a third woman. Two already lie dead on the ground, their blood flowing into the drains.

Well, at least that explains the screaming.

I lower my axe.

"I thought you weren't going to kill anybody," I say.

Mikail's eyebrows go up. "When did I ever say that?"

He dumps the girl onto the floor. She lands clutching her throat but bleeding out on top of the others. She's the one who served him the poisoned plate.

The three guards Mikail had sent into town show up at the outside kitchen entrance. Mikail wipes the blood off his sword and sheathes it as they take in the scene.

"Attempted regicide by poisoning." Mikail points to the women and curls his lip with disgust.

"We'll add them to the funeral pyre, then," one of the guards says. He snaps his fingers, and the other guards get to work moving the first body out.

Mikail turns to the rest of the household staff. Three dozen or so huddle together on the other side of the kitchens. "The rest of you may continue to serve me, but you now know the cost of treason. I will free this island and bring glory to the realm. Gaya will be independent again, but I cannot do it alone. And it won't happen if I can't be safe in my own house. Be loyal or leave now."

The staff shuffles back into the palace, except the ones who work in the kitchens. I don't know how many will quit—they'd be announcing themselves as traitors, but it would be better than bleeding out on the floor.

Mikail leans with his palms against a steel table. His whole body shakes as he grips the edge. What's happening to him?

I look at Aeri, whose eyebrows are raised in concern. Sora takes a step closer, but then Mikail relaxes. Everybody pretends like nothing happened as he drinks a glass of water rimmed with salt and filled with limes. He doesn't complain, but it's clear he's in a lot of pain— in his head and body.

"Hana, are you still working for Rune?" he asks.

She shakes her head. "No. Have a man follow me, if you want proof. I have nothing to hide. When you escaped from Rahway, Rune stopped being useful to me, and our deal was off. The only reason I gave him information was because I wanted to help you and Sora."

I rub my temples. These scheming women make my head hurt, too.

"Lie to me, and I promise you'll end up like them," Mikail says, gesturing to the two women still on the floor. He sounds more exhausted than anything else.

He steps toward us and then stops by Hana. "Come with me. We have other things to discuss."

She nods and follows him. Sora watches her leave out of the corner of her eye, but she doesn't say anything.

The four of us stand quietly in the kitchen.

"Well, I could use a bath," Aeri says. She slaps her hands against her legs.

I turn and look at her—always the weirdest person in a room. She stares back at me and darts her eyes over to the doors. She wants us to leave. I look at who's left, and I realize she wants to give Sora and Tiyung a minute alone. They haven't spoken since he showed up here, and I'm sure there's plenty to say.

"I'll scope out the room," I say.

Aeri smiles that joyful grin, and my chest feels lighter. She brushes against me as we pass through the doors. That spark I feel when we touch flows along my body. It's almost enough to make me forget that fresh blood continues to trickle down the drains.

CHAPTER FIFTY-ONE

SORA

ROSE PALACE, GAYA

eri and Royo rush out of the kitchen in the least subtle way possible, and that leaves me alone with Tiyung. I haven't even been able to process the fact that he's standing in front of me. Or that he's here at all. He died in Idle Prison, and I had accepted that. Well, not entirely, but I knew it as a fact. The same way I knew Hana was dead. And Daysum. The same way I knew my parents sold us.

I press my hand to my forehead. I don't even know what's real anymore.

"Are you actually here?" I ask.

"I am, Sora." He takes a step closer to me, and I lean away. He reaches his hands out but keeps his distance, which is good. I don't think I could handle him touching me right now.

"I don't understand," I say.

He told us the whole story in the living room, and everything made sense, but it all still feels like a fever dream. Like the vivid dreams Daysum had as a child.

And now I wonder: Is she even dead? I want to hope she isn't, but in my heart, I know she is.

The kitchen staff busies themselves cleaning up the blood. Within moments, it's clear we're in the way, and Tiyung gestures for me to follow him out. We leave the kitchens and the servant quarters and enter the main palace. This place is unlike anywhere I've been before, with the outside blended inside from the cool stone walls to the fragrant flowers. It's both grand and earthy. Undoubtedly the home of a god, yet natural.

Tiyung tries the first door we come across, and it opens to a study. On second thought, it's not a study but a war room. The main feature is an enormous central table. Tiyung lights the lamps because it's pretty dim in the green-painted room, even with the rays from the sunset streaking in through the windows.

On the table, there's a map of the island with figurines of soldiers and arms. Most of the soldiers are off the island, sent to Khitan. A map of the four realms occupies the entire western wall. Books and scrolls line the eastern wall, and there is a bureau with ten drawers that I imagine are also full of strategic maps.

But I don't care about strategy at the moment. I stare at Tiyung from across the war table. He seems different, but I can't put my finger on how. His eyes are the same shade of blue, his black hair is short the way it was, but his air, his manner is different.

Yet I know it's him standing in front of me. First Hana, and now him.

"I'm sorry," I say, lowering my chin. "This is a lot."

He nods, looking a little disappointed, but then he clears the expression. "It is, Sora. Today has been a great shock for you. I was so excited to see you that I hadn't considered what you would feel on seeing both of us again. But I had to find you. You are what saved me in prison."

"Me?" I ask.

He slips a card out of his pocket. It's dirty, and the paper has been bent and wrinkled dozens of times, but I know my own hand. It is the message I sent to his father when we first arrived in Khitan. I was trying to tell him that the plan to kill King Joon failed and Tiyung was in prison.

Tiyung slips the note back into his pocket, unwilling to part with the letter.

"I knew you were alive and still trying to help me," he says. "It was enough to get me through the darkest times."

He shudders, and I realize that's the difference—Tiyung is more haunted, less convinced of the goodness in the world.

He's more like me.

I sigh. "I couldn't even think about what you were going through."

Shame floods me, sending heat into my cheeks. I was all he thought about, and I couldn't bring myself to think about the realities of Idle Prison.

"Of course not," he says. "You were on a very dangerous mission. You still are. But I'm with you now, Sora. Whatever comes our way."

He takes a step closer to my side of the table. A part of me wants to fall into him. I missed him, and I'm so tired of being strong. I wouldn't have to keep holding myself together if I fell into him, because he'd wrap me in his arms. But I stand straight. I can't—for so many reasons.

"Your father killed Daysum," I say.

He draws a breath. "I know he sold her to Lord Sterling. And Hana told me when she died."

"He was responsible," I say.

He nods. "I know. I'm so sorry, Sora. I wish I could've done something, anything to have prevented it. I wish I could have found her indenture or smuggled her away to Khitan. I should've. I could've done so much more. It's as much my own failure to act as anything else."

It isn't his fault—not at all. But I don't have the grace or kindness to say that aloud. Not now. Not when it comes to her.

"I'm going to kill him." I stare at Tiyung, waiting for a reaction.

He blinks but doesn't break eye contact. "I know."

I search his face, still handsome despite the broken nose that was never properly set. But that can't be it—that can't be his full reaction to me wanting to murder his father.

"Seok is who he allowed himself to become," Tiyung says as his fingers trace along the map. His expression is grave, his forehead lined. "I don't pretend that he's a good man. To ask you for mercy for someone who never showed you a drop of kindness isn't fair. I know who you are, and I know who he is. I also know what he deserves."

I'd forgotten this side of Tiyung. How reasonable and fair he can be. This is why Mikail wanted him on the throne—because, in the end, he is a good person with a kind heart. He grew to be different from the soil he was raised in.

He is not his family.

"What do we do now?" I mutter.

He takes another step closer and reaches out slowly, his hand seeking mine. When I don't do the same, he lets his fingers fall onto the table. "We survive. And then maybe there will come a day when there can be more than survival."

I force a smile. "That's a nice fantasy."

His ocean-blue eyes scan me, and then he frowns. "You have to believe in hope, Sora. Otherwise, what's the point?"

"Revenge—that's the only goal."

He shakes his head. "Vengeance is a fire without warmth. And you deserve warmth."

It's a sweet thought, but it's unrealistic. I pull my hand away from his and run it through my hair.

His fingers curl in, and he nods, dejected. I hate causing him pain, but there's no room for love and affection when all I feel is rage and emptiness.

"I need to go lie down," I say.

He nods, and I leave him alone in the war room.

CHAPTER FIFTY-TWO

MIKAIL

ROSE PALACE, GAYA

I walk through the palace with Zahara, who is actually a poison maiden named Hana. I'm surprised I didn't pick up on it before, as she is beautiful enough to be one of Seok's poisoners. But I suppose she's not the first royal spymaster able to hide their real identity. I'd excuse the lie, but I haven't even been crowned, and there's already been an attempt on my life. I can't allow anyone to be close if I don't fully trust them.

And I don't trust her.

We find the staircase that leads up to the watchtower. The top of the tower is five stories above the palace and the highest point on Gaya. I remember seeing the tower from my village as a boy. At the time, it felt comforting, like there was always someone watching over us.

Hana and I climb until the stairs become a spiral, and we go all the way to the open-air lookout. The evening is cooler, and the wind smells of the salt of the sea. The sun is setting, but nearly the whole of the island is visible from here. I eagerly search for my seaside northern village, but there are no signs of it. No buildings at all.

My breath catches. There are no northern villages. Instead, it's charm fields as far as the eye can see. Yusan slaughtered tens of thousands of people and then erased them from the face of Gaya.

I stare as my heart pounds, anger seeping through my bones.

Yusan razed the homes and replaced them with the drug plant like nothing ever happened. Like Gayans never existed.

Across the water, to the northeast, are the lights of Tamneki. I grip the ledge. I swear I'll see it burn before this is over. I will pay them back body for body.

Hana moves, and I feel her next to me. The poison maiden, the spy, the double agent working for both Joon and the western count.

"Rune specifically said that Fallador was feeding him information?" I ask.

"He didn't name him," she says. "Rune said he was working with someone in your group, and then he didn't have any solid information once you left Rahway, so that is my theory."

That's confirmation enough.

My heart squeezes as my head falls. There's real pain in my chest, and I don't know why I'm so disappointed. Fallador has lied to me since we met. Another deception shouldn't come as a shock. But he and Gambria betraying me cuts the deepest because they had been my only remnant of home.

I inhale a breath of sea air. It doesn't matter. I am home now.

But how long will I last? How long until the might of the other realms comes crashing down on us? How long until the soldiers on the island figure out that I have taken the palace? How will we defend it with a handful of guards and three relics?

I continue to stroll around the tower. From the southern end, I see the tops of the black wood forest and the mist that covers the sacred woods. Once upon a time, it must have been beautiful, but now it's a ghastly reminder of what was stripped away.

I lock my jaw. Joon will pay for this.

The ones we hate die first.

"Is Rune in an alliance with Seok or Joon?" I ask.

"I don't know."

Surprised, I turn and face Hana. She looks sincere, but looks are deceiving with spies.

"Rune should arrive with his army in Tamneki within a day or so," she says. "But the Weian warships will reach the capital around then as well. Knowing Rune, he will wait and align with whomever he thinks is likely to win. Seok has Qali, but Joon has Wei on his side, as well as the Immortal Crown."

It does sound like that desert snake to wait and throw his support when the battle is already decided. We could also let Seok and Joon destroy each other and then take on the weakened victor—it's the smart play.

"What will you do?" she asks.

There's nothing in the world that could make me tell her my actual plans.

"I'm going to hang the governor from the city gate, and then I'll decide," I say. "On second thought, I'll behead him and throw his skull into the sea first, as he did to my family. And then I'll crown myself king. After that, I'll hang his body."

Hana nods.

I stare directly at her. "Because of the aid you've given me in the past, and even tonight, I'm giving you this one opportunity to flee."

"Mikail..." She stares at me, and then she tilts her head and sighs. "I can't prove my loyalty to you, can I?"

"No, you cannot, and I can't afford another traitor in our midst. The safest place for you would be Khitan, as whether Seok or Joon wins this war, neither will be interested in seeing you alive, and Wei and Fallow are no place for Yusanian women."

"You know, Sora and I once had a dream to escape to Khitan together, but now..." Her voice breaks, reflecting her heart. She swallows hard and shakes off the memory. "Safety in death, my friend."

"Safety in death," I say.

Hana hesitates, seemingly wanting to say more, but there's nothing more to say. She takes the stairs back down.

A part of me wants to stop her, but this is no time for

sentimentality. It's no time for emotions at all.

I stay in the tower until it's dark and I can no longer see the island except for twinkling lights. Alone, I plot our next moves in this dangerous game.

CHAPTER FIFTY-THREE

ROYO

ROSE PALACE, GAYA

After baths, we sit down to a big dinner spread, ready to eat like these servants didn't just try to poison Mikail. A few bells ago.

I run a hand down my face. I feel like I've gone mad, but I sit in a chair next to Aeri.

Sora tastes and smells every plate and goblet. She's almost done when I realize the other poisoner isn't here. It's only the five of us. I look around, but no one else seems concerned that the girl is gone. Mikail sits on the throne at the end of the table, and then there's me and Aeri, and Sora and Ty across from us.

I want to ask where Hana went, but she upset Sora so bad that I decide not to bring it up.

Aeri looks over at me with mischief in her eyes. She walks her fingers over to my thigh under the table, and I remember flashes of getting into the bath with her a couple of bells ago. She called me in like something was wrong, but instead of being in trouble, she was trouble, standing there, naked in the clawfoot tub. And how was I supposed to resist that? She hooked her finger at me, and I took off my clothes and got in with her. Her body was slippery against mine as she straddled me.

I shift in my chair. Not the time for these thoughts.

It almost feels wrong, having this happiness when our friends are so sad. But I don't move her hand from my leg. We've struggled for this. I'll hold on to what little joy I can. I place my hand over hers, and we mesh our fingers together.

Tiyung sips his wine and looks from me to Aeri. He smiles into his goblet. The guy is a hopeless romantic. I'm glad he's back with us.

I'll be honest. I thought Tiyung was just a useless nobleman at first, but he's got more grit than I realized. He has to in order to have made it out of Idle Prison in one piece. He broke down in tears when he talked about Mikail's father dying for him, and even I got a lump in my throat. Mikail's father knew what he was doing and died to protect him. That says more about both men than I ever could.

Mikail has been handling all of this suspiciously well, but everything rolls off him.

Until it doesn't.

Sora stares at him. She has a way of seeing through people's bullshit.

"Are you all right?" she asks.

Mikail is leaning back with the top two buttons of his shirt undone, but once she speaks, he sits upright. "Leave us, all of you."

The servants all bow, and Mikail eyes them exiting the dining hall.

"This time tomorrow, all of our enemies will be in Tamneki," he says.

"What do we do?" Aeri asks.

Mikail taps the massive black table. "I've been pondering just that. I think we send an emissary to Joon, offering an alliance."

I shake my head. I couldn't have heard him right, and he is speaking real low, so maybe I didn't. But everyone else pauses, too.

"To King Joon?" I repeat. "The guy who threatened to torture and kill us all like a month ago? Or is there another Joon I haven't met yet?"

Mikail sighs. "A usurper sits on his throne. Joon will need alliances beyond Wei. I was his spymaster, Aeri is his daughter, and Seok put the bounty on us. He could believe we want to align with him over the count."

"And what are we actually doing?" Sora asks.

"We're arranging a meeting so I can take the Flaming Sword of the Dragon Lord."

The table goes silent. I grip my goblet, glad it's metal, not glass, because I would've cracked it.

Ten fucking Hells, we're stealing shit again? This never goes well, but I guess we have to get it right once? I pinch the bridge of my nose. My scar hurts.

Mikail downs another glass of water. "I see no one loves this idea."

"Why do you need the sword?" Sora asks.

Yeah, why risk getting outsmarted by King Joon again? We have the palace. We have three relics. Let him and Seok fight it out and destroy each other. It's not worth jumping in.

"In order to free the island, I need more power than the Water Scepter," Mikail says. "With the Flaming Sword, I could use fire to protect Gaya, and with two relics, who knows what I'd be capable of? You've seen what Aeri can do. I need the same multiplication."

I lift my eyebrows. He doesn't need the sword. He wants it. But he can't see the difference because his ambition is in the way.

This is going to end well.

"But the cost." Aeri shakes her head. She hasn't frozen in time lately, but she also hasn't used the relics since Rahway.

"Let me worry about that," he says with a wave of his hand.

Nobody at this table is worried about old age. But I want a future. One with Aeri and the rest of them. With Mikail as king, we could have that. We could live comfortably here in the sunshine where it doesn't even monsoon. None of us had a family until now—not as adults. And I don't wanna lose it. But it's really hard keeping someone alive who doesn't give a shit about dying.

"Let's say you get this meeting," I begin. "What's going to stop King Joon from killing you and Aeri to make himself the Dragon Lord?"

Mikail's face falls. Everyone gets quiet.

Sora and Tiyung turn to Mikail. He and Aeri are powerful, but they don't have the Immortal Crown. They aren't gods. There's nothing that would guarantee that either one comes back alive from a meeting with King Joon, even if Aeri is his daughter. And if Mikail goes alone, he'll die, and King Joon will come after Aeri with all his might because she'll be the last piece he needs.

"Can't you just use the stick to pull Joon's ship away from the fleet, kill him, and take the sword that way?" I ask.

"Well, when you put it that way…yes." Mikail smiles.

I sit back, surprised he took my idea over his own. Aeri beams at me as she spoons marinated tofu onto her plate.

"So we'll strike tomorrow, then, when the ships reach Tamneki?" Tiyung asks.

Mikail shakes his head. "There's no rush. Let Seok and Joon battle first. The war on Tamneki and the siege of Qali will take several weeks, or more likely months, and there will be massive casualties, weakening both sides. Yusan will be too distracted to worry about Gaya. We can wait until the battle for Tamneki is nearly over."

Ty shakes his head. "Those casualties are people, Mikail. Men trying to make a living as soldiers and innocent civilians—elders, women, and children, in the capital."

Mikail slams his water glass down on the table with a loud thud. "Those 'men trying to make a living' raped, murdered, and pillaged this island—or their fathers and uncles did. You'll forgive me if I don't have sympathy for soldiers being killed when they signed up for murder."

Oh shit.

Only Aeri is making a sound right now. She's slurping down noodles without a care in the world.

Ty sighs. "Mikail, past atrocities, especially unconscionable ones, can always justify future acts. Your people did nothing wrong twenty years ago. Neither did the women and children in Tamneki today. Tonight, they will sleep in their beds, not knowing they will die tomorrow. But the gods have blessed you with a unique opportunity. You can break the cycle and end the violence before it begins."

Sora blinks, turning like she's just seeing him now. I haven't heard anyone talk like this since…well, Tiyung when we were in Oosant. Even Aeri tilts her head. But she could just be looking at which dish to sample next.

"It's a rather convenient stance to save your father," Mikail says.

Tiyung runs his finger over the wineglass. "There's no saving my father."

Mikail leans on the table, staring down Ty. Tiyung holds his gaze. The tension in here is thicker than egg custard, but the thing is, neither of them is wrong. Terrible shit was done to this island, and letting Seok and Joon fight it out and weaken each other is the smart play. But the reality is, it won't be Seok and Joon. It'll be thousands of soldiers and tens of thousands of innocent people dying if there's a war.

"Everyone's letting this good food get cold," Aeri says, tossing down her chopsticks. They clatter onto the wooden table, and everybody stares at her.

"I mean…this is a pretty important conversation," Mikail says, his eyes wide. She's succeeded in weirding him out.

"It isn't, though," she says. "It's a pointless theoretical debate. You're both right, and you're both wrong. You could argue this until sunrise, but there's dinner on the table now."

Her ring clangs on the table as she smacks her hand down.

Ty opens his mouth, and Mikail tilts his head, but no one says a word.

"I guess I'll explain it." Aeri's all frustration as she stares at Mikail. "You want—not need, *want*—the sword, and we can't meet for a parley because Joon will kill us. We aren't safe as long as my father is alive, especially not with him having both of the other relics. This isn't new—we've known this since Quu Harbor. He'll always want to become the Dragon Lord. So, we'll take a crew of trusted men and attack his boat in the middle of the night. We'll pry off his crown and kill him when he least expects it—and that'll be when he's just arrived in Tamneki. Not during a siege, when he knows he's a target. Then we'll take the sword and the crown and come back to Gaya. There's not a lot to discuss."

Everyone sits silently, reasoning through what she said. Aeri didn't grow up in the palace, but she speaks and thinks like a ruler.

She picks up her chopsticks. "Now, could someone please pass the squid? It looks really good."

Ty shakes his head and then reaches out for the plate as Sora and Mikail continue to stare at Aeri.

"You're the rightful queen of Yusan," Sora says. Mikail nods.

"They can have it. I have all I need here." Aeri gestures around the table.

Sora clutches her napkin in her fist. "But…"

"Sora, I promise Seok won't be able to leave well enough alone," Aeri says. "Men who love power always want more. He'll come for the relics and the island, and then he'll burn. I swear it."

Apparently, that's enough of a promise. Sora takes a breath, releases the napkin, and nods.

One corner of Mikail's lips rises in a satisfied smirk. "To Queen Naerium." He lifts his glass.

"And King Adoros Miat," she says.

We all drink, and I can't help the stomach-churning feeling that runs through me. They've never been closer to sitting on their thrones, but I just got a terrible sense that all of this is about to go to shit.

CHAPTER FIFTY-FOUR

AERI

CITY OF JEUL, GAYA

There comes a time when everyone just needs to go the fuck to bed. We hit that point bells ago, and it's been nothing but nonsense since.

"Should we sleep in shifts?" Royo asks as we stand in the hall outside the second-floor bedroom suites.

"We're going to," Sora says. She points to herself and Tiyung. They said at the end of dinner that they're going to watch over Mikail, despite his protests.

"All right. We will, too," Royo says. "Be well."

He and I head into the same bedroom as before. I mindlessly unwrap my dress and let it fall to the floor. Hopefully we'll be here long enough for me to order a new wardrobe and actually wear it. I think I still have tailored clothes in Tamneki somewhere. Plus, the clothes we left in Rahway, and the ones set on fire, lost in the woods, and abandoned in Khitan.

Royo looks the other way as I walk past him. I guess he's back to pretending he's my professional guard. Like we didn't just make love in the tub earlier today.

I'll try again tomorrow. For now, I slip under the soft covers on the feather bed. These villas and palaces always have the best food and bedding. As hideouts go, this one is pretty great.

Royo remains standing in the middle of the room.

"Come to bed." I pat the sheets next to me.

He shakes his head, raising his chin. Ever since dinner ended, he's been very official. It's so disappointing.

"I'll take first shift," he says. "I'll sleep when you get up."

"No. That's no fun at all."

He rolls his eyes so hard his head falls back. "Yes. I have to keep watch. I won't sleep tonight anyhow, so I might as well."

"Why not?" I ask, yawning.

"Because I don't think that getting rid of the governor and a few guards is enough to take and hold the city. I expect there will be trouble. I think the others do, too—that's why Sora and Tiyung are in Mikail's room. But nobody wants to be the one to say it out loud."

I think through what he says, and it makes sense. I was expecting soldiers, too, earlier.

"Maybe I should wear something to bed, then," I say.

He nods. "That would be a start."

I toss off the sheets and get out of bed. "You weren't complaining about me being naked before."

He blushes, staring at the floor. "We were in the bath."

"Decorum first," I say.

I get a nightgown out of my bag, slip it on, and turn out the light. My whole body aches from everything we've been through. I fluff the pillow and lie back. These beds really are nice.

I'm half asleep when Royo calls my name.

"Aeri," Royo says.

"I'm fast asleep," I answer.

"You're the worst is what you are," he says.

I open my eyes and see that he's sitting on the other side of the room by the windows. He looks like a king on a throne the way he fills out that armchair. I want to do unspeakable things to him, but sadly he's in guard mode.

I smile. "Yes, Royo?"

"I... I'm worried about Mikail."

It wasn't what I thought he was going to say, but it's valid all the same.

"Because you're smart," I say.

He shakes his head. "Nobody calls me smart."

My heart squeezes for him, for the people who don't understand his value, but it's their loss.

"Because they're not paying attention. You were the first one to realize that Mikail's plan wasn't going to work. You're smarter than you give yourself credit for—you have been from the start. But what specifically about Mikail worries you?"

I sit up a little so I can see him better.

"I just don't think he's okay," he says.

I raise an eyebrow. "I mean, which one of us is doing great?"

"No, I think he's driven by his ambition." He pauses and looks at me. "Why are you smiling?"

"I'm enjoying being right about you. People see muscle and mayhem and they don't realize how observant you are, how you analyze a situation. It's like a secret power."

He doesn't crack a smile. I sigh. Of course he doesn't.

Royo leans closer. "I think he won't hold back. He'll do anything to free this island, even if it means using you."

"Oh, he definitely plans on using me." I thought that was obvious. Mikail wants to have powers like mine, but to use in conjunction with me, not alone.

Royo slaps his hands against his legs. "Why are you so calm about it?"

I shrug. "What else am I going to do?"

"Aeri, I swear, I'm going to kill you myself."

I lie down fully and stretch out. "Ah, what a fitting end. She died as she lived—pressed on a bed under Royo. Not a bad way to go, if you ask me."

He slouches and looks like the most cursed man in the four realms. I laugh.

"Aeri, I need you to take this seriously," he says.

"I promise I am. I know I sound glib, but in the end, no matter what Mikail wants, I control how much of my power is used. He can want the East and West Sea, but I have to choose to give them to him. He can't do it alone. Be more worried about what happens if he actually gets the Flaming Sword. And I guess be super worried about what happens if he doesn't."

Royo goes quiet. I guess they aren't great thoughts—Mikail with that much power or Mikail failing to get the relic. Both are terrible, just in different ways.

"What I mean is—" I begin.

Royo raises a hand for me to be quiet. At first, I'm offended, but then his shoulders tense and he stares out the window.

Goose bumps run down my arms, and I slide out of bed. I walk up to his chair and peer out the window. Then I look at his face and back again.

"Do you see that?" he asks.

I don't. Apparently, he has better vision than I do.

He points, and I squint until I finally see it. There, in the distance, is a flame. But as I watch, the fire is moving. It's not one flame but many. And they're coming closer to the palace. If I had to guess, it's the soldiers Mikail said were still on the island. They're marching and carrying torches.

I put my wrap dress back on.

So much for getting a good night's sleep.

CHAPTER FIFTY-FIVE

TIYUNG

ROSE PALACE, GAYA

We're in the king's bedroom suite of the palace, which is absolutely enormous. I grew up in the grandest villa in Gain, and my bedroom wasn't a quarter of this size. I don't think my father's bedroom was half this large.

Mikail and Sora have taken baths and gotten ready for bed. I agreed to take first watch so they could get some sleep. I'm tired, but Mikail is bodily exhausted from wielding the scepter, and Sora is emotionally wrung out.

He's on the enormous black wood bed—I think it's two king-size beds put together, but it could be larger than that. The canopy frame nearly reaches the high ceiling, and it has roses and leaves carved into its dark wood. Mikail's scepter is to his right, and his sword is on the nightstand. I'm sure if I looked I'd find a dagger or three under his pillow.

Sora is lying on a daybed at the foot of his bed. I think ordinarily, it's for a servant to use.

Neither of them is asleep, but they're resting. I stand over by the dressing table and chairs. All the drapes are closed except for the sitting area, where I'll keep watch until I wake Sora.

"Tiyung," Mikail says, reaching for his lamp. "I didn't say it before, but you are worthy of my father's sacrifice."

Tears immediately well in my eyes. I shake my head. I don't know why he thinks this. I don't know what I did to deserve this kind of compliment when we just argued at dinner. Why me? Why now?

"You reminded me of what I actually believe," he continues. "I have said in the past that the atrocity of one people does not justify atrocity to the next. It's harder than I realized to keep your ideals when it's your people who suffered and you have the power now. But you were my compass when mine broke." Mikail stretches and relaxes in his bed. "Thank you."

I blink back tears and nod. "I... I'm glad I could help."

Feeling Sora's violet eyes on me, I turn away. I don't want to cry in front of her.

I take a few breaths and attempt to gather myself. Mikail turns out his light, and now I don't have to worry about them seeing me, but it's uncomfortably dark in here. There are a few candles lit, but I grab an oil lamp by the dressing table. My hands shake, so it takes me a few tries to light it.

Once the lamp is lit, I sit by the window. I swear I can still feel Sora looking at me, but she doesn't say anything. As much as I want to talk to her, I also want her to rest, so I pretend not to notice.

They both get quiet and fall into that steady breathing of sleep. Sora sleeps like a doll, but Mikail moves around a lot. It's not long before he's thrashing in bed so violently that I'm afraid he'll hit her. I'm about to get out of my chair to wake him, but finally, he settles.

It's around a bell later when I spot something strange in the distance. I squint. I wish I had a spyglass, but Hana took that.

I startle in my seat as soon as I think of her. Hana. I haven't seen her since the kitchens. Where did she go? I can't believe I forgot about her until now, but so much has happened.

With a deep breath, I slow my heart as I try to think. Last I saw her, she and Mikail went to talk. I don't think it's a coincidence that she wasn't at dinner. I don't think he killed her, but I also don't put it past him.

No. I shake off my own thought. She was a source for him,

and even tonight she stopped him from being poisoned. I have to imagine he let her go.

There's an odd flicker again outside the window. I turn down the oil lamp so that it doesn't reflect in the glass. Heart racing, I squint at what appears to be a fire in the distance—that can't be good.

"Mikail, Sora," I say.

They both sit up before I even get the words out. Sora might not have been asleep at all.

"What is it?" Mikail asks.

"There are flames. I think they might be torches—"

I'm cut off by the door opening. Royo and Aeri burst into the room. I should've locked it. I thought I did. Actually, I'm certain I did. Aeri must've picked the lock.

"There's trouble coming," Royo says, small spyglass in hand. Aeri probably stole it from somewhere.

Mikail already has his sword as he takes the spyglass and looks out the window.

"Soldiers are marching toward the palace," he says. "It doesn't look like that many. Maybe three hundred. Judging from where they are, they'll reach Jeul in a bell."

My stomach drops. Three hundred soldiers sounds like a crisis to me when we have five guards and just five of us. I start to sweat, but Mikail doesn't look worried at all.

"What are you going to do?" Sora asks as Mikail dresses.

"I'm going to meet them by the sea. I have to throw the governor's head in anyhow." He shrugs on his shirt.

"Well, it's good to multitask," Aeri says.

Sora shifts her weight foot to foot, and Royo runs his hand over his face, but this is just the way Aeri thinks. It's Mikail, who appears unsettlingly calm.

Sora goes into the bathroom and reappears, dressed again.

"You don't all need to come with me," Mikail says. "I will settle this with the Yusanian king's guard." He grabs the Water Scepter and stares at the sapphire on the top.

"You're not going alone," Royo says.

Sora shakes her head. "We are with you until the end."

"You need us," I add.

"We're coming," Aeri says. "One man, even a powerful one, is too easy to ambush."

"Well, I thought I'd offer," Mikail says with a smile. "So much for playing the hero. Let's go and be villains."

CHAPTER FIFTY-SIX

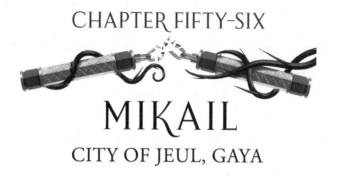

MIKAIL
CITY OF JEUL, GAYA

Despite my minimal protests, the four of them come with me. We take halibred horses from the stable and ride through town and out the city gates. In truth, I do need them, but I did want the others to stay safe at the palace. I suppose self-sacrifice on my part will have to wait.

Royo has his axe strapped to his back. Sora has nothing but poison, but I've seen the damage she can do with that. Aeri has her relics in case things go wrong, and Tiyung is…here.

We ride until we reach the beach bordering the Strait of Teeth. It's the middle of the night, but the giant monsoon moon illuminates the water and white sand. The sky is filled with thousands of stars, and hundreds of soldiers are marching from the east. They will have to come this way along the Perimeter Road to get to Jeul. This is a good place to wait for them.

Once the group stops, I ride onto the sand and fling the bag containing Yong's head into the sea. He was the one who ordered the same for my family—not even releasing the souls of the children. I'll hang his body from the city gates after I finish with this.

I feel strangely detached as I watch the spot where the bag disappeared. The rings of moonlit ripples dissolve into the regular rhythm of the sea as his head sinks. I hope the iku enjoy the snack.

My friends join me on the sand, facing the road. I look through the spyglass. The soldiers are close now. They'll reach us in a few minutes.

"Are you drowning them all?" Aeri asks. There's no judgment in her tone, just curiosity.

Tiyung, however, eyes me like this is a test.

"I will give them a chance to surrender," I say.

He relaxes his posture slightly as he holds his reins.

But then he twists around in the saddle to look back, and my entire body tenses. Footsteps approach us from the opposite direction—from the other side of the Perimeter Road. Did we fall into a trap?

The scepter hums, begging to be used.

There are more torches, and they're much closer to us than the soldiers coming from the east. I look through the spyglass, and Aeri puts out her hands. I know she'd turn them all to gold to save us, even if it would doom her.

But as I look, I don't see standards or king's guard uniforms. Instead, they're Gayan civilians with clubs, pitchforks, torches, and swords. Leading the group is the groundskeeper I spoke to earlier. He's marching alongside Teo and Calier.

"Allies," I shout.

At least, I hope.

I ride toward them, and Aeri spurs her horse to keep pace with me. She doesn't say it, but she's acting as my bodyguard.

"Your Majesty," the groundskeeper says in Gayan. He drops to one knee.

"Uncle," I say. I wait for him to fill in his name.

"Fremo," he says. "We saw the soldiers marching and gathered to fight. We, the rebels of Keen Hill, are with you."

The other three or four hundred men and women take a knee to me as one.

My chest expands, and a new feeling flows through my veins. It's like euphoria, but it's warmer and more addictive, like laoli. I don't recall ever feeling as good as I do now with loyal citizens behind me.

"Your loyalty to Gaya and the Miats will be rewarded," I say. "But I will handle the soldiers with the aid of Alta and the God of the Seas. Watch tonight and witness who the gods favor now."

The Water Scepter pulses in my hand, ready. Every muscle in my body aches from the dehydration and lack of rest, but I've also never felt so alive.

Aeri and I ride back to the others. By the time we reach them, the soldiers have assembled on the road, maybe a hundred to two hundred yards away. There are more than I thought—probably four hundred men. The captain must have gathered all king's guard within a day's march of Jeul. They have two rows of archers, and I'm slightly worried about the crowd behind us. They're within striking distance, but the soldiers' bows and arrows won't matter soon.

I will do whatever it takes to protect the people.

The soldiers hold, but the captain rides out of the line. Another man trails him. That has to be his aide or second-in-command.

I urge my horse forward, and the five of us close the distance to them. It's time for a parley, I suppose. This should be interesting.

"Criminals!" the captain of the guard says.

It's a strong opener.

"Mikail of Yusan, Naerium of Yusan, and Sora of Yusan, throw down your arms and surrender by order of King Seok," the aide says.

I laugh to myself at Seok calling himself a king. Obviously, none of us drop our weapons. Ridiculous suggestion.

"I am Adoros Miat, the rightful king of the realm of Gaya," I say. "You are trespassing on this island and raising arms against a sovereign. I will give you one chance to surrender, or I swear by the stars that you and your men will die tonight."

The captain barks out a laugh. "We will bring you to justice by force, then, and hang the rebels who have joined you." At his gesture, the lines of archers move forward while the rest of the soldiers remain in place. The archers in the front row kneel to give the back row clear shots.

"Perhaps I didn't make myself clear," I say. "Allow me to demonstrate what I mean."

"All right. *Demonstrate*, then." The captain smirks.

I smile. I love someone convinced they're invincible.

I ride out onto the sand and then dip the scepter into the ocean. Immediately, the water responds to me, the sea churning and begging for direction, a plaything in my hands. I pull the water into the shape of a drowning wave. In a matter of seconds, an unnatural surge builds and crests over the captain, his aide, and the rows of stunned archers. One hundred paces behind them, the army breaks rank to run away as the sixty-foot-tall tidal wave glimmers in the moonlight, hovering and waiting for my command.

Whispers of awe and prayers to the God of the Seas flood in from the rebels with us. The captain of the king's guard fights to control his horse, his jaw dropping in astonishment.

"Surrender!" I yell.

"Never!" There's no smug mockery in his tone now. Behind him, several of the archers have summoned enough courage to raise their bows again, prepared for his signal.

So I let the wave fall and send a smaller wave to wash out the road behind the army, cutting off a quick escape. The water crashes with such a force that mist hits my face from this far back. The captain, his aide, and the hundred or so archers are now flailing in the Strait of Teeth.

They shouldn't do that. It will attract the iku.

Come to think of it, that's a good idea.

I dip the scepter into the water and then send a riptide to pull them deep into the strait, where the iku love to hunt.

Without even looking to see what happens to the men, I ride close enough to the remaining soldiers for them to hear me.

"Let me repeat myself: surrender or die," I say.

Almost as one, the soldiers throw down their swords and raise their hands in surrender, their arms shaking.

I still consider drowning them all—these men are far from innocent. But it's not worth the argument with Tiyung. Braya said to give the people something to believe in. They can believe in my power but also my word.

"Flee," I say. "Leave your weapons, return to Yusan, and tell them that Gaya has declared her independence."

I turn and ride back to the rebels. The others turn, too. Royo is last, making sure the soldiers leave their swords and don't try to attack with our backs turned. I appreciate that he's thorough, but there's no threat from men who soil themselves in front of real power.

I canter toward the crowd of Gayans and raise the Water Scepter.

"En Gaya!" I yell. "The cowards' weapons are yours."

They cheer as they run to collect the swords, and their joy drowns out the screams of the men struggling in the water.

CHAPTER FIFTY-SEVEN

SORA

ROSE PALACE, GAYA

I finally had a full night's sleep, and I feel like a new person.

After the events of the midnight beach, the five of us all went to bed. The Gayan rebels who'd followed us lined the streets of the hill, standing guard until we awoke. The human wall was more security than we've ever had.

The five of us had breakfast at noon, and a bell later, I finally find a chance to talk with Mikail. I want to ask the question that's been weighing on my mind, and I'm also worried about him after the way he used the scepter last night.

He and I stroll the gardens where they burned the governor's guards and the women who tried to poison him. The firepit and the manicured grounds look no worse for wear. The pyre is already dismantled, the ashes cleaned up.

I walk holding Mikail's left arm. It trembles, but so does mine sometimes, so I say nothing about it. The same way I said nothing about the small convulsion he had in the kitchens yesterday.

The sun is warm and pleasant on my face, and Mikail seems at peace in this land. At least as much as he ever is. His brow is smooth, and his gait is relaxed.

"Come this way, down to the Fountain of Life," he says.

I glance over at him, worried he'll use the scepter that's in his right hand. He hasn't bothered with concealing it inside the walking stick today.

"I'm told a miracle occurred overnight, and I want to see it for myself," he adds.

Horrors and miracles. At least it's the latter.

Rather than scaling the walls like when we came here, we take the gentle stone steps of the terrace. It doesn't take long to notice the abundance of red roses blooming in a perfect circle around the Fountain of Life.

I blink, clearing my vision. Those flowers weren't there yesterday. I stood feet away from the spring, and there was nothing but green grass—not even a bud or a thorn.

Mikail smiles, his eyes filled with wonder.

We reach the roses, and we stop and stare. Each bloom is so large, it would take both of my hands to cup one. I lean down and breathe in the smell. It's like rich perfume. I stroke the petals, and the flowers feel like the smoothest, softest velvet. They are beautiful and impossible, each one in full, perfect bloom.

"They're fantastic," I whisper.

Mikail nods. "The people have taken them as a sure sign that the goddess has returned to Gaya, or at least that we have her favor again. My home is called Rose Palace because riots of these roses used to encircle the columns. They haven't in two hundred years."

He stares at the palace with an appraising eye, and I can picture it. How different the white structure must've looked covered in flowers—the true home of an earth goddess. Mikail reaches down and caresses one of the roses, and then he touches his hand to his forehead in homage. He offers me his arm again. I take it, and we amble back toward the palace.

"But you didn't ask to speak with me about flowers or miracles." He looks at me out of the corner of his eye. "What's on your mind, Sora?"

"Well, I did want to see how you were feeling after last night's tidal wave," I say.

It was as fantastic as it was terrifying.

Mikail smiles as he half closes his eyes. "I'm in a tremendous amount of pain. I'd take laoli if I weren't well aware of how addictive it is. I drank charm tea at breakfast and ate salted fruits to ease the aches, and it does help some. But nothing stops the toll. I saw you notice the seizures. They're getting worse, but right now, they're still blessedly short."

I stop on the path and turn toward him. "Oh, Mikail."

He shakes his head. "It's okay, Sora. I've been through worse. And if I had to make the decision to use the scepter again, I'd do the same."

I don't doubt it. Mikail doesn't waste time on remorse. Not even in drowning a hundred men.

We continue to walk, slowly meandering back. With everything that happened yesterday, I didn't get a chance to appreciate how stunning the views are from the hill. The entire city of Jeul is laid out around it, mostly small houses and shops lined in black timbers, and then the sea in the distance. The gardens, although not what they once were, are equally as beautiful, verdant and manicured. And the sky is the brightest blue I've ever seen.

When I was first brought to Gain, I couldn't believe how things could grow in the southern sunshine of Yusan. Hana felt the same, since she came from the western desert. There was so much abundance that we could never understand the hoarding, torture, and betrayal just to have more.

"What happened to Hana, Mikail?" I ask.

His mouth moves in such a way that I know he was waiting for me to ask. He raises his chin and takes a breath. "I thought it was best for her to leave us. I can't trust someone who was working for the western count and who could still be working for Joon. I didn't want her to be at risk in Yusan, so I suggested a ship to Khitan. If she left for the northern realm, she is safe."

He studies me, and I can tell he wants to gauge if I'm all right with his decision. One he didn't consult with me about. I don't know how I feel, though. I was so hurt and betrayed by learning Hana has been alive this whole time that the lie was all I could focus on. Yet my stomach twists at the thought of her going to Khitan, of her leaving me again. I don't know what to do with all of this emotion. Nothing seems right, and maybe that's just what happens when the love of your life deceives you like this. Yet, as far as Mikail goes, I understand his reasoning. It was the same thought behind getting rid of Fallador.

I bite my lip. It's yet another impossible web of lies and emotion to untangle. I simply push it to the back of my mind, hoping one day I have the time and space to unravel it all. Mikail puts his hand over mine, but then his gaze darts to the side.

Teo and Calier approach us as we come up the last set of stairs. They carry silver trays filled with envelopes, both eagle post and courier from the island. Most of the letters are addressed to the governor, but some are for Mikail—probably intel from rebel sources.

"Bring the letters to the war room, please," he says.

"Yes, Your Majesty," they reply.

The brothers bow low before they leave, and there's reverence in their expressions. The lore of Mikail has already begun. They think he's a demigod because of what he did last night and because of the roses returning.

Maybe he is.

Mikail smiles and nods.

"It suits you," I say.

"What does?"

"This role as king of Gaya."

He smiles, but then he sighs. "It doesn't, Sora. It is fine for now because I'm not actually ruling but grasping for power. In the end, I am a killer and a spy. I don't understand diplomacy or governing a people. No matter how much I love them, the scale of this is over my head. I understand how to bring down realms, not how to restore them. I can kill enough men for the island to be free, but someone else will have to worry about what comes after."

I take a step back, startled, but I suppose his answer shouldn't surprise me. None of us actually want a throne or power over others. We just can't live with things the way they are. I'm beginning to wonder if anyone good ever *wants* to rule, or if it is always morally devoid men like Seok and ruthless women like Quilimar.

But thinking about kings and queens brings up new questions and concerns.

"We attack tonight?" I ask.

Mikail nods.

I take a deep breath. The plan is as simple as it is impossible. Scouts have been tracking the progress of the Weian fleet. They are swinging around Gaya, taking the South Sea. The Gayans suspect they're sailing this way to avoid detection by Yusan. Mikail thinks the fleet will wait in the Strait of Teeth until dusk. Once it's nightfall, the ships will move into Tamneki Harbor. We will find King Joon's ship, use the scepter to isolate it, climb aboard, and kill the king.

My stomach knots, and I worry the fabric of my dress, because nothing, not my poisoned kiss or even the flood in Quu Harbor, has been able to put an end to King Joon's life. And even if we succeed, his death will only legitimize Seok's rule. But what choice do we have? Aeri is right: we aren't safe as long as the king breathes. One enemy at a time.

"I'd rather you and Tiyung stay here tonight," Mikail says.

I shake my head before he finishes the sentence.

He pats my hand. "I know, we go together, Sora, but I thought I'd express my pointless hope. You are both valuable hostages if things go wrong—too much so for comfort. With all the love in my heart, I wish that you'd stay here."

I ignore the sting of his words.

"We don't let things go wrong," I say. "You'll kill King Joon, take the sword, and put an end to this."

He nods, but there's chilling uncertainty in his eyes. Simple plans have a way of getting complicated in Yusan. I shudder in the heat, and my mouth goes dry.

"What else is troubling you?" Mikail asks.

"Oh, nothing really." I smile. "Everything is just fine. A normal day."

He laughs, and I do as well.

Tiyung rounds the corner just as Mikail and I are laughing together. He looks from me to Mikail without smiling. I don't know if he mistakes our friendship for something else or if our closeness bothers him regardless.

Mikail holds himself straighter when he notices Tiyung. "What is it?"

Ty clears his expression and his throat. "There's someone here to see you, Mikail."

I look toward the palace. This can't be good.

"Who?" Mikail asks. His earlier mirth becomes a memory.

"Fallador, the exiled prince of Gaya," he says.

Yes, that is definitely not good. Fallador should be with Rune in Tamneki. What is he doing here? How did he know where to find us? I immediately think Hana betrayed us again, but Mikail did just spare hundreds of soldiers. Someone could have easily reached Tamneki and spread the word about Mikail by this morning.

Still, Mikail stiffens, his biceps hardening. I search his face, but he's not looking at me. He's staring up at the palace.

"Very well," he says. "Show him to the throne room, please."

I touch Mikail's shoulder. "What if it's a trap?"

He shrugs. "Everything could be. But I have some questions for my old friend. Don't worry, Sora. I'll bring my guards and Aeri and Royo. If you'd like to come, too, you can. I'm in no peril from an audience. We are the most dangerous people on this island. Not him."

I'm not sure that's true, since love has a way of cutting the deepest.

Tiyung turns on his heels, walking without us. Mikail and I exchange glances, and then we make our way back to the palace.

CHAPTER FIFTY-EIGHT

ROYO

ROSE PALACE, GAYA

We're in a throne room again. I never thought I'd see one palace, let alone three different ones, but here I am. A strongman, standing next to the king of Gaya. And somehow it feels like just another day.

Life is really fucking weird.

Mikail isn't crowned, but he looks like a king on that throne. The throne of Gaya is carved out of a single blond tree that used to stand here, according to Mikail. The back of the throne reaches all the way up to the high double ceiling, but it's not plain wood. Carved on it is the goddess Alta and her lovers, the God of the Seas and the God of Knowledge, founding the realm. It's kinda like that giant painting in Khitan, but the whole chair is decorated. The arms and legs are covered in carved vines and roses. There's a white cushion that Mikail said used to be the green of the Gayan flag, but Yusan changed it when they took over.

Aeri sits on the black wood queen's throne to Mikail's right. I don't love it, but it's because she has the relics. Even I can admit that she's the best protection for him.

Sora and Ty stand off to the side in the airy white room. The brothers, Calier and Teo, wait by the massive doors.

All this, and in front of us is just one guy—Fallador.

I grit my teeth. Today got tense in a hurry.

"Your Majesty." He takes a knee in his white slacks, but his eyes take in this room. I wonder why he has that longing expression, but then I remember he grew up in the palace. It's gotta be like looking at a house other people moved into. But Fallador was never going to sit on the heir's throne. He said at the inn that when he was young, his sisters slipped and told him he wasn't the real prince. The king and queen then confirmed it.

"Fallador," Mikail says. He seems casual, but I know he ain't.

Now acknowledged, Fallador stands and smiles. "The throne suits you, Adoros. It makes my heart happy to see a Miat in this room again."

The guy seems genuine, but he's looked that way this whole time. I narrow my eyes and study his relaxed expression. What the fuck is he doing here? What's the play?

"What brings you home?" Mikail asks.

Fallador stiffens a little. "I am here as a messenger for the western count."

"What else is new?" I think. Unfortunately, I also say it out loud.

Everyone stares at me. Teo and Calier look ready to faint. Heat rushes into my face, and it takes all I got not to put a hand over my mouth. I wasn't supposed to talk shit or say anything, really. I look at Mikail and grimace.

"He has a point," Mikail says with a shrug.

Fallador's chin drops. "Adoros, I thought that working with Rune would ultimately help you, but since you left, I can see where I was wrong. I should've told you what I was doing. I've been thinking about why I held back from you. I suppose I thought you'd object to the alliance because of how you feel about the Yusanian nobility. But maybe it was baser than that. Perhaps it's just that I wanted to have importance for myself. Either way, I didn't give you a choice. I deceived you again, and for that I am truly sorry. But please believe I thought I was only assisting you."

Fallador's got a way of speaking where everything sounds

reasonable. He's smooth, and I'm nodding along at his heartfelt confession. But what he's really saying is he betrayed us to help Mikail. And that doesn't make sense. I grip my axe tighter.

Fuck this guy.

"The noblest of intentions can still be treasonous," Mikail says.

"I don't disagree. But I believed Rune to be the lesser of the evils with so many powerful enemies assembled against you. I *still* believe that—it's why I'm here."

"What is your message?" Mikail asks.

"The count has reached the outskirts of Tamneki, and he waits there with fifteen thousand men. Between you and me, I think it's closer to ten, but it's an impressive number of soldiers at his command. I have to imagine he's been raising a private army for a decade now."

I raise my eyebrows. That's as many men as Wei had originally. Mikail said over a thousand people died in Quu Harbor, but most were Khitanese. Who knows what Wei's got now? Either way, that's a lot of soldiers for a count to control. And it's a fuck of a lot more than we've got.

"Let him know how thrilled I am for him," Mikail says.

Fallador smiles. "He knows you are the real king of Gaya, and he desires an alliance."

"How'd he find that out?" I ask.

I really gotta stop talking.

"Mikail left with the Water Scepter, which was a dead giveaway. If that weren't enough, it's not every day that a hundred soldiers are drowned and eaten in the Strait of Teeth. People wind up talking." Fallador shrugs, then grins. "It struck fear into the heart of Yusan. They're speaking of a lost colony and a found prince."

Pride shines in Fallador's eyes even though he didn't have anything to do with it. Well, he did help us get the scepter, so maybe he had some part.

"Does this alliance include marrying me?" Aeri asks.

"Actually, no, it doesn't. This one is purely with Mikail, although I'm certain Rune's ardent feelings for you still stand."

I curl my hands into fists. I'm going to punch Rune in the throat.

"What are the terms?" Mikail asks.

Fallador stands straighter. "Rune is ready to support your rightful claim to the throne and your bid for an independent Gaya. He offers you the use and protection of his soldiers either on this island or after the siege of Qali Palace. Your enemies will become his."

"I can't wait to hear what his generosity will cost," Mikail says. He taps his fingers on the arm of the throne.

Fallador's lips curl up, but then his smile fades. The ball in his throat bobs. "In return, he expects your full support of his campaign for the throne of Yusan. Once you succeed, Gaya would pay a seasonal tribute of laoli to Yusan with continued free trade."

So, freedom ain't free. But what else is new? Independence always costs blood or money. People like us usually have to pay in both.

"After the siege?" Aeri says, her golden eyes shining. "He still plans on aligning with my father?"

"He remains unaffiliated," Fallador says.

"So he will wait outside of the theater of war and then conquer the weakened victor," Mikail says. "This sounds familiar."

I raise my eyebrows. It's exactly what Mikail had wanted to do before that argument with Tiyung. Because it's smart, so long as you don't give a shit about human life.

Mikail looks over at Tiyung. Aeri and Sora also eye him. Ty sighs.

Fallador spreads his hands. "You know Rune is pragmatic."

"Yes, to a fault." Mikail shifts on the throne, leaning to the other side. "What do you think about all of this?"

Fallador tilts his head. "The alliance?"

Mikail nods. "If you were king, what would you do with this generous offer?"

"I was never going to be king." Fallador shakes his head and looks at the floor. Sunshine streams in and highlights some of the pain on his face. For the first time, I feel for the guy. It's gotta be weird to know that you were the odd man out. That none of this could ever be yours.

"You have far more experience being royal than I do," Mikail says. "And you came across the Strait of Teeth with this offer. If I know you, you have thought about it from all angles."

Fallador smiles. "I think the siege of Qali and who ultimately sits on the serpent throne are irrelevant to Gaya. It's one tyrant versus a would-be tyrant—there's no difference to the island. The real problem you have is the Water Scepter. Whether King Joon or Seok ultimately wins, you will have to deal with Wei. Priest King Uol is dead, and Uolson, the Weian prince, can't claim the throne having lost millions of mun in tribute in addition to the Dragon Lord relic—his own people would rebel. Sooner or later, the Weian fleet and their impenetrable steel will come for you. This island will need protection to keep the relic, and even then...a war could be a slaughter with how they are armored and trained. You need a powerful friend. It doesn't have to be Rune, but given what's occurred, I don't see you forming an alliance with anyone else."

"And if I sink the entire fleet?" Mikail asks. "Would I need friends?"

True terror flashes in Fallador's eyes. "No. No, Adoros. Using that much etherum would kill you. You saw what it did to the water bearers in Quu Harbor."

Sora's mouth drops open, and Aeri grips her armrests as both women turn to Mikail.

Mikail shrugs. "Every man dies."

Fallador slowly closes his eyes. "There has to be another way. Consider Rune's offer. Let his soldiers die instead."

"And remain chained to Yusan? Not solve the scourge of laoli infecting this island? Owe my throne to another realm the way the Miats lived for two hundred years? Just sit here, a fatted goose, ripe for the slaughter?" Mikail shakes his head. "What's the point of living that life?"

"Living." Fallador's eyes plead with Mikail. "Carrying on because this island needs you."

"I'll take it under consideration."

He's not. Not even a little. No one is more comfortable with Lord Yama than Mikail.

Fallador sighs with his entire body. "Rune expects me to return with an answer by sunset."

"Then I take you hostage," Mikail says with a wave of his hand. "You're forbidden from leaving the palace until I release you."

The little line appears on Sora's forehead. It's nothing compared to the ridges I feel on mine. Is he serious? Are we kidnapping people now?

Fallador smiles like Mikail just said *I love you.* Then he bows. "I am your political prisoner, then."

"Good." Mikail stands. "Go pick a bedroom and let the servants know if you're hungry."

CHAPTER FIFTY-NINE

MIKAIL

ROSE PALACE, GAYA

That was an interesting audience. For the life of me, I'm still not sure where Fallador's loyalty lies. Maybe I'll figure it out with time. Regardless, it is better to hold Rune at bay for now, because in the worst-case scenario I might need him. And if I'm honest, having Fallador here, safe and accounted for, is one less worry.

Good thing I'm rarely honest.

I invite Fremo, Teo, and Calier to join me in the war room. Teo said Fremo has been involved in the rebellion cause for decades. He was the one who rallied the people to meet us on the beach. I never heard of him during my time as spymaster, which means he was clever enough to escape detection, and that makes him very valuable as a leader.

It's a little cramped in the war room with Sora, Aeri, Royo, and Tiyung also in here—which means this space is useless. It was probably a study that Yong altered. If I had to guess, the new tuhko court is where the real war room used to be.

I'm glad I hung his worthless body from the gates.

"What is your report, Fremo? What have your scouts seen?" I ask.

After the beach last night, I asked Fremo to put trusted rebels at the four corners of the island to report on the movements of the Weian fleet.

Fremo steps forward with his head high. I doubt anyone during his sixty years has recognized his full worth, but I can do so now.

"The warships sail the South Sea, well off the shore of Hallan, Your Majesty," he says with a bow. "We expect they will arrive in the Strait of Teeth before sunset."

"What is the likelihood of Jeul being the target?" I ask.

"It is unlikely, Your Majesty," he says with another sharp nod. "The ships have been within range of our forts for a full day now. If Gaya were the target, they would've attacked from the East Sea. It is our belief that they circumnavigated the island to avoid detection by Yusan."

I relax my shoulders some. Fallador's warnings about Wei and their steel are still fresh in my mind. He is correct that we wouldn't survive being invaded by them. Not at the moment, anyhow. Once I have the Flaming Sword, our chances will dramatically improve.

"Thank you, Fremo," I say. "A group of us will prepare to strike the fleet from the Port of Charm at one bell."

I reach down and move the model ships and soldiers to the northern port on the map. The Port of Charm sits directly across from Tamneki. It is where the ferry docks and where laoli is transported to Yusan.

I'll burn it down once we're done.

Royo furrows his brow. "Why one bell?"

"Because the fleet's attack on Tamneki will commence between four and five bells," I say.

"How do you know that?" Calier asks, then hastily adds, "Majesty."

Teo gives his brother a hard look, and Calier takes a step back. His face reddens, and his chin drops. He spoke out of turn, but I don't care about the formalities. It was a reasonable question.

"Experience," I say. "Yusanian generals are taught to use the cover of night to move into place and then begin their assault to catch the enemy unaware. They take advantage of daybreak to continue their strikes. If we attack at one, the soldiers will be asleep in preparation for battle except for a skeleton crew of the least experienced men.

We will pull Joon's ship to us, board with a small group, and kill him without engaging the entire fleet. I have battled Weian steel before. It's not a fight we want."

Teo and Calier nod. Pride and hunger shine in Fremo's eyes. My four friends look less than certain.

"And if our attempt goes wrong?" Tiyung asks.

I spin the scepter in my hand. "Then I'll sink Joon's ship."

Sora whips her head in my direction. "You'd risk losing the relics?"

I don't care about the crown, but the thought of the Sword of Gaya drifting to the bottom of the sea makes me ill. But then I think about Joon sinking with it. When he rose to the surface, I would spear him like a fish, rip the crown from his head, and finally have my vengeance.

"If it means putting an end to Joon, yes I would," I say.

The room falls silent.

"Fremo," I say. "Gather the six rebels you trust the most, strong men who can fight, to accompany us."

He stands as straight as possible and formally puts his hands to his forehead to salute me. Then he marches from the room, his knees high.

I smile. I like him.

I stare at the map of Gaya—everything I want to protect, the place I call home. How do I do it? I'd give my life, but will that be enough?

"Six guys?" Royo's eyebrows rise. "These boats carry a hundred men apiece."

"Yes, but if we do this right, they will be asleep aside from ten men, split between above and below deck," I say. "A small team allows us to move quickly, strike, and then get out."

"We request to accompany you as your personal guards, Your Majesty," Teo says. Calier looks at him with a questioning glance, but then his expression clears and he nods.

I eye them, looking from one to the other. Stars, it's like I can feel Euyn standing by my shoulder, questioning their loyalty. Teo is the older brother, the one calling the shots. Calier seems less certain, but I simply haven't known them long enough to tell. If they are Gayan through and through, they have every reason to give me their allegiance, but if this is a ruse, they would have me alone, able to dispose of me and claim I died in battle.

No, I wouldn't be alone. I'll have Aeri and Royo with me.

"Granted," I say.

The brothers salute me and leave the war room. Calier looks behind at us as he goes. There's a flash of hesitation in his eyes, but he follows his brother.

"So, it's settled, then?" Aeri asks.

I nod. "It will be over tonight."

No one smiles. Including me. The pit of my stomach twists, and sweat dots my forehead. Tremors start, and I tense my muscles to try to make them stop. Maybe it's remembering what happened in the arena—how the decoy crown broke into two and yet Joon still lived. But I don't believe it will be as easy as I just laid out. Something will go wrong, and that normally means death in Yusan.

Or maybe it's simply worsening convulsions. I grip the table, and eventually they subside. I'm certain they all saw, but no one says a word.

"All right, then," Aeri says. "We'll meet you for supper later."

I nod. My chest feels tight, but there's nothing more to say. The four of them move to leave.

"Sora, stay behind for a moment, please," I say.

She turns to me, her eyes wide and searching. "Of course."

Aeri and Royo exchange glances in a silent conversation before walking out the door. Tiyung eyes both of us, but then he turns with a resigned look on his face. He closes the door behind him.

Sora and I both wait until the door clicks shut. She has on a light-green dress that makes her look like the hope of spring. We continue to stand silently, letting time pass until someone listening at the keyhole would naturally give up.

"What's on your mind?" she asks, her voice low.

"I brought this up before, but I need you and Tiyung to stay here tonight," I say.

She sighs, doubtlessly tired of this conversation. "Mikail…"

"I need someone I can trust to keep an eye on Fallador, and I need Tiyung to stay here—you happen to be the perfect person to accomplish both."

She frowns.

"With what Fallador said, with so many players in this theater, things are bound to go wrong," I continue. "Tiyung is Seok's only heir, and you know he's not valuable in a fight. I can't bring a man like that on this mission, and I know he won't agree to stay without you."

"You underestimate him," she says. "He survived Idle. He killed in Oosant. He's not the useless nobleman you think."

He's not useless, but survival is a different skill set from being a wartime killer. I suppose Aeri isn't a trained fighter, either, but she's more of a natural murderer than even Royo. She's second only to me, seemingly feeling no regrets about it. I happen to love that about her.

"I will tell Tiyung that we need him here to signal us from the watchtower," I say.

She narrows her purple eyes. "Signal for what?"

"Danger. If the soldiers from Berm march north, or if you spot the fleet moving toward Jeul, I want you to flash a lantern three times. It's not out of the question for the Weian fleet to attack Yusan and Gaya at the same time—and that would be disastrous for us."

She presses her lips together. "I don't know that he'll buy that. Any one of the rebels could stay here and signal you."

I take a step closer to Sora and rest my hand on her delicate shoulder. "That's why you'll help me convince him."

The truth is, they're both key hostages, and although Sora can kill, she can be replaced by another Gayan rebel for a fight like we'll face tonight. More importantly, though, for my heart, I couldn't take losing her. I have to take Aeri, and Royo will not accept being separated from her, but Sora, I can save. I need her to stay safe here just as much as I want Tiyung to stay behind.

She sighs, her chin falling. "All right, Mikail. I'll do what's necessary."

CHAPTER SIXTY

AERI

PORT OF CHARM, GAYA

Well, I guess it's time to go kill my father.

Yeah, that thought is a little weird, but it's midnight, and we're leaving Rose Palace to go do exactly that.

As we ride under the last monsoon moon, I search my heart for any regret or doubt, but honestly, I feel nothing. My father was just fine with my rape, murder, or various demise at the hand of his brother, and I've come to be less than concerned with his well-being.

All things being equal, I'd rather not be the one to kill him, but in the end, the choice is him or the people I love. That's an easy decision.

The warm, salty breeze blows through my shoulder-length hair, and I remember the cold winds of the Light Mountains in Khitan. This can't be the choice between loves that the amarth prophesied. But with how the mythical birds protect their eggs, maybe they assumed I had a relationship with my father.

The joke's on them.

"Are you okay?" Royo asks.

It's the sixth time he's asked that question tonight. His scarred face is troubled, his eyebrows knit, but I love that he cares.

"I'm good," I say with a smile.

We ride along the Perimeter Road past where Mikail drowned those soldiers last night. I search the stone and the beach, and nothing is left of the archers. Something about that strikes me as sad, even though I know they would've happily slaughtered us.

Mortals are but shadows and reflections.

The thought comes from somewhere inside my brain, but it didn't sound like me. So, that's weird. It was almost like hearing voices.

I shake off the oddness. I don't have time for this right now.

It takes around a bell for the twelve of us to reach the Port of Charm. It's me and Royo, Mikail, Teo and Calier, Fremo, and the six men he found. The men range in age from fifty to the youngest, Duval, who is around my age. They all said their names before, but I don't remember them except for Duval, who has dark skin and a smattering of freckles.

We reach the port, and it's a far simpler space than the Port of Rahway or Quu Harbor. The main purpose is obviously docking the barges of laoli. The port holds a variety of other ships and docks, along with a large building at the end. This is also where the ferry comes in from Tamneki.

As I look across the water, the lights of the capital burn in the distance. Well, not all of them. Around ninety-five Weian warships block some of my view. Their sails are all folded, the ships as sleek as possible to avoid detection.

Mikail leads us down a dock. The twelve of us are dressed in black and nearly disappear into the night. Well, other than Royo's heavy footsteps on the planks.

Sora and Tiyung aren't here—they're still at the palace with Fallador. I was surprised that Sora agreed to stay behind, but we do have a hostage to watch. Sort of. It's more like safekeeping. Mikail likes Fallador more than he'll admit, even to himself.

Best not to think about that whole complicated thing right now. We have another deadly mission starting in moments.

A man in a boat signals us. I recognize him—he's the head of household of Rose Palace. Wan, I think is his name. But why are we getting into a rowboat? I thought we were pulling the ship to us.

"Aren't we running the ship aground?" I whisper to Mikail.

He leans toward me, still staring at the capital. "No, because the soldiers would be jolted from their beds as their ship hit the beach and then we'd have to battle a hundred men. If we row out and raise our boat to the king's ship, we can use stealth. It's fewer lives and less danger."

Fair enough, I guess.

"Your Majesty, I beg your pardon." Fremo makes a deep bow.

"Granted," Mikail says.

"Which boat is King Joon's? With their sails and flags down, they all look alike."

He tries to be extra formal with Mikail. It's sweet, really.

"Joon's ship was leading the fleet through the strait," Mikail says. "I assume his will be the one closest to Tamneki, but we'll look for the flag as we get closer. Only two ships have them."

My mouth drops open, and I catch Royo's eye. I thought Mikail already knew which one we were targeting. He seemed so certain in the war room that I didn't question him. Joon's boat could be front and center in the fleet, like he thinks, but it could also be at the very back, since kings normally command from the safest location.

My palms itch, and an icy feeling takes hold of me. I stare out at the identical ships. This is the equivalent of finding a needle in a haystack. A one in a hundred chance, and all our advantage will be lost if we choose the wrong one.

We'll also probably die.

I can't—no, I *won't* risk Royo.

"Mikail, we need to abandon this," I say. "We need a new plan."

He knits his eyebrows. "You said yourself that it has to be tonight."

I sigh. "Because I thought you knew which ship was his. We have to know for certain. We need daylight and the flags up. Maybe if we wait here until daybreak, we can use the chaos of the battle to—"

Mikail shakes his head. "He could be leading the fleet, and there would be no way to discreetly get to him."

The gold of the Water Scepter shines in his hand under the moonlight. These fucking relics. Mikail is not thinking clearly. Either the toll or the need for vengeance is muddling his mind. He wants blood and power, and his ambition is causing him to be overeager. The chances of my father actually leading a Weian battle are almost nothing.

I ball my hands in fists and fight the urge to scream. His impatience and his relic lust will result in blood being spilled. I really don't care about who he slaughters, but I won't gamble Royo's life.

My relics start to warm, but I'm not in danger of anything other than losing my temper.

Thinking about the relics gives me an idea, though—a wild one. From when I woke up in the skiff, I could feel the Water Scepter. It has a distinct pull, a hum and vibration all its own. I could also feel the ring, especially once it was in Euyn's hand. And that means…

"Wait," I say. "Everyone quiet."

No one was talking, but everyone stills, staring at me.

I close my eyes, breathe through my mouth, and try to eliminate my senses one by one except for the way I feel etherum. It's a call, a draw to magic and god force. The amulet at my chest and the ring hum on my skin. The Water Scepter vibrates to my right, an entrancing pull. I need to ignore it. I step forward on the dock. One step. Two. Then I cast my senses out into the night.

Where are the other relics of the Dragon Lord? Where is the Immortal Crown? Where is the Flaming Sword?

I hold my breath and put out my hands.

"What is she—" someone whispers. A hush swiftly cuts them off.

Where are the other pieces left behind?

Startled, I open my eyes. There's the voice again, like someone is speaking inside my mind. I'm hearing things, which isn't great because I'm weird enough as is. But I close my eyes. Maybe the voice can help.

Where are the relics? Show me where you are.

I call and reach out with my arms as if to embrace them. I'm just hugging air. Nothing. There's nothing at all. But it was worth a shot.

Suddenly, a pull yanks at my chest like someone has a rope tied to my ribs. I need to go there. Etherum. It calls to me like the cirena wanted Royo.

It's the relics.

I turn sharply and take a step. Then another. Then arms wrap around me and I can't walk anymore. But I want to. The crown and the sword are out there, and I need them. I need them like I've never needed anything before. My fingers scrape at the air, and I struggle to break free.

"Aeri!" Mikail says.

I blink and shake my head. Mikail holds me firmly, my back against his chest. As I look down at my feet, I realize I've stepped halfway off the dock.

I almost drowned myself. Again.

He studies me, and his jaw drops.

"Get her in the boat now," he says. "She'll take us to Joon."

Everyone moves quickly. Royo hops into the rowboat. He extends his arms, and Mikail lowers me to him as the other men jump in. Mikail is last, Water Scepter in hand. He and I move to the front of the rowboat, and Royo joins us.

"All right, Aeri. Show us where to go," Mikail says.

I sit at the bow as six of the men pick up oars. They're waiting, Mikail is waiting, but I don't feel the sword or crown anymore. Whatever connection I had before, the relic lust, has faded. I can't guide us because I don't know where we're going.

I shake my head.

"We have time," Mikail says. There's nothing but determination in his eyes.

"You can do it, Aeri." Royo rests his hand on my knee. The warmth of his palm spreads along my skin. His face is innocent, trusting. He believes in me. But more than that, his life depends on me. All their lives do.

I swallow hard. I have to try again because I'm not going to be able to convince Mikail to abandon this plan.

"She was going west on the dock. Row that way," Mikail says to the men. Then he looks at me. "You can do this. You mentioned before that you can feel the scepter, and when my mind is quiet your relics create a buzzing sensation in my head. I feel a pull, but I know it's not nearly as strong as what you feel. Quiet your mind, and then you'll be able to find the crown and sword."

With a frustrated huff, I close my eyes. I focus on the relics on my skin, then the pull of the Water Scepter. It's too strong. This close, it's all I feel. My fingers curl. I want to rip it out of his hand, no matter the cost. The desire floods through me, and I hold on until it's a pulsing need.

I lean forward and cast my senses into the shadowed fleet.

Okay, voice in my head, where are these fucking things? Where is the crown of my blood? Where is the Sword of Gaya?

At first, there's nothing. Just the constant draw of the Water Scepter. I'm about to ask Mikail to move to the back of the boat when a new sensation hits me. My eyes are shut, but the crown feels red and beats like a heart. I reach my arm out.

Come to me.

"Row to exactly where she points," Mikail says.

Eyes still closed, I pull a throwing knife from my vest.

All right, voice. I'm coming for you.

CHAPTER SIXTY-ONE

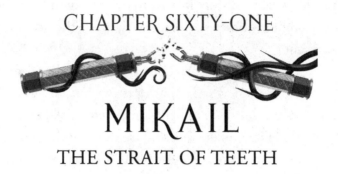

MIKAIL
THE STRAIT OF TEETH

We follow Aeri's motions as if she's a compass needle, rowing straight and then changing direction until she points us to ships that are nearly in the Strait of Teeth. Joon's ship is not at the front like I'd thought. It's not closest to Gaya, either, but hidden away to the west. I should've known better. Of course Joon wouldn't risk leading the attack. The forefront sustains the most casualties, and he wouldn't stick out his own neck any more than the other rulers—despite having the crown. Instead, he's in position to casually observe the battle unfolding.

Coward.

Once Aeri has homed in on one ship, we have him. My heart speeds up, my muscles twitching. Now, I don't have to just sit and observe. This mission falls on me.

And I wouldn't have it any other way.

I strike the Water Scepter into the sea. The ocean responds just as it did last night, and a quiet contentment fills me. All my aches and pains vanish, replaced by the swaying of currents and swell of waves, by brine and primordial power. The only time I feel well is when I use the relic. It does explain how the Weian scepter bearers used the relic continually until their deaths—it's more painful not to.

I command the water to bring Joon's ship to me.

Even though I know the scepter is controlling the tides, I still marvel at the Weian warship floating to us on a smooth current. The flat-bottomed boat effortlessly drifts away from the fleet despite its dropped anchor.

I pull Joon's ship until it's about two hundred and fifty yards away from the nearest vessel. That's just within range of the best archers of the fleet, but it's a difficult shot even for skilled marksmen in the dead of night. I'll take those odds. There's only so far I can go. The more I move the ship, the more likely it is that someone aboard will notice and call out an alarm.

"Ready yourselves," I say.

The men in our boat drop their oars and grab their weapons.

Even the brief break in wielding sends pain shooting through my muscles. I grip the side of the rowboat with my free hand and breathe hard as my body shudders painfully. It's another convulsion. I grit my teeth, waiting for it to pass.

When it finally does, I focus and command the sea again. The water responds, and my pain subsides as I gather the wave beneath us. I let out a low moan of relief.

Gasps fill my ears as the men ride the miracle of one ship being raised by the sea. I continue to lift us until we're even with the cabin of the warship.

On my signal, we spill out onto the deck. I'm last, and I let the boat drift back down to sea level. Wan, the head of my household staff, stays in the craft. This is his rowboat, and he'll keep it in place, waiting for us until the job is done.

The twelve of us press ourselves against the exterior back wall of the cabin. Ordinarily, this should be the captain's quarters, but if this is Joon's ship, he will be in here. He wouldn't deign to mingle with the commoners below deck, so this is the only other option.

My heart hammers my chest as I press against the varnished wood of the ship. I take deep breaths of salty air and attempt to slow my heart rate, but excitement and anticipation course through my veins. So much so that I can't even feel the pain that should be shooting through my limbs. I've waited for this moment for nearly my entire life. Victory is tantalizingly close, but I can't rush things. I can't ruin the mission again with impatience. This must be slow and methodical, or we'll lose.

Footsteps thud along the deck, accompanied by the jangle of steel. The sounds are moving closer—a guard.

I gesture to Duval, the youngest of the rebels. He's closest to the left side, where the guard will come around the cabin. Duval nods, a serious look on his round face. He launches and grabs the soldier. Before the guard can scream, Royo pulls out his nunchuka. He wraps the metal chain around the guard's neck, strangling him. It's not the normal use, but I'm not complaining.

The guard is dead within a minute, and the two of them gently lower the body onto the deck so that his steel doesn't make a sound.

I can't tell the color of the armor, but the red plumes mark him as a Yusanian palace guard. We have the right ship.

The men all exchange glances. Fremo puts his hand on my shoulder. He smiles and nods approvingly.

My hands shake. I want this so badly I can taste it. I can feel Joon's blood spray and the thrill of a near twenty-year mission finally coming to its end. I will kill him tonight.

I wave my hand. On my signal, four men toss the body overboard. We don't need a guard discovered right now.

The Water Scepter is in my left hand; my right is on my sword hilt. My heart pounds against my ribs, but I'm ready. I survived the Festival of Blood in order to kill this tyrant. If I fail, I should've died that day.

We make our way in two lines to the port side of the cabin. I lead one group, and Teo leads the other. And there, at the end, is the door. Just one piece of wood stands between me and the bloodletter who robbed me of everything, including my name.

I gesture for Royo to kick it down, but Aeri puts out a hand for us to stop. I tilt my head. She followed orders up until now. I suppose it was too much to expect that to last.

She moves closer to the door. I'm about to pull her back when she reaches into her sleeve. She takes out a pin set and then kneels by the lock.

Clever thief.

I don't ask why she has a lock-picking set on her—no need to question a gift. If she can silently open the door, it will give us the element of surprise. We might kill Joon in his bed.

The rest of us watch for patrolmen or other dangers, but it's quiet on the ship. The sea laps against the boat, gently rocking it. There's no chatter from a crew, as the men are mainly asleep. Other footsteps resound on the deck, but they're on the aft side.

A soft click lets me know Aeri was successful. Royo immediately picks her up and carries her away from the door.

Teo and Calier file in close to the door, and Fremo reaches for the handle.

As soon as his weathered hand hits the metal, the little hairs on my neck stand. I grip the hilt of my sword tighter. I don't want him to be first in, but I don't have a reason to tell him to stop.

He swings open the door, and we flow in after him. One moment later, the lamps light in the cabin.

That's when the shooting starts.

CHAPTER SIXTY-TWO

AERI

THE STRAIT OF TEETH

This is all wrong. The lamps are lit in the room, and two palace archers stand across from us with crossbows at their shoulders. I have one second to absorb that we walked into a trap before bolts fly. One hits Fremo directly in the chest, and another is off aim. It strikes Teo in the thigh. Teo goes down on his knee with a groan. But the bolt that hits Fremo must pierce his lung, because he starts spitting up blood. He staggers forward, remaining on his feet to try to fight as crimson drips down his chin.

It's so very brave.

The six rebels he picked rush at the archers as they reload. I want to sprint forward, but I'm trapped behind Mikail and Royo, who stand still.

We're all inside the cabin, but the room is L-shaped—we can't see around the corner until we get past the archers. Two more guards come out of nowhere and attack the rebels.

I gasp as the space becomes a frenzy of blades and blood.

The palace guards are armored in steel while we don't even have leathers. It's not close to a fair fight.

A guard swings his sword, and Fremo blocks the blade, but he doesn't see the second one coming. With a slash of another sword, Fremo collapses to the ground, a huge gash spanning from his neck to his chest, exposing white bone and sinew. He shakes and gasps as blood pools on the wood floor, but I can't do anything but watch as the light leaves his eyes. All in a matter of seconds.

Mikail's face goes ashen, and then his sword flames to life. He tosses the scepter to me and joins the fray. It buzzes in my palm like a trapped bee, bound to Mikail but tempting anyhow.

Royo drops his axe and pulls me behind him as I try to rush forward. I struggle to break free, but his hands have me in a vise grip. I know he cares. I know he doesn't want me involved, but he needs to let me go. I can use my relics to end this. The ring and amulet vibrate to the point of shaking me, but I'm afraid to use them when Royo has my wrists and I can barely see around him. Will I have control, or will I accidentally kill our men?

I can't risk finding out.

Instead, two more rebels die anyway, their bodies crashing onto the floor. That much, I can see.

Royo uses one hand to pick up his axe, and I get out from behind him. He grabs my wrist again. I stand to Royo's side just in time to see one of the archers reload his crossbow. He shoots, and another rebel falls.

But Mikail joining the fight evens the odds. He runs his sword through a guard, then engages another, moving as fast and fluid as he always does.

Yet the other rebels are struggling, and Royo and I are doing nothing. He moves from side to side, searching for a threat, but I don't need protection—the rebels do. Calier is also standing guard by his brother despite Teo trying to wave him off.

Blood soaks his black pant leg, but Teo grits his teeth. With one pull, he yanks the bolt out of his thigh. Then he stands and raises his sword.

I look at Royo, so angry I could burst. "I didn't come here to sit like a doll on a shelf. Let go of me *now*."

I stare at him, fully resolved. Expressions war on his face until he relents, dropping my arm.

By the time I'm free, it's too late. Nearly all the fighters are dead. The archers, five rebels, and both palace guards bleed out on the ground.

Tears sting my eyes as I take in the scene, but it's not sadness—it's frustration. I didn't help. I didn't save anyone. I put all my hurt, all my useless anger into the stare I give Royo.

He looks away.

Mikail and Duval breathe hard. They're the last men standing from the fray. Duval looks like Tiyung right now—shocked at what he just did—but when Fremo died, something changed. He went from being a boy to hacking like a butcher.

I know the feeling.

At Mikail's signal, the four of us, plus Calier and Teo, make our way around the corner in a sweeping motion. I hold my breath, my heart pounding. I carry the scepter but put out my other hand, bracing for an attack.

It doesn't come.

Mikail pulls up short as we reach the end of the room. Standing at the back wall by the bed are four people: two palace guards with their weapons drawn, my father, and…Hana.

Good gods, what is she doing here?

Her arm is extended. The poison-maiden-turned-spy has her fingers on a rope—the rope for an alarm bell.

Ten Hells, we're dead.

CHAPTER SIXTY-THREE

TIYUNG

ROSE PALACE, GAYA

S ora insisted that we stay behind at the palace while the others went on a mission to murder King Joon. Mikail claimed that we were needed here, but I have a feeling she is just my nanny for the night. He and the others don't think much of my fighting ability, and compared to them, I suppose they are right. He still sees me as either soft or too valuable a target.

Maybe both.

It's difficult to change first impressions, especially when they were correct.

I wouldn't have agreed to remain at the palace without Sora, and I assume Mikail knew that, too. But there are worse jailers than her.

We've been up in the watchtower since midnight. It's dark, other than the lights of Jeul beneath us and a small lantern on the floor. None of this sits well with me—not the darkness, not their mission, not staying behind. Mikail believes he needs the sword in the way that Seok believes he needs more power. That endless hunger creates its own battles. But if they do take the relics tonight and kill King Joon, they'll stop the war before it begins. His greed is for the greater good.

I think.

My skin turns to gooseflesh in the cooling night air. I wish I could shake this feeling of doom, but it wraps around me like a cloak.

Sora and I aim our spyglasses toward Tamneki. The moon glows on the water, and it's just enough light for us to make out the silhouette of a Weian ship lying in wait. The fleet has their sails down. If we didn't know to look for them, I don't think we'd spot them.

Every now and then, Sora and I change positions and scan to the west and south of the island, but there's nothing of note.

Still, the air crackles with tension. Sora hasn't said much, but I know her heart. She'd rather be with Mikail, Aeri, and Royo than here with me and our hostage. She keeps straining to see the Port of Charm even though it's too far and too dark to make out anything.

"What do you think about Fallador coming here?" I ask.

Sora lowers her glass and turns toward me. "Do you know him?"

I shake my head. "Not really. I met him once before with my father when we were in Khitan. I really believed he was the prince of Gaya."

"Everyone did. Including Mikail," she sighs.

The way she says his name makes me wonder about when I saw them in the garden. She and Mikail were laughing together, standing so close that their foreheads nearly touched. And then there were the glances they exchanged in the war room.

My stomach turns again.

Mikail is handsome and charismatic, so I see why she'd fall for him, but he was in love with Euyn the last time I saw him. I can't imagine that their love has faded enough to be replaced by another. But Sora is no ordinary woman.

"You've grown close with him," I say.

The bitterness I can't hide seeps into my words. I can't seem to keep my resolution that I want her to be happy regardless of how she finds that joy. This close to her, and I only want it to be me.

I grind my teeth. So much for striving to be a better person.

She shrugs. "No more so than the others. We've all grown close. It's how we survived in Khitan and ever since."

Curiosity bubbles and bursts inside me. I want to ask more

questions. I want to know exactly what he means to her and what she means to him, and it's deeply none of my business. I press my lips together to keep the words in.

"Mikail is grieving the one dearest to him," she says. "So am I." She stares into the distance without a spyglass, and her fingers grip the stone railing of the wall. "It's a deep, dark pit, especially when you feel responsible. We share that double bond of love and loss. If you're implying that it's romantic, though—no, it is not."

I wish that didn't make my heart lighter. I wish I didn't suddenly view Mikail in a better light. He did love Euyn for a decade. I was right—that kind of consuming love doesn't disappear when a body burns. Instead, it lurks in the corners of your mind, chaining your heart. He and Sora are both saddled with grief and thirst for revenge, but together, their load is lighter. I know that feeling. All the sadness and desperation in Idle was far easier when I had Ailor with me.

"I'm sorry," I say.

She tilts her head. "For what?"

"For making assumptions."

She smiles slowly, and it's hypnotic. This is the grin she gives when I've pleasantly surprised her. It's the one I strive to see.

"It's all right," she says. "You've been through so much as well— Idle, escaping and traveling to Khitan, and then trying to reach your father. You could have fled to safety, but you came here to find us. To find me. I… I'm glad you're here."

She hesitates, but she drifts a step closer and then another. I make myself hold still. I've been longing for weeks to hold her—for nothing more than to have her safe in my arms—but as much as I want her, I need her to want me, too.

I lean on the half wall, and she stops two feet away. She holds the railing. I move my hand closer on the stone until our fingertips touch.

She looks down at our hands, and she smiles. Her grin erases the darkness around me.

"You're really here," she says, her beautiful voice filled with wonder.

I nod. "I made a promise to you that I would wait for anything."

She looks to the side, frowning. "Promises are just words to most people."

"Not to me."

She scans my face and then sighs. Our eyes meet, and for the first time since I've seen her again, I feel that she wants me closer. She wants me here with her. She takes a small step, but it feels like she's closing miles of distance between us.

I slowly reach toward her face, and her eyes drift closed.

I'm about to touch her cheek when she whips her head to the right. Startled, I pull my arm back, but she's not looking at me—she's staring at the entrance to the tower. I was so lost in the moment that I didn't hear the footsteps racing up the stairs.

But I do now.

My breathing speeds up as person after person jogs closer. This isn't Mikail and the others. And that can only mean trouble.

With their steps comes the jangle of metal and coordinated breathing. It's soldiers—I'm certain of it. But we didn't spot any king's guard marching from Berm or anywhere else. The fortress in Jeul is manned now by rebels, and they should have intercepted any soldiers. Where did these men come from?

It doesn't matter. They're almost here.

I drop my spyglass and push Sora behind me before I draw my sword. The glass falls on the stone floor with a crack. Sora sets hers down and pulls out a dagger.

We stare at the archway. Only two people can pass through at the same time, which makes our numbers even. If I strike as soon as they appear, I could kill them two at a time. But how many until my strength gives out? And what if they're on our side?

I don't have to wait long to find out.

Two men in black leather armor reach the top of the tower.

They're Yusanian king's guard. That means there are at least ten more men behind them, since the king's guard moves as a twelve- or fifteen-man strike team.

I hold my sword, waiting, my palms sweating. For the life of me, I don't know how Mikail handles this so casually—the moment before an attack, when you resolve to murder another human being. My chest throbs to the point I think my heart might fail. I don't want to kill anyone, but there's Sora. She's breathing behind me, and I won't let them hurt her. If I die protecting her, it would be a worthwhile ending.

I make my decision, ready to swing.

One of the men raises his hand. The medals on his chest glimmer in the moonlight—he's a captain.

"Sora Inigo and Tiyung Gamesong, you are to come with us."

To where, exactly? Are they soldiers from Berm or are they Rune's men? If they are Rune's, did Fallador betray us? Or was he merely a decoy while the count moved his men in to take us hostage? They obviously want us alive; otherwise, they would've attacked already.

"I don't think so," I say.

"Lay down your sword or we will remove you by force," he replies.

I need time to figure out how to get Sora to safety. We are far too high up to jump. And their men occupy the only exit. There's no option. We'll have to go with them and then try to escape once we're in the palace.

"On whose authority?" I ask.

The more they talk, the more time I'll have to formulate a plan. The longer we spend here, the greater the chances that the others might return and slaughter all of them.

The captain tilts his head slightly as if it's a wild question. "On King Seok's authority."

My shoulders drop, and my heart falls. No. No, these can't be my father's men. They must be soldiers trying to collect on the bounty.

But the doubt makes me loosen my grip. The second my sword

tips, the king's guard rushes me. I regrip the hilt and slice at the soldier's waist where the armor ends. He falls to the ground with a scream. Horror and victory flow through me, but more guards appear before I can even recover. Four king's guard pull at me and Sora, separating us. Our eyes meet—she's terrified. I reach for her, but a guard knocks my sword from my other hand. Weaponless, I ball my hands into fists and punch whoever is near me.

I won't let them take her.

While I flail, a fist flies at my face. Next thing I know, I'm seeing stars and clutching at my nose.

A voice rings out. "Enough!"

Everyone stops moving.

"The king's son was not to be hurt! Those were the orders." The man's voice carries authority and is laced with irritation at his underlings.

I look up as a man in gray steel walks onto the tower. Red feathers decorate his helmet. Oh gods, that is a Qali Palace guard.

These *are* my father's men.

Sora goes still, her jaw slack. She stares at me with betrayal in her eyes. I wonder why she's looking at me like that, but then I realize she thinks that I knew or that I am a part of this. I don't have a chance to deny it before the king's guard carries us out of the tower.

CHAPTER SIXTY-FOUR

AERI

THE STRAIT OF TEETH

Hana holds a rope as white as her dress. If she pulls it, the brass bell will tip and ring, waking all the men below deck. Ninety more soldiers will surround this cabin. We might be able to kill my father before we die. Probably not.

I stare at Hana's beauty and remember how heartfelt she was, sitting in Rose Palace, confessing what she'd done over the years. How she'd tried and how she had failed. She'd seemed honest, open.

My stomach bottoms out as I exhale my disappointment. I really thought she was on our side. I believed she loved Sora and had done everything for her. But I guess there's only one side to Hana—her own.

Mortals are fickle instruments.

I sigh. Really? Not now, voice. I have a lot of shit to handle as is.

Whatever happens, we can't let anyone ring that bell. I think about turning them all to gold, but it wouldn't affect my father, since he has the crown. And I know him well enough to be sure that he'd step over corpses to get to the bell.

What do I do? I need a diversion. Something, anything.

"Father," I say.

"Daughter."

My father stands in gray satin nightclothes, although he wears the Immortal Crown over his black hair. The Flaming Sword of

Gaya must be the golden blade slung on his hip, no doubt hastily grabbed when they felt the boat being pulled or whenever they heard us coming.

"We are here for the sword," I say. "Give it to us, and no one else will die. You have my word."

I hold my chin high as if we're the ones in control. Mikail's eyes dart over to me. It wasn't what we agreed on, but we're now in desperate times. If we get the sword and leave with our lives, that's a huge victory. I don't care how badly he wants to kill Joon. That will have to wait for another day.

My father smiles. "What a queen you would've made, Naerium—between the harbor and this." Then his grin fades, and his expression turns grave. "Instead, you and your friends will die tonight."

He actually manages to look sorry for us, and then he turns to Hana. I take half a step forward.

"Euyn has already gone to the Kingdom of Hells," I say. "You'd kill your last remaining child?"

My father's brown eyes shift just enough to reflect his confusion. My face tingles as blood leaves my cheeks. Euyn wasn't his. If Quilimar told the truth, that means he was Omin's son.

"Euyn was my brother, not my child," Joon says. "And I gave you two chances to be recognized as princess of Yusan, but you could not be loyal. You made your choices. I will have to make mine."

He gestures to Hana.

My relics vibrate. I will have to use them and hope we can kill Joon before he reaches the rope. But Hana's eyes dart to the king and then back. Twice. She's signaling to someone, but it's not me. She lets go of the rope and, at the same time, grabs for the Immortal Crown.

What is happening?

A blur moves to my side—Mikail. He runs and then launches to strike. Hana lifts the crown off Joon's head, and my breath catches. My father's hands reach up to take it back. One heartbeat. Two. The palace guard standing next to Hana turns toward her, his sword already drawn. The relics heat my skin. The guard moves forward to strike. I put my hand out.

But Mikail's sword cuts through the air. The entire world stops as the blade careens toward my father's neck. His aim is true. His sword strikes my father so hard, he's nearly decapitated. Blood sprays out like a fountain, and Joon's crownless head lolls to the side. His eyes stare at me as he falls to the floor.

The Immortal Crown is in Hana's hand. I forget to breathe, completely frozen. Whatever I thought I'd feel, it's not this pitiful shock. I watch as the light leaves Joon's eyes.

The scrape of metal fills my ears, calling me back into the moment. Calier has drawn his sword. But it's not to attack Joon or the guards. He's aiming for Mikail's back.

No. He's going to kill him.

I exhale and shake off the shock. I call to my relics.

Turn enemy hearts to gold.

A golden glow fills the room. The glow becomes an orb around Mikail. He shades his eyes, but the light quickly fades. Three men fall to the floor, clutching their chests—the two palace guards and Calier.

Mikail turns just in time to see Calier's sword nearly strike him before the man crumples onto the ground. Then he stares at me, his mouth dropping open. It's not the first time I've saved him. It's what we do.

Somehow, we've succeeded. My father is dead, and we're still standing. I don't know how other than to say the gods must be on our side.

A gasp that's more like a moan draws my attention. I think it's Teo reacting to his brother's death, but he's frozen still. No, it's not him.

It's Hana.

I look at her, and horror stabs at me, just like the sword protruding from her chest. Her eyes are wide and terror-stricken as red blood seeps down the front of her white dress. The palace guard struck, spearing her with his sword before I could kill him. Because I hesitated. In her hand, she still clutches the crown. But she's not royal, so it can't save her.

"No!" I cry.

Hana had played the king, acting the part of a trusted spymaster, just like Mikail. I don't know if even Mikail realized that she was one of us before she signaled to him. Either way, in the end, she was true. And she was killed because I didn't act in time.

It was all my fault.

"No. Please, no." I plead to no one, because there is nothing any of us can do for her. All this magic, and none of us can save a life.

I can only kill.

Hana's eyes are open, and tears roll down her cheeks. But I don't think she hears me. She's gone somewhere else.

"Sora," she whispers. It's more like a rattle as she falls to her knees, but the sound is full of so much love that it shatters my heart.

Hana collapses, and the crown drops out of her hand and rolls on the ground.

It's the last thing I see.

CHAPTER SIXTY-FIVE

MIKAIL
THE STRAIT OF TEETH

It wasn't supposed to be like this.

Joon is dead at my feet. I struck the tyrant down with my own blade, avenged my people. We won. This is all I've wanted, but as I stare at Hana's eyes, all I can think about is what I've lost to get here. It doesn't feel like a victory at all.

I reach down and lower Hana's eyelids. Gods guide her soul.

"Aeri!" Royo cries.

He catches her as she falls.

"Aeri! Aeri," he cries. "Mikail, help. I don't think she's breathing."

She's stiff as a board as he cradles her. Her eyes are closed this time, but he's right—she's not breathing. She's frozen in time, and it's worse than before because she used her powers again to save me.

I shake off my stupor and grab the Immortal Crown. It's speckled with blood, but the drops are hard to see on the rubies. The relic is surprisingly light in my hands. The fake was much heavier.

I go to place it on Aeri's head, and Royo pulls her back, away from me.

He bares his teeth like a dog. "You don't know what that'll do to her."

No, but we also don't have time to debate this.

"It's true, I don't," I say. "But it'll save her life right now."

Lines mar Royo's face—his scars and his worries. He looks at her, then the crown, and then her face again. He gives me a short nod as pain swims in his eyes. Our choices are between bad and worse, but without this, I'm certain she will die. Anything is better than that.

"I trust you," Royo says. He moves Aeri closer to me.

The weight of his words hits me. I hold my breath as I slide the crown over her hair.

The second the crown meets Aeri's skin, the metal completely changes, flowing around her.

Stars.

It was a crown with peaks and gems. I just held it in my hands a second ago. Now, it's a solid gold diadem on her forehead with a ruby and diamonds in the center. I touch it, but I already know that it's now fused to her like the other relics. Something happens when a person has more than one. Some merger with the etherum. It doesn't just multiply powers; it melds the relics to the skin.

As strange as that is, the most important thing is that her chest suddenly rises and falls. Royo and I both sigh in relief.

"Thank you," he says with tears in his eyes.

I nod and put a hand on his shoulder. At least that's one problem solved. There are around ninety of them still asleep downstairs.

I don't understand why Joon didn't ring the alarm bell the second he saw us. Maybe he actually cared about Aeri, or maybe he wanted to toy with us, or ultimately, he wanted the relics beyond logic. It doesn't matter. I don't have the time to stand here and wonder.

I grab the Water Scepter from where Aeri dropped it, and then I approach Joon's dead body. I swing my blade and cut the Sword of Gaya from his belt, then kick him to the side. His head rolls last, since it's barely attached.

The Flaming Sword of the Dragon Lord is a beautiful blade of pure gold with gems embedded in the pommel. I reach down and grab the hilt.

Instantly, power like I've never felt before surges through me. Images of Gaya flash through my mind. As a child playing on the island, I was always told to run back home when thunderstorms rumbled across the sky. One day, I saw why. A boy was outside in the charm fields, and all of a sudden, a bolt came out of the clouds. Lightning struck his body, and he literally glowed with all of the energy.

This has to be a similar feeling. Every inch of me feels lit from within.

My vision clears just in time for me to watch as both the sword and the scepter become liquid, snaking up my arms like bangles. And then they become solid once more. The scepter is now a blue metal rope circling up my forearm, and the sword has become a gold band on my right. Duval and Teo drop down to one knee, which is not easy for Teo, since he was shot.

They are my last men still alive. I need to keep them that way.

"We have to go," I say.

Duval rises, and Royo stands, picking up Aeri.

"But…" Teo begins. He clamps his mouth shut as he colors, but his eyes dart to his traitor brother. Calier's body is on the ground, and I can't say I care much about releasing his soul, but there are also the bodies of our fallen nearer to the door, including Fremo.

But we don't exactly have time for a pyre and prayers.

As soon as I think of fire, the gold relic vibrates on my arm. Right. There's a far easier solution.

"I'll light the entire ship on fire once we're on the rowboat," I say.

First things first, though. I take my sword and swing it downward to fully behead the king.

"Baesinga," I whisper.

Joon's head comes clean off with the snap of bones. I lift it up by his hair and then nod to the remaining men.

The four of us proceed in a sweeping motion, stepping over bodies, until we reach the cabin door. I take a deep breath, grabbing my sword in my free hand, and then we spill out onto the deck. Duval grabbed one of the crossbows. He holds it up to his eye, meaning...he has no idea how to use it. Teo stands ready with his sword, ignoring the pain in his leg.

The night is still as we silently skirt to the back of the cabin. I can't see the rowboat, but that was the point. I reach my left arm out and call the sea to me.

Nothing.

I try again. Still nothing at all. No tides or swells. The water doesn't move aside from the usual waves.

I can't touch the sea from this high up, but there's no feeling. The relic doesn't hum or respond. The command isn't there.

My stomach drops. What is this? I thought two relics together were supposed to multiply power, not lessen it. But there's no time to think this through. We're too exposed out here.

Two guards shout from down the ship. Footsteps come pounding toward us. We are out of time.

"Can you all swim?" I ask.

Teo and Duval nod.

Royo shakes his head. "I can, but she can't."

Duval shoots at the guards and actually manages to hit one. But I wish he hadn't. The man cries out with a terrible howl.

Stars, he's as loud as the alarm bell.

"She won't drown," I say. "We need to jump—now."

Royo looks around as if trying to find another means of escape, but there isn't one.

I give the signal, and we all jump overboard, landing in the cool water just as daggers chase us.

As soon as I dive under, I remember we are too close to the Strait of Teeth for comfort. Monsters don't respect artificial borders. If Wan was killed or captured, it'll be a long swim back to the Port of Charm.

I surface and search for the boat. Echoing across the water, there's a faint whistle. I stare in the distance but spot the rowboat just twenty yards away. Wan must've seen us jump and rowed closer.

I want to help Royo swim with Aeri, but I'd just get in the way. With fast arm strokes, I make it to the boat, then climb aboard. Wan and I both assist the others scrambling in.

"What is that?" Royo asks. He flails in the water as I take Aeri from him. Duval and Teo get her onto one of the benches.

I scan the water, but I don't see anything.

Wan and I both struggle to help Royo in, which is hard because he's floundering.

"Ten fucking Hells, I swear that was an iku." Royo thrashes as he throws a leg over the side of the boat while we tug his arms.

"It was probably just a fish," Wan says. "Iku don't come this far."

"It was definitely a fucking iku," Royo insists, now completely in the boat. "I almost got eaten because you rowed away!"

They begin to bicker, but I'm staring at the Weian warship. I still need to release the souls of our fallen, but I couldn't even call the sea. I need the ship to catch fire, but the Flaming Sword is now a decoration on my arm.

The gold band begins to vibrate, an irresistible hum filling my mind. I raise my arm almost on instinct.

Light on fire.

Then I snap my fingers.

In a whoosh and flash of light, the white ship is completely engulfed in flames, a bonfire on the water, illuminating all the ships around it.

Stars.

I stare at my arm, and now I see what I can do with two relics.

Royo and Wan stop arguing. Everyone is silent as Fremo, Hana, and even Calier's souls are released, and the men below deck start screaming. They will be released soon, too, but not Joon. Never him. When I jumped overboard, I dropped his head to the bottom of the sea.

CHAPTER SIXTY-SIX

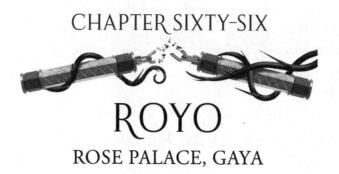

ROYO
ROSE PALACE, GAYA

Mikail and I ride back to Rose Palace with Teo and Duval behind us—the only other guys who survived. In the distance, the king's ship and the Port of Charm burn, smoking into the night sky. But I don't give a shit about the fires Mikail set. Aeri has been unconscious for over fifteen minutes.

"Aeri. Aeri, please. Come back. Come back to me," I whisper.

Tears stream down my face, drying in the wind. I ride holding her against my chest. She won't die because the crown saved her, but no matter what I say, I can't reach her. She's like the tide slipping through my hands.

We gallop toward the city walls of Jeul. Mikail rides just as hard as I do with the relics encircling his arms.

We got all the relics. King Joon is dead. We were supposed to have won, but it doesn't feel that way. Nobody's said a word as we speed back to the capital. That nice old guy, Fremo, is dead, Calier was a traitor, and Hana died trying to help us. Everybody's quiet, trying to deal with what happened. But more than anything, if Aeri doesn't come back, it doesn't matter how much we won—we lost. I draw Aeri tighter, like holding her against my chest will help the ache there.

The headless body of the governor hangs chained to the top of the city gates as we ride into Jeul. It seems to take forever to get up the hill, but minutes later, we're back at the palace. We ride up to the front steps.

I hand Aeri down, and Mikail holds her while I get off my horse. As soon as I'm on my feet, I take her back. I kiss her lips and stroke her hair.

"Come back to me," I say. "Please. I beg you."

Her eyelids move. Mikail startles, taking a step back, then stares at me. My heart jumps—he saw that, too. I thought I was just imagining it, but the stable boys stop and gape as well.

"Keep talking to her," he says. "She can hear you…wherever she is."

Hope surges through me, speeding up my pulse, and I hold her tight. "Come on, Aeri. Come back. Stay with me."

Her lashes flutter, and then, finally, she opens her eyes.

I throw my head back and let out the longest sigh of relief. She woke up. She's not frozen in time anymore. She didn't leave me.

"Royo?" she asks. There's a question in her voice that I don't understand.

"It's me."

"What are you doing here?" she asks.

"We're at Rose Palace," I say. "You passed out on the warship, and we came back to Jeul."

"Oh." She runs her hands down her face, but then she slides her fingers upward, toward her forehead. She explores the gold band with her fingertips.

"That all really happened?" She's not surprised that the Immortal Crown is now fused to her. Not at all. She sounds more exhausted than anything else.

"Let's get her inside where you can lay her down," Mikail says.

It's a good plan.

Mikail leads the way, and I carry Aeri as she snuggles against my chest. My heart pounds hard, but in a good way as I feel her nuzzle me. Teo and Duval follow us up the stairs to the front entrance of the palace. They're good guys, both of them.

We've just reached the doors when Fallador comes running out. Teo and Duval grab their weapons, but Fallador gestures with empty hands. Actually, he doesn't even have shoes on. His eyes are wild, and his wavy hair is straight, it's so wet. I think he just got out of a bath.

"What happened?" Fallador asks.

"It's done. We killed Joon," Mikail says.

Fallador is barely listening, looking past us. "No, what happened to them? Where did they go?"

Mikail tilts his head. Fallador is so frantic, he hasn't even noticed the relics.

A chill settles on my shoulders. This ain't good. I look at Aeri, but she's barely paying attention. She blinks hard and then smiles up at me.

"Where did who go?" Mikail's calm, but there's the rattle of danger in his voice.

"Them! Your friends—Sora and Tiyung," Fallador says. "I was in the bath, and I heard men in the palace. I figured they were rebels, but then I heard a scream. A man's scream. By the time I was dressed, Sora and Tiyung were both gone. No one was here except for me. What happened?"

It takes me a second to get what he's saying, but Mikail storms right into the palace.

He's already inside by the time I realize Sora and Tiyung were taken.

CHAPTER SIXTY-SEVEN

MIKAIL

ROSE PALACE, GAYA

I stride through the palace, ignoring the servants who bow to me, and then I throw open the door to my bedroom. All of Sora's and Tiyung's things are still here—not that he would need anything if he did, in fact, betray us.

Calier. Gambria. Fallador, to some extent. Was Tiyung a traitor, too?

He was so in love with Sora that I never suspected he could be working for his father. But was he? As soon as Fallador said they were gone, I began to wonder: Were they taken, or did he arrange for them to leave? And did I play right into his hand by having him stay behind with her?

With no clues in the bedroom, I sprint up the stairs of the watchtower. I breathe and move without agony, which gives me a lightness I haven't felt since Khitan.

When the Flaming Sword bonded to me, it took away all my pain. But I might've also lost the ability to wield water. So much happened tonight that I can't even stop to think about that. I'm sure I'll pay some terrible price for using two relics, but right now, I don't care. All that matters is finding Sora.

I reach the top of the tower, and I search for any sign of her. Two spyglasses, one broken, and a small lantern litter the floor. And there's a stain. I tap the wetness on the stone. It's blood—a lot of it.

Fury rises through me, but I force myself to exhale. It's probably not hers. Whoever took them wanted them alive, or I would've found their bodies. And Fallador heard a man's scream. This is likely someone else's blood.

Once I finish checking the tower, I take the stairs back to the palace. There are a few spots of blood, and then they stop. I take a deep breath, trying to exhale my anger. If they hurt her, I'll burn down the world.

There are three possible groups who could have targeted her: Rune's men, bounty hunters, or Seok's men. If it was Rune, what did Fallador know? He seemed frenzied when he ran out of the palace, but was it all for show so that I wouldn't suspect his involvement? I don't think he could fake that, but he convincingly acted like royalty for years.

I must know, and there's only one way to find out.

I call him and the entire household staff to the throne room. Aeri and Royo also join us. I don't need her protection now that I can summon fire, but I know they want to be here. They care about Sora just as much as I do. And that lessens my rage…somewhat.

The staff files in. Most are dressed in white cotton nightclothes and rub sleep from their eyes, but some were awake. They will all answer to me.

"Two of my guests were taken from the palace tonight," I say. "I need to know what you saw. What you heard. Give me anything that will be useful in helping us locate them, and you will be rewarded."

I wait on the throne, but the cavernous room is silent. No one speaks.

After a few seconds pass, I exhale and lean forward. "Am I to understand that not one of you noticed a group of men invading this palace and leaving with two hostages? No one investigated the scream Fallador heard from the bath?"

More silence greets me.

I tap the armrest, my patience wearing thin. "How interesting that none of you heard or saw a thing. Perhaps because you were complicit in their kidnapping." I sharply change my tone. "May I remind you all that you pledged your loyalty with your lives."

The line of servants reacts. Some pale while others go wide-eyed, but either way, they stay silent. I allow a full minute to pass, slowly scanning down the line.

"You have all witnessed how I handle treason," I say.

My impatience mounts with every second. Maybe I should've dismissed them when we first arrived. We are more than capable of cooking and cleaning for ourselves. Instead, I accepted these strangers' vows but cast Hana out. And she was loyal in the end. Yet she died and they all still live.

I stand. If I can't solve this as a king, I will resolve it as a spymaster.

I pull my sword, and it flames to life. The men and women gasp and stare. I suppress a laugh. They're awestruck by a gimmick as the real Flaming Sword warms on my skin, begging to be used. With a snap of my fingers, I could light all of them on fire. In the recesses of my mind, I consider it. The relics vibrate like my own heartbeat, but using etherum isn't necessary when a blade will do.

"Where are they, and who took them?" My voice thunders in the room.

Thirty-six of my household servants stand silently. Wan, my head of household, stayed at the Port of Charm to report on the fleet.

"Adoros," Fallador says. "The men who took them were in and out within the span of a bath. Without hearing the scream, I wouldn't have thought anything of it. It's possible none of them saw anything."

It's also possible that everyone is lying—him included.

There's always a way to get to the truth, if you have the stomach for it. I grab the girl closest to me and hold her so she faces the staff. She's a chambermaid around Aeri's age. Yulia—the cook's daughter.

"I take your silence as complicity and judge you guilty of conspiring against the throne." I bring my sword closer to her neck. She sweats and whimpers.

Some of the servants shake their heads. Others immediately start crying. They saw what I did to the women who tried to poison me. The memory and current threat should be enough to make someone turn on the others.

The flame on my sword dies out as I wait. They are either being truthful or fear someone else's retribution more.

"No, please," the cook says, falling on his knees. He wrings his thick hands, his round face lined with pain. "Spare her. She did nothing wrong. She was asleep, and I heard nothing in the kitchens."

"Tell the other servants they need to come forward, then," I say. "Because someone heard or saw something, and she will be the one to pay for it."

Desperate, he looks around at each of them. He really didn't hear or see anything despite being awake. That means it wasn't bounty hunters—they would've been far sloppier. The blood on the floor also indicates a tactical strike where a soldier fell, but the men refused to leave a man behind.

Rune or Seok, then.

My thoughts are interrupted by the loud cries of the girl. I haven't hurt her, but she's wailing. Her cheeks are stained strawberry red.

I stare at her. Maybe I should put her out of her misery.

"Mikail." Aeri rises from the black wood throne and walks toward me. "Enough. Let the girl go. They don't know or, more likely, they're too afraid to talk."

"They're too afraid to obey their sovereign?" I grip the girl's arm, and she yelps, crying in a pitch so high I instantly regret it.

"Yeah, that's pretty much what I'm saying," Aeri replies. "This isn't the way, and you know it." She shakes her head and lays her hand on my shoulder. "Every second we waste in anger is one that could cost Sora her life. You knew this in Oosant; you know it now. Whoever took Sora and Tiyung must be bringing them to Yusan. The question is whether they're going to Rune's encampment or Qali Palace."

I stare at Aeri, but she doesn't flinch or look away. She's right, and

I do know it, but I'm furious. I sliced off Joon's head and threw it into the sea, and it didn't make a dent in my anger or grief. Instead, I lost Fremo and Hana, and I was betrayed yet again. Good people died tonight, and killing a bad man didn't erase it.

It was supposed to be a victory.

With a sigh, I let go of the chambermaid, sending her back into the staff. I know killing an innocent girl won't help, either.

Aeri nods once, and then I ball my fists. I was the one who convinced Sora to stay behind. It's my fault she was here, but I'd rather strike at anyone else than blame myself.

"S-sire," a stable boy says.

Aeri and I both turn toward the kid. He's probably eleven. He takes a deep breath, puffing out his narrow chest as much as he can, then steps forward.

"Speak freely," I say.

"I… I don't know if it has anything to do with anything. But I found this on the steps before you came back. I just thought it was pretty. But maybe it's something."

He reaches into his pocket and pulls out a red plume.

My heart stops when I see the feather. Blood drains from my face, and tendrils of fear creep along my back. We just got rid of one tyrant king, but the other now has Sora.

Stars.

Aeri closes her eyes for a long, pained blink. It's the worst possible answer. Rune, at least, would've kept Sora alive as a bargaining chip. Seok will kill her.

"Qali?" Royo asks.

I nod. "Seok has them."

The three of us stand quietly.

"You're all free to return to your duties or beds," I say to the staff.

They back away slowly, then scurry from the room like rats from a fire.

I sheathe my sword, then stare at the hilt. I allowed my anger to get the best of me tonight. This isn't the way of a king—at least one hoping to not be a tyrant. I want to offer something to the chambermaid and the stable boy, but I don't know what.

Because I don't know how to rule.

The heavy weight of despair makes me sigh.

"Money," Fallador says, eyeing me. "You give them money, and they'll only think about your generosity."

I nod and then wonder how he knew what I was thinking.

"I've known you for years, Adoros." He smiles. "I know when something is troubling you. When you are less than who you are, it haunts you."

Hard to say who I am right now. Sora is the one who reminds me.

"Send word to Rune that I accept his terms," I say to Fallador.

Aeri and Royo look over at me. We hadn't discussed this, but we are now out of choices.

Fallador's eyes shift, but eventually he nods. "All right."

"Let him know that you are to remain here as collateral," I say.

He gives me a small smile as he bows. "Yes, Adoros."

There was something sad and resigned about him when he agreed. This is probably another trap. But odds even out on a battlefield. If Rune crosses me again, I'll cut him down myself.

Once Fallador leaves, Teo and Duval also bow and go. Duval is now my most trusted guard, having proven himself on the mission, even if I'm certain he couldn't grow a full beard if he tried. I trust Teo as well, but he is grieving his brother.

Aeri and Royo are the last ones left in the throne room.

"Thank you, Aeri." I say it and I mean it. Euyn would call me a demon when I was angry like that, and she went toe to toe with me for what was right.

She gives me a kind smile. "I'm worried about her, too, but we need loyalty now, not fear."

Aeri continues to be the biggest surprise, born to rule as a queen but raised outside of all the excess and corruption.

"We will get them back," Royo says.

"I know. It's why I agreed to Rune's terms. Yusan will come for us now that Joon is dead and there's no risk to Seok's only heir. It's no coincidence that both happened tonight, so either Calier sent word that Tiyung was unguarded or we have yet another traitor in our midst."

Perhaps Seok was paying far more attention to me than I imagined. Or maybe he's working with someone who knows me well. Someone like Tiyung.

"What do we do?" Royo asks.

I stare at the Gayan throne. The wood carved by the gods who abandoned us long ago. I think about my parents, who sat there, and all the Miats before them.

All dead except for me.

"We try to survive," I say.

CHAPTER SIXTY-EIGHT

SORA
THE EAST SEA

The Qali Palace guards wrap a rope around the central mast of the fleet ship and then tie me and Tiyung to it, giving us a few feet of length to move around. Really, it's just enough to sit down. It's better than the dark, covered wagon they threw us into in Jeul, but not by much.

I count the guards as we set sail into the East Sea. The guard who Tiyung struck down in the tower died, but there are nineteen more king's guard and ten armored palace guards aboard this ship. We never stood a chance. Not without Mikail and Aeri.

The timing couldn't have been a coincidence, but how did they know we'd be alone?

I glance over at Tiyung. Were palace spies following him? I have to assume they were. So the question becomes: Did he know? Was he in on this plan? I wouldn't think so, but he was supposed to kill me on our first trip together, and if I've learned anything, it's that everyone is capable of deceit and betrayal. Even the ones you trust the most.

"Did you do this?" I ask.

Tiyung's brow furrows, and then he points to his nose. "No."

"How did they know we'd be alone?"

"Either Fallador or someone else betrayed us, or my father had spies watching me. But if I was being followed, I had no idea. I'm sorry, Sora. I swear I'll find a way out of this for you."

A chill settles over me, and it's not the late-night air or the sea spray. It's that I don't believe there will be a way out. Not this time.

My knees buckle, and I drop until I'm sitting on the deck. No matter who betrayed us, this is my fault—all of it. I had the chance to kill Seok in the armory in Khitan. He held me as we danced, and I had poison on my lips. I could've leaned forward and kissed him. But I didn't do it, and people like me don't get multiple chances to slay a monster.

"Sora?" Tiyung leans to the side as he looks at me.

"I'm sure you'll try."

My voice sounds exhausted because I am. I'm tired of running, of never being safe, of losing everyone I love. I'm tired of life. I'm not the girl who dreamed of living at the country villa with Daysum. I no longer have a sister, and I'm tired of shattered dreams. I know Tiyung will try to stand up to his father, but in the end, I don't really care. For twenty-one years, I've battled, and I have nothing to show for it. More than that, I have nothing left to fight for. There's only so much that can be stripped away before there's nothing left of you worth keeping. Even the strongest blades can break.

"Don't give up," he says.

"Why not?"

He exhales, and then he sits near me. The sea spray drips down his broken nose. Or it's the rain that started as we sailed closer to Yusan.

"I suppose I can't give you a real reason," he says. "I need you, but that's my reason, not yours. Daysum would want you to go on, but you can't live for losses." He pauses, his eyes looking up at the moon. "I guess because, in the end, you deserve more. You deserve ten times as many years of happiness as you have spent suffering."

Mikail also wanted me to have a long life, but for what? Life is filled with pain and heartache. And what happened to him tonight? What about Aeri and Royo? Are they all dead or captured, too?

Probably. We're trying to fight the world. With so many odds stacked against us, I'm not sure how we ever thought we'd win.

I stare at the back of the ship, looking toward Tamneki Harbor, where the friends who became my family are all probably dead. Then suddenly, there's a fire on the water—a blaze as large as it was instant. I blink the rain out of my eyes.

Just as I reopen them, another huge fire lights—this one on the Gayan coast. It's tall as the Oosant warehouse blaze. Maybe larger.

The soldiers on this ship run around as the lookout calls overhead. Because of the fires, the Weian warships are now visible. Boots thud on the deck, and the men take up oars down below so we can move away from the fleet faster.

Those unnatural fires can only mean one thing: Mikail got the Flaming Sword.

I stare at Tiyung, and his eyes move side to side, alternating between the two flames. Then a smile spreads over his face.

"They did it," he whispers.

I think they did.

They're still alive. Maybe all of them. And King Joon is almost certainly dead.

I stare at the flames in the night, and hope flutters through my chest. Just a little thing, delicate as glass wings, but it uplifts me. We already took the relics and killed two god kings. Maybe, just maybe, we can win.

Tiyung reaches his fingers out on the deck. He holds his palm open, waiting for me. I give him my hand.

I just have to hold on.

CHAPTER SIXTY-NINE

AERI

ROSE PALACE, GAYA

It's over a day since Sora was kidnapped, and while we have sent messages to Qali demanding her release, there has been no reply. Mikail is losing his mind, but none of us are okay. I want to ask him if he's hearing voices, too, or seeing an ash road now that he has two relics, but...he has enough to deal with.

We're gathered in the throne room. It's early in the morning and we haven't had breakfast yet, but Rune arrived on Gaya and immediately "requested" an audience.

I, for one, am very surprised he's still alive. I thought Sun-ye would've poisoned him days ago. But the doors open, and a long-winded soldier announces the western count with his eight noble titles. After a dramatic pause, Rune walks into the throne room, striding down the stone aisle with a smile.

"Your Majesty," he says with a deep bow.

He smiles and greets Mikail like they are the best of friends. As if he didn't try to trap us in Rahway, but whatever. We have bigger problems.

Rune's snake eyes focus on me, and he issues another formal bow. "Princess Naerium, you are looking exceptionally well. I remain your most humble servant."

He places his hand over his heart.

I purse my lips into some semblance of a smile, but he's not looking at my mouth. He can't keep his eyes off the ruby on my forehead. I have to admit, I rather like the look with the gold of my eyes. But it's the power of the relic that he's hungry for, not the jewelry.

Ugh, I can feel another marriage proposal coming.

"Your Grace," Mikail says, acknowledging him.

Rune is in his finest cream-colored suit with his noble collar on display. I can only respect his tailoring. Fallador stands to his side, pleasant as ever. Royo is on Mikail's left. He's grinding his teeth so hard he might lose a molar. I'd laugh, but I'm still bitter about what happened on the warship. Royo holding me back cost lives. Good people died while I stood idle.

"Thank you for the warm welcome," Rune says. "I'm pleased that you accepted my offer, and I look forward to our long, prosperous friendship."

He means prosperous for himself, of course.

"Are your men having any difficulty navigating the Strait of Teeth?" Mikail asks.

I'm certain he already knows the answer. He instructed Rune to have his army cross at Cetil because the Weian warships still occupy Tamneki Harbor. They have neither attacked Yusan nor turned for home, which is unsettling at best.

"No issues at all, Your Majesty," Rune says. "I conscripted ten ships to ferry men across. My full army will be encamped on Charm Beach by sunset."

Mikail nods—they're on schedule. Charm Beach is the area by the former Port of Charm, directly across from Tamneki.

"What news of Qali or Seok?" Mikail asks casually. He won't mention Sora to avoid tipping our hand to the western count.

One corner of Rune's lips rises. "Here I was thinking you had your own sources in Qali."

Mikail shrugs as his reply, but Hana deserves more than a shrug.

"Hana is dead," I say.

And that remains your fault.

So…that's the other thing that has happened since I was crowned. The voice is with me *a lot*. It can't be a good thing, but I haven't mentioned it to anyone else—not even Royo. It would just worry him, and it's not like he can do anything about it.

Rune raises his eyebrows. "I'm sorry to hear that."

I'm not sure he has that emotion, but he's pantomiming it well enough.

"My sources tell me Prince Uolson of Wei met with Seok yesterday and forged an alliance," Rune continues. "All of the king's guard has been called to Tamneki."

"All of it?" I grip the armrests of my throne. That's a hundred thousand men. It will take weeks, maybe over a month, to move those soldiers to the capital, but eventually, the full might of Yusan will descend on us.

My empty stomach tightens.

Rune nods. "I highly doubt they will wait for the soldiers, though, if I know Seok."

Mikail doesn't blink. "Then we will fortify the beach today, in the event they attack before dawn."

"And if the fortifications aren't enough?" Rune asks. "What is your plan for the Weian guard?"

I raise an eyebrow. I thought the point of aligning with Rune was to get an army at our disposal. But Royo told me about how Mikail battled with the Weians in Quu Harbor and struck death blows on their steel without them falling. If hundreds of them are armored that way, Yusanian soldiers don't stand a chance. Wei's ten thousand would fight like one hundred thousand.

"If the Weians attack, I will sink their ships," Mikail says.

Rune smiles that snakish grin.

I look over at Royo as Fallador pales. From just that one sentence, I know: Mikail is planning to die to kill them all.

CHAPTER SEVENTY

TIYUNG

QALI PALACE, YUSAN

It took a day to reach Qali because the fleet ship had to sail up to Trove in order to avoid Tamneki Harbor. From the docks, we were placed in a carriage and brought to the palace. We arrived in the middle of the night, and guards locked us into two holding rooms. I panicked when they separated us, but I could hear Sora next to my bedroom suite.

We spoke through the wall, Sora telling me about the Temple of Knowledge in Lake Cerome as I moved the pillows and blankets from the bed onto the floor. I must've fallen asleep because I startle awake when my door is opened. I look up to find palace guards in the doorway.

"Tiyung Gamesong, your father requests an audience," one says.

"Requests" is surely the wrong word, but I'm worried about what they'll do to Sora if I refuse. I get up. My body aches, especially my nose, but I make it to my feet and walk out with them.

I stare at the room next to my wall. It's not a bedroom, like I'd thought, but a storage closet. They didn't even give her a bed and bath, and she said nothing. I wait, but they don't open her door.

"Where is Sora?" I ask.

Neither guard answers me. I stop moving, locking up my limbs. The guards grab my arms. The older guard sighs as I struggle to get free. But the younger one is gentler. He looks familiar. I recognize his wide eyes and the red birthmark on his cheek. It takes a moment, but I realize that I served with him in the king's guard.

"She'll meet you in there," he whispers. "Your father wants to see you first."

I stop struggling, then jerk my shoulders away, wordlessly demanding to be released. They exchange glances, but ultimately, they let go of me. I adjust my bloodstained shirt, then walk with them again, holding my head high. I look at the younger guard out of the corner of my eye. Beom, I think. I won't forget his kindness.

They bring me to the gilded doors of the throne room. I'm not announced, but I don't need to be because the room is nearly empty.

Dread pools in my stomach as I walk inside. I try to keep my chin up and my steps measured, but memories haunt me. I wish I could say this was my first disastrous trip here.

At the end of the room, my father sits on the black serpent throne. He wears imperial red and a gold, ruby, and diamond crown. It's the same style as the Immortal Crown but far smaller. I think it's the heir's crown that had belonged to Euyn. I wonder where Seok found it.

My mother sits on the golden throne next to him. Her blue eyes fill with sorrow as she takes me in. Her gaze stops at the bloodstains on my shirt. She gasps, then covers her mouth with her hand.

I lock my jaw to keep from shaking. I don't know how I'm going to speak, but suddenly, my parents both look past me. I turn as the doors open again and Sora is brought in. Her hands are still tied from when they put us on the ship.

Outrage flows through me—they left her hands tied all night and threw her in a storage closet just to be cruel.

Sora walks with her head high even though guards hold her arms. She glides effortlessly until she's nearly even with me. I look her over, and aside from her wrists, which are red and chafed from the ropes, she seems all right. I let out a sigh of relief, though anger churns in my stomach.

"Kneel to royalty," the palace guard on her right says.

"I will when I see any," Sora replies.

Admiration lifts my spirits, but the guard grins and then flings Sora to the ground. Because her hands are tied, she can't brace her fall. Her face hits the tile. When she looks up, her lip is bleeding.

Fury—the kind I've never felt before—bursts in my chest. I lower my shoulder and barrel forward at the guard. I hit with enough force to knock him onto his back, his steel clanging against the mosaic tile. Then I start punching any place his armor doesn't cover. My fists connect with his cheek and his eyes, his groin, but I can't feel my hands. All I feel is rage.

Hands try to pull me off him, but I don't care. I kick at him. He smiled as he threw a defenseless girl. He made Sora bleed. I will end him right here.

Bloodlust fuels me, and I slip from the guards. I get another crack across the guard's jaw, but it's not enough. I want him dead. I won't stop until I send him to the Kingdom of Hells.

"I will smile at your pyre," I say.

"Enough!" Seok says. His voice echoes in the room.

More guards grab me and Sora. They force us apart and both to our knees.

"Father," I say, panting. "You wanted to see me?"

I stare at the guard I bloodied, and then I focus on my father.

Seok blinks like he's confused, then shakes his head. I'd think it's the change in my demeanor, but it doesn't seem so simple—it's something else that's puzzling him. Different expressions cross his face until it seems like he's at war with himself.

This is what my mother meant—he's not in his right mind. And then I realize what's wrong: he truly believes I died, but at the same time he knows I'm kneeling in front of him. It's a similar look as when Sora saw me for the first time in Gaya. But this shock has a madness to it.

Cold dread seizes me. My father was ruthless under normal

conditions. I can't imagine what he is now. I hazard a glance at Sora and find her frozen with fear.

"Captain," he says.

The captain of the king's guard who seized us in Gaya steps forward.

"Geon," Seok says.

The palace guard from the tower comes forward as well.

"Job well done," Seok says. "You've brought in a dangerous, rogue assassin and found my son. You and your men will share a two-million-mun bounty."

They both salute him.

"Now, lock her in Idle Prison, until I have time to deal with her." He stares at Sora as he waves his hand.

"No!" I shout.

The room is silent as all eyes turn to me. But I don't fear Seok. Not anymore. Or maybe I don't dread anything as much as Sora having to endure that place. "If she goes, I go with her."

My father grips the arms of the throne. I can feel how badly he wants to strike me with the back of his hand.

So, he's at least somewhat the same.

I hold his stare. *Come and try.* I am not the same man who left Gain.

My mother turns in her seat. She clutches my father's arm. One second goes by, two, and then he finally looks at her. She silently pleads for mercy.

She'd have better luck bleeding a stone.

But my father's head eventually drops in a nod.

"Very well, Olivia." Seok touches my mother's hand, and there's some softness in his expression. Some part of him remembers her. Then he turns toward Sora and me, his brown eyes hardening with hate. "There's surely a better use for her."

"You are correct, Your Majesty," a woman's voice says. "She is the so-called king of Gaya and Princess Naerium's closest companion.

They would do anything to get her back."

A petite woman with blue eyes and curly dark hair steps through the side entrance of the throne room. Sora's eyes widen with recognition.

"Gambria?" Sora says.

The woman looks at her as if they barely know each other, and then she focuses on Seok. "No harm would come to you, Your Majesty, if she is aboard your ship."

Sora shakes her head, hurt flooding her features as her face flushes. I wonder why until I realize that this is the woman Mikail spoke of. The one he thought was Fallador's cousin who later betrayed them for the Queen of Khitan. But now she has a trusted position at my father's court.

Whose side is she really on?

"That is also what I observed in Rahway," Sun-ye says, stepping into view. "They were quite the close-knit group—far too sentimental for war."

Sora seems less than surprised to see Sun-ye. She sighs and stares like she smells something rotten. Sun-ye stares right back, but there's just a slight change in her expression when she notices Sora's bloody lip. She cares. I'm not sure who is double-crossing whom, but something strange is going on here.

My father strokes his clean-shaven chin. "Very well. My son and this assassin will both accompany me to Gaya. They, and all the realm, will witness what it costs to rebel against the king of Yusan."

He looks at the palace guard who brought us in—the one he called Geon. "Put them on my ship."

Sora is pulled away first. Her gaze meets my father's. Hate meets unbridled hate. But then Seok smiles a cruel grin. As he looks at her, I know for certain: he's going to kill her.

CHAPTER SEVENTY-ONE

ROYO
CHARM BEACH, GAYA

I've been setting up wood all damn day.

Yesterday, Mikail ordered trees cut down and for spikes to be made to protect Gaya. Hundreds of people turned out to help chop, but now we actually have to build these beach fortifications.

I'm leading a group of locals while Rune's men also drive spikes into the ground to protect the archers. A guy digs a hole, I put the spike in, another guy fills it, and then we do it all again until there's a wooden shelter where the crossbow archers can hide. Then we move on to the next one. We gotta build a hundred.

The sun is relentless, but being oceanside is nice. Well, except for the fact that we can see the Weian fleet sitting in the harbor. But more and more of Rune's troops arrive, and it starts to feel like a fair fight.

My shoulder muscles strain, but this beats the hells out of sitting on our thumbs in Rose Palace worrying about Sora. I don't think Seok will hurt his own son, but the count has wanted Sora dead for a while now.

I strangle the spike in my hands. If she dies, I'll kill him myself.

Not that I'd get the chance. No, if she dies, Mikail will leap over the strait to kill him, and Aeri will be right behind him.

She and Duval are around two hundred feet above me on the overlook. This part of the land drops off sharply to the large beach below. Workers are cutting back the charm fields up there to clear room for the longbowmen and for us to watch the battle unfold. Other guys are setting up a big tent for Rune.

I shove another spike into the hole in the sand. Aeri, Mikail, and I are doing our own things because we've been snapping at one another nonstop since Sora was taken. We all feel guilty. We're all worried. After losing Sora, I don't want Aeri anywhere near here, but she's gonna be, no matter what.

So fuck me, I guess.

We're also still off. It's the worst feeling in the world—her being upset with me. But I've got nothing to apologize for.

The sea breeze cools my skin, but I still can't shake the look she gave me after I protected her on the warship. I was only trying to keep her safe, and I'd do it again. It's the whole fucking reason I'm here to begin with. She's the one making things difficult. How do you guard somebody willing to die to save everybody else?

You can't. It's impossible.

So why do I feel so fucking guilty? My chest squeezes, and I ignore it, grabbing another spike. My legs itch to run up the hill to her, but I'm not gonna apologize for doing what I'm supposed to do.

No way.

It's sunset by the time I get back to Rose Palace. I'm sweaty, sandy, and I smell like a mule. All I want to do is take a bath and curl up with Aeri. But the bath is all I'm getting.

The stable boy takes my horse, and a servant opens the huge doors. I take a step through, but then I walk backward. I caught a blur of red as I came in.

What was that?

I go back down the stairs and look at the entrance. Roses circle two of the columns—huge ones—and that shit wasn't here this morning.

"Mikail!" I yell, striding into the palace. "Mikail!"

My voice and feet echo. Mikail comes out of the war room, and

Teo follows him, walking with a slight limp. They both look puzzled. I guess it's weird to yell for a king, but I don't care. Aeri also appears out of nowhere. I think she was in the library—probably stealing more books.

"Come see this." I wave them toward me.

We all walk outside, and I point to the columns.

"These weren't here before, right?" I ask.

The three of them stare.

"No, no they were not," Mikail says. "Not for a very long time, anyhow."

He and Teo both get down on a knee. They put their hands to their foreheads. Fallador also comes out of the palace. He looks at the columns, and his jaw drops. He takes a knee, too, while staring at Mikail. Meanwhile, Aeri touches the flowers, then sticks her nose into the petals.

"The goddess," the men say almost in unison.

Aeri looks at me, a smile gleaming on her face. Her golden eyes are filled with wonder.

Ten Hells, she's beautiful.

I wipe sand and sweat from my brow, like that'll make me more presentable.

Mikail stands. He looks at me and then Aeri and smiles to himself. "We'll have a midnight supper before we leave. I suggest you rest before then…or whatever it is you want to do."

There's only one thing I want to do. All right, two with the bath.

The men go inside, but Aeri remains, gently touching the roses. Her fingers twitch. She probably wants to steal one, but she holds back. Once plucked, the flower won't be the same. Sometimes you have to accept things as they are and admire them for what they are.

Ugh, fuck me.

"I'm sorry," I say.

She stops and tilts her head. "For?"

"I… I just wanted to protect you."

"Oh." She looks far into the dusk. I can tell she's thinking about that night, the men we lost, Hana's death, and Mikail killing her father. I don't think she cares much about King Joon's death, but she's gotta feel something.

She shakes her head and then sighs. "I was upset at the time, but mostly at myself. You were just trying to keep me safe."

"You're the most valuable thing in the world to me," I say.

More than gold. More than the blood that got spilt. More than my own life.

Her lips spread into a smile. "In a strictly-friends way, of course."

"No."

She closes her eyes and inhales like she's breathing in the moment. Then she takes my hand, weaving her fingers with mine.

"I'm gross." I start to pull my hand away.

"I don't care."

She holds on to me, and we walk into the palace together.

CHAPTER SEVENTY-TWO

AERI

ROSE PALACE, GAYA

Royo insists, absolutely insists, on taking a bath—alone. What a killjoy.

But he was working hard today. Duval and I were up on the overlook with Rune's generals, listening to them prepare for the war, while Royo was doing real work. He was driving heavy spikes into the sand. He had his shirt off and his pants rolled up, his body bronzing and sweating in the sun.

Duval caught me not paying attention twice, and he smirked both times. But I saw him looking as well and arched an eyebrow. Who could blame him? It's quite a sight.

As I stood on the overlook, though, I realized how much I like this island. I started daydreaming, imagining a life for us. One beyond all this, where there were no Weian ships in the distance—a future in which we won. My father is dead, and while Rune is arguably more of the same, Royo, Sora, Mikail, and I could be safe here on Gaya. We could live out our lives and have boring, idle days. All right, not Mikail, since he's king, but Gaya would be free with the alliance. Royo and I could have a peaceful existence where I bother him during the day and we make love all night.

I mean… Where do I sign up?

Maybe we'd have children one day, or maybe it would just be the two of us, but either way, we'd always have a warm home. I'd never freeze, never be alone again. Royo would complain he had no place for his three necessary outfits while I took up three wardrobes, and our biggest argument would be about what to eat for dinner.

I revel in the commonness, the boringness I want so badly, because it wouldn't be boring—it would be heavenly. It would be everything I ever wanted.

Just as I'm thinking of it again, Royo comes out of the bath in a towel. I'm sitting on the bed, and I stare at him from his wet, short hair, to his muscled shoulders and broad chest, down his abs to where there's, unfortunately, a towel blocking the rest of him.

"Stop it." His face reddens.

"What?"

"You're eyeing me like I'm dinner," he says, looking away.

Gods, I've made him blush! I bite my lip to keep from laughing as joy curls my toes. Instead, I tilt my head. "I mean, you could be."

He groans, but he's starting to remove the towel. I try to keep my cool, but I crawl toward the edge of the bed closest to him. If I wasn't eyeing him like a meal before, I definitely am now.

I want to taste him, lick him, bite him, if I'm honest. I just want to consume him and be consumed by him.

Royo runs his thumb over my bottom lip. I stare up at him and dart my tongue over the tip of his finger. He smiles, and then his eyes change. He pushes me back on the bed. I fall with a laugh, but he moves with me, and his towel falls, too. I look down and whimper—I'm *that* eager and also shameless, but who cares? It's just me and him, and the throbbing between my legs is intolerable. It feels like I'll burst if I don't have him this instant.

All we ever get are moments. Dreams don't always come true, and memories fade. What we have is right now, and I'm going to have him.

Royo laughs, and it's the best sound in the world. I soak it up like a sponge, filling my mind with the echo.

"I want all of you," I say.

He grins as he delicately unties my dress. "Only if you give everything to me."

He leans down and kisses me, tasting my mouth. I've never been kissed like this before, where it's all I can think of. His lips are gentle, but his tongue swirls around mine. A content hum builds in my throat, my arms around him. Then he kisses down my neck, and I squirm with pleasure as he hits the sensitive skin by my pulse. He continues his kisses until he gets to the amulet. Then he looks up at me.

There's desire in his eyes but also concern. The amulet saved me, but it also doomed me until I found him.

"You already have all of me," I say. "You have from the start."

Royo stares at me with so much love in his eyes. He might not ever say it—I honestly can't imagine the words coming out of his mouth—but it doesn't matter. I feel it from my heart to my core, and that's what's most important. *I love you* is just three meaningless words unless there's feeling behind them.

I wrap my legs around him. "Please, Royo."

"Impatient little thief," he whispers.

"Pretty please?" I try.

He laughs, and then he continues to kiss down my body, taking his time as I dig my nails into the bedsheets.

CHAPTER SEVENTY-THREE

MIKAIL

CHARM BEACH, GAYA

We leave the palace after a quiet supper. Without Sora or Tiyung here, and Fallador off with Rune already, we are down to three of us. Even Aeri is subdued. It's not uncomfortable, though, as we mount our horses in our silver chest armor. It feels like everyone is savoring the last moments and thinking about what's to come. Nothing will be the same after today. That much is certain.

Euyn used to say that last moments make you want to live, and now that I'm ready to die, I think he's correct. And if I'm right, maybe I'll see him again.

As we ride away into the night, no one is left behind at Rose Palace. Either we will win, or all will be lost. I take a final look at Jeul—the palace on the hill and the lights of the city. The home I lost and then regained. My heart fills with love for the capital, for the realm.

We ride through the city gate, and I stare at the governor's headless body. Hael birds have started pecking him apart. Good for them.

I've cut off the heads of Joon and Yong and launched them into the sea. As a boy, I would've called that an unqualified success—but as a man, I know there are always more enemies, more tyrants, more wrongs. Fallador asked what I would do when I was done fighting the world, as if that were even possible.

But I also have more to protect than I'd ever imagined. Sora is out there somewhere. Teo rides beside me. He's been my constant guard, although at night I've heard him quietly crying, mourning his brother. Aeri and Royo are behind us, and Duval is last. And then there is this entire island.

On Fremo's death, Duval, who was actually his grandson, took the reins of the rebellion. Every Gayan person willing to fight will meet us at Charm Beach tonight. Thousands follow us from Jeul and Hallan. More are coming from the eastern villages.

It's all I ever wanted.

I wish it were enough.

"I want you to keep an eye on Fallador and Rune until the war is over," I say to Teo.

"Yes, Your Majesty," he says. "About…about—"

He ends in silence, probably thinking he's speaking out of turn. I don't enjoy this part of being royalty.

"Speak freely, please," I say. "We're headed into battle. I don't have time for court formalities."

"Yes, Your Majesty," he says. He takes a deep breath. "I am at a loss for how my brother could betray you, betray us, betray all of Gaya and the memory of our ancestors. I am ready to atone for his disloyalty in any way you see fit."

Oh, was that all that was on his mind?

"Everyone is capable of betrayal," I say. "His disloyalty wasn't yours. There's nothing to atone for."

He swallows hard and nods, but he looks discontent. Like he'd prefer I whip him at a post instead. Men seeking atonement are odd. They'll do anything except forgive themselves.

By two bells in the morning, we reach Rune's field tent on the overlook. It's well behind the archers, far removed from the actual battlefield.

Stable boys take our horses after we dismount. There's a makeshift paddock off to the side.

We walk through the remains of what were charm fields, toward the towering ivory tent. No flags fly from the top. Gayan flags were long outlawed, and this isn't Yusan anymore.

"Let us be first inside," Teo says. Duval nods.

"Why?" I ask.

"In case it's a trap," Duval answers.

I gesture for them to go ahead. If it were a trap, they'd allow us in to lull us into a false sense of security and then they'd attack. But I don't bother saying that. With a snap of my fingers, I'll light them on fire, or Aeri can turn them all to gold…or whatever her power is now with the crown.

I don't think any of us want to find out, but these are about to be desperate times. We may have to.

We enter the tent, and it's just a luxurious war room with Rune, Fallador, and generals of Rune's army inside. There's also a host of servants to attend them and musicians playing a soothing tune. Somehow, Rune found the time to bring over furniture. There are fine couches, tables, chairs, a four-poster bed, and woven rugs. A chandelier hangs from the center.

I stare up at it. The man brought crystal to a war.

"Your Majesties." Rune strides to us and then bows.

All the other men and servants bow as well.

"Please speak freely. This is a war," I say. Even though it looks more like a living room.

"My sources report that Seok has left Qali," Rune says. "We expect an imminent attack."

I'm surprised Seok has the gall to come with his fleet, but then again, he doesn't have an Immortal Crown, and the loyalty of the palace guards must be shaky at best. He's as likely to get murdered there as he is in a war.

Rune's four generals give full reports, which take a shockingly long time. I try to focus, but I keep listening for war drums. No attack comes, but it's well after three bells by the time they finish.

We're constantly offered refreshments, but without Sora here to poison check, we all decline. No need to make it that easy on anyone.

Now that the reports have been given, it's a waiting game. The generals pass the time with strategy talks and hypotheticals, which, apparently, Rune loves. He eagerly moves the models around on the table, planning for different contingencies. I listen for a while and then discreetly gesture for Aeri to take my place.

"But what if they attack from the east first?" she asks.

Rune busily resets the table as I step out of the tent for air. Duval and Royo's eyes track me, but they stay in place.

It's after four bells, now—closer to five, and worry creeps in. The attack should've already begun. The sky is already lighter with the predawn. The air smells crisp, the ground dewy in the quietest part of the day. I soak up the peace even though I can feel the coming war.

The tent flap moves, and Fallador comes out with Teo following on his heels. They both stop right next to me.

"It's all right," I say to Teo.

Teo looks conflicted, but ultimately, I spoke. He bows and turns back inside, trying his best to walk without a limp. But Euyn was also shot in the leg. I'm well aware of how much pain he's in.

Fallador watches Teo leave. "He's a good man."

"They are chronically in short supply."

I am, of course, referring to both of us.

He smiles that easy grin. We're so alike. Too much so, perhaps. Maybe that's the problem.

"I received word today that you should know about," Fallador says, suddenly serious. He leans in closer, that familiar scent of home surrounding me. "Your friends are aboard Seok's ship."

"You're absolutely certain?"

He nods.

The only source he'd be certain of is Gambria, which means she didn't go to Khitan as I suggested. No one did. Instead, she wormed her way into Qali Palace. But whose side is Gambria on?

Euyn had more than one rant about how women were masters of deceit. I'd kindly point out that the skill wasn't limited by gender, but between Aeri, Sun-ye, Gambria, and Hana, I'm not sure.

What is her end game? Telling me Sora is on the ship means I won't sink it, but is that to save Seok's life or Sora's? What would benefit Quilimar more? Because that is the ultimate motivation behind Gambria's actions.

Just as I'm contemplating these riddles, the scouts bang the war drums. The sound reverberates along the island and into my spine. The time for questions is over. Now, we're in a war. Our troops have been ready for a bell, and Yusan is late. By the time the ships reach us, it will be dawn.

It's a mistake that could allow us to win. Or at least I hope so.

I move to go back inside the tent, barely noticing the way Fallador reaches out for me as I pass.

CHAPTER SEVENTY-FOUR

ROYO
CHARM BEACH, GAYA

The war drums beat until they rattle my skull. I really want to go the rest of my life without hearing this shit again. The percussion goes right through me, stomping on my last nerve.

Mikail comes back into the tent, and everybody snaps to attention. Everyone but Aeri. She's curled up on a sofa with a book.

"It's time," he says.

He puts his hand out for her. She rises from the couch, but she turns and gives her hand to me. We both step forward.

Mikail smiles, and it's genuine.

Teo and Duval fall in line with him, and I hold Aeri's hand. The five of us step out into the breaking dawn. The breeze carries the smell of salt and moves the fleet closer. They're fully visible now—a sea of ships.

"Promise me something," I say to Aeri.

"It'll depend," she says. "There's not a lot, but there are a couple of things I can't promise you."

She side-eyes me, and I know she's talking about the night we killed the king.

"Don't use your relics unless you have to," I say. "You don't know what it will do now that you have the crown, and there's no telling how long you'll get frozen in time...or worse. It's gotta be a last resort."

Her golden eyes look everywhere but at me. "All right, Royo. Unless we're in danger, I won't use them."

I flatten my lips. That promise has more holes than lace, but it's as good as I'm going to get.

We make our way to the overlook, and the line of archers breaks for us to stand in the middle.

Out on the water, the Weian fleet is still hundreds of yards away, but there's a lot of them filling the harbor.

The dawn sky lights up in pinks, oranges, and gold. I grip Aeri's hand while I can. It won't be long before she has to stand ready, before the ships are within range of our archers. But we have this quiet moment.

My heart pounds like the war drums. What I wouldn't give to run. To bring Aeri to my shack on the Sol and hide out there. But we're long past that option. We're in this now.

Mikail pulls out a spyglass and scans the waters. I'm not sure what he's looking for, but he takes his time before he lowers the glass. Whatever it was, I don't think he found it. The only thing I can figure he'd look for is Sora.

Maybe it's better that she's not in this.

We wait. One hundred longbowmen stand in a line and breathe with the five of us. The thick air hangs on all of us. I want to scream, to take my axe and run at an enemy, but we just stand here waiting while they creep closer and closer.

Minutes crawl by, and then Mikail takes a step forward on the grass. He stands alone. I wonder what he's doing, but then he slowly sweeps his right arm out in front of him. The closest Weian ships catch fire. I mean in the blink of an eye, ten ships become bonfires on the water. The flames are so large, it hurts to stare at them. It's the same way the port caught fire—unnaturally ablaze from god magic.

My breath catches. Ten fucking Hells.

The overlook and Charm Beach below are dead silent. Mikail just took down a thousand Weians with one move of his arm.

Aeri squeezes my hand. We can do this. We can win this thing.

Hope surges in me, filling my chest. I look at Mikail. He smiles but coughs. Then he waves his left arm—the one with the blue metal that used to be the Water Scepter. The row of ten ships behind the first wave lights on fire. Mikail's eyebrows move just enough for me to know he's confused. He didn't expect fire.

He expected water.

But the men don't know that. A chorus of cheers rise from the beach and through the archers. The people chant: *Adoros, Adoros, Adoros.*

We can't hear screams from this far away, but I'm sure there's plenty on the water. Men are on fire, and the twenty Weian warships begin to break apart and sink into the sea. That means we have two thousand fewer Weians to worry about. Even if they survive the fire and can swim, their steel and the wreckage will bring them down.

Two thousand as good as dead in seconds from one guy. I rub my forehead. Maybe he really did need the sword. We've been used, played, abandoned, and left for dead. But this time is different. This time, the gods are on our side. Maybe, despite everything, we're gonna come out on top.

I smile at Aeri just as Mikail drops to his knees. His chest heaves, and he puts his arms out on the grass to brace himself. His face turns light red, then crimson.

Fuck, he can't breathe. Fear seizes me, making me stand still.

"Mikail!" Aeri says.

Before I can even move, she dives to the ground next to him, then sits back on her heels. Her light skin gets even paler.

Mikail pukes. Water comes out. A lot of it. And he didn't drink anything in the tent.

Aeri's face morphs in horror as she looks at the ground and Mikail, who's coughing now.

"Water turned against you the way time turned against me," she says. "That's why you don't have control over the sea anymore. This is the cost of multiplication. This is the new toll—using the relics is slowly drowning you."

Goose bumps coat my skin as I think back to the hot spring in Khitan, the man pulled from the Sol, and my mother's body in Tamneki.

Mikail sits up, wiping his face. "It's okay. Fire will be enough."

I stare out at the sea. There are dozens and dozens of ships left. I say a silent prayer that he will be able to do it, because there's an entire Yusanian fleet behind them.

CHAPTER SEVENTY-FIVE

AERI

CHARM BEACH, GAYA

Winds blow, rippling my skirt. They carry the scent of burning wood up to the overlook and bring the Weians closer.

Fallador runs up to us and kneels with me, his green eyes filled with concern. We both put our hands on Mikail's arms to help him up. He shakes us off. Fallador's eyebrows knit at the rejection, but Mikail rises to his feet under his own power. The men cheer again.

I exchange glances with Fallador—he loves Mikail, and he wants to help, but the men needed to see him stand on his own.

Or he needed it.

Fallador falls back into line. Teo side-eyes him as he takes his place by Rune's side.

No one trusts Fallador just because he betrayed us, and that seems unfair. People make mistakes. I did.

Mikail takes two deep breaths, and then he waves his right arm and his left in rapid succession. He's trying to pay just one toll, but relics don't work that way.

Twenty more white ships catch fire, engulfed in red-and-orange blazes on the water. It's incredible, but I'm not looking at the flames of etherum or the sea. I'm staring at Mikail. He doubles over in pain. Water drips out of his nose as he leans forward, and he grips the metal armor on his chest with both hands.

No one has wielded both the sword and the scepter, so we

don't know how long he can last. But I can guess. I do the terrible calculations in my head. At the start of the attack, there were ninety-five Weian ships. Fifty-five remain. With the toll increasing from every use, there is no possibility of Mikail sinking all of them. He'll die first.

My stomach twists, and I shake with a chill. He would. He would happily die to sink them.

Mikail coughs violently until he vomits water again. I wring my hands, utterly useless. I want to help, but I can't. I know better than everyone else—nothing stops the toll. I squeeze my hands until they hurt, but there's nothing I can do. I have to stand here and watch my friend suffer through a relentless torment of pain. I remember the agony of drowning in the hot spring, and Mikail is doing it slowly.

I shudder as the soldiers below us cheer. The twenty ships Mikail just lit aflame are sinking, but the overlook is silent as Mikail's limbs visibly shake. He tries to stand up straight, but he grimaces, losing the fight against his own body.

I look over at Royo, and pity scrawls across his face. He can see it, too—Mikail can't keep this up or it will kill him.

My relics vibrate as I stare at Mikail and then the sails—the blue of Wei and the red of Yusan in the distance. There are around forty Yusanian ships sailing far behind the Weians.

What do I do?

I can't just stand here—that much is certain. My relics hum and heat up. I could try to turn the remaining Weian fleet to gold, but I don't know if I could even reach all of them. And what will happen now that I have the crown?

I made a promise to Royo that I wouldn't use etherum unless I have to. Is this a need? We're safe up here, for now, but I also can't let Mikail kill himself.

The ships drift ever closer. I shift my weight, staring at the sea. What do we do?

Mortals are born to die.

I groan and look up at the sun. Thank you for that, voice in my head. I assume it's the voice of the former kings of Yusan, since it picked up so much after I got the Immortal Crown. Military strategy tips would be a lot more useful right now.

But as I stare down at all the men below, I realize what the voice is saying. It *is* strategy. I take a deep breath. There's another horrible calculation to be done. We have fifteen thousand people between Rune's soldiers and the Gayan rebels. Mikail said Yusanian boats carry sixty men, and the Weian ships, one hundred. We have nearly twice the soldiers they have. If we let them come ashore, we can overwhelm them with greater numbers. More of our people will die, but it will save Mikail.

There's no choice to be made. We have to let the soldiers fight like the kings and queens before us. Even right now, the prince of Wei is at the back of his fleet. Seok beyond that. And Quilimar is safe in her palace. Only Mikail is actually fighting this battle.

"We have to let them come, Mikail," I say.

He shakes his head, but he still can't talk, so weakened by the toll. I steel my spine, my resolve only strengthened.

"I'll buy you time, then."

I don't mean it. We have soldiers and arms ready for war. We can't idly stand by and watch Mikail battle for us.

I turn and face the archers. "On my signal."

It's a gamble. I'm not the commander of this army, but Rune has referred to me as the Relic Queen.

The captain of the bowmen looks at Rune, who, of course, stands safely behind everyone, but he's been observing everything. I hold my head high and raise an eyebrow at him. This is my throne we're fighting for—the one he desperately covets. Are we allies or not? He hesitates, but he nods, giving permission to the captain to follow my command.

Pages set a line of oil aflame, and the longbowmen light their arrows. Their bows are enormous, the arrows, too. They each appear to have around a dozen of them.

I stare through my spyglass. The fleet is close now but in disarray, trying to navigate around the sinking ships. I wait a few seconds to make sure we can hit two rows of targets.

Hitting warships and killing men is not much different from the rigged tuhko rings at the night carnival. At least, not from up here. Maybe I should be horrified that it's all a matter of angles and trajectories, but I glance at Royo. I have too much to protect to worry about morals.

War is always a game.

Great. I raise my arm and then drop it. "Loose!"

One hundred fire arrows launch into the air. They arc into the sky, and I hold my breath. Mikail is still coughing, but he raises his head for long enough to watch the barrage. The arrows begin to fall, striking two hundred yards away, give or take. Some of the arrows miss, sinking into the water instead. Most hit the decks of the warships, barely doing any damage. But some hit the sails or light other flammables on fire.

We have to adjust.

"Aim for the sails," I call out.

I give the command to loose another barrage as the Weian crews scramble on their decks. We need to take advantage of the chaos and make sure they sink. I raise and lower my arm, and the archers release another hundred flaming arrows.

Then another hundred.

Men die and fires light as I watch it all like a play from the safety of the cliff.

"Ready the men," Rune says to his generals. They salute him and ride the path down to the beach.

Eight warships are now on fire. The flames are far slower, smokier, and less devastating than Mikail's etherum, but it's still a success. The men on the beach cheer each one as it sinks.

A rush of victory hits me, but then I count, and my stomach

turns. The cold truth makes me shiver. There are far too many blue sails still billowing on the sea. It's not nearly enough.

Forty-seven Weian ships left. Nearly five thousand Weian soldiers will soon hit the beach.

We must keep trying.

As the ships come into range, arrow after arrow flies through the air, but still, Weians continue toward our coast. They sail right past their dying brothers, not pausing to take on drowning men or to put out the flames.

The closest ships are now only fifty yards from our shore. They will beach any second.

Archers with crossbows wait behind the spiked fortifications. Regular bowmen stand with the infantry a few hundred yards from the shore. We have two lines of defense before our soldiers will have to battle theirs.

It will have to be enough.

My pulse pounds, doubt seeping in, but we have numbers. Numbers are what matter in a battle—it's why we fear the full Yusanian king's guard descending on us. Why we need to win today.

I hold my breath as the first Weian ship runs aground. It's one moment, two, before the Weian guard drops planks into the surf.

The first Weians barrel down onto our shore. They are all outfitted in steel from head to toe. And this isn't the royal ship. Blood drains from my face—how can that be?

As soon as the Weians appear, the archers fire arrows. Their aim is true. The Weians are hit from multiple directions. I wait for them to fall as they're struck in the chest, the thigh, the helmet.

Nothing happens. They continue to run forward.

I gasp, my fingertips icy and my relics humming. Two Weians who were unlucky enough to be shot in the face fall, but everyone else proceeds. The arrowheads just glance off their steel. The crossbow archers begin to fire, but the Weians have shields.

Nearly all the first Weians make it off the ship and onto our beach. And four more ships have run aground.

Mikail finally stands straight and looks at me. For the first time, there's fear in his eyes.

"We can't beat them," he says.

I hold my chin up, pushing away my doubt. "We can. No steel is impervious."

The Weians pour from the galleys of the other ships. Our crossbow archers hit some, the bolts penetrating, but not nearly enough— maybe two dozen total. The Weians run toward our fortifications as we continue to shoot in waves.

Rune's generals give the call for the first line of infantry to advance. War cries rise up from both sides. One thousand of Rune's soldiers run from our side of the beach, kicking up sand. A single sound comes from the Weian guard—*oorah*.

I ball my hands in fists as the lines of men crash into each other by the fortifications. Sword meets sword and body meets body. Bolts fly when our archers have a clean shot.

I scan, hopeful, waiting as I hold my breath. We can do this. We sent twice their number. But as the fray continues, the Weians begin to advance, cutting down our men. There's not a sound on this cliff as blood begins to soak our shore. The Weian guard is far better armored but also better trained, and that combination is unstoppable.

Another thousand of Rune's men run in to bolster our front line. It should be enough. We now have four of our men to each one of theirs. My pulse beats in my neck as I observe, waiting.

It doesn't matter. Our men fall at a horrifying rate. Screams and death pleas reach us up here. How is this possible?

Mikail's teal eyes widen with pain as he takes in the scene. This is not a battle—it's a slaughter.

This is what Fallador warned us about. And now we're here with dozens more Weian ships about to invade our shore.

Mikail throws his arm out, staring at Charm Beach. One hundred

Weian soldiers suddenly catch fire on the sand, screaming as they're burned alive. As they contort, our men use the distraction to attack. We temporarily gain ground. But Mikail hits the grass until he's lying flat on his back. He starts to convulse. His eyes are open, but he can't stop shuddering, his limbs moving uncontrollably. Royo takes a knee next to him as Mikail's face turns purple.

And there's nothing I can do.

All of this power, and I can't fucking help him. My stomach churns, and my hands are balled in fists so tight that my nails cut into my palms. I'm useless. I can't find Sora. I can't help Mikail. I didn't save Hana. I've watched man after man die on the beach. Men I didn't know but who will never return home to their families because I thought some might die, but I was good with that cost.

I have to do something. Promise or not. Yes, we're safe on this cliff, but we won't be for long when a small group of Weians can take the beach.

Ten more Weian ships will land in seconds. The rest of the fleet behind that. And even if we could somehow withstand the Weians, Yusan is behind them with fresh men and a would-be king whose reign would be solidified with our deaths.

It never stops.

Gods, it never fucking ends.

Royo puts Mikail on his side, and his convulsions ebb. It's a relief. But if he uses the relics again, it will kill him. I'm certain of it. I'm also certain he'll try.

As soon as he can breathe again, Mikail crawls forward to look down at the beach and then out at all the ships. There are still too many left—too many ships, too many enemies.

Mikail grins from where he kneels in the trampled grass, but he's not happy at all. He's done the math, too. We can't sustain this.

We can't win.

But we have to try, because we have no other choice. Actually, we do have one option. I can try to sink the last Weian boats no matter the cost.

I raise my arms but not for the archers. I look at Royo and purse my lips. I'm sorry. I really am. But I have to do this. We are simply out of time.

His eyes widen, and he's just started shaking his head when Mikail stands.

"Aeri," he says. "I need you to kill me."

CHAPTER SEVENTY-SIX

ROYO

CHARM BEACH, GAYA

"What the fuck, Mikail?" Aeri and I say at the same time. The longbowmen fire another round of arrows, but it's hard to even pay attention to the flames because what did Mikail just say? My stomach knots, but I couldn't have heard him right. No way did he just ask her to kill him.

Mikail holds out a dagger. "Take this and put it into my chest or I will. It's easier if it's one of you, because I can guide your hand."

"Thanks, but I'll have to pass on murdering you today," Aeri says.

I'm so stunned that I stumble forward. "Get that away from her. Have you gone mad? Why would you even say that?"

Mikail looks at me with sad eyes. "If she kills me, she can take the sword and the scepter and become the Dragon Lord."

Aeri and I are both silent. Mikail coughs and then continues, "I don't want to die. Really, I don't. But Aeri is the last Baejkin—the last of the line who can wear that crown. Aeri, if you become the Dragon Lord, you can win this war and save my people. It's all I want."

"She's not fucking doing that," I say.

"We've lost." Mikail turns toward the beach. He stares with a mournful expression. "We lost because I couldn't sink the fleet—not without controlling the sea. Look at the men down there dying. You both have seen how the Weians can fight. There's no chance of winning. Not with the rest of the fleet coming. And what matters isn't my life—it's saving the people we love. Sora is somewhere out there. As the Dragon Lord, Aeri can save her. Aeri can let everyone on this island live to see another day. Or we can all get slaughtered by the Weians, including the three of us."

I shake my head again, but more and more Weian guard make it to the shore and fall in line. They already took out the fortifications we built yesterday—most of our archers are dead or running. The Weians march right over the bodies of our men and their own, trampling them in the sand like they're seaweed. It's heartless and efficient. The beach is now made of blood and bone, and it's combed with screams. At least five hundred, maybe a thousand men are already dead. More will be soon.

Aeri unclenches her fists, shaking out her hands. Her palms have red crescents from where her nails were digging into them. I want to kiss the welts away.

She looks at Mikail and sighs. Dread seizes me—she's giving in. And she can't. It's too high of a price.

Mikail takes another step closer. "It's the only way, Aeri. Believe me, I've thought it through. If my death puts an end to tyrants, everything, every single thing I endured, everything and everyone I've lost, was worth it. I know you feel the same."

A tear rolls down her cheek, and she sniffles. No. He can't talk her into this. I can't let this happen. Because he won't be the only one who dies.

I step between them. "No, Mikail. If she becomes the Dragon Lord, she'll die, too."

"You don't know that," he says. "It hasn't been done before."

I gesture to the two of them. The relics have tried to kill them. Time turned against Aeri, and now water is drowning Mikail. I don't know why he thinks five relics would be a fucking picnic, but he's wrong. She'll die. All of the etherum put together is gonna kill a human being.

There has to be another way.

Aeri looks down at the battlefield and out to the sea. Then she looks at me. "We have to do this, Royo."

"No."

Her expression softens, but I can tell she's made up her mind. "Look at all those men moaning for mercy, Royo. And Seok has Sora. Even if we could somehow get her and win today, even if we find a way out of this, none of this will stop, because we have the relics. It will be war after war. We're going to die either way—let us choose how."

Mikail nods.

Panic runs through me until I'm shivering in the heat. I'm going to lose her. This is what I felt when I was searching for her in the hot springs. And it's worse because she's choosing it. She's choosing to leave me.

"Aeri, no," I say. "No. You promised." My voice breaks, and I clutch her hands. "Please."

She closes her eyes, and her shoulders slump. "Your face has so much heartbreak, and the worst part is, I know I'm causing it." She opens her eyes, draws a breath, then reaches out and cups my cheek. "I don't *want* to do this. I want tomorrow and tomorrow and tomorrow with you. I want to annoy you for the rest of our lives. I want boring days and warm nights next to you. I want to win every hard-fought smile of yours and to have your hand in mine for all time. I want to have kids and grow old with you. On a throne or not. Married or not. I just want you."

Tears stream down her face, matching the trails on mine.

"You have me," I say. "All of me."

"But we're not going to get that life, no matter what." She sniffles and swallows hard. "I wish we could have it. Gods, I wish we could. I'd live a thousand lifetimes by your side." She stops and kisses my hand. "But I won't let you die by mine. And I won't let Sora and the men and women down there be slaughtered when I can stop it."

If she cut into my chest with Mikail's dagger and ripped my heart out, it would hurt less.

"But I love you," I say.

A smile breaks through her tears. "That's the first time you've ever said that."

"No, it's not." But as the words leave my mouth, I realize I've never said them out loud. I never told her. What a fucking chump. I should've told her every day.

"I've waited my whole life to hear that," she says. "I love you, too."

I squeeze her hand. "Then stay with me."

She looks away just slightly, because the answer is no. My heart breaks in two, and I know: it'll never heal.

"I'll always be with you," she says. "But it's me or it's everyone. Look at them." She points down to the beach, to the soldiers running into a hopeless fight. To the bodies and the wounded crying out. Eventually, the Weians will kill everyone down there and come for us. Aeri and Mikail are right, and I know it.

"It can't be everyone else. I love you, Royo, but it just can't be." She stares up at the sky, and then she focuses on me. "Oh, Royo, this was the choice of love the amarth said I'd have."

I grit my teeth. Those fucking parrots. But Aeri told me she'd always choose me, and yet here we are. She wants to do this to save me, but there isn't a life without her. Not one worth living.

A million arguments race to my mouth, but they die on my tongue as her eyes meet mine. I know that look. This is a done deal, and there's nothing I can say or do to change her mind. Maybe I shouldn't try. Maybe she's making the right decision for the greater good. Maybe it's selfish that I'd let everyone else die instead of losing her, but I don't really give a fuck. I'd drown the world to save her.

But I also can't stop her.

"It's us," Mikail says, stepping forward.

Aeri manages a smile as she cries. "That's right. It's us. It's us or it's everyone."

I wipe my face—not that it helps much when I can't stop these tears. These cursed relics and that fucking prophecy. What do those birds even know? Aeri had offered the Sands to try to save me, but the amarth wouldn't take it. And now I'm going to lose not just Aeri but Mikail, too, because Aeri can't take the sword and scepter while Mikail's heart still…

"You don't have to die." I point to Mikail.

The corner of Mikail's mouth rises. "Oh, but I do."

"No, that's not what they said. Your heart just has to stop."

Aeri stares at me and then gasps. Her heart stopped when she drowned and I brought her back. I could stop Mikail's heart and bring him back, too.

"Put the knife away, Mikail," I say.

CHAPTER SEVENTY-SEVEN

MIKAIL

CHARM BEACH, GAYA

"I think I'm a little lost," I say. "How is stopping my heart not killing me?"

"I can drown you just until your heart stops and then revive you," Royo says. "I did it with Aeri."

I look over at Aeri, and she nods.

I rub the back of my neck. I suppose it makes as much sense as anything. If they're right, stopping my heart should undo the binds of the relics. Aeri would be able to take the sword and scepter, just as the crown bound to her once Joon was dead. And if they're wrong, well, I die either way.

Then an idea hits like a lightning bolt. "Wait—can't it be Aeri, then?" I ask, hope rising. "You can stop her heart, and I'll take the amulet, crown, and ring from her. I'll become the Dragon Lord instead."

Royo stares at her with all the hope in the world in his eyes.

She purses her lips and shakes her head. "You said yourself I'm the last Baejkin. We don't know what the Immortal Crown would do to you."

"I'm willing to gamble," I say.

Royo nods, maybe a little too eagerly, but I get it—he doesn't want to lose her. I don't, either.

"I'm not," she says. "If you died from the crown, I'd still have to become the Dragon Lord, and then neither of us would go on. Your people wouldn't have a king, and you'd be ashes for nothing. We know I can be the Dragon Lord. Put the knife away, Mikail. Let's be done with this."

None of it makes sense because we can't bring people back from the dead; otherwise, I'd have Euyn still here with me. But I suppose in the worst case, I stay dead. Sounds good to me.

I sheathe my blade.

"All right. As to drowning me, do we go to the beach? Because…" I gesture to the war below us.

Royo shakes his head, his eyes and nose still red. "It only needs to be a few inches of water. Duval, can you see if you can find anything?"

Duval runs to the tent and then brings back a large green-and-white ceramic bowl. We use those to wash blood off our hands after the fighting ends.

I want more time to think this through, but it's in short supply. Every second I delay, more men and women die trying to protect my realm. More of my people suffer. I exhale as I make my choice.

I kneel and stare at the bowl, then laugh to myself. Royo is going to drown me in here. Not quite the blaze of glory I'd hoped for. But this might as well happen.

Duval bows to me and then holds the bowl steady. "En Gaya."

"En Gaya," I say.

I lower my head until my face is nearly touching the surface, and then I take a last breath. I dip my face farther, until my nose and mouth are covered in cool water. Royo's hand clamps on to the back of my neck.

I try to maintain my calm. At first, it's easy, but then I quickly run out of air. My heart races as my lungs begin to burn. The desperate need for survival takes hold. My relics vibrate so hard that my arms shake. It feels like another seizure, but it's not. I need to get up and breathe. I need air. My fingers itch to light Royo on fire and to save myself at any cost. But I can't let that happen.

This is the plan. This is what we agreed to. I inhale the water before I can hurt anyone.

I thought I knew pain, especially with using the two relics and all I've endured. Apparently, I did not. My throat and lungs feel like I swallowed fire as my chest is racked with the worst agony I've ever experienced. I try to flail, but I'm held in place. And then, when I can't take it anymore, it stops.

Suddenly, there's nothing. No pain. No hand gripping me. Nothing at all.

When I open my eyes, I'm standing on a road made of ash and bone—human ash and bone. It's neither morning nor night. Instead, the sky is an unnatural shade of red. Bare black trees like the ones in the sacred woods line the road, and people shuffle past me.

But they aren't quite people—they're nearly see-through.

This is the Road of Souls.

So I died after all.

I smile, peace filling my mind. Royo drowned me, and he wasn't able to bring me back for whatever reason, but with my death, Aeri will now become the Dragon Lord. She'll defeat our enemies, and then I will see her again in the Kingdom of Hells, or maybe, hopefully, she'll find a way to survive. If anyone can escape through a loophole, it's her. She's capable of so much more than she's given credit for.

I start walking. I don't need directions, since the road only leads to one place. I can't see the Ten Hells as much as I feel them. Maybe, after I'm judged by Lord Yama, I'll be with Euyn again. I'd rather suffer torment with him than live in paradise alone.

As soon as I think his name, a figure begins to move against the crowd. He's different from the rest of the souls who mindlessly shuffle down the road. Most of those are the Weians I lit on fire. But this figure is walking toward me with purpose. I reach for my sword, but then I remember that blades don't matter when everyone is dead.

Perhaps it's Saja, the Soul Reaper.

When he gets closer, though, I know who he is from just the way he holds his head too high.

Euyn.

My heart fills, but I temper my joy. Euyn died weeks ago. He's been judged by Lord Yama in the Kingdom of Hells by now. His three years of doubtless punishment have already begun. So is it some other malicious spirit? Am I simply imagining what I want to see?

He gets closer, and it truly looks like Euyn. Maybe it could be him. I suppose no mortal knows the afterlife for certain. We believe souls reincarnate after three years, but by the time you experience the Ten Hells, it's too late to share your story. Maybe there's a waiting period. Maybe it's not three years.

"Mikail?" he asks. He sounds as uncertain as I feel, but it's his voice.

"Euyn?"

He smiles widely, and then we finally embrace. I wrap my arms around him, and he does the same. Stars, it really is him. I'm surprised that I can actually feel him without a body. But it makes sense—we love with our souls.

I hold him as an incredible comfort fills me. It's the joy of a warm bed on a cold, rainy night. I savor every second, pressing my hand against his head, his back. I forgot how much I missed this. No, that's a lie. I've known the emptiness since the banquet room. I just couldn't dwell on it.

And then I kiss him. It's not quite the same without a body, but it's like I touch his soul. It's better, more beautiful.

"I've missed you," I say. I thread my fingers through his. "There's so much to tell you."

"I'm sure there is." He smiles. "There have been quite a few souls lately who have spoken of a lost prince of Gaya who was once a Yusanian spymaster."

"They've mentioned me? I'm flattered."

He shrugs. "Souls often talk about the way they died."

With nothing to say for the body count, I shrug back at him. He laughs.

"How are you still here?" I ask, though I can't stop smiling. "I thought souls go right to the Kingdom of Hells…or at least that's what we're taught."

"Normally they do, but I died bonded to a god relic, so I've been able to stay on the road, despite the Soul Reaper's pull. I lingered because I thought I might find you. And now, I'm sorry I have."

"Why is that? We're together now." I hold up our entwined hands.

He shakes his head. "But we're not. You have so much life, Mikail. Even now I feel it pulsing through you. I'm not sure how you wound up on the road, but you shouldn't be here. Not yet."

Just as he says it, I feel a pull, like a tear through a slip of paper. Royo's voice fills my mind. He's trying to call me back to Gaya. Back to life.

No.

I ignore him. I found Euyn. I want to stay. There's nothing in the realms worth more than this.

"I know what you're thinking, Mikail," Euyn says with a frown. "No. It's not your time."

"It wasn't yours, either. I should've…"

I think of all the ways the audience with Quilimar could've been different if Euyn had told me his plan or if I'd picked up on it faster. I would've gotten him the crossbow. We could've fought our way out, side by side. But instead, Quilimar murdered him in front of me.

"It was my time, Mikail." He strokes my face. "It was."

I shake my head at the unfairness. The gods aren't fair, and I know that better than anyone, but this was a murder that had nothing to do with them.

"She killed you."

"Oh, I'm aware." He laughs. "But Quilimar made a mistake. I saw it in her face before I died."

The others have tried to tell me this—that she believed he was reaching for a weapon—but I disagreed. It didn't look like a mistake to me, yet it's hard to deny Euyn's own words.

Once again, I feel my soul being yanked from the road. I fight to stay, to keep my feet in the ash.

Gods damn it, Royo is insistent. He needs to leave me alone.

"Go," Euyn says.

"No."

He stares at me, unamused. "You must. There's so much for you to do in this life still. I won't let you cut your time short for me. I'll be yours in the next life, too."

Euyn sounds so certain, but how can he be? If we go to Lord Yama together now, we'll reincarnate at the same time, no matter the punishment. Otherwise, everything is left to chance.

"But what if we don't find each other in the next life?" I ask. "What if I live long past you? What if we miss each other in time? What if we keep missing each other? What if—"

He smiles. "Mikail, you're worried about the wrong things. I used to do the same, but you and I, we are meant to be. You were a Gayan village boy who found me in Qali. I will find you again. Worry about your life now, not what's in the future. Now go. You don't belong here."

"Euyn…" I don't want to leave him. Not when I have him here with me. I can't.

"Do this for me."

Stars. I tip my head back because what am I supposed to say to that?

"I love you, Mikail." He leans forward and kisses me. My soul fills with that pure joy only he brought me.

"I love you, Euyn," I say.

"In this life and the next," he says.

"Forever."

We lock eyes. I want more time. Just a little more time.

"Go," he says.

"You're insufferable."

The corner of his mouth rises as he lets go of my hand. "I'll see you again."

When the next pull comes, I give in. I let go of the road, and Euyn fades from view.

I open my eyes, and I'm lying on green grass with Royo's face extremely close to mine. I just miss his nose as I vomit up water.

CHAPTER SEVENTY-EIGHT

AERI

CHARM BEACH, GAYA

The scepter and sword fall from Mikail's arms as soon as he drowns, shifting from bangles back to their full sizes. His body goes still, and there's a fatal pull in me that's desperate to grab the relics, to possess them. But once I do, I will become the Dragon Lord. And deep down, I know I won't come back.

I stare at the beach as Royo tries to bring Mikail back to life, hitting his chest and breathing for him. The men down there continue to fight and die, so many that the water and the sand are bleeding red. So many that I can't count them—well over a thousand.

They will always war for more.

I sigh. Not now, voice.

Suddenly, Mikail pukes and Royo sits back on his knees, breathing hard. I exhale, finally relaxing my shoulders. It worked. It actually worked! Royo brought his soul back.

He's the only one of us who can save someone.

Royo wipes sweat from his brow as Mikail catches his breath. Fallador gets off his knees and gives thanks to Alta again. He ran up to help Mikail but stopped once we told him what we were doing.

Now it's time for me to do my part…only I really don't want to. I savor the breeze of the warm sea air, feel the softness of the green earth beneath my boots. I see Royo. Only Royo. The man I love who just said "I love you"—everything I've wanted to hear. I see the life that I wanted with him, all the days and nights, curling up beside him as I read and he sharpens a blade. Being held in his arms and finally feeling safe. And then I say goodbye to it all.

I close my eyes, and a single tear rolls down my cheek.

Enough. I made the decision already, and there's no time for doubts. It's me or it's everyone, including him, and that's still an easy choice to make.

"Stars, I can't believe that worked," Mikail says, panting. He looks at his bare arms. They shake from dying—probably from relic lust, too, but he's free now.

Royo picks up the sword and scepter. He stands and comes closer to me.

"I wish I could get rid of these things," he says.

Most people wouldn't. Most people want them above reason. The rulers have warred for more relics, for even a chance to acquire them. They want the power, but not him and not me. Yet we're caught in it all the same.

"I love you, Royo." I touch his hand, his face, memorizing the feel of his skin. I hope I can take this memory with me to the next life. Just this one.

He closes his eyes, pain etched into his face.

He swallows hard, and then he extends the relics to me. "I love you, Aeri."

I smile.

"I'll find a way to bring you back again," he whispers in my ear.

I can barely hear him, though, because once I touch the relics, power surges through me with such intensity that I lose my senses. My eyes fill with a golden glow, but somehow, I know it's coming from within me. I can't hear or see now, but something is pulling me upward, trying to lift me toward the sky. I don't struggle. It feels right, inevitable.

I'm not really a person anymore. I'm becoming something else.

I begin to levitate, my feet leaving the grass of the overlook.

Once I'm in the air, my sight returns. It's just in time to see a red creature coming down from the heavens.

The red being descends through the sky like a falling star, but it's no star.

That's the Dragon Lord.

I tip my head back as I soar upward to meet him. He's part man, part creature, but entirely a god. He's so beautiful but at the same time absolutely terrifying. I can't look away. I'm frozen with fear but also comforted. I don't think mortals can process seeing a god, but I'm also not exactly mortal right now.

He draws me to him, my body rising higher in the air. And then he collides with me with the force of an explosion. It's shattering, but not in a painful way.

Sparks twinkle around my eyes, but I'm in the clouds. Or I'm somewhere. I don't really know, but I'm not alone.

Naerium Baejkin, finder of the relics of my power.

As soon as he speaks, I realize how familiar the feeling is.

"You're the voice that's been in my head," I say.

At times.

I don't know if this is better or worse than thinking it was a bunch of dead kings.

The relics call to me and connect us. Why have you summoned me? What is it you wish, my child?

I shake the strangeness of speaking with a god and look down. The clouds part, revealing the swells of blood on the beach, bodies littering the sand, half buried like stones, and the ships smoking and sinking. This is the rot of death the amarth mentioned. Royo and Mikail stand on the overlook, as does Fallador. From way up here, I can see clear to Qali Palace. This is why my father wanted the relics by the end of monsoon season. Without the rains, I can see the realms clearly. And then I remember Seok and that Sora is on his ship. Maybe Tiyung, too.

"I want to save them all," I say.

Even your enemies? The ones who make war against you?

"Even my enemies. And then I want you to destroy the relics."

I can feel his surprise lighting up like a sky after a storm.

"As you said, men will always war for more," I explain. "Etherum will always cause death and hardship, because in the end, humans aren't meant to have this kind of power. But there's one more thing…"

Very well, Naerium.

"Actually, it's Aeri."

CHAPTER SEVENTY-NINE

SORA

TAMNEKI HARBOR, YUSAN

I'm chained to the deck of Seok's ship, human protection for the man I hate most in the world. If I could dive into the sea or put an end to my own life somehow, I would. Tiyung is confined to the galley below. He has been since he tried to unchain me not long after we set sail.

I've watched as Weian ships have caught fire and sunk, but this fleet keeps advancing. We're close enough now for me to see that the Weians are taking the beach. I wonder if my friends are alive. I pray they are, but I don't know how much longer they can hold on. I also don't know how much longer I'll be a hostage. I don't think I'll make it through the day.

Gambria walks up and stops beside me, looking out at Gaya. The guard assigned to me eyes her, but he says nothing because she's Seok's spy.

Disgust floods me. We trusted her.

"It was the only way to keep you out of Idle," she whispers.

I laugh. "Yes, this is much better."

I jangle the heavy chains attached to the metal handcuffs that bind me.

She stares out at the beach. "It is. Mikail and the others will move earth and sky to save you."

I raise both eyebrows. "You're on our side again?"

"Believe me when I say I am never on the side of Yusan."

She speaks with such venom that I do believe her. Maybe that's foolish, but it will hardly matter for long.

As she turns to leave, she slips a small switchblade into my palm. Is she trying to give me a weapon so I can take my own life?

"For me?" I arch an eyebrow.

"Stars, no," she says. She meets my eye, and I know who it's for.

I grip the weapon in my hand. It's not much, but if Seok comes close to me, it could be just enough. She really is on our side.

As I think of him, the demon arrives on the deck.

"What a beautiful day." He inhales and smiles, staring out at the destruction.

He didn't ask a question, so I don't have to reply. I flip open the blade in my hand and hide the weapon at my side.

I wish this chain were longer. I can't reach my arms up high enough to strike his neck, and that's the only fatal place I can hit with a blade this small.

"We'll take the island by sunset," he says. "Well...I will take it. You, my dear, won't set foot on land again." He turns to the guard he called Geon. "Kill her the second we make landfall and then dump her into the sea."

Geon salutes him.

Seok turns to walk away. Fury rises through me like a ship bursting into flames. He's not even man enough to kill me himself. I aim the blade. I can't reach his neck, but there are organs in his lower back. I can get at least two jabs in before they kill me.

I'm about to stab him when there's a fire in the sky.

No, that's not fire. There have been plenty of flaming arrows—this is different. I stare up at the heavens as something impossible happens. A golden person levitates from the coast of Gaya, and then a red comet comes falling out of the sky.

The men all stop and stare. The blade clatters from my hand, falling onto the deck, but no one notices because both the person and the comet disappear into the clouds. Then, an enormous blackbird soars through the air. It's like a hael but a hundred times larger.

The massive bird swoops down, flying low over the ships as if it's searching for something. Seok's men are too startled to shoot at first, but then they recover. The best of the Qali Palace archers are on this ship. They aim for the bird, but the bolts and arrows simply bounce off the black feathers.

It's a samroc.

This is exactly what Mikail and Euyn described—a bird with steel-like feathers. But it's hard to think of why there's a mythic creature overhead because…Kingdom of Hells…because I think Aeri rides on its back. I gasp. Yes, it's Aeri, and she's on fire—or at least glowing red.

Awe and terror fill me as I realize what she's done. Oh gods, no. She's become the Dragon Lord.

I drop down to one knee in submission but also sorrow.

"Lay down your weapons or die," she says.

Says isn't exactly right. She speaks in a god's voice, and it echoes in my mind. I'm certain every soldier can hear her because they react immediately.

Most of the men drop their weapons and raise their hands, but flames rise from the ones who don't surrender. A thousand flames go up at once on Seok's ships and the Weian fleet. More on the shore.

The bird circles and then dives down on my ship. I think it's coming for me, but the samroc grabs Seok in its talons. He screams as the claws dig into his skin. My mouth falls open as the samroc lifts him up. His heir's crown falls off his head and lands in the sea. I wonder if he'll be eaten, but I don't have to wait for an answer. I watch as the bird drops him on the Gayan coast, behind enemy lines.

I exhale, my hands shaking. In just seconds, Seok was defeated. But what's happened to my friends?

I'm still struggling to comprehend what I just saw when Aeri appears, flames emanating from her as she stands in front of me. I lower my head to the deck, bowing to her. I want to embrace her, but it's not Aeri. Not really. She's merged with the Dragon Lord, and I don't think I can touch a god.

She smiles and then frowns at my chains. With a single motion of her fingers, my shackles fall off. Then she draws them to her and forms a ruby crown. A new crown of Yusan. She reaches forward to place it on my head.

Kingdom of Hells, she is trying to crown me as queen of Yusan.

I put my hand up. "No, please."

I don't want the throne. I never have. I hoped that if we won, I would live a short life. Now she is asking me to be the new ruler of the realm.

I couldn't want this less.

"It has to be you," she says. "Or nothing changes."

"Aeri, please," I beg. But I don't know what I'm begging for. She's saying my own words back to me. But it was supposed to be her. She is Baejkin. She had the blood and the relics. She was supposed to rule. She was the one who would change things.

But she won't survive being the Dragon Lord. That is why she's trying to crown me. I can read it in the kind sympathy in her eyes.

"I love you, Sora," she says. "You are everything this realm needs. And nothing it deserves."

Tears stream down my face, but even with tears in my eyes I see that she's fading. Her flame is dying out. She gave her life to stop this war, to defeat Seok, to save me.

"I love you, Aeri," I say. "Please don't go."

"I'll stay in your heart," she says.

They're the last words she says to me before she vanishes. I hold in my breath and my scream of sorrow. She is gone. Yet another person I love is dead, and I'm still left here. Perhaps I deserve this. Perhaps living is my punishment.

My ship and the ships around us are silent. There's not a sound on the water.

"Hail Queen Sora—the first Dragon Queen of Yusan," Tiyung says. I stare at him as he emerges from the galley.

We survived, the two of us, against all odds, because in a world of hate, there was love.

He takes a knee on the deck. Everyone, as far as the eye can see, suddenly kneels to me. I raise my chin, ready to carry on.

CHAPTER EIGHTY

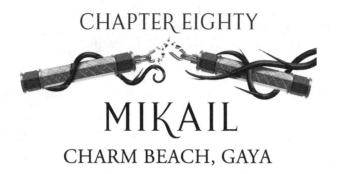

MIKAIL

CHARM BEACH, GAYA

Stars, what is a samroc doing in Gaya?

I'd just gotten my legs under me, and now my knees are weak as the enormous black bird flies toward us. Memories of the attack in Fallow resurface as the smell of blood and fowl returns. I can almost feel the grit of the desert sand on my hands, hear the hamels cry in my ears. Only this time, I don't have Euyn to shoot it.

Fighting the logical urge to run, I plant my feet. This is my home—I won't flee. And what's dying again, anyhow?

The creature comes even closer, the iridescent feathers at its neck shining in the sun. I pull my sword from its scabbard, and the blade flames to life. It won't do much against this beast, but I can try.

It flies closer until its shadow covers me, Royo, and the entire overlook. Just as the longbowmen pull back to fire, a man falls from its claws. The body rolls onto the ground, and the samroc soars away.

Everyone except the man dropped from its talons remains silent as the samroc disappears from view.

I blow out a relieved breath and try to stop trembling. Lord Yama, I think Euyn's bolt was still in its eye. But no, it can't be the same creature, right?

I shudder off the thought as Seok flails, screaming like he's still falling, even though he's on dry land. Rune strolls over to him.

"Seok, my old friend." He smiles down at the would-be king,

beaming as if he were responsible for our victory.

I stare at the southern count as he bleeds on the grass. Seok crowned himself king of Yusan, poisoned all those girls, and kidnapped Sora. But Aeri, as the Dragon Lord, just delivered him at our feet. Seok is swarmed by guards and put into chains, but where is Sora?

I clench my jaw. If he hurt her, I'll drop him into a samroc nest myself.

My pulse pounds as I search through the spyglass. Where is she?

Almost in unison, the men in the boats turn and kneel to someone. Even the Weians. Following their direction, I find who they are submitting to.

Just one woman stands on the deck of a Yusanian ship.

My heart leaps. Sora! She's alive, and so is Tiyung. He's kneeling closest to her.

Praise the gods—somehow, they made it through.

I'm so overwhelmed with joy and relief at seeing her, it takes me a moment to notice the red crown on Sora's head. My breath catches, my pulse skipping.

Aeri made Sora the queen of Yusan.

Stars.

I'd never considered it, and now my heart drums as I think of the possibilities. It was supposed to be Euyn, then Seok took the palace, and Rune warred and schemed to grasp at it, but Aeri chose Sora to sit on the serpent throne.

For the first time in a while, I feel hope bloom inside my chest. It feels...warm, comforting. Aeri might've been the wisest of us all, because if anyone can change things for the better, it's Sora. Maybe, just maybe, she and I can make all of this worth it. Or at least we can try.

We were both ready to die, but perhaps it's braver to live on after loss.

I look down at the beach, no longer shaking. We have two realms to watch over now. It's the time for strength and valor.

Queen Sora the First. May there be many more.

I take a knee, and everyone on the overlook follows suit. Well, everyone but Royo. He's standing still, too heartbroken to move. He has remained frozen ever since Aeri levitated off the ground. I ache for him—for his pain that I know all too well. We only won by him losing the person he loves the most. It's not much of a victory when it costs your heart.

We're all still kneeling when Aeri returns. There was no one there a second ago, and now she's here, standing in front of Royo, surrounded by flames.

She's so bright, it hurts to look at her, but also, I can't take my eyes off her shimmering god form.

"Royo." She smiles.

He steps forward and seems to take his first breath since she rose to join the Dragon Lord.

CHAPTER EIGHTY-ONE

ROYO

CHARM BEACH, GAYA

Aeri came back to me. My chest expands with love, and I reach out to take her hand in mine. My fingers go through the air, smacking my side when I can't touch her.

I blink hard and reach for her again. Her hand is right there, but, even though I try, my fingers just catch the air. I can't hold her.

She's changed.

My stomach knots as I keep trying, unable to accept it.

"Royo," she sighs.

My heart squeezes, shrinking in defeat. It's not really Aeri—well, not the one I held in my arms last night—and she's not really standing but flickering in front of me. She's sometimes solid, sometimes see-through, but already out of reach. I don't know what to do with my heart. It's filling and breaking at the same time, because even though she's here, she's not really here. She merged with the Dragon Lord and left me.

It's like there's a giant boulder crushing my chest, and I can't breathe. My voice comes out as a whisper. "Aeri."

She smiles. "I couldn't leave without saying goodbye."

Agony claws at the shards of my heart when she says the word "goodbye." I wanna scream out in pain, but I know it won't do any good.

"Then don't," I say. Tears stream down my face. "Don't say

goodbye and don't leave me." I know she has no choice, but my heart doesn't.

"Everything will be okay now."

No. *No.* Nothing will be okay. Not without her.

I shake my head. I shouldn't waste this time arguing with her, but she's just wrong. I don't give a fuck about the war or the kings. I just want her to stay. Life without her isn't worth shit. Take the fifteen thousand souls down there and just give me hers. Or let me die with her.

She tilts her head like she read my mind. "I want you to go on, Royo."

"To do what? I'm nothing without you." My chin falls, my shoulders dropping with it. What's the point? A world without her is black desert. I've wandered it before, living without color or life. Now that I've had her, I can't go back to that.

She doesn't touch me as much as use the air to raise my face to hers.

As I look at her, she's flickering hard. Somewhere in my mind, I know she's almost gone. I can feel it. And there's nothing I can do to stop it. I grip my own hands because I can't hold hers. I'd break my fingers to touch hers.

"You're everything and so much more than you know," she says. "Thank you for loving me."

Tears flood my eyes, making her beautiful face blur to nothing, but it's not my vision. I blink hard, trying to hold on, but she's fading. Just another minute. Just one more. I won't get a life with her. Just give me another second.

She smiles. "I'll love you for tomorrow and tomorrow and tomorrow."

And then, before I can say anything else, she vanishes.

"No!" I cry.

I grab the air where she was just standing, but there is nothing. I look down, and my arms hug emptiness. I turn in a circle, hoping to see her just one more time. Just one. I search the sky, and there's nothing. I lost her.

She's gone.

I'm all alone.

I fall on my knees as my heart goes with her. The pain in my chest is unbearable. I scream until there's no more air left in me, until the world is nothing but a blur. She's gone somewhere I can't follow. I pound the earth with my fists, wishing I could crack a hole straight to the Ten Hells. Wishing I could do anything with this useless agony.

Mikail rests a hand on my shoulder. "She saved us all."

I eye him with all the hate I feel for this world, this place, and those relics that took her from me. "It wasn't worth it."

Real empathy shines in Mikail's eyes. If anyone understands what this is like, it's him.

He exhales and shakes his head. "Maybe not, but it's what she wanted."

I can't... I can't even think about her choosing this. We won, but a hundred knives stabbing my chest would be a relief right now. Tomorrow will be worse. Tomorrow, I'll have to wake up in a world without her.

I crumple lower, sinking into my grief.

Mikail sighs as he takes my hand. His palm firm and warm. I think he's going to try to get me to move or say something to make me feel better, but he doesn't. He just holds my hand as we watch the surrender.

CHAPTER EIGHTY-TWO

SORA

IDLE PRISON, YUSAN

ONE WEEK LATER

This place is pure evil. Despite it being empty, torture and death cling to the stone walls of Idle Prison.

Mikail walks by my side. We are a few steps into hell before I realize that he's familiar with this place. He walks with the certitude of someone who memorized these halls.

"You were down here as spymaster?" I ask.

He gives me a quick nod. He's far more himself now that Aeri destroyed the relics a week ago. I have missed her every minute since. We all have—Royo most, of course.

"Not often, but yes," he says. "It was worse when Joon was in power. This place was full."

Kingdom of Hells, I can't imagine it. Or maybe I just don't want to.

We take a ramp and pass a foul-smelling pit.

Mikail shakes his head. "Don't look down."

I don't.

Idle Prison is a warren with tight corridors, but I follow Mikail. We pass into vaulted, open spaces, and I can finally take a full breath, until I realize we've entered torture chambers.

"Interrogation rooms and…tools of the trade," he says.

We pass a series of cages. The stench still lingers, blood caked on the chains along with other filth, and I grimace, far too well trained to gag.

"Those held people?" I ask.

He looks down and smiles but not in a happy way. Maybe I should just stop asking.

I swallow hard and draw my gaze away from the four-foot-high cells. The horrors men are capable of inflicting on each other are endless. "I'm going to shutter this place once this is over."

I've considered it since Tiyung told me about the torture here, but I'm certain of it now.

Mikail sighs. "Don't. It's an admirable wish, but your throne will have enemies. To keep a kingdom, prisons like this are a necessary evil."

I shake my head. "If this is the cost of keeping the kingdom, the realm isn't worth it. And the soul of Yusan can't afford it."

"All right, Sora. Have it your way."

I side-eye him. Mikail gave in far too easily. What he means is he'll make his own plans to keep my throne secure and he just won't tell me about them.

He catches me staring, and I raise an eyebrow. Mikail is Adoros, king of Gaya, but I wonder if he will ever stop being a spymaster.

Probably not. Ultimately, we are who we are.

"He is in there." Mikail points to a door that has a metal slot about three feet off the floor. There's a transom window up high. The door is heavy wood and iron. I brace myself. It looks barely fit for a beast.

"Joon held Tiyung in here?" I ask.

"And before him, Euyn," Mikail says.

I draw a breath, forcing down my horror. The only reason I haven't dealt with Idle Prison before now is because of how busy

I've been. The remaining Weians were allowed to return home after full and unconditional surrender. General Vikal and her soldiers were also permitted to return to Khitan once we entered into an everlasting peace accord. New treaties and terms were negotiated and signed. Then I burned the colonial treaty and granted Gaya its full independence.

It's been a lot.

Now, I have one last thing to deal with before I'm officially coronated. One last piece of history before the new realm is born.

Mikail lingers in front of me, wearing regalia and the crown of Gaya. I found the emerald-and-platinum crown in the palace vault. I've arranged for the return of all of Gaya's looted treasures that I could find. No one can ever be made whole after an atrocity, but we can still try. Our shared goal is to build a world worthy of Aeri's sacrifice—no matter how impossible that is.

Mikail stares at me, obviously wanting to say something.

"Yes?" I ask.

"Sora, I can take care of him, or there are any number of executioners…"

I meet his eyes. "I survived just for this."

All the poisonings, the torture, the murders, the close calls. I endured losing everything I loved just to see Seok destroyed. I have lived far longer than I've wanted to for revenge. No one will pry this from me.

"Very well, Your Majesty," he says with a bow. "He's chained in there."

I nod. "Open the door."

"Yes, Your Majesty," the four guards in front of us say.

Some of them served Seok and Joon, but most of my palace guards are former indentures I freed as soon as I got back to Yusan. Thousands rushed to enlist into my service.

One guard turns the key, and another pushes the door in.

I wait as the hinges creak. I've dreamed about this for a dozen years—imagined what I'd do and say in this moment hundreds of times.

I'd expected to feel giddy anticipation flutter in my chest, maybe a little fear or trepidation along with righteous anger, but now that the moment is here, I feel...nothing. Nothing at all.

Strange. I blink and focus on the feelings in my chest—or the lack thereof. There's a vague sense of obligation in my mind, because this is what needs to be done, but aside from that, there's nothing. It's like I'm hollowed out.

Tiyung and I spoke about what to do with Seok. We both agreed that for as long as he is alive, Seok will try for my crown. The realm won't know peace, and neither will I until he is dead. But the triumphant joy I expected isn't blazing in my chest. Seok is just an unpleasant reminder of my past that I will be rid of today. I was once a line item on his ledger, but he is nothing more than a debt on mine.

I'm just ready for this to be done.

As light from our torches hits the cell, Seok blinks, then struggles to stand, balancing himself against the stone wall with his arms and legs chained.

Gods, the smell. I place a hand in front of my nose.

They must not have cleaned out his wounds from the samroc claws. The odor of rot and infection makes my stomach turn as I step inside.

Seok closes his eyes, his face scrunched in pain. For the first time, I'm seeing him dirty and unkempt. I pause, not because I care for him at all, but because this is what Tiyung must've looked like when he was kept in here. My heart falls—they do bear such a strong resemblance to each other. No matter what Rune claimed, Tiyung is undeniably Seok's son. But Ty was in here because of his father's schemes and ambitions. Seok is here purely because of his own.

My former owner has fallen from grace, but he still has much further to go. I swore I'd show him what it feels like to be powerless. And I will keep my word.

"Close the door, please," I say to the guards.

They hesitate, and I glance over my shoulder, vexed to be disobeyed. Everyone, including Mikail, bows, and then a man with a red birthmark on his cheek quickly shuts the door.

I put my torch in a holder on the wall, then take off my cloak. I have on a plain white cotton dress. The gold coronation gown that Sun-ye and her twin sister finally agreed on lies on my bed. Aeri would've loved it, but I don't care about fine dresses and tradition. If it weren't for decorum, I'd just wear this. It's the kind of simple dress I wore in my cottage when Hana and I stayed together, pretending we were free.

She came to this place, braving the screams and filth to help Tiyung. Royo, in the rare times he's sober enough to talk, has told me about what Hana did on the warship that night. How she helped them live and how she paid with her life. My name was her dying breath. He and I drown our sorrows together even though I still don't drink. We cry and we remember. We share our regrets, of which we both have many.

Too many.

Somewhere in my mind, I escape with Hana to Khitan. In that corner of my dreams, none of this happened. They're all still alive. I'm going to the market with her and Daysum, not about to torture someone to death.

I shake myself out of the daydream and square my shoulders. Right now, I'm very much in Yusan. In Idle Prison. I turn my attention back to the man chained in front of me.

"So you've finally come," Seok says with his head high.

Even chained, about to die, Seok still believes he has control over me. He still believes he has power. I sigh and shake my head at his delusion as I reach into the bag.

"This is for her."

I toss down a whip.

"This is for them."

I drop a boning knife onto the filthy stone floor.

"And this is for me."

I reach into my pocket, pull out a bottle of poison, and show it to him before I set it down next to the knife.

He laughs but then coughs until he's out of breath. "You see, torture is easy once you've lost your soul."

I tilt my head, staring at the man who used to make me freeze with fear. There was a night in Khitan when he did break my soul. Aeri was the one who helped me put myself back together. And then, as her final act, she made me queen.

Now, I remember her kindness—the light, not the darkness. I feel joy at having known her more than the pain of losing her.

"I still have my soul," I say, my voice smooth and steady. "After everything you did, I have the throne you wanted. I have the love of your son, which you lost, and your wife has been left at my mercy. I swear and I vow, I will destroy every single thing you built within a sunsae. There are no indentures, and your rank will be next. All of it will be gone, and no one will remember your name."

Seok frowns, his mirth gone.

He finally looks me in the eye, and I casually hold his gaze. Fear, true fear, flashes across his face. If I were angry, screaming, righteously vengeful, I don't think it would've frightened him as much as the fact that I just don't care anymore. I've become something that he can't touch, and that terrifies him.

I pick up the whip. Let's get this over with.

I strike the air to get the rhythm down. But the crack of the whip jolts me into a memory.

Seok lined up his entire household and then pulled Daysum out of formation and threw her onto the gravel in front of his villa. He was going to whip her, but Tiyung volunteered to carry out the punishment instead of Seok to try to spare her some of the pain. All of it was done to punish me after I fled to the Xingchi forest. I had to watch in horror and guilt as the whip shredded her skin until I couldn't bear it anymore. I crawled to Seok, kissed his shoes, and promised never to flee again.

I stare at the wooden handle of the whip in my hand.

He deserves it. There's not a doubt in my mind—he deserves all the pain I planned to inflict and more. I wore this dress because it's cheap and I could dispose of it or keep it as a blood-soaked reminder of what I've endured.

But the thing is, I'm already well aware of what I've suffered. In truth, I'd really rather forget.

I press my lips together as a new feeling takes hold. One of peace. Maybe peace is being beyond the reach of your past.

Hana used to say you are more than what you endure, and I know that I am. The problem is that no matter what I do to him, it won't bring her back. Mikail chopped off Joon's head himself, and it didn't bring back a single Gayan soul. Doing this won't lessen the suffering of any of the girls I knew. I won't get to live in a country villa with Daysum or ride horses with Hana, even if I carve him up after whipping him to death.

My shoulders droop. Tiyung said vengeance is a fire without warmth, and maybe I'm just tired, but I don't seem to need it anymore.

I toss the whip down.

I step over the knife and leave the poison behind, and then I knock on the door.

The guards immediately open it.

"Wall it off now," I say.

"Yes, Your Majesty," they answer.

I glance at Seok's shocked face, then at the poison and the knife that are just out of his reach. He won't be able to do anything but wish for a faster death as he suffers alone with no one to hear him.

I take the torch from the wall. I don't spare Seok another glance or thought. Mikail offers his arm, and he escorts me out of the prison.

CHAPTER EIGHTY-THREE

MIKAIL

QALI PALACE, YUSAN

Sora and I take the stairs up to the palace. She walks with her head held high and not a drop of blood on her. She surprised me. I thought for certain she would torture Seok to death. I would've. But she has always been the better person. Far better than this place deserves.

I am, of course, referring to both Idle Prison and Yusan as a whole.

By the time we reach the door, the tower chimes four bells. It's time for the high priest of the Divine Temple of Kings to formally coronate Sora. Not that she needs it, since she was crowned by the Dragon Lord herself, but traditions hold sway.

"I assume you'll want to dress before the coronation," I say. "I'll tell them that—"

"No, I'm ready now," she says.

I pause. She's stunningly beautiful, always, but she's in the type of dress a commoner would wear with her hair in a simple braid.

"I'll take the throne as myself," she says.

My lips turn up in a smile.

Stars, what a queen.

"Very well." I bow to her.

Royo meets us by the doors to the throne room. He eyes Sora's rough cotton dress and then shrugs and sways a bit. He might still be drunk, even though he was supposed to dry out for this. I'm concerned about his drinking, but I'm in no position to tell anyone how to live.

Trumpets blare, and gilded doors open. I guess we're doing this. I offer my arm to Sora, and she takes it.

The crowd stands and turns, but whispers spread as Sora gracefully walks in her simple calf-length shift.

Well, this is one royal event no one will forget.

Ambassadors from Khitan, Wei, and Gaya stand off to the right side of the throne room. Fallador, the Gayan ambassador to Yusan, smiles, as does Gambria, the Yusanian ambassador to Khitan. Sora told me of how Gam tried to help her when no one else could. We've both buried old betrayals in favor of a united future.

Sora's ladies in waiting stand to the left. Sun-ye stares daggers, unamused, and her twin sister, Rayna, seems dismayed as we pass them. All of that work picking a dress and hairstyle for Sora just for her to wear exactly what a girl from a mountain village would pick for a holy day.

Sun-ye and Rayna are free, of course, like all indentures, but chose to remain here to look after Sora. I'm told that they all sleep in the same room to ward off nightmares. It makes sense. It's easier to face the darkness together.

As a sign of her mercy, Tiyung also stands in a place of honor. Seok's heir being allowed to survive signals to everyone that old animosities won't dictate her new rule. She spared his mother, too, sending the countess back to her country house.

Tiyung's eyes drink her in. He's also here because they have some kind of love between them. Who knows what that means or what it one day will become? They've said they're taking things moment by moment, but when their eyes meet, there's the promise of tomorrow.

My chest fills. That's exactly what Sora is—a hope for a better dawn.

We reach the stairs, and she takes the steps up to the serpent throne alone. She sits, adjusting her hem, and Royo and I stand to either side at the bottom of the stairs.

The high priest begins the ceremony, and he eventually climbs the steps and lifts the ruby crown. All of the palace guards kneel to her, saluting her as one.

Unusually, the entire throne room, the ambassadors included, takes a knee to Sora.

"All hail Sora Daysum Naerium," the priest says. "The sole rightful ruler of Yusan, uniter of the land, blessed by the gods, beloved of the people—the first Dragon Queen."

"Long live the queen!" The sound echoes through the room and out into the palace.

I glance at Royo, who's watching the queen. We will both do what's necessary for Sora to have a long reign. We all will.

The three of us are family with bonds forged by blood and tears, but also mercy and hope. Together, with the people we loved, we changed the world. Now, we'll make it worth the ones we lost.

EPILOGUE

ROYO

THE TEMPLE OF KNOWLEDGE, YUSAN

TWO YEARS LATER

I'll find a way—that's my motto and the words I live by.

New scrolls come in every day, documenting Queen Sora's rule. She is, of course, everything a ruler should be—fair and wise. It's no surprise that everybody loves her, and Yusan has never known this level of peace and prosperity.

I load the scrolls onto a cart, and with a grunt, I haul it to the scroll room. We really gotta invest in a wheelbarrow, but I'm just the muscle here.

My bloodwork days are long over, but I carry heavy things. I move tables around and shut large doors. Basically, I do grunt work for the priests of the Temple of Knowledge. In exchange, the Yoksa feed me and let me stay here.

I've taken worse jobs.

It's also my responsibility to greet pilgrims. In one of her many changes to the realm, Sora allowed public access to all the books and scrolls we keep. She said the people must know their past to avoid repeating it. It's true enough, but these scholars are a pain in the ass. They do come all this way, braving the sheer cliffs of Cuesta

Mountain, so I guess it's only right to let them in.

For a little while.

It's dusk now, though, so I can tell everybody to get lost. No, I don't say it that way, but they get the point. They pack their shit and scurry out. They can come back after sunrise tomorrow.

Once they're gone, I close the massive black wood doors. Any time I touch them, I think about Gaya—what we gained and lost there. I remember that the world only changes when people with really good hearts are willing to die for each other.

I wonder how King Adoros is doing. I mean, I see the scrolls and reports come in. He, like Sora, is beloved. He's made some missteps, but at his core, he loves the island from the farms that replaced the drug crop to the souls of the people. But I wonder how Mikail really is after all the shit he's been through. After all the shit we've been through together.

Sora sent word that Mikail raised a golden statue to the Dragon Lord Naerium. Pilgrims from all over journey to the overlook on Charm Beach to leave roses and pray for Aeri's soul. Sora invited me to go, but I said no. A statue isn't the same.

Nothing is the same.

I sigh as I turn the green temple key, then lumber down the stairs to my bedroom.

The bedrooms are built right into the orangey rock of the mountain. It's kind of a tomb, but I don't care. My axe and my nunchuka hang on the rock wall, unused since Gaya. Sora gave me a gold band of friendship before I left the palace, and that hangs there, too. It's as good as making me a nobleman, even though she got rid of all titles right after her coronation. A lot of people were unhappy, but because we don't owe Wei tribute anymore, she was able to buy them off.

Like Ambassador Fallador said, money solves a lot of problems.

Sora made Rune Yusan's prominent ambassador. He travels all three realms but spends most of his time in Khitan. I still think she should've killed him, but whatever. No one agreed, and I've got bigger issues.

I take a book out from my desk drawer and continue trying to translate it. It's the forty-first book I found on a gateway to the Kingdom of Hells. Scholars think it exists—a way to get from our world to the Ten Hells without dying—but so far, no one can tell me where the fuck it is.

If there's a way to make it to the Ten Hells, I'm going to do it. And then I'm going to bring Aeri back.

Somewhere, the road to hell exists, and I've got nowhere else to be.

The End

ACKNOWLEDGMENTS

It is bittersweet to finish the series that changed my life. A million thank-yous to the amazing Liz Pelletier. None of this would've happened without your brilliant guidance and constant support. I'm so blessed to work with you. Thank you also to Jen Bouvier for your ideas, feedback, and for making this series possible.

Thank you to everyone at Red Tower for your tireless efforts in shaping this series. Thank you to the amazing edit team including: Mary Lindsey, Rae Swain, Hannah Lindsey, Stacy Abrams, Nancy Cantor, Jessica Meigs, and Aimee Lim. Thank you to the incredible art team including: Bree Archer, Juho Choi, Jennifer Valero, and Britt Marczak, but especially Elizabeth Turner Stokes. Thank you to Curtis Svehlak and Viveca Shearin in production. And thank you to the fantastic publicity and marketing team including: Meredith Johnson, Heather Riccio, Ashley Doliber, and Brittany Zimmerman. Special thank-yous to Aaron Aceves and Nicholas Macoretta for your valuable input, and thank you to Nicole Resciniti for bringing this series worldwide.

Many thanks to my agent and agent assistant, Lauren Spieller and Hannah Morgan Teachout, for your notes, guidance, and support!

Thank you to my four children, who inspire and delight me. I am blessed to call you my family. Thank you to my mother for instilling hard work and dedication and leading by example. With every page,

I hope to make you and Dad proud. Thank you to my sister, aunt, and cousins for your excitement and love.

Thank you to my friends who've been there for me through the highs and lows of this wild author ride, especially Karen McManus, Alexa Martin, Sabina Khan, Rachel Van Dyken, Matt Weintraub, Susan Thibault, and my sprinting buddy, Carissa Broadbent. Thank you to Jenn Kocsmiersky for your beautiful art.

Thank you to all the influencers, booksellers, reviewers, and most of all readers for making this series an international bestseller!

Last, but most importantly, thank you to John Coryea for your patient love, for being my rock in this storm, and for giving my heart a home. Without you, I couldn't write a story about love because I never really understood it until I found you. Tomorrow and tomorrow and tomorrow.

BEING THE SPARROW ISN'T AN HONOR.
IT'S A TRAP.

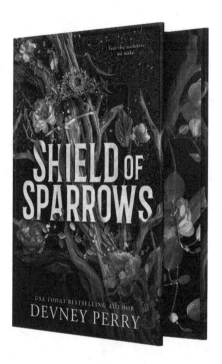

Long ago, the gods unleashed monsters upon the five kingdoms of Calandra to remind us that humans are insignificant—that we must pray to the gods for mercy throughout our fragile, fleeting lives.

I didn't need a deity to remind me I was powerless. Being a princess had never been more than a performance—twenty-three years of empty titles and hollow traditions. My sister revels in the spectacle, basking in the attention and flawlessly playing her part. I was never asked to be part of the charade.

Until the day an infamous monster hunter sailed to our shores. The day a prince walked into my father's throne room and ruined my life. The day I married a stranger, signed a magical treaty in blood, and set off across the continent to the most treacherous kingdom in all the realm.

That was the day I learned that not all myths are make-believe. That lies and legends are often the same. And that the only way to kill the monsters we fear was to *become* one…

THE GODS LOVE TO PLAY WITH US MERE MORTALS.
AND EVERY HUNDRED YEARS, WE LET THEM...

I have never been favored by the gods. Far from it, thanks to Zeus.

Living as a cursed office clerk for the Order of Thieves, I just keep my head down and hope the capricious beings who rule from Olympus won't notice me. Not an easy feat, given San Francisco is Zeus' patron city, but I make do. I survive. Until the night I tangle with a *different* god.

The *worst* god. Hades.

For the first time ever, the ruthless, mercurial King of the Underworld has entered the Crucible—the deadly contest the gods hold to determine a new ruler to sit on the throne of Olympus. But instead of fighting their own battles, the gods name *mortals* to compete in their stead.

So why in the Underworld did Hades choose me—a sarcastic nobody with a curse on her shoulders—as his champion? And why does my heart trip every time he says I'm *his*?

I don't know if I'm a pawn, bait, or something else entirely to this dangerously tempting god. How can I, when he has more secrets than stars in the sky?

Because Hades is playing by his own rules...and Death will win at any cost.

CONNECT WITH US ONLINE

⊙ @redtowerbooks

f @RedTowerBooks

♪ @redtowerbooks

♥   ♥

Join the Entangled Insiders for early access
to ARCs, exclusive content, and insider news!
Scan the QR code to become part of the
ultimate reader community.

RED TOWER
BOOKS™